Ben Elton has proved himself the most popular and the most controversial comedian to emerge in recent years. As well as his own stand-up routines, Ben's numerous writing credits include *Blackadder II*, *Blackadder the Third*, *Blackadder Goes Forth*, *The Man From Auntie*, *The Young Ones*, *Gasping*, *Silly Cow* and the internationally bestselling novel *Stark*. *Gridlock* is his second novel.

PRAISE FOR *GRIDLOCK*:

'He combines passionate espousal of a cause with the machine-gun narration of a stand-up comic, peppered with good jokes and with the energetically managed, funny and violent action of a manic strip cartoon'

Ned Sherrin *Standard*

'Perfect fodder for the politically correct holidaymaker'
Time Out

'Leaves you wondering why our more up-market novelists can never be bothered to write about something as obviously important, topical and politically resonant as the nightmarish growth of the motor industry'   *Guardian*

'Hugely enjoyable . . . very funny, frequently perceptive and often thought-provoking'
Yorkshire Evening Post

GRIDLOCK

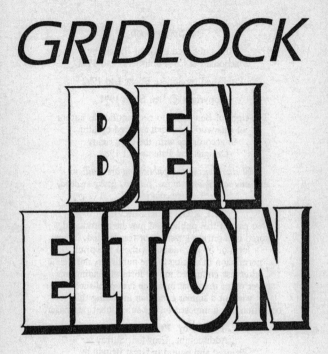

BEN ELTON

SPHERE BOOKS LIMITED

A *Sphere* Book

First published in Great Britain by
Macdonald & Co (Publishers) Ltd 1991

Published by Sphere Books Ltd 1992

Typeset by 🅐 Tek-Art Ltd,
Addiscombe, Croydon, Surrey
Printed and bound in Great Britain by
BPCC Hazell Books
Aylesbury, Bucks, England
Member of BPCC Ltd.

ISBN 0 7474 0568 9

Sphere Books Ltd
A Division of
Macdonald & Co (Publishers) Ltd
165 Great Dover Street,
London SE1 4YA
A member of Maxwell Macmillan Publishing Corporation

For Sophie

AN OFF-PLANET INTRODUCTION

Before beginning this story proper, a story which has its fictional feet very firmly on the ground, it is worth taking a moment to look upwards, high above the teeming masses of rush-hour London where most of this story is set. Above the tired office workers, tired of office working; the tired media lunch-eaters, tired of eating media lunch; the strange cockney philanthropists, who are prepared to offer you not one gold watch, not even two gold watches, but three gold watches for a tenner. Up and away from the deep carpet of burger boxes and homeless people. Up through the dirty air, over the satellite dishes currently receiving fifteen different Italian game shows, some with bikinis. On, up past Nelson, through the flock of pigeons with the telescopic sights on their backsides, past the great crowd of 747s playing aeronautical Russian Roulette on their way to Heathrow. Through the hot, sticky fog of greenhouse gases, sadly no longer through the ozone layer, past the awesomely sophisticated satellite technology currently employed in transmitting fifteen different Italian game shows, some with bikinis. Up up up and out into space, for it is here, in space, that there recently hovered a spaceship.

This spaceship contained a group of television researchers from the Planet Brain in the process of analysing humanity, in order to compile a three-minute comedy item for their top-rated television show, *That's Amazing, Brainians*, which followed the early evening news.

The researchers were pleased, they had noted much which was amusingly amazing, and they assured each other that Earth had provided the easiest bit of researching that they had done in aeons. Brain is populated by beings of immense intelligence and so far it had taken them only a quarter, of a quarter, of a single second to assimilate and comprehend humanity.

All those things which we on Earth believe to be complex and difficult had been simplicity itself to the beings from Brain. The situation in Beirut; what Hamlet's problem was; how to set the timer on a fourteen-day video-recorder – these things were not mysteries to the Brainians. In that quarter, of one quarter, of a single second they had answered it all. Although, in fairness, it must be added that two weeks later, back on Brain, the researchers would discover that they had managed to record a documentary about Tuscany rather than *Dirty Harry* which they really wanted to watch.

But such slight slip-ups aside, the Brainians had humanity taped. They understood the rules of cricket, how the stripes get into the toothpaste and the reason why there is no word in English for the back of the knee. In that quarter, of one quarter, of a single second the research team had answered all the great philosophical questions. They knew whether an object still exists when you are not looking at it (it does); whether there is a God (if you want); and why people eat Kentucky Fried Chicken even though it makes them feel ill (human beings are stupid).

But then, they were stumped. They had encountered one aspect of human activity which astonished and mystified even those hardened researchers. Researchers who thought they had seen every illogicality and lunacy that the universe had to offer. On this very planet they had seen pointless wars and pointless destruction; they had visited the Tate gallery; they had listened to modern jazz; they had read the novels of James Joyce; they had seen ice-creams which claimed to be shaped like faces but were actually shaped like amoeba – and they had understood it all. But this one had thrown them. This one had them scratching their multiple thought podules in a perplexed manner and saying '*akjafgidkerhs lejhslh hei!*', which translates as 'Bugger me, that's weird!'

3

The problem was one of transport.

The Brainians could see the long, thin arteries along which the humans travelled. They noted that after sunrise the humans all travelled one way and at sunset they all travelled the other. They could see that progress was slow and congested along these arteries, that there were endless blockages, queues, bottle-necks and delays causing untold frustration and inefficiency. All this they could see quite clearly.

What was not clear to them, was why.

They knew that humanity was stupid, they had only to look at the week's top ten grossing movies to work that out, but *this* was beyond reason. If, as was obvious, space was so restricted, why was it that each single member of this strange life-form insisted on occupying perhaps fifty times its own ground surface area for the entire time it was in motion – or not in motion, as was normally the case?

The super intelligent beings transmitted their data back to the producer of their programme and they received a right earful in reply (which was rather a lot because, although Brainians are only eight inches tall, their ears are the size of wheelbarrows and have to be rolled up like blinds).

'You're mad,' bellowed the producer using his inter-galactic portable phone because, like producers the universe over, he was having lunch.

'You're trying to tell me that they're all going in the *same* direction, travelling to much the *same* destinations and yet they're all *deliberately* impeding the progress of each other by covering six square metres of space with a large, almost completely empty tin box?'

'That's exactly what we're trying to tell you boss.'

'You're drunk,' shouted the producer, and he was so annoyed that the binding on one of his ears snapped and about six square feet of flapping lughole flopped into his pasta.

'We're bloody not drunk,' responded the aggrieved researchers. 'They're all stuck down there, beeping and screaming at each other and working themselves into a frenzy, not getting anything done, not producing anything, just stuck.'

'Oh go on then, let's have another bottle of wine,' said the producer, which naturally rather confused the researchers, but in fact the producer hadn't been speaking to them, his last remark was addressed at his lunch companion. Having another bottle of wine is something else which producers do the universe over – except in Los Angeles where people who, ten years ago, took cocaine in their coffee now give you the phone number of Alcoholics Anonymous if you ask for a beer.

Returning to his telephone conversation, the producer allowed himself to be mollified.

'You mean it's really true?' he said. 'A society sufficiently sophisticated to produce the internal combustion engine has not had the sophistication to develop cheap and efficient public transport?'

'Yes boss,' said the researchers, 'it's true. There's

hardly any buses, the trains are hopelessly under-funded, and hence the entire population is stuck in traffic.'

'Well that's amazing,' said the producer.

'Yes boss, it is amazing,' the researchers agreed.

'Get your asses back to Brain,' said the producer, 'we got a show.'

Chapter One

THE MAN THEY TRIED TO KILL

LOVELORN EGGHEAD

Geoffrey sat alone in the big open-plan office of the Institute of Industrial Research where he worked. He was surrounded by computers and they all winked and flashed at him, but, despite being intimately acquainted with every one of them, Geoffrey neither winked nor flashed back. He wasn't thinking of computers. He was thinking of a beautiful girl, and how one day in the not too distant future, he, Geoffrey, would set that girl free and by doing so would win her love. He would achieve this end with his fantastic research development. A research development so colossal and stupendous it made Penicillin look positively mouldy.

There was a bottle in front of Geoffrey and he was allowing himself a small toast, a little celebration, to mark the imminent realization of all his wildest dreams. Not all of them obviously, not the one set in a nunnery where all the novices turned out to be

7

Dolly Parton for instance, nor the one about the recurring ostrich, but all the ones fit to print. The dreams about success, peer group respect, enormous mountains of serious cash and setting free the most beautiful girl in the world, hence winning her love. If that wasn't worth a sloosh of pop whilst alone in the old research lab, then Geoffrey wasn't the man he thought he was. And Geoffrey certainly was the man he thought he was, because Geoffrey's was a thorough and precise mind and it wasn't the sort of thing he would make a mistake about.

So there he was, warm glow of satisfaction in his gut, love for a good woman in his heart, a little drinkie on the table, and bent over the arm of his chair staring at the carpet and dribbling.

UNWELCOME VISITORS

There was a buzz from the intercom. Obviously somebody was at the door. Geoffrey was a bit annoyed. He had no wish to be disturbed by anyone, unless of course it was by the girl of his dreams, or possibly Dolly Parton in a wimple, but since these were both rather unlikely, any visitors were unwelcome. Actually Geoffrey had no idea just how unwelcome these visitors would turn out to be. For they were professional killers – which is nearly as bad as having the Jehovah's Witnesses knock on your door.

With difficulty Geoffrey got up, or at least partly

up. He managed to get to his feet but it wasn't what you would call a particularly perpendicular performance. None the less, it was the best Geoffrey could manage under the circumstances. He fixed his eye upon the intercom some thirty yards across the room. A room crowded with obstacles. Getting across it was going to take some concentration. There were computers, printers, swivel chairs, kettles, stuffed Snoopies and amusing stickers proclaiming that you didn't have to be mad to work there but it helped.

These stickers were originally developed by psychologists as a test to enable office managers to determine an employee's utter dullness. If, for instance, the manager is seeking to find a person to whom may safely be entrusted the organization of the coffee-making rota. If he needs a reliable sort who will ensure that a good tin is provided for the sugar so that the office does not end up with a soggy paper bag containing forty-seven congealed brown sugar globules. All the manager has to do is spy out the employees with the sticker on their computer amusingly proclaiming that 'You don't have to be mad to work here but it helps'. That person will be guaranteed dull, dependable and sane as a pair of corduroy trousers.

Geoffrey lurched forward towards the vast expanse of potential croppers that lay between him and the buzzer. His work place was one of those modern open-plan areas where everything is rendered much more frank and relaxed by virtue of there being no nasty walls to divide people or doors to intimidate them. The actual result of course being that everyone develops nervous ticks due to never knowing who's eavesdropping on them and never feeling safe to have a really good bitch.

An added disadvantage of these spaces, especially if you happen to be in the condition that Geoffrey was in, is that plug and telephone sockets stick up out of the floor in the most unexpected places and there are wires everywhere. It was whilst attempting to negotiate a particularly tangled bit of technology that Geoffrey skidded on the bit of pizza that was left over from a leaving bash which had taken place on the previous Friday evening.

THE LEAVING BASH FROM HELL

Geoffrey lay on the carpet tiles, with his head in a waste-paper bin, quietly cursing. The leaving bash from hell had returned to haunt him.

All leaving bashes are awful. Perhaps not as awful as birthday bashes where one is forced to annoy an entire restaurant by singing *Happy Birthday* whilst a waiter proudly brings forth a mound of whipped cream with a sparkler in it, but pretty bad, none the less – and this leaving bash was worse. The nightmare had started with the card. Geoffrey had barely known Suzy, the lucky recipient of all that office warmth, symbolized, as it was, by a large picture of Snoopy holding a horseshoe. However, he had felt obliged to rack his brains for twenty minutes trying to think of something witty to write. Eventually he had decided on 'I don't know who you are, but very best wishes'. The biro had scarcely come to a standstill when he deeply regretted his decision. Paranoia consumed him, the phrase was too hard, too dismissive. The scrawled sentence Geoffrey had written seemed to dissolve before his eyes and reform into the words, 'Bugger off, nobody'. After all, that was what his message implied wasn't it? In that instant Geoffrey convinced himself that the girl would be very hurt and that the rest of the lab would despise him for messing up their nice card. Already he could feel the icy hand of social ostracism fingering his collar.

In desperation he opened a bracket. Impulsively he wrote, 'Just joking, really, it's been great working with you'. Geoffrey closed the bracket and descended fully and completely into the paranoid zone. Talk about making a bad thing worse! Maybe he should just go have a shit in the poor woman's pending tray! The first joke had been merely tasteless, now he had turned it into pure hate mail. Everything he had written seemed to just deliberately and maliciously draw attention to the fact that he had scarcely ever spoken to the girl and did not care whether she lived or died. Frantically Geoffrey considered a second bracket, a square one, just a simple and affectionate message to repair the damage of the previous two efforts. Perhaps something along the lines of, 'Actually I want you to be the mother of my children! . . .' or, 'Listen Suzy, name your price to forget about the whole thing.' Fortunately for Geoffrey reason returned to its throne. He realized that there would not be sufficient brackets in a book of algebra to extricate him from the tact swamp into which he had dived. He would simply have to let it go.

Geoffrey firmly closed the card and, with a weak smile, handed it back to Denise, unofficial social secretary for the whole building and the girl with the 'mad' sticker on her desk.

Denise, who had about as much tact as the Wehrmacht, reopened the card and read Geoffrey's message. 'Oh that's *lovely*,' she said, in a voice that you could have beaten down and forged into drill bits. 'I'm *sure* Suzy will see the joke.'

Attending the 'do' itself had been worse than writing the card. There is a type of white wine which is produced in continental Europe specifically for leaving do's in Britain. It is described as 'an elegant, delicate, fruity dry' which is Euro-plonkspeak for abrasive and it is made by putting sandpaper and lemon juice into a blender. Within two sips from his or her plastic cup the unhappy imbiber's throat becomes coated in a thick layer of bitter tasting phlegm which can only be removed with a pan scrubber. Unless of course you happen to be talking to the boss, in which case the phlegm will instantly leap out of the back of your neck and cling desperately to his tie.

This wine also contains a special kind of alcohol that cannot get you happy-drunk but can only get you bored-drunk, which was the state that everybody was in when the 'do' finally wound down at about eight-thirty.

This is an appalling time for an after-work social to end. Up until eight-twenty everyone has spent the entire time making desperate conversation and wishing they were somewhere else. Then suddenly, with no warning, people are sufficiently bored-pissed on plastic cups of warm French expectorant to agree to go on for a curry.

It is a strange factor of this kind of euphorically dull drunkenness ('Oh go on then, sod it, why not? The evening's buggered anyway.') that it lasts for only twenty-five minutes. This is exactly long enough to get trapped in a curry house between two people you have absolutely no desire to talk to, who are on a different table from the person you have vaguely begun to fancy, while you watch one person order three – no better make it four – popadums each, and someone else order a large brandy. All of which you know you are going to have to pay for a fifteenth of, even though you're not particularly hungry and you can't drink any more yourself because you're driving.

All of this had taken place on Friday night, and now it was late Sunday afternoon and the leaving

bash from hell was back. Like some evil curse from
a darker age it refused to let Geoffrey be. Having
caused him untold worry, bored him stupid and cost
him over twenty quid, it had now dumped him down
with a thud on the carpet tiles and left him with his
head in a waste-paper basket, wherein, a polystyr-
ene cup was in the process of pouring half an inch
of cold coffee with a fag end in it, up his nose. How
much more could one leaving bash do to a man?

ENGLISH COMPREHENSION

The buzzer was still buzzing, Geoffrey wanted to
shout 'All right, hang on, where's the fire, dick-
heads,' but he was a realist and in his condition he
didn't reckon he would be up to making himself
understood. If you're going to start being brusque
with people, the last thing you want is them looking
puzzled and replying, 'You what?' It detracts from
your impact.

With some difficulty, Geoffrey extricated his head
from the waste-paper bin that the pizza had
dumped it in, and continued his uncertain stagger
across the room, finally arriving at the intercom
buzzer.

On the second attempt Geoffrey managed to press
the button . . . 'Yurgh,' he grunted into the microphone. Which translated meant 'Yes, who is it?'.
However, since no interpreter was available at the
other end, the two killers waiting on the pavement

had to make do with 'Yurgh'.

'Uhm yeah,' shouted one of the killers, for the traffic was loud in the street, 'we're looking for Dr Geoffrey Peason. He around?'

'Yes, that's me, come on up,' said Dr Geoffrey Peason – or rather he didn't because he was having a bit of trouble getting his tongue and larynx to cooperate with each other. The sentence had departed from his brain in perfect condition, but by the time it struggled out of the intercom into the street it had become 'Urg-ats-mm-uhmonup'.

The two men in the street did not know what to make of this cryptic message. They couldn't see the condition Geoffrey was in so they just presumed that they were dealing with a foreigner, or perhaps a mental defective.

The more talkative killer began again, employing the accepted method of communication employed by the British whenever they encounter someone who does not appear to understand English. He raised his voice.

All over Europe, each summer, can be seen the sad picture of frustrated, purple-faced Britons screaming in the faces of non-comprehending natives, 'WHERE . . . IS . . . THE . . . PUB-LIC . . . CON-VE-NIENCE'. The curious theory that a strange language can be rendered under-standable by increasing the volume at which it is spoken is one of the great mysteries of the British abroad.

In Paris the cause of the commotion is slightly different. Most Parisians do in fact speak some English, but out of pure bloody-minded snobbishness they refuse to do so in the company of the British. When accosted by a desperate, sweaty, confused Brit asking, 'Excuse me, but do you speak English?' the immaculately dressed Parisian will raise a languid eyebrow and enquire, 'Yes, do you speak French?'. It is a little known historical fact that it was this irritating habit which was the principal cause of the Hundred Years War.

Anyway, in an effort to make himself understood, the man in the street raised his voice. Since he had already been shouting to get above the traffic noise the effort caused veins to stand out on his forehead. He accompanied this tonsil-tingling rant with an elaborate pantomime, this being another aspect of the standard British method of getting your message across to foreigners – scream at the top of your voice and wave your arms about in massive but vague physical gesticulations.

This sad display provides mainland Europeans (again, particularly, the French) with endless entertainment. Outside the Georges Pompidou Centre in Paris, there can always be found a cluster of extremely dull mime artists in tights and bowler hats with flowers sticking out of them, miming walking into a high wind. These irritating performances are invariably accompanied by a clutch of Americans, Brits and Japanese delightedly assuring each other that the bowler hatted one indeed looks *exactly* like he's walking into a high wind, or quite anyway. The locals of course, know that far more fun can be had watching a British tourist attempt to mime 'Can you direct me to the Museum of Contemporary Sculpture please?' and what's more he won't shove his bowler hat under your nose at the end of it.

JUDGING A BOOK BY ITS COVER

So there they were, the two men on the pavement, one of them roaring at the intercom and miming wildly. Geoffrey, deciding that actions speak louder than words, even words as loud as the ones making the intercom shudder, pressed the lock transmission button, thus providing the first clear message of the whole communication.

After the obligatory electronic lock dance, in which a person and door push against each other to the tune of a buzzer going on and off, the door swung open and the men stumbled in.

They took the lift to the floor marked 'Transport, Fuel and Engine Research' and emerged from it to find Dr Geoffrey Peason waiting for them. Geoffrey held out a shaking hand and tried to greet them cordially but he wasn't really up to it and the two men clearly weren't very impressed with him. However, at first they made at least a pretence at the easy good manners which killers are wont to adopt before unmasking themselves as the angel of death.

They enquired again after Dr Geoffrey Peason stating that they had business with him regarding his recent application for a patent. Dr Peason, also attempting easy good manners but blowing it by dribbling a bit, again replied that he was the said Peason, Doctor of Physics and patent applicant, and what could he do for them? Unfortunately Geoffrey still was not making himself very clearly understood and the visitors' tone became impatient.

'Now listen Sonny, we haven't got a lot of time to waste, so you pull yourself together, all right? And tell us where Peason is.'

Geoffrey was suddenly very tired. He hated being patronized and he hated being dismissed as of no importance. It was always happening to him. He turned his back on the men and staggered back to his chair. Plonking himself down rather heavily he knocked his bottle onto the floor.

'Bollocks,' he said, or rather 'Burgles', an exclamation which he accompanied with an impulsive looking gesture of despair.

Faced with this incoherent hurdle to their enquiries the two men's tone became markedly more intimidating.

'Where's Peason?' the talkative one barked. 'This is where he works isn't it? Our information is that he's always here Sundays.'

Again Doctor Peason tried to explain that he was the man they sought, but the men just did not have the patience to listen to him. They had been briefed to pay a visit on a brilliant scientist and inventor. A man who had invented something quite brilliant and scientific. Confronted by this slurring, unpleasant, uncoordinated young man in a leather jacket and torn jeans, they assumed that the doctor was out. However, since the dribbling rocker was clearly their only available source of information they had no choice but to continue their clumsy enquiries.

Advancing towards Geoffrey one of the men slipped on the pizza.

'I just did that,' said Geoffrey trying once more to be friendly, but still failing completely to make himself understood.

'Don't laugh at me you disgusting little git,' barked the man. He grabbed Geoffrey's cap from Geoffrey's head. Geoffrey was wearing a cap he particularly liked, it was a comedy cap. It had a stuffed arm holding a hammer emerging out of it which appeared to be beating the wearer on his own head. The man wiped the pizza from his shoe with Geoffrey's hat.

Geoffrey may have been having more trouble than usual making himself understood that day but this last gesture confirmed an understanding that had been dawning on him for some time: that he was in the presence of a couple of potentially very dangerous people.

Pizza-shoe roughly crammed the hat back on Geoffrey's head.

'Where's the Doc zit face?' he demanded.

Geoffrey gulped.

'He can't tell you nothing, can he,' said the other, speaking for the first time.

'Look at the state he's in. Let's search the building.'

And with that Geoffrey's interrogators stalked from the room, leaving Geoffrey rather shaken by his unpleasant encounter. Not as shaken as he would have been if he had realized that, had he not been a spastic, he would have been murdered. But none the less, pretty shaken.

Being a spastic had not done Geoffrey a lot of favours in his life. In fact it could be said to have been a total and utter drag from start to finish. However, in that brief moment, being a spastic had actually made up for quite a number of its short-comings as a physical condition. It had unquestion-ably saved Geoffrey's life, because if Geoffrey had not been a spastic, or CP sufferer as some people call it, the two thugs would certainly have killed him.

This is not to say that they refrained from such a course of action out of any sense of sympathy; they did not say to themselves, 'Oh look, hell, the poor bugger's been knocking glasses off tables all his life and probably never been able to masturbate prop-erly. Let's give him a break, eh?' No, the two thugs in question were far too hard of heart for that. It was simply that it never occurred to them that the strange, guttural sounding, twitchy chap sat before them could be the brilliant scientist and inventor whom they had been ordered to murder. But he was.

People with disabilities are very used to being looked through, over, and around. Judged by their covers so to speak. They no longer find it surprising when it is presumed that they have little or no potential and nothing to add to a conversation (other than a conversation on the subject of disability). This is not to say that it gets any easier to put up with, spending one's entire life being underestimated never ceases to be anything other than a horrendous strain, but people with disabilities certainly recognize the attitude. Geoffrey did, he was always being either ignored or patronized and on this occasion he was extremely fortunate that it was the case.

Chapter Two

WHAT IS IN A NAME?

There is a debate surrounding the word 'spastic'. This concerns its appropriation, by those who do not suffer from cerebral palsy, as a term of contempt. There can scarcely be any able-bodied person who has not used, or at least failed to confront the use of the word 'spastic' as an insult.

It is normally a youthful insult, particularly beloved of small farty boys ('Cripes spew face, you're such a spastic'), but it resonates throughout the population. We all know that to call someone a 'spastic' means that they are stupid, worthless and beneath contempt. Hence the debate for those who actually *are* spastics about what to do with such a tainted term. It's their word, it describes a condition from which they suffer, but it has been stolen, and the question is, do they want it back? Being as how the word spastic has come to imply an all-encompassing and extremely negative summation of a person's abilities and personality, is the word any longer of any real relevance to those who suffer from cerebral palsy? Has the very word itself not become yet another cross that people with this condition are fated to bear?

Some say yes. Some say that the word has been debased beyond redemption. Some say that it must be discarded as a lost cause, and that a new, untainted word or phrase must be found. They suggest 'CP sufferer' for instance, a phrase which certainly has the advantage of clearly only describing an aspect of a person, and not appearing to sum up their entire personality. On the other hand, there are those who insist that the word 'spastic' must be reclaimed. It must be wrested from the mouths of thoughtless little boys and restored to its true meaning. These people look to a day when they will be able to say 'I am a spastic' or 'my daughter is a spastic' without it sounding a bit like a gag.

Geoffrey was of the latter faith. Ever since he had first understood the nature of his severe disability, he had laboured to escape from the social stigma that such a condition engenders. He knew he could not escape from its physical limitations but he could definitely try and stop people thinking that he was a thick, useless, embarrassment.

His method, not one that would work for everyone, had been to take the linguistic battle to the aggressor. He proclaimed himself a 'spasmo'. He had had the words 'Geoffrey Spasmo: Satan's Hell

Dog' written in studs on his first leather jacket and worn it to school. Geoffrey, who always found walking quite difficult, had in his youth sometimes been pushed around in a wheelchair. To his mother's intense embarrassment he had the word 'spasmobile' beautifully inscribed on the back. He had done it in the same lettering as the famous Triumph motorbike company logo, and it looked very cool.

It was at this time, during his wild youth, that Geoffrey had attempted to set up the first wheelchair chapter of the British Hell's Angels. The Angels, who have a highly developed outcast mentality themselves, were quite sympathetic, but Geoffrey dropped the notion when it was explained that besides kissing the arse of a dead chicken, he would be required to piss on his jeans and wear them forever.

Geoffrey's aggressive confrontation of other people's attitudes to his condition upset and annoyed some people. His parents had been terribly upset when he had wanted to officially change his name from Peason to Spasmo, so he hadn't done it. Other spastics, or CP sufferers, were also ambivalent about it, some considered that it played into the hands of the enemy, and Geoffrey conceded that this was possible. However Geoffrey wasn't doing it on behalf of the whole spastic community. He was doing it for himself, to create his own style and his own identity. He was Geoffrey Spasmo. Even now, as an eminent physicist, his leather jacket still spelt it out in studs. His shades, his Sex Pistols T-shirt and torn jeans still spoke of the time in the mid-seventies when he had emerged from his shell and begun his personal rebellion. Geoffrey's had been the only wheelchair to make it to the front of a gig on the Clash's *White Riot Tour* in '77. His Dad had to hose it down to get all the gob off afterwards.

Chapter Three

MAN ON THE RUN

THIEF

In another part of London Sam Turk sat alone in his office. Sam had no physical disabilities, unless you counted a copious beer gut, but he did have a seriously retarded soul. It was this moral deficiency that had led him to unleash the killers on Geoffrey.

Sam was not naturally a killer, it was circumstance which had made him deadly. Circumstance in the form of a great sheaf of diagrams and computer printouts which lay before him in his office. The diagrams were complex, and Sam was a good enough engineer to realize that to fully understand their subtle intricacies would take months, perhaps years. However, even a superficial perusal had been enough to convince Sam that what lay before him was a revolution, a revolution that would change the world.

Sam's mind reeled at the almost limitless potential of what had fallen into his possession. Limitless is a word that comes more easily to a copywriter than an engineer, but Sam knew that on this occasion it was apt. Fame, power and wealth without boundary of constraint were his for the taking. First, however, Doctor Geoffrey Peason would have to die.

MISTAKEN IDENTITY

Dr Geoffrey Peason was considering his position, a broken lemonade bottle at his feet and two extremely aggressive looking thugs wandering around the building.

Geoffrey was, of course, unaware that these two men wished to kill him, on the other hand it was pretty clear that they were not intending to give him a great big French kiss and a little box of choccies either. Their attitude had been distinctly aggressive. Geoffrey was reluctantly forced to conclude that the two men had intended to do him no good; possibly the beating up, robbing and leaving for dead type of no good. Geoffrey did not know how he had come to annoy them or what they could want. In fact he was quite certain that the whole thing was a mistake and that they were after an entirely different Geoffrey Peason. Possibly Geoffrey 'chainsaw' Peason who had managed to cross some shadowy 'Mr Big' on some matters of drugs, whores and unpaid gambling debts. Now, however, Geoffrey realized was not the time to sort the matter out. Now was the time to clear off and have a bit of a think, what's more speed was of the essence. It was Sunday and the research facility offices, the labs and the little tea making areas were empty. It would not take long for the two thugs to discover this. Then perhaps they might put two and two together and work out that 'dribble lips' in the computer room might just be the person they thought they were looking for. Actually Geoffrey thought that this was fairly unlikely because, as he well knew, changing the first impressions that people form of those with disabilities was well nigh impossible. As far as the able-bodied community was concerned, if you twitched, and spoke with difficulty, you were a retard. People say that first impressions are so important, for people with disabilities they are a ten foot wall to climb. Which, if you happen to be a quadriplegic, is a bloody difficult thing to do.

None the less, on the off-chance that one of the thugs might be sufficiently enlightened to make the chasmic mental leap required to realize that a spastic might also be a brilliant physicist, Geoffrey thought it wise to get out.

POPULAR DEMOCRACY

Geoffrey scurried out onto the Cromwell Road, which was where he worked, and started looking for a cab. Normally they were pretty frequent around Kensington but on this occasion there were of course none to be seen. Geoffrey waited, nervously glancing back at the door of his office, caught in the classic cab dilemma, should he start walking and look for one? or should he stay put and look for one? Geoffrey agonized. If he started walking what was the betting that ten would arrive where he presently stood. On the other hand, perhaps the same ten were at that moment hiding around the very next corner. This dilemma is in fact a principal cause of urban pedestrian fatalities, because people will sometimes throw themselves under a bus rather than make a decision.

On this occasion however, Geoffrey managed to pull himself together and had just decided that he would be better off getting away from the two thugs even if it meant walking, which was something that he found quite difficult, when a cab pulled up. Unfortunately, as Geoffrey got into it, the two thugs having tired of their search, emerged from the office. They had not yet freed their minds sufficiently to realize that Geoffrey was Dr Peason, but they had decided to interrogate him further, and on finding him gone from the office had begun to wonder whether their bird had flown.

'There he is, the little bastard,' they cried unkindly, as Geoffrey's cab pulled away and they ran for their car.

'West Hampstead,' stuttered Geoffrey, 'and step on it' – a phrase he had never imagined anybody actually used.

Unfortunately, in London, stepping on it is a very rare achievement (as opposed to stepping *in* it, which is almost impossible to avoid). London is, of course, the capital traffic jam of the UK and even though it was a Sunday the streets were still very busy. Unusually so in fact, and as Geoffrey's cab drove up Queens Gate things became positively teeming. A great colourful mass of people streamed down both pavements heading away from the park. Some braver souls were even venturing to colonize those parts of her Majesty's highways reserved exclusively for cars. Geoffrey was taken aback for a moment, as one aggressive youth pointedly lingered in the act of crossing the road, thus causing the cab to stop, and the cabby and the youth to engage in a brief exchange of views conducted wholly in Chaucerian vernacular.

'Funny thing innit?' the cabbie opined to Geoffrey after the youth had flicked his last V sign. 'Here's this lot all wanting to protest about road building plans. So how'd they go about it? Create a bleeding traffic jam, that's what. I mean that's like screwing for virginity isn't it? If ever there was an argument for building roads, it's a traffic jam. I mean, a traffic jam shows the road's inadequate doesn't it? London needs more roads, there's just no arguing with that.'

Despite this predicament Geoffrey took a moment to go through one of two stock emotions people reserve for when they are sitting in the back of cabs.

Not the one about being convinced that the driver is taking you on an eight mile detour which will cost two hundred pounds, but the one about totally disagreeing with some horrendous prejudices that the cabbie has glibly spouted but not having the moral fibre to take him on. Geoffrey did not think that London needed more roads and heartily agreed with the principles of the rally which had been called to make this point.

It was widely believed that the government had a massive hidden agenda on road building. Nothing was known for certain, but then again nothing is ever known for certain about the actions of the British Government. Whitehall makes a positive fetish out of secrecy. Many a fresh young Civil Servant has had their first day ruined because no one will tell them where the toilets are. None the less, despite the absence of any real proof, there was a growing conviction amongst environmentalists and public transport unions that large sections of Britain were in danger of being submerged beneath concrete.

Of course, the government strenuously denied it. Indeed it went so far as to employ its most open and accountable means of communication; the private, off-the-record briefing. In these private, off-the-record briefings, a senior Civil Servant (in this case Ingmar Bresslaw, Chief Permanent Occasional Over Under Secretary to the Cabinet Office) hands out a private, off-the-record statement, with which the Prime Minister is in no way associated but which he none the less expects to see in the following day's national newspapers.

The private, off-the-record statement which Ingmar Bresslaw handed out, of course, completely dismissed environmental fears regarding road building, but none the less spoke suspiciously in terms of reviewing the 'infra structure', reconsidering the 'road to rail relationship' and 'seeking always to protect the inalienable rights of the private motorist'.

It was this rather inconsistent statement that had provoked the protest in which Geoffrey found himself caught up. A protest which, under normal circumstances, he would gladly have joined. Geoffrey, like many people with disabilities, was dependent on public transport and did not relish the prospect of having to hobble half a mile along a six-lane suburban motorway to get to the footbridge (and frog-tunnel) so that he could cross over, in order to hobble the half mile back down the other side, to get to the bus stop. However, sympathetic though he might be, for the time being Geoffrey had more pressing matters to contend with. His cab was still stationary, behind it was a lorry, behind that, Geoffrey guessed, lurked his pursuers.

'I've changed my mind,' Geoffrey said. 'How much do you reckon to Harlow, Essex?'

'In this traffic,' said the cabbie, wincing as if in pain, "s'gotta be twenty notes hasn't it?'

'Fine,' said Geoffrey, handing over the money. 'I want you to deliver this hat to Harlow Town Hall,' and, having perched his comedy hat on the back shelf of the cab, Geoffrey slipped out of the door and into the crowded street. Geoffrey was a small man, he sat low in a cab, he felt fairly confident that from behind, it would appear as if he was still in his seat with his hat being the only part of him that was visible.

Geoffrey was soon deep in the crowd, jerking his way past the numerous vans dispensing salmonella in a bun. He passed the inspiring and beautiful trade union banners depicting tools that nobody used any more and solidarity that nobody felt any more. He passed the punky-looking kids surrounded by photo-journalists trying to persuade them to throw bricks. He passed London's community policeman, with his big community smile. The same kindly chap produced by Scotland Yard for all such events, who every year at the Notting Hill Carnival got his picture in the papers, dancing with a black woman who was wearing his helmet. Then there were the coachloads of non-community policemen hiding in the side streets. Confronting these, snarling and spitting at them all the while, were the inevitable knots of anarcho/punk/hippy/skinhead arseholes, hoping to provoke a confrontation so that the police would overreact, there would be a riot and they could nick a TV from Rumbelows.

Every cliché of liberal dissent was milling around

Hyde Park that day and Geoffrey felt the inevitable sinking feeling that anyone who has ever attended a protest march feels. That niggling voice in the back of the mind that says 'Do we all look like a bunch of utter gits?'

Rallies are a very double-edged sword. On the one hand, they can serve as a powerful demonstration of popular feeling, on the other, they can simply make everyone look a bit pathetic, it's a thin line. Some types of protestor are entirely counter-productive. Worse even than the middle-class pseudo-punk demanding class war, is the over-excited student who insists on leading chants that nobody wants to join in with.

'Digby Digby Digby,' Farty would scream, invoking the name of Digby Parkhurst the Minister for Transport and principal hate figure of the rally. 'Out out out,' a few loyal comrades would shout in weary reply. 'Digby Digby Digby,' Farty repeats in his hoarse yell, clearly feeling the need for further elaboration. Again, a now diminishing gang reply, 'Out out out.' 'Digby,' bellows Farty, honing down his debating style somewhat. 'Out,' comes the equally succinct reply. 'Digby,' repeats Farty, pressing the point. 'Out,' reiterate his pals, as all around them gnash their teeth. Finally, just to make his position absolutely clear on the subject of Digby, Farty returns to the original rhythm, shouting 'Digby Digby Digby,' and the gang again rewards him with three rousing 'Outs'.

That is the chant as heard on many a march in the last few years. It always emerges at some point – presuming the hate figure in question has been considerate enough to have a two syllable name, 'Theophilus Theophilus Theophilus,' not having quite the same rabble rousing feel. The problem with the chant is that most 'outers' go along with it only out of a sense of duty and to avoid being embarrassed on Farty's behalf, in the way that an audience will murmur at a joke they find unfunny, just to get through the embarrassing silence. They go along with the chant but they feel pretty stupid doing it, and thank God when they get to the final 'Out out out' and can return to silent anonymity.

Unfortunately, what inevitably happens is that Farty, emboldened and intoxicated with his new roll as cheerleader, rabble rouser and street-fighting man, tries to go for the whole thing again. This condemns it to an inevitable and eggy petering out which renders the entire exercise so limp as to actually work against its intention. At the end of the chant, any non-aligned observers would definitely be left with the impression that Digby, far from being 'out out out', was more entrenched than ever.

NOT QUITE JERUSALEM

'Oh God,' thought Geoffrey, 'please, please don't let anybody strike up "Here we go".'

'Here we go' is a football chant performed

vaguely to a fairground barrel organ tune which, during the Miners' Strike of 1984, did useful service warming people up on 5 a.m. picket lines. Since then, however, it has been adopted as a kind of catch-all anthem of protest and has been heard near missile bases, outside hospitals in danger of closure, inside town halls where new cuts were being announced and at the end of Labour Party meetings. Indeed such a contribution did this chant make to the cultural backdrop of protest in Britain in the eighties that it is worth recording its lyric in full, that posterity might not forget the depth and subtlety of its message. The text runs like this:

Here we go, here we go, here we go,
Here we go, here we go, here we go-oh.
Here we go, here we go, here we go,
Here we go-oh, here we go.
(Repeat until your cause is lost.)

Where we were going is not touched upon, why we might want to go there is also left to the imagination, the one salient point is that we are off. Sadly, never was a lyric more apt. 'Here we go' would be sung, and pits, jobs, services etc., duly went.

Compare this turgid, lifeless effort with 'Jerusalem', or 'We Shall Overcome' and it is possible to see what a momentous own-goal in public relations this chant was. Mindless as 'Oompah oompah stick it up your jumper,' but without the biting wit. So mindless is it in fact that the only possible explanation for its continuing emergence year after year at every possible protest event, is that it is the result of infiltration by *agents provocateurs*. Just at the point at which the audience at a protest are at their most emotionally and intellectually moved, a right wing infiltrator in a bobble hat will ruin it by striking up 'Here we go'. It works every time. The hall groans inwardly, but none the less joins in under the mistaken impression that not to do so would give the appearance that the event has no unity, soul or fervour. The impression actually given is that the event is made up of a bunch of parrots without an original thought between them.

MESS: THE ULTIMATE SOLUTION

Geoffrey got on the tube at Marble Arch and, by coincidence, arrived home at almost exactly the same time that a bemused cabby found himself standing on the steps of a firmly locked Harlow Town Hall, holding a comedy hat, whilst behind him two furious thugs stared into an empty cab.

Geoffrey let himself into his ground floor maisonette and began to pick his way carefully through the mess. Any stranger opening the door of Geoffrey's place would have presumed that Geoffrey had just been burgled by a hyperactive burglar who had taken a line or two of speed to get him into a good burgling mood. The place was a mess. It could not have been in more of a mess if it had been occupied by a fifteen-year-old girl who had decided to rebel against the bourgeois mentality of her parents because neither they, nor indeed anyone else in the world, understood her.

In choosing to live in a manner that would cause a punk sewer-rat to raise a dubious eyebrow, Geoffrey was unlike many other people with disabilities, who treasure order. Because simple functions are more difficult for them it is important to them to know where everything is and to make sure that wherever that is, is the most convenient place. If you are in a wheelchair for instance and want to read your book, it is obviously less hassle to know where the book is and also to have a clear, uncluttered path to reach it.

Geoffrey was not in a wheelchair, but he did move in a vaguely unpredictable way, which meant he often knocked things over. He really only became truly aware of the mayhem this can cause when he left home to go to university. Like every other new student Geoffrey discovered, to his astonishment, that clean socks do not organically form inside drawers and that mugs left around the house do not magically bathe themselves thoroughly and then levitate back onto a hook – they go mouldy. Geoffrey, like many an eighteen-year-old before and since, was forced to realize just how many of the true facts of life his mother had been keeping from him.

Facts like, sheets go yellow if you don't wash them, the rims of toilets become encrusted with dust and pubic hairs if you don't wipe them, meals do not grow on the table and, in Geoffrey's particular case, if you don't pick things up, everything you own eventually ends up on the floor. Geoffrey struggled against this problem for many years, just as his mother had done before him, endlessly picking things up in order to knock them over again. Until one day the futility of it all suddenly dawned upon him. He felt like a philosopher contemplating war, or a British gymnast contemplating the Olympics. He realized that there was no point. He realized that the solution to knocking things over, was simply never to pick anything up, thereby depriving himself of ammunition. From that day on, Geoffrey allowed the bulk of his worldly goods to remain on the floor.

Geoffrey was of course lucky, he had a wonderful cleaner who, after initial reluctance, had agreed to apply Geoffrey's method. The rule was very simple, she cleaned up anything wet, and left anything dry. Geoffrey never cooked, either eating out or having pizza delivered, so the system worked pretty well.

ROBO CUP

Geoffrey's passion was mechanics and, in particular, robotics. Perhaps because his own motor mechanism was so faulty he took a peculiar delight in clever and smooth-running machinery. His little maisonette was filled with fantastically complicated electronic gadgetry; a mass of bits of mechanical arms, half-finished vacuum cleaners that were supposed to do the hoovering by themselves, concertinaed platforms designed for lifting heavy objects. Geoffrey had work to do on most of his gadgets. At present the lifting platform was a touch enthusiastic. It lay almost flat on the floor and was designed to lift a wheelchair up a step for instance, or simply raise a heavy suitcase. Unfortunately such heavy-duty hydraulics are rather expensive, so Geoffrey was experimenting with pistons loaded with small explosive charges. Geoffrey would have been the first to confess that he was having trouble getting the pressure right, also the balance. In fact on the last attempt the suitcase had been catapulted out of the window and into the front garden. Geoffrey was grateful he hadn't tried it on a person in a wheelchair.

Geoffrey sat down, not unnaturally, still ruminating over the threatening manner of his two interrogators. He decided to have a glass of wine to facilitate thought. Sitting in his chair, he took up a little remote control device with switches and a joystick; Geoffrey's cerebral palsy was not as severe as for some and he had one fully working hand. He flipped a switch which activated his new mechanical corkscrew. Geoffrey liked his drop of sauce of an evening, and getting bottles open was a major drag for him, so he had invented a mechanical arm with a needle on the end, a needle attached to a canister of compressed air. The idea was that the radio-operated arm manoeuvred the needle over the cork and then plunged it down into the bottle, the downward movement causing the air to flow from the canister into the bottle, thus forcing the cork out. The machine was on the sideboard next to his booze stash. From his armchair on the other side of the room Geoffrey positioned the needle and sent the arm plunging down, there was a hiss of compressed air, but sadly the cork was a stiff one, the bottle gave out before it did, exploding with a loud bang and sending broken glass and Rioja everywhere.

Geoffrey was used to failure, he could not possibly afford the equipment required to make his equipment foolproof. He decided to have a cup of coffee instead. There was a pot all brewed in the coffee-maker. The pot was attached to an extendable robotic arm. Geoffrey's mug was where it always was, on the arm of his chair, he did not take milk or sugar so it was never washed. With a twiddle of the remote Geoffrey began to manoeuvre the coffee pot through the air towards him. When it was positioned perfectly, he twiddled again and the pot tilted. It was a triumph, a brimming cup of scalding coffee without leaving his seat. Geoffrey sent the pot flying home, put in his straw and head jerking a little, took a careful sip. Relaxing, perhaps for the first time since the intercom had gone off in his office, Geoffrey continued to muse on that afternoon's disturbing encounter. For a moment he toyed with the idea of reporting it to the police, but then, what was there to report? Two men had enquired after him at his place of work. Certainly they had been unpleasant, but that isn't a crime. If it was, the courts would be packed with television astrologers and BMW drivers. Burglary is, however, a crime, and it was as he sat pondering that Geoffrey first noticed that he had been burgled. As has been pointed out, Geoffrey's place always looked as if it had been burgled, which is why it took him so long to realize.

It was not a bad burglary as far as Geoffrey could see. In fact, when he considered some of the horror stories he had heard, he reckoned he had got off fairly lightly. The burglars had been a thoughtful and professional bunch. They had refrained from having a crap on the coffee table or masturbating into Geoffrey's underwear drawer. In fact all they seemed to have taken was his television.

Geoffrey steeled himself to make the phone call, he hated ringing up people he did not know.

'Hello police? I've been burgled,' said Geoffrey, adding, as he always did, 'and I talk this way because I'm a spastic.'

Chapter Four

GOING TO THE PARTY

OFFICIAL BOOZE UP

Whilst Geoffrey was being pursued by murderers and discovering the theft of his television, Sam Turk, the man responsible for this mystifying harrassment, was in the back of a luxury car on his way to Brighton. Starting on the morrow, Brighton was to play host to a Party Political Conference, or Party Political Piss-up as the more honest politician would concede.

There is a similar institution in the world of marketing, it is called a 'sales conference' which, despite its business-like title, is a corporate institution whereby the staff get the opportunity to become legless at the company's expense and the sales reps have a chance to try and shag the secretaries. Of course this is denied absolutely when the Inland Revenue queries the drinks bill. Then much corporate gobbledegook is spouted concerning 'late night policy sessions', 'target dinners' and 'strike-unit damage control briefings'. None the less, the sales conference is a piss-up. And why not? It is a small reward, a chance to get out of the Ford Sierra and into the bar; to get away from the typewriter and into a little black cocktail number. It forges *esprit de corps*. The Japanese have their company songs and exercise sessions; the British have their eleven pints of lager and at 3 a.m. attempt to break into the hotel swimming pool. People need a chance to express themselves.

Party Conferences are the political world's equivalent of these fine corporate institutions. The only difference being that they last a week and provide an excellent opportunity for behind the scenes wheeler-dealing. This was why Sam Turk was going to Brighton.

KILLER ON THE LOOSE

Sam was not a politician, not in the elected sense anyway. But he certainly dealt in power. He was a carmaker.

He worked for Global Motors, a US based multi-national auto manufacturing company, and he had come to London the previous year with the declared intention of kicking some English bottoms at Global Motors UK. The British motor industry, as Sam well knew, was still residing in the 1920s which, considering the US motor industry had made it as far as the 1950s, meant that Sam had a lot of work to do. The Japanese motor industry is, of course, in the 1990s. It was Global Motors' secret target that by the year 2015, they would be in the 1990s too.

For the moment however cars were not on Sam's mind, but killing was. In his briefcase lay hidden the most exciting designs that he had ever come across. However, in order for Sam to realize their full potential, he needed their creator dead.

'D'yah knock out the professor guy?' Sam asked Springer, his loyal Lieutenant of many years.

Springer winced a little at this abrupt enquiry. He had not enjoyed the task of organizing a murder one little bit. In fact he had for the first time in all his loyal service attempted to defy Sam. It was only after Sam had reluctantly shared the momentous secrets of the plans with him that Springer had steeled himself to the task. It was immediately clear to Springer that the good of the company, indeed the good of the entire economy of the United States, might be at stake.

'I guess he must have bought the farm by now,' Springer replied. He had served in Korea and loved to talk like a soldier.

Sam nodded with grim satisfaction, none the less, he could not help but feel a pang of something. One wouldn't go so far as to say it was actual remorse, but it was definitely regret. Sam had led a pretty rough life in the paranoid world of the US motor industry and he had done wicked and unpleasant things. But he had never before had anybody killed.

45

'I can't help feeling that bumping the guy off was wrong,' he said.

Springer was surprised, it was most unusual for his boss to be tormented by doubt.

'I can get the driver to haul ass to a church boss. It might be best to let a priest handle this,' he said sympathetically.

'I ain't talking morally wrong,' said Sam. 'We had a serious situation, and we made a move. That's business, that's what I'm paid to do, my conscience is clear. But was it the *right* move I ask myself? Death *is* kind of radical. I still can't believe we couldn'a bought the damn thing off the little fuck'n' brain box.'

'I'm telling you Sir, there's no way he would have sold,' said Springer. 'We ran a full background make on the guy, major reconnaissance. He's a public transport nut, he hates private cars, reckons we should all be sat behind each other on stinking buses, picking the chewing gum off our pants.'

'Mother of God ain't people sick?' said Sam in disgust. 'The guy's probably into free love too.'

'I guess he would be at that,' Springer agreed.

'You want someone like that having the right to ball your old lady?' Sam was working himself up into a fine state of self-justification. 'Smoking his pot and corrupting college kids? He got what was his. We did the world a favour.'

'We had to do it, Sir,' Springer affirmed. 'His invention in the wrong hands could take out our entire operation. They'd be sending Global Motors home in a body bag.'

This last analogy was sufficiently ghoulish to re-concentrate the minds of the two men on the human cost of their business decisions. They lapsed into a brief silence.

'Yeah,' said Sam eventually. 'The little commie sure had it coming.'

DELAYS

The knock-on effects of the protest rally which had impeded Geoffrey's escape continued to paralyse part of London. Traffic jams are strange things, they resonate. As when a stone is dropped in a pond, the matter does not end with the initial plop. Six feet away some frog on a lily gets a series of rhythmic ripples up the back flap and hops off going *ribbit* and looking for something semi-aquatic to shag. It is the same with traffic. It's quite possible for a person to miss a train at Waterloo because half an hour previously a one-driver bus on the Strand was confronted with someone who didn't speak English, only had a twenty pound note and wanted to be taken somewhere that provided traditional English scenes, haddock and tea-time. Traffic jams never actually end, they merely expand and contract, merging into one another, endlessly connected by frustration and grinding synchromesh. There is a little bit of the very first traffic jam in every one that has happened since.

Sam was caught up in the ripple effect. His car, like his industry, was at a standstill and he was getting impatient.

'Jeez,' he barked, lowering the electric window which separated him from the driver. 'I never seen the city this bad. It's Sunday goddamit, doesn't anyone in this damn country worship the lord any more? What the hell's going on?' The driver explained that the traffic was particularly bad that day because there had been a huge protest rally in Hyde Park and the effects had fanned out across the city.

'A *protest* rally? What, like a hippy thing?' gasped Sam in astonishment. 'I don't believe this fucking country! It's like it never left the middle ages! A *protest* rally! What's there to protest about, there ain't no war or anything? Sometimes I just want to throw in the towel. The whole of Eastern Europe comes to its senses and kids in the West are still shouting about Ho Chi Minh.'

The driver explained to Sam that the protest was to do with the suspected new road plans for London and the South-East of England. Sam knew all about these plans. In his capacity as boss of Global Motors UK he was on very close acquaintance with Digby Parkhurst, the Minister for Transport and whole-heartedly supported his policies. This was something which Digby took great pleasure in. It did not occur to Digby that it was perhaps a little unhealthy for a person whose function was to represent the best interests of the people in the area of transport, to be quite so close to one of the country's largest car manufacturers.

Sam was delighted.

'A protest about the road plans! Well that's great,' he cried. 'That is my kind of protest. What is it, they don't think it's radical enough? I told that stupid son of a bitch Parkhurst that nobody gives a damn about Nelson's column.'

The driver was forced to disillusion Sam as to the political slant of the march. '*Objecting* to roads!' said Sam in astonishment. 'But that's crazy! What are they gonna object to next? Food? Don't they want to be able to get from A to B!'

'I think that they're concerned that there should still be an A to come from and a B to go to Sir,' replied the driver who cherished his individualism.

'What did he say?' enquired Sam who, as was his wont, had only been asking a rhetorical question.

'I think he said that he'd better button his lip or get fired,' said Springer, raising the sound-proofed electric window again.

Sam looked sadly out at the rag-bag of protestors making their way home. 'I don't know,' he said wearily. 'People. You try to make a better world for them, and what do they do? Throw ball-bearings under police horses.'

It was while Sam was having this philosophical ponder on the ingratitude of 'the little fellow' that

Springer's personal phone rang.

'This is it Boss. News from the dead professor,' said Springer.

'You got hit-men calling you here? In *my* car!' replied an astonished Sam.

'Relax,' said Springer. 'This is a brand new portable phone, after this call I chuck it in a river.' He answered the phone.

'What's he say? What's he say?' Sam demanded impatiently.

Springer's face had fallen.

'He says the Gerbil is still twitching.'

'And why did he say that?' asked Sam, not unreasonably.

'Because the guy ain't dead yet. They missed him,' Springer admitted.

Sam grabbed the phone in a fury.

'Now listen here, you lazy, Limey fruit!' he shouted. 'When I employ tradesmen I expect them to get the job done and get outa my face, not to ring my car to say some hampster is still doing the rumba. What you doin' you English fuck? Taking a *tea-break*? On a frigging *strike*? Jesus Christ, what is it with you English? You can't make cars, you can't kill people, how the hell d'you ever get yourselves an empire? I'll tell you how, you got the *Scots* to do it for you! That's how.'

'*Pardonez moi, monsieur*,' said the impeccably polite French voice of the contract killer on the end of the line. 'I am Anatole Chiraud of Euro Despatch and I can assure you that the gerbil which you require to be sedated has only been briefly mislaid. The contract will be completed as soon as possible.'

The line went dead, leaving Sam frustrated and bemused.

'A French hit-man?' said Sam. 'What is he going to do, breathe on the guy?'

CONCRETE AND STEEL

Digby Parkhurst, the Minister for Transport, friend of Sam Turk and the man at whose image the students had spent the afternoon chanting 'Out out out', was preparing for his departure to the conference at Brighton. He was a little sad because he was going to have to leave his beloved models behind him. They were beautiful models, mounted on trestle tables all through his department, and he loved to touch them. He loved to feel the long, grey ribbons and stick his fingers in the tiny little tunnels. The models were of bits of the British Isles, although a native of those same islands would have been hard put to recognize them as such. Hills had been removed, villages relocated, lochs drained, and in their place were roads – long, empty, beautiful roads.

Well not quite empty, here and there on the larger scale models the architect had placed a tiny model of a car. Just one, and a lovely looking car at that. One could imagine it carrying a family off to have a picnic. Perhaps the family were planning to have the picnic under one of the little trees that the architect had thoughtfully placed on the beautiful models.

THE CATERPILLAR AND THE BUTTERFLY

The architectural model is like the sluggish, hairy caterpillar that turns into the beautiful butterfly. Unfortunately, it happens in reverse. Take a stroll round something large and concrete in any neighbourhood, and then, with the image still in mind, rush round to the planning department of the local council and demand to see the original model and drawings. It will be a strange experience. For, although the dimensions of the building you have rushed from, and the model you are shown, will be the same and the colours similar, none the less the two images will *bear no resemblance to each other whatsoever*.

The transformation between fiction and reality is as stark as that which drunk strangers, who screw each other after parties, go through during the night. How beautiful they had appeared in each other's eyes after a bottle or two of Spanish, but reality must be faced in the morning. Any little boy who has been entranced by the picture on the front of a soldier-kit box, the brave GI with gun blazing, will be familiar with the architects' trick. He will know the disappointment of Christmas morning when the box turns out to contain a squashed plastic hat and a gun that does not even go 'click'. Just as residents (and no doubt the architects themselves) know disappointment at the appearance of great rust streaks down the concrete walls and puddles of piss in the lifts.

It is not always the fault of the architect, planners give them impossible briefs and inadequate budgets, but they might make their failures more easy to bear if on the original models, instead of lots of pretty little trees and a tiny motor car, they placed models of hundreds of cars, three dead trees, a little discarded supermarket trolly, some model dog turds and plenty of damp.

KING OF THE ROAD

Digby wandered like a dreamer from one pristine model to another, touching them gently, stroking their contours. In this exquisite private moment he even knelt down and pressed his cheek against the cool surface of a miniature flyover. As he stood up, a faraway look crossed his features. He could see clearly in his mind's eye, a sunny day, a crowd of dignitaries standing on the spotless concrete, a long, blue ribbon of delicate silk stretched across the ten proud lanes, he himself sternly holding the golden scissors. Digby's eyes grew misty. 'I, Digby Parkhurst, Her Britannic Majesty's Minister for Transport, do hereby declare the UK orbital ring road open.'

It was a delicious dream, to be immortal, to be set in concrete. One of Digby's recurrent fantasies was that he would be remembered as 'King Of The Road', that school-children would be taught of his great achievements . . .

'And this infrastructure,' Digby said to himself, assuming the personality of mythical teacher of the future, 'was set in place by Digby The Road Builder. Yes class, Digby Parkhurst, the King of the Road.'

Chapter Five

FIRST BLOOD

WICKED WORLD, SIR

As Sam Turk angrily slammed the phone down on the French hit-men, the object of his concern was still very much alive and the reason that the Gerbil could not be sedated was that the Gerbil was, at present, in the company of the Police. This is a state of affairs likely to impede any murder. One of the first things they impress upon rookie hit-men during their hit-man basic training is, that if you are contemplating perpetrating a homicide, it is advisable to avoid doing so whilst there are uniformed bobbies present.

Unfortunately for Geoffrey, his protector was on the point of departure. 'We'll be in touch if need be, Sir,' said the copper, having looked at the forced window-pane and noted the absence of a television.

'Is that it?' said Geoffrey astonished.

He had perhaps not expected an immediate arrest but he wouldn't have minded some small indication that an arrest might one day be within the bounds of possibility. Geoffrey could not help feeling that he would have got more investigative vigour and commitment to law and order if he had called in the Brownies.

'That's it for the moment, Sir,' said the policeman.

'But this is absurd,' Geoffrey stammered, struggling to keep his speech comprehensible. 'Where are the blood-hounds? The lines of dungareed cadets beating the undergrowth? Surely you'll need a sample of my semen so that you can rule me out when you start the genetic fingerprinting?'

Detective Constable Collingwood smiled his weary smile. He was used to outraged householders demanding action. It always comes as a great shock to people, perhaps second only to that of the actual burglary, to realize that there is virtually nothing the police can do about it.

A population raised in the comforting company of *Dixon of Dock Green*, fondly imagine that the police have sufficient resources to do their job properly. George Dixon was a policeman who was not only happy to investigate minor crimes but also found the time to deliver lengthy philosophical monologues on the nature of the villainy he encountered. Sadly, the real police force, in the real world, were long ago forced to recognize that their chances of keeping up with the thousands of burglaries committed each week are non-existent.

'This mean city's a bubbling cauldron of sleaze and crime,' said DC Collingwood, who enjoyed the occasional Batman comic. 'Our job's to keep the lid on, Sir. I have to ask myself what is more important: your telly, or some slime-ball pushing crack onto a teenage girl to get her hooked and turn her into a piece of filthy human wreckage, so that she can be lured onto the game?'

Put that way Geoffrey began to feel a bit guilty about having called the police at all. The last thing he wanted was to be the cause of a teenage girl becoming a piece of human wreckage. Geoffrey had been about to mention the two men who had visited him that afternoon but he decided to forget it.

'As I say, Sir,' continued Collingwood, 'we'll call you if we find anything out,' but he knew that there was no chance. Much as they would like to, the police don't investigate burglaries any more. They write them down in a big book and then, at the end of each police year, they take the big book to their annual conference, show it to the Home Secretary and ask for more money, which they get, but only if they promise to spend it on riot gear.

Of course, if the young detective had had any idea as to where Geoffrey's small burglary was going to lead; if, for a moment, he could have seen into the future and caught a fleeting glimpse of the mayhem and destruction that would eventually stem from this one tiny entry in the big police burglary book; if DC Collingwood had glanced into a convenient crystal ball and seen the murder, mayhem and environmental catastrophe that lay at the end of the chain, which began with the theft of Geoffrey's telly – he would have had a look round for some fingerprints and stuff, he would have got down on his knees with some tweezers and started putting bits of fluff and fag ash into envelopes, he would probably have accepted Geoffrey's kind offer of some semen. But Constable Collingwood didn't know, so he went on his way. Leaving Geoffrey feeling rather rotten and depressed.

But Geoffrey's time of trouble had only just begun. He was destined, in a very short while, to feel a great deal more rotten and depressed. It was only, in fact, to be a matter of minutes before Geoffrey would be looking back on that vague sensation of feeling rotten and depressed as a positive high point of his day. He had not, as of yet, made any real and concrete connection between the theft of his television, and his unpleasant experience with the two thugs at the lab. But he was about to.

ROBO CUP 2

Finishing his coffee, Geoffrey got up and wandered into his study. It was only then that Geoffrey noticed that the hard disc drive had been removed from underneath his computer. He had not noticed before, because the computer itself, which was by far the more valuable item, had not been stolen, neither had an extremely expensive laser printer borrowed from the lab. Only his hard disc had disappeared and also, he now noticed, all the back-up floppy discs as well.

Why on Earth would any burglar wish to steal discs?

Geoffrey came to the rather worrying conclusion that they were after his research. The television had been either mere opportunism, or a blind to cover up the true purpose of the burglary. Geoffrey now understood that the two fellows he had encountered at the office were not acting under any misapprehension. They had mentioned Geoffrey's patent application, and now, on the same day, all his work, all his electronic files had been stolen. The conclusion was dawning on Geoffrey that somebody did not like his invention, and in fact, disliked it enough to steal it, and send thugs after its inventor. Geoffrey thanked his lucky stars that he had already submitted the project to the patents office. Whoever it was who had stolen his work would not be able to suppress his brilliant invention simply by pinching it.

Geoffrey returned to his armchair pondering his predicament. Should he tell the police about the threatening men? about the theft of his work? He supposed so, but it was a tiring prospect. Long and bitter experience had taught him that it was extremely difficult for spastics to get themselves taken seriously. People often didn't even want to talk to them, let alone hear about their problems. The first thing to do, Geoffrey felt, was to get away from his house. Clearly something was very wrong and he needed peace to consider it. He had just decided to go and spend the night at a friend's place when he heard the unmistakable sound of his front door being kicked down.

Geoffrey's life had demanded from him a peculiar courage and strength: but it had not prepared him for having violent thugs kick down his front door – and he was shit scared. Years of being demeaned and patronized had caused Geoffrey to develop a very thick skin, but he knew it was not thick enough to withstand physical assault. Geoffrey shrank into his chair as he heard the sound of heavy feet in the corridor and, before he knew it, his two companions of earlier in the day were standing before him. Geoffrey could not believe his stupidity for hanging around in his house. Obviously, if they knew his work place, they would know his home. He could have kicked himself. As it happens, he was kicking himself because the tension of the situation had caused him to lose a degree of control over his lower limbs.

'Stop fucking twitching,' said a thug, disgust in his voice.

'He can't, can he? Look at him,' said the other, adding 'makes you wanna puke dunnit' thus dispelling any suspicion that his rough exterior might disguise a sympathetic soul.

'So you're the bleeding egghead then?' continued the thug (whose name was Frank). 'Who'd of bleeding thought it?'

'He looks like a total spastic, dun' 'e?' said the other.

'I am,' said Geoffrey, trying to keep his head still.

'Shut your face you mongol,' barked Frank. 'We've wasted a whole bleeding afternoon looking for you. We followed that taxi all the way to Harlow.'

'Let's kill the pathetic little bastard and piss off,' said his colleague (whose name was Gary) as he produced a gun.

Geoffrey was slightly stunned. He had no idea that the stakes were quite so high. It appeared that these men were actually going to kill him.

'Probably doing you a favour, eh, Professor? Put you out of your misery, eh? Jesus, look at the state of it, eh?'

In truth, Geoffrey was in rather a state. Small and twisted in his armchair, he was jerking and dribbling and his voice was not working.

'Och och och,' he grunted for no apparent reason. Adding, 'uuuurrrrgh.' In fact, Geoffrey was pleading for his life, but this was somewhat lost in the translation.

'Come on, Frank, kill it and shut it up,' urged Gary unkindly. 'Makes me sick that noise does.'

Geoffrey had always been aware that many people found him distasteful, that their stomachs weakened at his twitches and grunts and they longed to be away from him – but no one had ever been so up front about it before. On another occasion, following his policy of confronting his Cerebral Palsy head on, Geoffrey might have applauded such honesty. However, on this occasion, he was too scared to applaud anything.

'Can't kill him, can we?' said Frank to Geoffrey's intense relief. 'Not until we've tortured him,' he added, which somewhat mitigated Geoffrey's enthusiasm.

'It won't need torturing mate,' said Gary the death enthusiast. 'Look at it. It's shitting itself,' an observation which was not far from the truth. Gary crossed the room and, sweeping away the broken glass from the exploded wine bottle, perched himself against the sideboard. He addressed Geoffrey with exaggerated slowness, as if talking to an idiot . . . 'Here Spaso,' he said. 'Have you got any other work stuff stashed away, besides what we nicked before . . . Dribble for yes, twitch for no . . . ha ha ha.'

Geoffrey was not in a position to answer, every ounce of his concentration was pinpointed on his good hand. It lay underneath his twitching body and in it was the remote control. Very slowly, and with all the dexterity gained through years of doing the work of ten, Geoffrey's five good fingers were gently teasing the tiny joystick.

With his chin, seemingly, attached to his collar

bone and his small body rigid and jerking, rattling about in the stiff leather of his jacket, Geoffrey did not look dangerous. But he was.

The laughing man's bottom was perched next to the wine bottles, Geoffrey could see the big fold of flesh from the sideway's view that his tilted head allowed him. The man was still laughing at his brilliant dribble gag as the little hydraulic arm that Geoffrey had made, silently came to life and hovered across the sideboard. The needle came to a halt above the fold of Gary's plump backside, squashed as it was against the polished wood.

Geoffrey flipped a switch, the shaft of steel plunged downwards and Gary's cruel laughter turned to a scream as the vicious needle buried itself in his flesh. The needle hissed like a snake and the man fell dying on to the floor. As luck would have it, the snake had found an artery, and ten cubic centimetres of compressed air had been pumped, at high pressure, into Gary's blood stream.

Frank spun round, astonished.

'Jesus Gazzer, this is no time to have a bleeding heart attack.'

Even at this moment, Frank could not get over his prejudices. He still could not quite believe that the small, twisted wreck in the armchair could have had anything to do with the besting of his tough, able-bodied colleague. Then Frank saw the jointed robotic arm hanging over the edge of the dresser. He saw its one finger, a long thin spike, crimson with blood, pointing down at the dying man. A stern, accusing finger calling Gary to book for his life of sin. Frank looked from the needle to Geoffrey; then at his now dead colleague – and he began to wonder.

'Did you do that, you little bastard?' he shouted at Geoffrey. 'You're supposed to be some sort of bleeding professor, ain't ya?'

Frank had drawn his gun and his face spelt murder. But Geoffrey wasn't looking at Frank's face, he was looking over Frank's shoulder to the space behind, where a pot of scalding coffee was slowly crossing the room on a long arm.

'All right mate, that is it. You are dead, you hear? I don't care whether we've got all your research stuff or not, you ain't going to be telling anyone about it because you are bleeding dead.'

Frank held up his pistol, and for the first time in his life Geoffrey found himself staring down the barrel of a gun. Except he wasn't really staring down it, his eyes were fixed on the space above his assailant's head. Could the arm reach high enough? Fortunately, it had also been designed for getting things down from the top of wardrobes.

As the man cocked his pistol the coffee pot appeared from behind him and levitated upwards until it hovered above his head. Geoffrey had literally only seconds in which to act, but, to his lasting credit, he found the time to be cool. Making a huge effort to gain control of his voice he enquired . . .

'Do you take sugar?'

Without waiting for a reply Geoffrey again hit the button on his remote, and a pint of boiling coffee descended on Frank. Fortunately, Frank did not fire, instead he screamed in agony and began to hop about. Geoffrey's plan, as far as he had one, was at this point to try to get to the door, praying he would have time to stumble out before Frank recovered sufficiently to kill him. However, as Frank hopped about, fate hopped in beside Geoffrey and offered him an altogether more satisfactory course of action. Frank's agonized jumps had landed him bang on top of the explosive lifting platform. Geoffrey had intended the platform to be used for purposes such as getting wheelchairs into buses, or the paralysed into bed, but he had no objection to it being employed to fight murderers. It was the work of a moment for Geoffrey to hit his remote for a third time. There was an explosion and the unfortunate Frank sailed out of the window – following exactly the same trajectory that Geoffrey's suitcase had done on the previous occasion. He landed head first in a flower-bed and broke his neck.

THE SMALL MIND OF THE LAW

Detective Constable Collingwood was absolutely delighted.

'I rather think this bears out the point I made

earlier, Sir,' he had said proudly, 'regarding the fact that this city is a murky melting-pot of sleaze and crime. I mean there you were, not an hour ago, with nothing more to complain about than a pilfered telly, and now you've got a couple of raving deadies on your doorstep. Welcome to life at the sharp end, Sir.'

'Shut up, Collingwood,' said the Superintendent having finished his inspection of Geoffrey's cork-screw. 'All right, Doctor Peason. Let's have this story again, shall we?'

For a long time it had proved impossible to make the police believe that Geoffrey had despatched the two thugs alone. However, after he had painstak-ingly demonstrated the process by which he had achieved his victory they scratched their heads in awe.

'Well it's a neat bit of work, Sir. A very neat bit,' said the Superintendent. 'Especially considering as how you're a, well a . . .'

'Spasmo,' prompted Geoffrey.

'Yes, that's right,' the policeman replied. 'A disabled gentleman. I mean these two are well known to us. And very hard cases they are too. I wouldn't have wanted to face them if I had a shotgun. You done 'em with a bottle opener and a pot of coffee.'

'I think me being a spastic put them off guard,' said Geoffrey modestly.

'Yes, well, we could do with a few more like you on

the force,' the Superintendent replied. But he didn't really mean it. Impressed though he was, he would never have trusted a spastic with the famous tit helmet.

'I reckon the papers will go wild for this one when they hear,' DC Collingwood interjected.

'I'd really rather they didn't hear,' said Geoffrey. 'I mean if somebody wants me dead, the lower a profile I keep the better, don't you think?'

'Oh I don't think it's you they wanted dead, Sir,' said the Super with an annoying tone.

Geoffrey enquired, as clearly as he could, if the copper would like to suggest an alternative interpretation as to why the two men had broken into his house and pointed pistols at him.

'I think it was probably some sort of mistake. After all Sir, why would anybody want you dead? You're a . . . disabled gentleman. Either way I'm sure we'll sort it all out once we get down the station.'

And leaving Geoffrey's flat filled with pathologists and photographers and men with bits of chalk, whose job it was to draw lines round dead bodies, Geoffrey was trooped off to the police station – at present two nil up against the forces of darkness.

ASK NOT FOR WHOM THE BELL TOLLS

As Geoffrey and the two police officers emerged from his front door, the London night was, as usual, filled with the ringing and wailing of various alarms.

'Listen to that, Sir,' commented DC Collingwood. 'Like I said, this mean city is a seething, writhing, bubbling hotbed of a satanic melting-pot. Your two raving deadies are just part of the Devil's mosaic.'

In fact the Detective Constable was the only person to pay any attention to the alarm bells (except of course the thousands of people with pillows wrapped round their heads screaming 'Turn them off! *Please* turn them off!' into the darkness of their bedrooms). Everyone always ignores alarm bells, which is a shame, because if they didn't Sam Turk might not have found it quite so easy to burgle the Office of Patents and hence he would have had no cause to attempt to have Geoffrey murdered. A little social responsibility can go a long way.

Chapter Six

PARTY BUSINESS

CHIEF EXECUTIVE

Digby Parkhurst, the Minister for Transport, prided himself on being a quiet, well-ordered, law-abiding citizen. Hence he would have been astonished to learn that through his unprofessional relations with Sam Turk he was the man who had unwittingly set in motion the events which led up to the deaths of Frank and Gary, the alarm bell ringing at the Office of Patents and Geoffrey being forced from his home.

At present though, blissfully ignorant of the mayhem he had unleashed, the Minister was stuck in the same traffic jam that had caught both Geoffrey and Sam Turk – the one caused by the anti-road protest. It was lucky for the Minister that his car had darkened windows, for had he been recognized by the crowds milling about along the road, he might have been lynched. Fortunately, the leather-lined opulence of his Ministerial limo offered all the privacy Digby required, for it was a spanking new Panther 'Chief Executive'.

The Chief Executive was the first car to come out of the Panther Motor Company since the Japanese had bought a majority shareholding in it – a deal which Digby had himself orchestrated. It was a wonderful machine. A fitting flagship for a great new partnership, a partnership which, as Digby had said at the time, built on the strengths of both nations. And of course it did; the Japanese contributing the technology, the design, the materials and the money; the British contributing the prestige name.

Names are very important in cars. Panther had agonized for months over the name 'Chief Executive'. It was most frustrating, all the really superior names had been done. Ambassador, Statesman, Senator . . .

'Come on, what are you paid for,' the chief executive at Panther had shouted at his hapless creative people. 'We need a power name, a smug name. We're losing our traditional predominance in the arrogant git end of the car buying market. I want a name that says "up yours" to every two-year-old family saloon on the road! I want a name that says "kiss my arse pauper!" to anything under three litres. I want a name that says that the chap in our car has four houses, five directorates, a six-figure income and a pork bayonet that measures seven inches in repose. All right? I want a name that is *well hung.*'

'The Presidential,' one creative person suggested.

'Sounds like a hotel suite,' barked the Chief Executive. 'The chap *sleeps* in the Presidential, the chap does not drive the Presidential. You're fired.'

'How about, The General Secretary of the Communist party of the Soviet Union?' another creative person offered timidly.

'Hmm,' the Chief Executive pondered. 'The Panther General Secretary of the Communist Party of the Soviet Union. It certainly has power.' But then he rejected the idea. 'No, the Soviet Union is falling to bits, our cars fall to bits anyway, we do not need to draw attention to the fact. You're fired as well, clear your desk and get out.'

'I know,' said a youthful enthusiast, taking an insane risk with his career prospects, 'Why don't we name it after you, Sir.'

'The Panther Kevin?' replied the Chief Executive. And there was a lengthy pause whilst the youthful enthusiast reflected that redundancy would at least give him time to lag the roof . . .

'Not bad, not bad at all.'

'Actually I meant "Chief Executive", Sir,' corrected the enthusiast. And so it was that the latest over-priced, personal wealth advertisement on the road came to be called the 'Chief Executive' (Kevin Class).

THE PARTY SPIRIT

So there was Digby, stuck in traffic in his Chief Executive, on his way to Brighton for his party's annual conference. The jam was likely to make him late, he hadn't planned for traffic (which would make it the only event in Digby's entire week at conference that wasn't planned, for the conference was to be so meticulously choreographed it would make a New Kids on the Block dance routine look like a spontaneous, free-spirited improvization).

(*Author's note*: As it is to be hoped that this book will have a shelf-life longer than a fortnight and will hence be around long after the New Kids on the Block's flame has dimmed and their ten testicles have descended, the reader is kindly requested to substitute whatever pimply teen sensation is currently charging a million quid for a tour programme, a crap T-shirt and about forty-five minutes of synchronized miming.)

There was a time when the three main British Political Party Conferences were very different. The Liberals were courteous and rather worried, Labour were rude and quarrelsome, and the Conservatives were positively robotic in their ruthless insistence on the serflike tugging of the forelock and towing of the party line. Sadly, as the years go by, all three parties are tending more towards the Tory version. A mindless, gung-ho jamboree being considered rather safer than a debate. Millions and millions of pounds are spent on elaborate security precautions. Delegates are continually being felt-up by members of the Constabulary. Ostensibly, all this compulsory groping is concerned with terrorism: the truth is that it is to prevent any delegate bringing an opinion into the building. The other reason is of course that some MPs rather like being felt-up by the constabulary.

The reason for this desperate desire to be bland is one of the great misnomers of modern political life – Party unity. It has become a cornerstone of British political thinking that the single and greatest ideal for any political party to aspire to is that of unity. We got the idea from Stalin. No conference can look to a higher goal than to maintain throughout the week an impression of complete harmony and bland acceptance of the party line. A conference that forgets itself so far as to allow discussion and differences of opinions is deemed to have been marred by rows, open revolt and damaging splits. The ultimate conference delegate would be a person who has no face and ten sets of hands to clap with.

POLITICIANS' GAGS

Anyway, Digby was nervously running over the rest of the speech he intended to give the following afternoon. There was, as has been said, no need for him to be nervous because he would probably have had to bugger a dog live on stage to fail to get an ovation. Even in that event, party loyalty would probably have held.

'I thought it a considered and statesmanlike speech,' the delegates would say to the news crews, as they left the hall . . . 'Perhaps slightly over long, I would probably have cut the bit where he buggered the dog.'

Perhaps Digby was nervous because he intended to speak on his very favourite subject. A subject much beloved of all transport ministers; the subject of freedom . . .

'I hardly think,' . . . the Minister muttered to himself, practising the toadyish sneer for which he was justly loathed by all right thinking people, and adored by conference delegates . . .

'I hardly think, *thnn thnn*,' he carried on muttering to himself, adding the little rhythmic nasal wheeze with which he habitually prefixed what he considered to be a humorous observation.

'I hardly think, *thnn thnn*, that the British public will be prepared to exchange the personal freedom that their motor cars invest them with, for a, *thnn thnn thnn*, donkey and trap.'

It was not, perhaps, a classic gag, in fact it was something in the nature of a turkey. A gag unlikely to qualify for entrance into even the meanest of Christmas crackers – the sort that contain a three centimetre high blue plastic Indian Chief that won't stand up.

Digby may have been aware that he was opening

his speech with a gag that would be unlikely to find favour, even with the studio audience of a television sitcom – a demographic group that has been known to laugh at an unoccupied sofa. If he knew, he certainly didn't care, because the jokes in Digby's speeches always went well. The fact that most of these said gags would, under normal circumstances, be unlikely to raise a laugh from a pill-popping hyena was irrelevant. For Digby was a politician and, as such, was not subject to the rigorous critical standards of humour by which the rest of us are judged.

With one or two rare exceptions, the average politician would not recognize a decent joke if they encountered it wearing a red nose, while sidling towards a banana skin and reciting the *Monty Python* parrot sketch. As a purveyor of turgid, swamplike non-humour the average politician is second only to game-show hosts and headmasters. And yet strangely, like headmasters, they are never brought to book.

The media collude in the fiction that those who hold over us the power of life, death and the new dog licence legislation, are possessed of great wit. They describe a speech which contains three snide little put-downs against the opposition as 'peppered with wry humour'. They use the term 'memorable' to sum up phrases which everyone has already forgotten. The reason for the perpetration of this flattering deceit is quite simple. It is in order to prevent revolution. If people were ever to realize just how mediocre the minds of most of those who govern us are, come the next by-election, we'd all vote for the joke candidate with a silly name, top hat and yellow tights who stands at the back and grins when the count is read out.

MISTAKEN IDENTITY

The conference would not be officially starting until the following day but Digby was in a rush because that evening he was to be a guest of honour at a dinner and booze-up organized by Global Motors to mark the occasion of the launch of their latest car. This was of course the real business of the conference. Elsewhere in town the Minister for Defence would be being entertained by arms dealers, and the Health Minister would be dining with drugs companies.

Digby booked into his hotel in a rush, something he hated doing. Normally he liked to luxuriate over it, checking out all the little treats in his room, the individually wrapped soaps, the tiny shampoo bottles, the sachets marked 'shoe shine' which contain a strangely impregnated tissue which leaves shoes entirely unaffected but makes your fingers unbearably whiffy right through dinner. Digby never tired of these small luxuries and would always pocket the soaps and take them home with him. He had a big wicker basket full of them in his bathroom.

However, on this evening there was no time to relax. Digby just shoved on a bow-tie and rushed off to the Global Motors reception where Sam Turk was waiting to greet him.

Sam had been told by Springer that the Minister was at the door and had hurried out into the foyer.

'Minister, Minister,' he said, rushing up and shaking the hand of the smug, obsequious looking fellow in the bow-tie.

'That's the head waiter boss,' Springer whispered urgently under his breath. 'Parkhurst's behind him.'

Sam never missed a beat. He looked about the room with a serious expression on his face and then gave the head waiter an American hundred dollar bill. 'Nice work, thanks bud,' he said, and, passing the waiter, he approached Digby who was on the point of being deeply offended.

'Simple security measure Minister, we do it for the President. Throw in a decoy and see if he gets shot. Today the guy was lucky,' said Sam. 'I know your cops are good, but frankly Minister, you're too important for me not to care.'

Of course Sam had met Digby on a number of previous occasions but Digby, like most cabinet ministers, did not really have a proper face. Even his mother had trouble recognizing him. In the early days of his career he would leave for work in the morning and say, 'Bye Mum,' and his mother would say, 'Who the hell are you?' Then Digby would say, 'I'm the Junior Under Sub Deputy Minister for

Fisheries Mum,' and she would say, 'Oh'.

Sam ushered Digby towards a glass of champagne.

'Well Minister this really is an honour, yes it is Sir. A heck of an honour.' Of course Sam actually considered Digby to be a pretty pathetic figure, but Digby's job involved the annual expenditure of fifteen billion pounds of public money. That was a figure Sam thought worthy of respect. He would have been honoured to meet a cockroach with a turd in its pocket if it had fifteen billion a year to spend.

'I am afraid you've just missed the video, Minister, but it was really something,' continued Sam. 'Yes Sir, it sure was something.'

Prior to Digby's arrival the guests at Sam's little soirée had been watching an obscene video. A really nasty one; a disgusting piece of exploitative filth, featuring human degradation and child abuse. It was the television advert that was to launch the new Global car on the market.

OBSCENE VIDEO

The star of the advert was a child. Not the sort of child any real parent would recognize. Not a child born on planet Earth. No, this child hailed from Olympus, she was a child of the Gods. So petite, so vulnerable, so clean and pretty, she just made you want to gather her up in all her pink and golden fluffiness, dump her in a bathful of mud, slip her twenty Benson and Hedges and send her off for an afternoon shoplifting.

'I like the kid,' Sam had said. 'Cute.'

Cute indeed. This little angel made Cabbage Patch dolls look like they had been sculpted by a stern-minded socialistic realist in a bad mood. If Barbie had escaped from the toy box and shagged her plastic boyfriend Ken behind a Fisher Price garage, and had so far forgotten herself as to forsake the principles of safe sex, the child that might have been produced could well have grown up to become the gruesomely cutesome little girl in Sam Turk's car advert. She was perfectly calculated to make every parent in the country wonder why they themselves had given birth to the dirt monster. And there, in the video, she stood, innocent and utterly vulnerable on a tough city pavement whilst her father, a lean, finely chiselled, confident man, locked the fortresslike front door of their apartment building.

It was important that this super-yuppy and his Cabbage Patch daughter lived in an apartment, as opposed to a flat. Despite being British actors, playing British characters in a British advert for a British car (which is officially defined as a car in which a minimum of the ashtrays and seat covers are fitted by British workers), the story was none the less set in New York.

The reason for this was because the director

wished to create an atmosphere of gritty realism, and New York will always seem more real than anything Britain has to offer. It is strange that, although the majority of British people have never seen a skate-boarding body-popper, an exploding fire-hydrant, or anybody dunk a doughnut, these things seem infinitely more immediate and happening images than that jar of Horlicks which has stood in the cupboard for forty years.

'New York is good,' Sam had said. Despite the fact that the new car would spend its life stuck in traffic between Redditch and Wolverhampton, Sam was concerned that it should have a global profile.

On the screen, the little girl's face, surrounded by golden curls, is a study of nervous fear. This was hardly surprising, as she appeared to live in the middle of an urban nightmare – leaves blow across the dirty flagstones in a sinister and forbidding manner, lights are on red, abandoned cars burn. A black man with no shoes sprays a wall, he is muttering to himself, probably having a quiet rap, prior to spinning round on his head. We can't tell because the sound track to the video is Italian opera, the reason for this was to make it clear to the meanest intelligence that the anonymous little hatchback in question has class.

The little girl continues her nervous perusal of the tough world she will inherit. An old man with a beard and the face of a philosopher sleeps in a cardboard box.

All cardboard box dwellers shot by groovy film-makers have the faces of philosophers – which is a good thing because, living in a cardboard box in the middle of an urban nightmare, you'd need to be a bit of a philosopher.

In front of the old philosopher a cop busts a hooker, we know she is a hooker because she is sensationally sexy.

In the video tape world, just as all tramps are philosophers, all hookers are gorgeous. Of course, in the real world, street-walkers (who are the poorest type of prostitutes) do not tend to look as if they've walked straight off a Pirelli calendar. Their sad, dispirited appearance tends to provoke either sympathy or disgust from most people, rather than lust. However, in the movies, from Louise Brooks as *Lulu*, to Julia Roberts as *Pretty Woman*, we are taught to recognize street-walking whores by watching out for the wittiest, prettiest, most flawlessly beautiful girl in view. She'll be the one risking her life getting into cars with drunk strangers and having to try and get a condom onto him with her mouth, while pretending to give him a blow-job because he doesn't want to use one and he might have AIDS.

'I like the hooker,' Sam had said. Great legs, real class.

The doll-like little girl continues to stare. She is such a beautiful little girl, with such sensitivity and intelligence that by the look of her she is in real danger of growing up to be a prostitute . . .

Daddy has finished sternly locking the doors of his fortress and with swift, strong movements he gathers up the bewildered child and places her safely in the Ghia (leaky sun roof) edition of a new, but utterly nondescript hatchback car. The door of the car slams behind the little girl and the gritty, grainy world of hookers, bare feet and graffiti is locked out.

So far the video has run for six and a half seconds.

'It's a little laboured,' said Sam, 'needs a tighter edit.' Daddy too is nervous and tense. And well he might be of course, considering that every possible cliché of urban decay seems to have elected to come and live on his street. However, we discover that this is not the reason for his discomfort. The fact is that his wife is about to have a child and, Daddy, being a thoroughly modern man, who cares, is anxious that he and the little girl should be present at this happy event.

Why, if he cares that much, Daddy has decided to leave his hospital dash to the very last pico-second, is not explained. Although, considering the man's entire relationship with the woman is based on a previous ad, in which he knocked on her door to ask to borrow some instant coffee, she's actually quite fortunate he remembers who she is.

The key turns and the engine jumps into life. With a flurry of sinister leaves and a knowing glance from the philosophical tramp (No doubt thinking to himself, 'At last, the meaning of life: a boring hatchback and a plastic daughter.') the car is away, whisking Chiselled Man and Cabbage Patch off through streets that are no longer in New York, but appear to have been lifted out of somewhere in Eastern Europe during the cold war.

'Good, I like Eastern Europe, it sells,' said Sam, adding, 'Tell them to turn up the opera, and see if they got any shots where we see more of the hooker's tits.'

The car screeches on through the misty night. Occasionally it is forced to brake on wet surfaces in order to let a flock of geese be herded across the road. Herded incidentally, by an old peasant, who by the look of him, could certainly have given the man in the cardboard box a run for his money in the philosophical stakes. If the two of them ever met they could probably crack the riddle of the universe between them.

Eventually Chiselled Man and Cabbage Patch end up at a private hospital where Mummy, who has a sensible bob hair cut and is not as sexy as a prostitute but makes up for her lack of raunchiness by being drenched in the honest sweat of her womanly duty, presents Chiselled Man with a new baby. (Well, she doesn't do it, the nurse does.) Mum just gives Chiselled Man a tired but adoring smile.

'Good,' said Sam. 'I'm glad the guy missed it. Never met a man yet who really went for all the mess and the slop.'

The scene then cuts to the next morning. Which was quite a good thing, because no doubt two seconds after the smile Mummy screamed at Daddy, 'Where the hell have you been! It's all very well coming in now all shaved and chiselled. Where were you when all the "Oh God it hurts, give me some drugs, push push push" was going on, and there was afterbirth everywhere?'

That bit of uncomfortable realism being avoided, the following morning Daddy pops Cabbage Patch, the sweating madonna (now dried off but still not sexy; proud certainly; vulnerable of course; doting; caring and ex-tremely sensible – but not sexy), plus the new sprog into the hatchback and drives off straight into what appears to be the location for a butter advert. There is a final caption . . . 'You can trust Global Motors with your most precious cargo of all.'

'Makes me want to puke,' Sam had said on first viewing. 'It's perfect.'

THE MOST PRECIOUS CARGO OF ALL

So why then was this an obscene video? It was offensive perhaps, tasteless, certainly, but why obscene? Because the men at Global Motors (a fictitious car manufacturer invented for the purposes of this book) had spent the previous twenty years actively campaigning against unleaded petrol and catalytic converters. This hypocritical bunch of low-life, had sat there congratulating themselves on their new advert which stressed family values and the protection of kids, and yet they had all been directly and personally involved in rotting the brains of countless children.

These wicked ogres had, of their own choice, brought about the production of an incalculable tonnage of appalling pollutants, every ounce of which directly affected the well-being of each and every child on the planet. They could not even claim ignorance of the facts, these wicked giants in their evil castle. In the United States, where Global Motors, like all car manufacturers, had been forced by legislation to fit the available safety equipment, children had been partially protected since the early seventies. In Britain however, and much of the rest of the world, unshackled by inconvenient legislation, Global Motors, like most other car makers, had elected to carry on damaging, and probably murdering, children. Perhaps not as perfect looking as the one in their advert, but children just the same.

The executives at Global Motors could scarcely have behaved more wickedly if they had prefixed their horrendous corporate decisions with the words 'fee fi fo fum'.

EUROSPEAK

The video had gone down terribly well. Everyone was congratulating the director, a fifteen-year-old

Dutchman with a pony tail and a crumpled linen suit. Everyone was assuring Sam that the car would no doubt be a huge success, but they knew that it wouldn't be, just as Sam himself knew and had already written the car off in his mind. The problem was the name. The new car was to be called the Global Crappee.

A car may stand or fall upon its name. If the Ford Thunderbird had been called the Ford Fluffy, one wonders whether it would ever have become quite the legend it is today. Had the E-type Jag been unwisely named the P-type Jag, surely it would have experienced greater sales resistance. If the tiny, girlie, Fiat Panda had been named the Fiat Cockroach, it seems unlikely that Penelope would have wanted one for her eighteenth. There are good car names and not-so-good car names. Calling a car the Crappee is marketing suicide.

It had come about through the noblest of motives. Global Motors UK, like most companies in Britain, were pursuing a Euro perspective. They sought to sell their cars in the shiny new Euro market. To this end, Global Motors had opened Euro offices and taken on Euro staff. They had concluded a massive, mutually supportive Euro deal with the Italian car giant Bianco and they had offered ludicrous salaries in order to poach an entire marketing team from the hugely successful Sportif of France. Global Motors' new hatchback was to be a Euro car down to the underseal. It was to have Euro styling, Euro engineering and a Euro name, the Crappee.

The Global Crappee. The French market research had reacted favourably, the Italians were enthusiastic, even the Germans seemed interested, although they would have preferred Krappy. However, the British, who still made up about ninety per cent of Global UK's market were unlikely to be impressed.

'How the hell did it happen?' Sam had spluttered when he first found out. 'Why didn't somebody notice?'

The reason nobody noticed was that the brief, right from the beginning, had been to let the Europeans get on with it. *No xenophobic interference* had been the order. Sam himself had set the tone.

'I don't want any limey bullshit about who won the war,' he had said. 'The US Battle of Britain up your polite British butts. The facts are, our European colleagues sell more cars in a week than Global Motors UK sell in a month. They are our friends and our brothers, even if they are a bunch of Wops. We need to absorb a little of their culture, their ambiance, and above all, their cash. So leave the foreign bastards alone and let them get on with it.'

That had been Sam's attitude only a year or so before when he had arrived from Detroit, but now, faced with an entire new model range called Crappee, he had changed his tune. His cringing minions attempted to defend themselves . . .

'It seemed so right,' they spluttered . . . 'The

Germans wanted something hard, something resonant of engineering. They suggested Krupp after the great arms manufacturer. But the Italian guys were looking for something light-hearted, something fun. Their suggestion was Caprice. The French reckoned everybody would be doing that. They wanted something multi-cultural, something ethnic, something cool. Their people suggested the Global Rapper . . . And, well, we all felt that Crappee combined all the elements suggested; being resonant of engineering, holiday fun and ethnic culture.'

'And shit,' said Sam.

Chapter Seven

APPLYING PRESSURE

THE GERBIL IN THE CAGE

All that had happened months before, but even then, the ads had been made, the styling completed and brochures gone out. Sam had been unable to stop the Euro decision. Now it was history. Besides, he no longer cared, he had bigger things on his mind. He had things on his mind so big that he was in danger of having to buy a larger hat, which was why he was trying to kill Geoffrey Spasmo.

The Crappee launch was in full swing, and whilst Digby Parkhurst buried his happy, shiny face in the champagne and dippy things, Sam snatched a hurried conversation with Springer.

'He dead yet?' demanded Sam.

'The gerbil's state of being is at present undetermined,' replied Springer slightly reprovingly. He felt that if you were going to go to the trouble of setting up a really great code like calling your murder victim a gerbil, you should try and stick to it.

'At present undetermined? Kind of enigmatic this "gerbil" ain't he?' mused Sam through gritted teeth. 'How come?'

Sam's knuckles were whitening around his glass as he struggled to contain his temper.

'I'm afraid I can't explain that, Sir,' said Springer, eyeing his exits. 'Euro Despatch have at present lost contact with their operatives.'

Sam's glass cracked under the pressure.

'You mean they fucked up?' he said menacingly.

'We certainly have to accept the possibility that there has been a degree of up fucking,' replied Springer very nervously. He hated it when Sam got glass-crushing mad – the next move tended to involve Sam reaching for something softer to crush.

Just as Springer was deftly acquiring an empty plate with which to protect the front of his trousers, Geoffrey Spasmo, the gerbil causing all the fuss, was still helping the police with their enquiries. Enquiries rendered more difficult, of course, by Geoffrey's communication problems. It wasn't that the Superintendent could not understand Geoffrey, with a little effort he could follow every word, it was just that he found it very difficult to bring himself to believe that anyone who sounded so thick could possibly have invented anything worth murdering for.

'You say that the hard disc containing your research material had been removed from your computer prior to the assault,' said the policeman.

'Yes,' jerked Geoffrey wearily.

'And you believe that the people who pinched your hard disc, and, I might add, your telly, were the same people who set the thugs on you?'

'Maybe,' said Geoffrey.

'But you have no idea who these people might be?' asked the policeman.

'No,' said Geoffrey.

'Or how they might have come to know about your invention?'

'No, as I've said about five billion times, I was keeping it a total secret from everyone until I got the patent, which I am in the process of doing.'

'And the invention concerns?' asked the policeman.

'It's a secret,' replied Geoffrey. 'That's the whole point.'

Eventually the police let Geoffrey go pending further enquiries. He had acted in self-defence so there were no charges. Obviously he could not return home for the present so the police offered him a hotel room.

'You'll be quite safe there,' they said confidently, mainly because they still did not really believe that Geoffrey had been the real target of the assault, mystery inventions not being high up on their list of credible motives.

Geoffrey declined the hotel room, he had other ideas. Late as it was he would go to see his good friend Deborah. He regretted having to place her in possible danger but he thought it unlikely that anybody after him would know of Deborah. Their friendship was a very private one and the thugs had not even known that Geoffrey was a spastic. Either way, he had to risk it. Geoffrey was convinced that, for reasons connected with his research, he had become the target of a murderous conspiracy, and since clearly the police were not at present intending to take him seriously, he felt he would be safer on his own. Giving the Superintendent his parents' address and refusing the offer of a lift in a squad car (even though he would have liked to have a go in one), Geoffrey took a taxi into the night.

Geoffrey believed that the only copy of his brilliant invention that lay outside criminal hands was with the patents office and he would not rest until he had secured a copy. He was destined for a very tiring time because, on the matter of the plans at least, Sam Turk was ahead of him.

THE LOBBY THROUGH THE LOBBY

'Find him and kill him,' said Sam to Springer before turning his attention back to the Minister.

Sam, although he was embarking on a plot of cosmic proportions, remained a dedicated, professional, car man. He knew that Digby Parkhurst was preparing a massive road building plan and this was something that, of course, must be encouraged. Digby had allowed himself to be cornered by the press and Sam waited courteously whilst the Minister almost dribbled with slightly tipsy self-importance.

'I think the Crappee is an absolutely super looking machine,' Digby gushed, 'and believe me, the people at Environment are delighted that Sam Turk here has made sure that all his people at Global Motors are committed to producing such a thoroughly green car.'

Digby had in his hand the press-pack which assured the public that the Crappee offered catalytic converters as optional extras on the top-of-the-range models and that, as always, Global Motors were striving towards ever greater fuel efficiency. Two promises which made the Global Crappee about as thoroughly green as an overipe tomato floating in a pot of strawberry jam against a particularly fine sunset. The production of a single private car consumes the sort of natural resources which could keep a famine threatened village in the Third World going for months. This, combined with the incalculable cost of the road it will require and the fuel it will consume, turns each car into an environmental hand grenade. Certainly we need cars. Certainly catalytic converters are very good things, but to imagine that fitting one will make a car environmentally friendly . . .? You might as well fit one to a bucket of napalm.

Sam extracted Digby from the mêlée of press . . .

'Any hints on the content of tomorrow's transport

speech, Minister?' they shouted.

'Wait and see, watch and learn,' said Digby, hoping nobody would notice that he was getting a little erection about how important he was.

'Perhaps you would like to come with me Minister,' said Sam Turk. 'It is a little crowded in here, isn't it? We have an executive dining area, perhaps . . .?'

Digby, who liked nothing better than being pampered by rich and powerful people, allowed himself to be led into a side-room. Besides, he had his own reasons for wanting to get Sam Turk to one side.

Sam led Digby through into a luxuriously appointed little room full of luxuriously appointed people.

'I'm sure there are no new faces here, Minister . . . Peter Logan, of Tar and Grit Road Construction, Jamie Saunders, the concrete man . . .'

There were oil people, tyre people, road haulage people, motoring associations people. All people well known to Digby, all good friends – good friends who had preyed upon his predecessors for generations.

For Digby was in the presence of the road lobby. A shadowy, unofficial alliance, difficult to define, difficult to pin down, but none the less one of the most powerful groups of people in the country. These people wanted one thing out of life, and one thing only – they wanted more roads.

They said that they wanted them to relieve congestion, to free the motorist, to make the nation more efficient. That's why they *said* they wanted them. But actually they wanted them so that they could sell more tar, more concrete, more rubber, more oil and, above all, more cars.

Private individuals make cars and pump oil, only governments can commission roads. Without roads all the people in the room surrounding Digby were finished. Their businesses, their whole industries meant nothing without roads. That was why they loved Digby so much – he commissioned the roads.

Vain, pompous, little Digby was an easy target for these clever, powerful men of the road lobby. They toadied him gruesomely. They made him feel so important, with their specious arguments regarding the massive human good that would flow from a six-mile extension of the M6 and their firm assertions that nothing less than the end of civilization would be the inevitable consequence if an extra lane were not added to the M25.

'And all these things Minister, these *world moulding* decisions,' Britain's biggest concrete mixer would say, his honeyed words massaging Digby's crotch.

'Are in your masterful hands Minister,' a man who owned three hundred car showrooms would add, his tongue extending three feet across a tray of nibbles to tease Digby's ear.

'Quite simply the choice between *freedom*, or a *new Dark Age*, is yours Minister,' the road haulers and the oil people would add, gently unzipping Digby's fly and delicately cupping his ripe plums in their hands.

'For the good of Britain,' chimed the whole gang, their heads full of millions as they went down on Digby . . . 'Build more roads.'

THE WORM TURNS

Normally Digby would have happily listened to this stuff until his trousers burst, but tonight there was something on his mind. Something that actually made the farty little minister assert himself.

'Later, gentlemen,' he said. Then, in a low voice, he snapped at Sam, 'I want a damn word with you Sam, and I damn well want it damn now, damn it.' Digby was better at saying *thnn thnn* than he was at swearing.

Sam thought, 'Oh Christ, what's got up the little shit's nose now?' But he said, 'Of course, Minister, is there a problem?'

They retired to a cosy corner.

'Listen, Sam, yesterday I had a very worrying call from the people at Patents. They say that damned invention I tipped you off about has damned well been pinched, damn it.'

'No!' said Sam, incredulously.

'Damn yes, and I don't like it, Sam! Damn it, these are *civil servants*, they're very vulnerable, they have the honours list to worry about and the subsidized canteen. They're hopping mad Sam. They don't believe it's a coincidence and frankly nor do I!'

'Minister,' protested Sam, 'Surely you're not suggesting that I . . .? That Global Motors . . .?'

'Oh come on, Sam! I'm sure you don't think I'm a fool,' snapped the Minister, who may have been sure, but he was certainly wrong . . . His voice dropped to an angry whisper. 'The patents people tell me about developments of interest and I tell you, I have no problem with that. We're all in the business of getting Britain moving. God knows we all want the best for Britain.'

'Well, of course, Minister,' Sam interrupted piously.

'But that doesn't stretch to burgling Her Majesty's property!' said Digby.

Sam was surprised. The Minister was actually being quite assertive. He had been so used to Digby's slimey mediocrity, he had never thought he would have to placate him. Sam remembered that even shit got stubborn when you were trying to scrape it off your shoes.

Sam, of course, continued to deny any knowledge of the break-in but it was a difficult process. Not because Digby was at all astute, but because it was bloody obvious that Sam must have organized the theft, or at least known the person who did, because he was the only person to whom Digby had passed the information about Geoffrey's invention.

Digby was having a wonderful time, slooshing top-notch plonk and being all stern and statesman-like. There he was, farty, inadequate Digby Park-hurst, who had been known at school as Shitsby Zitburst, dressing down Sam Turk the President of Global Motors UK, a two-fisted, big-bellied son of a gun. How Digby wished the teenage bullies of his unhappy school days, who used to give him Chinese burns and stuff radishes up his bottom, could see him now.

'Really Mr Turk, I'm afraid I shall have to consider very carefully the courtesies that the Department for Transport grants to the motor industry,' said Digby pompously, 'if they are to be abused in such a way.'

'Oh come now, Minister,' said Sam.

'Please do not adopt that tone with me Turk. May I remind you that I am a Minister of the Crown and not accustomed to being trifled with.' Digby slurped at his champagne. 'Perhaps, *thnn thnn thnn*, you think that Her Majesty's Government exists for your convenience.'

'Not at all Minister,' protested Sam, who wasn't even listening. He understood petty officials like Digby Parkhurst and was more than happy to let him have his moment of self-importance. That way he would get it out of his system and forget about it.

Digby, imagining himself to be having the most tremendous effect, happily accepted more champagne. There were flecks of filo pastry round his mouth and his fingers shone with grease.

'I am afraid I am going to have to consider this matter very carefully indeed. I am forced to ask myself whether the road lobby has achieved a sufficient maturity to justify its special relationship with Her Majesty's Government.'

'You're absolutely right, Minister,' said Sam absently, whilst casting an appreciative eye over the girl serving the drinks and wishing he was not such a staunch Catholic.

'Yes, I should imagine you are wishing you were somewhere else right now, aren't you Turk?' said Digby imagining Sam to be quivering in his boots.

'Well, to tell you the truth, I was, Minister,' answered Sam imagining the waitress quivering in hers.

'I'm glad you understood the seriousness of the situation. I have not decided what course of action I shall take but I commend you to consider what I have said most carefully.'

Of course, as Sam well knew, Digby had absolutely no intention of taking any course of action at all – but what fun he was having.

'Yes, Minister, certainly. I shall consider it most carefully,' said Sam, who had already forgotten everything the Minister had said.

'We shall discuss it again after my speech tomorrow,' said Digby. And draining a final champagne, he bid the road lobby goodnight and staggered drunkenly off to bed, imagining himself to be one hell of a fellow and actually being a git in a bow-tie.

END OF THE LINE

In another part of the hotel, a small forlorn group of men and women waited for Digby. They too had champagne to offer, although not quite such a decent vintage; they too had choice nibbles, although theirs were potted meat, not salmon.

'I don't think he's coming,' said one.

'He never does,' said another.

The forlorn group of people were the Chairman and senior management of Britain's railways.

Every year, at conference time, they mounted a sad little soirée for the Minister in order to put the arguments of the rail lobby. And every year the Minister did not come and the soirée got smaller and more depressed, like the railways themselves.

'Pretty soon we shall be having the rail lobby in the hotel lobby,' murmured the company gagsmith – but nobody was laughing.

The old man sighed.

'Well gentlemen, ladies. We did our best, we did everything they asked of us . . .,' And indeed they had. During the eighties the government had asked the railways to slicken up their act, to get modern, get groovy, get nasty – and the old man and his team had done it.

They were aware that the lucrative business traveller was ignoring the railways. Why was this? they asked. Was it because the railways were a crap, underfunded service? No, it seemed not. The problem, apparently, was simply one of snobbery. Top people, it was decreed, did not like travelling with scumbags. Britain used to have three classes on the railways, she would do so again! The old man and his team would reintroduce third class. Unfortunately the word 'third' is not a modern word; it is not a word that would much impress the Europeans; it is not a word that wins elections.

The solution of course was marketing. Marketing – that great decade-sized red herring which entirely replaced reality during the eighties. A first class seat would stay a first class seat; that, it seemed, offended none. But the second class seat disappeared, re-emerging bright and new as a 'full standard fare' incorporating the new *Silver* service (a free instant coffee). Finally, third class was revived after an absence of forty-five years, but it was not called third class, it was reborn as a Super Saver.

So there you had it, First, Standard (with free coffee) and Super Saver. First, second and third. The business traveller could now be as isolated as he was in his car, and no bollards or contra flows. It hadn't worked of course, no amount of marketing can modernize lines and put new rolling stock on them.

'I should have fought,' the old man said sadly.

'Why didn't I fight like a tiger?' he mumbled into his booze.

'Because you're a cowardly old git and you wanted to get knighted,' thought his team – but they didn't say it.

'I should have told them to stuff their restructuring up their collective bum holes,' continued the old man. 'You can't run a railway without government money. They understand that in Europe. The garlic-gorgers know it; the sausage-suckers know it; even the pasta-pukers are beginning to suspect – why can't the British work it out? The savings come later. Oh well, it's too late now.'

'Too late, Sir!' gasped the old man's team who thought more creatively than they spoke.

'Yes, I'm afraid this is my last lobby,' said the old man. 'Earlier today I spoke with Ingmar Bresslaw.'

'Ingmar Bresslaw!' gasped the old man's team, taking on the role of the Greek chorus at the tragedy.

And well they might have done, for Ingmar Bresslaw was the government's chief hatchet man. The most terrifying man in Whitehall. It was he who had been chosen to lie to the press about Digby's road building plans; and it was he who had carried the news to the Chairman of Britain's Railways that his industry was doomed.

'Ingmar Bresslaw informed me that tomorrow he will instruct the Minister for Transport to announce the formation of the BritTrak Consortium. Of course, I shall resign.'

'The BritTrak Consortium?' replied the team, still practising their echo effect.

'Yes, the BritTrak Consortium. What's more, ladies and gentlemen, it is my sad duty to inform you that there is no "c" in "trak" . . . Is nothing sacred to these despicable people?' the old man anguished. 'They reduce Britain to a single syllable and the word 'track' to four letters. What will they do to the railways themselves?'

The room fell silent. Well actually the room did not fall silent. The room went on playing the string arrangements of Simon and Garfunkel's greatest hits which it had been playing all along. The people in the room fell silent. They knew that what the old man feared had already come to pass. During the love affair with tarmac most industrial nations had neglected their trams and trains, and now, with eco armageddon looming, and oil producing nations holding the world to ransom, rail was needed again but was in no state to fulfil that need. In Britain, it seemed, the process of disintegration was not over yet.

Sandy Mackay, the youngest rail person, spoke up.

'What will the BritTrak Consortium do, Sir?'

The old man took a deep breath.

'It will reduce the rail network to a single high-profit track, running from the City to a decent little pub in Chobham.'

Sandy was a rail enthusiast. He had wanted to be an engine driver when he was six years old, and he still wanted to be one. His love for trains was wild and huge. He knew what it was that made people stand on the end of station platforms in anoraks, insanely taking down a series of meaningless numbers – it was the beauty of trains. He understood the man who spent thirty-six hours of every weekend in his attic watching Hornby models trundle through tiny tunnels while his wife took lovers in the living-room. It was the speed, the power, the romance of rail. And now it seemed that Digby Parkhurst had been instructed to finally destroy that romance forever.

Sandy decided to act.

BIG BEARD

Deep deep down in the bowels of the hotel, where the ancient, groaning heating system shuddered and hissed and made sounds which wandered round the pipes, giving the impression that a ghost was being sick in the radiator, there stood one man alone. Deep down in the forgotten underworld of an English hotel, with the great piles of moulding leaflets from failed 50s advertising campaigns (Isn't sunshine all the nicer for not having too much of it?) stood one solitary fellow with a bottle of rum in his hand. He was a huge, wild looking man with great gnarled fists and great gnarled arms. Everything about him was gnarled – the story of how his inside thighs came to be gnarled delighted the lads at the Frog and Gherkin every time he told it.

The man was clearly mad. His wild eyes sparkling over his huge beard. A beard which gave him the appearance of a man who was trying to swallow an Old English Sheepdog and not getting very far; a great tousled mass of steel-grey hair which was a sort of Bermuda triangle for combs and brushes. A great, strong, noble looking man, with a fearful, savage dignity – but mad. That's what they said.

'Old Big Beard,' the hotel porters said, 'bloody mad.'

And they were right, but not mad as in insane, mad as in angry. Old Big Beard was angry as a man with no head who gets a collection of balaclava helmets for Christmas.

'He hasn't come!' Big Beard roared in a voice so filled with passion that even the boiler stopped gurgling and listened.

'Another year goes by! and still he hasn't come!'

This was the annual conference soirée of the canal lobby.

'Hear me! Hear me!' thundered Big Beard, pulling mightily at his bottle and grabbing up thirty or forty cheesy nibbles in his hamlike fist. 'Britain has hundreds and hundreds of miles of canals! Dug with sweat and blood and . . . and . . . shovels,' he continued, slipping from his oratory peak for a moment. 'Dug two centuries ago, to transport goods

about the country. Today, we carry coal by road!!!'
Tears stood in the huge man's eyes. 'Are we mad!
A hundred million years coal lay still in the Earth!
and we take it on its last journey at seventy miles
an hour! Burning oil all the while! Choking the sky!
Scarring the land! Squashing the hedgehogs!' The
tears began to dive out of the old beardy's eyes,
making elaborate somersaults and pirouettes as
they fell and bounced off his oilskin coat – just to
make their point absolutely clear.

Behind Big Beard, mostly obscured by his huge
gnarled tummy, was a map of the British Isles. A
map which nobody but Big Beard ever saw. On it
were marked the canals of Britain and on each
canal was drawn a chain of barges covering its
entire length.

The point was, that although the very first barge
at the front of the queue might take weeks to reach
its destination, from that point on, if the chain were
not broken, barges might arrive every fifteen
minutes. This clearly would not do for perishable
products, but for coal, concrete, brick, wood . . .

'Imagine it,' the visionary screamed, 'a great,
noble shire-horse, running on high octane grass and
bramble, slowly plodding along, pulling perhaps
thirty barges! No fuel consumption, no pollution,
except the kind you can put on your roses . . . !'

'Listen to me! Listen to me!'

Of course there would be pretty considerable
practical problems, you certainly could not get that

volume of traffic through locks as they are currently designed. But then there are considerable practical problems to building motorways, and that never stopped anyone. Anyway, Big Beard was an idealist. He knew nothing of practical problems, mainly because nobody had ever bothered to discuss them with him.

Big Beard took another great sorrowful pull on his bottle and loosened his bow-tie. He fell over. The canal lobby soirée was over for another year.

Chapter Eight

NIGHT MOVES

SET-UP

'What are you doing Sandy?' said the young rail enthusiast's wife, sleepily.

She had gone to bed early claiming that she couldn't stand all the bullshit. She was right, there was a lot of bullshit, but Sandy's wife would have detected bullshit in a house brick, as long as it had been a London house brick. For she was a Liverpudlian, a Liverpudlian graphic design graduate who now lived in London and she had decided that London was entirely populated by bullshitters. Many arty London-based Liverpudlians share with arty London-based Glaswegians the deep-seated conviction that they, despite being artists and film makers quaffing champagne in the same bars as the native artists and film makers, somehow retain an honest earthiness and cynical sense of humour that is their birthright. The longer they live in London, the more convinced they become that nobody in that city is capable of communicating honestly. Whereas back home, a fishwife might be found sitting in a pub with a clothes designer and an ex-murderer discussing architecture. This is of course bollocks. All cities have an equal amount of bullshit, and an equal amount of honesty – and anyone who claims differently is bullshitting.

Anyway, Mrs Mackay was half asleep and she wanted to know what her husband Sandy was doing.

'Nothing,' he said. But he wasn't; he was doing something.

Sandy had spent the past hour trying to find a prostitute. It was his intention to either compromise or blackmail Digby Parkhurst out of announcing BritTrak on the morrow.

Digby was in his late thirties, and still single, but he was known throughout the party for his flirty ways with girls and his frequent, unpleasant and intimidating sexual allusions towards those women over whom he held power. Sandy reckoned that all this indicated, that underneath Digby was probably a sad, frustrated, little git. Also Sandy had seen Digby stagger to bed and knew him to be drunker than an eighteenth birthday party. If ever there was a time to get him, that time was now. At least that was what Sandy reckoned, but then again, he was completely pissed as well.

However, finding prostitutes is not really very easy in nice English towns, or probably anywhere for that matter. As the Global Crappee advert showed, the masturbating fantasies of video directors give the impression that gorgeous prostitutes are standing on every street corner, but of course they are not. Sandy had no idea where to look for one and after a nasty mistake with a late night doughnut maker had retired to his room rather than be done for kerb crawling.

But the defence of Britain's greatest public transport system was not over yet. Sandy had a different plan, an even drunker one. He was a slim fellow, with large eyes and fine bones, and he was desperate.

'Nothing at all, darling. Go back to sleep,' he said, stealing a pair of stockings from her bag.

'I have to pop down and do a bit more business.'

'Bloody bullshitters,' she replied through her sleep.

To Sandy's great good fortune his wife had purchased a wig that day, to wear at the end of conference ball. He took it.

'Quite important people actually,' he .said . . . 'Think I'd better have a shave,' and rolling up his trouser legs Sandy disappeared into the bathroom.

I HEAR YOU KNOCKING

Deborah could not sleep. It was one of those aggravating occasions when one is too tired to sleep. Having had a busy day, she had arrived home pretty exhausted and gone to bed early convinced she would be asleep in five minutes. And here she was, two and a half hours later, wide awake, listening to noises. It was one of those nights when for no particular reason a person feels more scared than usual. Anybody living on their own is going to feel nervous every now and then, particularly a woman, but tonight Deborah had it worse.

Every creak and rustle seemed imbued with murderous intent. The shadows of the trees thrown against her curtain by the street lights turned into a steady stream of mad axe murderers strolling past her window. It was almost as if the All England Federation of Mad Axe Murderers had elected to have their annual convention in Deborah's front garden.

The wind whispered under her front door, and the wind had a very sick sense of humour that night. What other reason could there be for it whispering 'Deborah I'm going to get you. You can't run Deborah, you can't run.' Unless of course it wasn't the wind at all, but an asthmatic sex fiend stretched out on her doormat getting his kicks. To Deborah's restless ear that whispering was beginning to sound more and more like the dickhead who used to ring her up before she got Telecom to put an intercept on her calls. Had he come to get her? Deborah longed to shout 'Piss off dickhead' but it was probably only the wind.

The fridge was particularly talkative that night,

it moaned and it burped, it burped and it moaned. It stopped moaning and burping, waited until Deborah's eyes began to become heavy, and then with a great moan and a burp started moaning and burping again. Eventually Deborah began to wonder whether this relentless cacophony of sound was the fridge at all. Maybe it was one of the mad axemen in the garden. Perhaps an unhappy one with a digestive problem had stepped over the asthmatic sex fiend, crept into the house and was standing in her kitchen by a silent fridge having his pre-murder moan and burp.

When the door bell rang Deborah's heart nearly stopped. Was it the axemen? Was it the neighbours complaining about the axemen? No way was she getting up to find out. Gingerly she reached for the radio that Geoffrey had made for her and tuned into the frequency of her door intercom.

'Hello,' she said, trying to sound like a heavyweight boxer with a gun. Deborah listened then smiled with relief, she would know that guttural stutter anywhere. The relief turned almost instantly to anger.

'Geoffrey,' she snapped into the radio. 'What the hell are you playing at? I thought someone was trying to kill me.'

'Someone is trying to kill *me*,' Geoffrey spoke into the intercom, rather enjoying saying such a momentous and cool thing. Unfortunately the impact was wasted because Deborah, who normally understood at least ninety per cent of what Geoffrey said, was too fazed to follow him.

'God knows what you want, but you'd better come in.' She pressed the button and the ingenious radio wave that Geoffrey had created opened the door for him. Deborah remained in bed whilst, with great care, Geoffrey made some coffee and brought it through into her room, then spilt it.

'OK, duvet head,' said Deborah sternly. 'What's the big idea busting in in the middle of the night? If you've come round here trying to get in my pants again I'm going to be real mad, OK, doughnut brain? I mean, ringing your mom, type mad, Geoffrey! and you know she hates it when you get horny.'

DEBORAH

Deborah was a citizen of the US. She used to refer to herself as an American, until she got trapped in a bar by a Canadian and a Peruvian who spent two mind-numbingly boring hours explaining to her that America is a continent not a country.

She was twenty-one years old and had been in Britain for three years studying, but the spirit of New York still seemed to hang about her. At any moment you expected her to say 'All right already'. Having had an English grandmother she had come to Britain to escape an over-protective Jewish family circle. Her parents were not rich but they had agreed to help her through her four-year course in textiles.

'You need to travel three thousand miles to learn how to make trousers and blouses?' her Poppa had complained. 'Trousers and blouses you can make in New York and live with your family. Is there a problem with New York I would like to know? Did we all suddenly get body odour?'

'Poppa there's nothing wrong with New York, if you discount the fact that a person can get shot putting out the garbage, and then the city can't even afford to pick up the garbage, so a person dies for nothing and rats move into the neighbourhood hanging around the trash cans taking steroids,' explained Deborah. 'I love New York. It's you and Momma I can't stand.'

'Hear her, Poppa, hear her!' Momma had wailed. 'Deborah listen to me. You turn your back on your family, and you desert your whole people, and your God. Nobody likes a Jew, family is all we got, read a history book.'

'Momma, I'm going to England, not joining the Nazi party,' Deborah had protested. She knew it would be OK, there was nothing her family liked more than a drama. If Deborah had not announced that she wanted to go to Britain her mother would have wailed about Deborah's neckline.

'Maybe you should hang them out of the window,' Momma would protest at anything saucier than a turtle-neck. 'I hear there are still people on Staten

114

Island who haven't seen your bosom.'

'Momma, I have tits,' Deborah would explain wearily. 'OK, I'm sorry, but they're stuck to the front of me. If I could keep them in a handbag I would.'

'So now it's OK to swear in front of your mother?'

Gradually, over supper that evening Deborah's parents came round to the idea of her studying abroad.

'I suppose New York *is* getting kind of dangerous,' conceded Deborah's mother.

'Kind of dangerous, she says!' said Poppa. 'Like Hitler was a little temperamental. Dangerous? I should go to work in a tank! Drugs, crack, bullets flying everywhere, nobody knows who'll catch a stray next. Last week, Gosha, the watch repair fellow, he was shot in his *own apartment*. Am I still living in America when a man isn't safe in his *own apartment*?'

'Poppa, Mr Gosha shot himself,' said Deborah. 'Crack didn't kill the guy, quartz did. He gave up the struggle when they started giving away watches inside cereal boxes.'

And so the conversation moved onto other topics, and Deborah was allowed to go to London. She was later to reflect on the irony of her parents supporting the trip partly on the grounds of New York's reputation for violence. For the night she let her friend Geoffrey into her home to seek sanctuary, she was letting in more violence than she would have got if she'd skipped London and joined the marines.

SANCTUARY

Geoffrey strenuously denied the accusation that his intrusion of Deborah's privacy was in anyway carnally motivated.

'Deborah,' protested Geoffrey. 'My motives are pure as the driven snow.'

'Oh yeah?' she replied, 'well I've seen snow in London. They mix it with gasoline and dog shit and pile it up in the gutter.'

Deborah was justified in being a little suspicious. Geoffrey had never attempted to disguise the fact that he craved her, and she had on numerous occasions had to dampen his ardour. It was not unreasonable of her to suspect that this was one of them.

'Pitch me Geoffrey, and it had better be good,' she said.

'Deborah,' Geoffrey replied. 'I'm in trouble, the twilight zone is here. Two men came to my house tonight and tried to kill me. But luckily I managed to kill them first.'

Deborah was flabbergasted.

'That is pathetic Geoffrey,' she said. 'Linda Lovelace wouldn't swallow that story, and she'd swallow anything. If you're going to invade a chick's privacy in the middle of the night you're going to have to do better than that. Go home and take less drugs.'

'No really, Deborah,' stammered Geoffrey. 'It's true.'

And pausing only to knock the glass of water off Deborah's bedside table, Geoffrey explained the events of the day.

I HEAR YOU KNOCKING TOO

Digby Parkhurst was having a restless night as well.

The booze and the comprehensive way he had put down the mighty Sam Turk had put a right ruddy firework in his jocks. He was restless and randy. Digby knew that elsewhere in the hotel, other, more important ministers were holding court and probably having an amazing time, but nobody had invited him.

He kicked round his room, wishing he hadn't left the road lobby soirée. They would probably still be drinking, probably having a really great time without him. Could he go back? Of course he bloody could, he was the Minister for Transport, he could do what he liked. But even dull stupid Digby knew that it would look a bit pathetic to sidle back now after his magnificent exit. Besides he might run into those dreadful railway people.

Digby realized he had shot his bolt. He dug a scotch out of his mini-bar and was vaguely wondering about whether he could be bothered to haul off his shreddies and have a bit of a twang on the old one-string bass, when there was a knock at the door.

So they weren't ignoring him after all! It was probably Sam and some of the guys from the road lobby come to crawl a bit more. Perhaps it would be a couple of his cabinet colleagues looking for a bit of a lads booze up. Digby opened the door with a big smile.

'I'm awfully sorry to bother you, but I can't find my room. Do you think I might come in and use your phone?' said the tall, slender figure with the tight dress, the flaming red hair and the husky voice.

Digby stared at Sandy. Sandy stared back. They were both very drunk, both for a moment lost in their own thoughts. After a few seconds Sandy felt the onus remained with him to continue the conversation.

'Oh I see you've broken the seal on your mini-bar, I'm gasping for a snort,' he said. Trying to say it through a sexy pout.

Digby, who appeared to have been struck completely dumb, came back to life.

'How did you know? Who else knows? Who the hell put you up to it?' His voice shook with guilt and fear.

Sandy had not really expected this, and did not know what to say next. So he said 'Uhm' and left it at that.

'Get in here now,' said Digby, realizing that his worst nightmare was now reality, and trying desperately to sober up.

'All right, sonny, you tell me, and you tell me now, who put you up to this. If you hold back I swear I shall turn you over to the police as a dirty little blackmailing whore, and hang the consequences.'

'Sonny?' said Sandy rather disappointed.

'Yes, sonny, now answer my question.'

'So you know I'm a bloke then?' continued Sandy, his voice returning to its natural brogue.

'Oh God, a bloody Scot.' Digby was a very worried man. 'I knew they'd get me. Is this because I'm planning to put a road through the courtyard at Edinburgh Castle?'

Sandy did not know what to do. His drunken plan had been to smite Digby with his girlish charms, get a tape recording of Digby propositioning him and then clear out before Digby had a chance to find the sausage. His instant unmasking as a gonad-packing, tackle-swinging member of the male sex had rather blown that out. Suddenly Sandy decided he had had enough.

'Sorry, wrong room,' he said and made to go.

'No you bloody don't!' said Digby, jumping up to stop him. 'Not before you tell me who the hell sent you and who the hell knows I'm bloody gay.'

For Sandy at least, those words seemed to fill the room with music, beautiful music, played on train whistles. He smiled a huge smile. He slipped a hand in his wife's handbag to ensure the tape was running.

In some ways Digby was a victim of his own

cowardice. His unquestioning acceptance that his sexuality must always remain a dreaded secret was the very reason that the revelation was so terrible now. It is true, that such are the prejudices of British society that, had he confronted it from the beginning, he might not have risen to the cabinet – but he might have done, and he certainly would not have lived a life of career paranoia and seedy intrigue. And now he was knackered anyway, his carefully cultivated jack-the-lad image making the truth about him all the more sensational.

'Come on, who's after me? Who knows I'm a gay transvestite! I only ever do it in Amsterdam . . .' Suddenly light dawned for Digby. Amsterdam! His last three trips to the Continent had been as a guest of the road lobby. They took him to motor shows, they took him to oil refineries . . . They left him alone in the evening. God, was this Turk's way of warning him not to dress him down in public? Was Turk warning him, in none too subtle a fashion, that he would burgle as many government departments as he pleased? How could Digby have been so foolish as to quarrel with a man like Turk?

'Listen,' said Digby, 'tell Turk, I understand and I'm sorry. Tell him he can pinch every patent in London if he likes, I'll stand by him. Tell him I'm very, very sorry and he won't need to warn me again. Do you understand?'

The years fell away from Digby. The arrogance of office evaporated. He knew he was still what he always had been, a sad scared little farty. Once again he was poor old Shitsby Zitburst pleading with the school bullies.

'Do you understand?' he said again. 'Tell Turk to call it off.'

'Yes, I understand,' said Sandy, who did not understand at all.

'You can go then.'

Sandy got up.

'OK then. It's been very nice.' He was about to leave, but he turned back to Digby once more. 'Just do me one favour will you Diggy? Remember this handbag, will you?' Sandy held up the handbag, and then left without another word.

Leaving a subdued and thoughtful Digby, Sandy staggered away, suddenly realizing how blotto he was. As he entered the lift a maid was coming out of it to collect the breakfast orders. Feeling rather exposed, Sandy confronted the situation with Scottish bravado.

'A bonny evening to you, sweet lassie,' he said.

'Good evening, Madam,' said the girl in a small embarrassed voice. Sandy felt pleased. So his disguise had at least worked on someone. Leaving the lift on his floor he crept back to his room and tried to get undressed without waking his wife up. He failed.

'Will you look at you,' she said. 'You've been living in London too long.'

SCUM ON THE BEACH

With the departure of the Minister the road lobby had soon broken up and Sam left the hotel to take a quiet stroll along the promenade and down onto the beach. He loved the sea at night, even in a town. At night you could forget all the crap that was in it and see it as men had seen it when they first set sail for the New World – shining and mysterious. It was a clear night and Sam turned his head to the stars. Despite the lights on the pier, quite a number were visible and Sam was just contemplating that he would probably soon be able to just about afford one, when Springer scuttled up beside him.

'Boy oh boy,' he panted, 'that wasn't too comfortable with Parkhurst there, for a minute.'

Sam kept looking up at his star.

'Who gives a fuck what Parkhurst thinks?'

'Well I was just thinking . . . What with the . . .' but Sam cut Springer short.

'I do hope you're not going to be stupid enough to mention our little project Springer.'

'Well, no, of course not. But I mean, when it comes on line . . . when we start building the thing . . .'

'Building the thing?' asked Sam.

'Yeah . . .' answered Springer, hesitantly. 'Building the thing.'

Sam looked at Springer quizzically.

'Listen, Springer,' he said, 'Digby Parkhurst is a low-life little cockroach. We kiss his ass while he's a Minister so he builds us roads. That's it, that's all. He has nothing to do with our future plans.'

'But . . . but he slipped us the . . .' protested Springer.

'Exactly, Springer. He gave us the information. So what's he going to say? That he tipped us off to make a robbery? Then he's an accessory and no one will believe he didn't take a piece. Besides, like I said to Parkhurst, we haven't stolen anything. Do you see any stolen property? I don't. What have we got to do with anything?'

'Yes, but when we start to build it, well then it has to come out doesn't it?' Springer persevered.

Again Sam looked at Springer quizzically.

'You just haven't thought this through at all have you son?' he said.

Chapter Nine

BLACKMAIL, THEFT AND DIRTY PHONE CALLS

THE POWER BEHIND THE THRONE

Digby woke up the following morning with a monumental hangover, but apart from that he didn't feel too bad. On reviewing the incident of the previous night he reckoned he had got off pretty lightly. Turk and the road lobby had only warned him of their knowledge, as long as he played ball and was a good boy they would have no reason to use it against him.

Besides, Digby had even scarier things to consider. He had been summoned to attend an early breakfast with Ingmar Bresslaw, the Prime Minister's eyes, ears and Doc Martin boots. Digby knew that, despite being a non-elected Civil Servant, Ingmar Bresslaw had more influence on national policy than the whole of Her Majesty's Loyal Opposition, every protest march and petition ever organized plus the European Court of Human Rights, put together.

On his way to the dining-room, preparing himself to genuflect before the great man, Digby encountered Sam Turk. Digby saw his opportunity to establish his puppylike loyalty to the road lobby beyond doubt.

'Uhm . . . Mr Turk,' said Digby nervously.

'Yes, Minister,' replied Turk, expecting a resumption of the ticking-off he had received the previous night.

'I just wanted to say . . . Sam, that you're the boss, OK? I know that Ministers for Transport may come and Ministers for Transport may go, but car builders, well, they stay forever . . . I know that now, it was stupid of me to forget it, and well . . . I'm sorry.'

Sam was mystified at Digby's change of attitude, but he was a man who took his good fortune where he found it.

'Yes, well, what you say is very true, Minister. And I guess if we have to liberate the odd patent for the good of Britain, what the hell, eh? It's only ethics for Christ's sake.'

'Exactly, Sam, exactly. It is, as you so very rightly say, only ethics,' replied Digby. 'And if I come across any myself, rest assured I'll slip them in my pocket for you . . . Patents that is, ha ha, not ethics, good Lord, you wouldn't be needing them . . . I mean . . . Well anyway, ha ha *thnn thnn* . . . Oh and by the way, that working paper the Road Federation presented, the one about turning all of

London parks into car parks, I've been thinking about that one hard, do memo me.'

'I will Minister, I will and good luck with your speech,' said Sam Turk.

'Well that's very kind Sam . . . and, I can forget about uhm . . . last night's little Scottish visitation can I?' said Digby.

'Why sure Minister, you can forget about whatever you please.' Sam had not the faintest idea what Digby was talking about and only the very slightest interest.

Digby, believing he had set matters straight with Sam, went into the dining-room for his breakfast with Ingmar Bresslaw.

'Good morning Ingmar,' he said. Ingmar Bresslaw did not even look up from his bacon, which he was viewing with utter contempt.

'They only ever do it on one side!' he growled in fury.

'What was that Ingmar?' enquired Digby.

'Without doubt the three most misleading words in the English language are "Great British Breakfast". It is a global bloody con and it should be exposed! Us boasting about our breakfasts? It's like the Russians boasting about their cars! We do worse breakfasts than any other nation in the world! The bloody Australians do better breakfasts than us and do you know why Minister?'

Ingmar did Digby the courtesy of addressing him as Minister, but only in the manner that an all powerful, regimental sergeant major might call a nineteen-year-old subaltern 'Sir'.

'Uhm not really, no Ingmar, no I don't,' a nervous Digby replied, desperately wondering what the answer was that Ingmar wanted to hear, and conscious that Ingmar could swat Ministers like flies.

'Because we only grill the bacon on one bloody side!!!' Ingmar said in a voice taut with emotion. 'From a transport café to a four star hotel it is considered enough that the bacon *looks* done. If it looks done the work shy bastard in the kitchen reckons it *is* done and he's off the hook. Is a car finished without the engine? It *looks* finished. Is a man dressed without his underpants? He *looks* dressed. So why is it considered acceptable to grill the bacon only on *one* bloody side!!! I like my bacon *crispy*, damn their bloody eyes!'

'Uhm . . . perhaps you should send it back.' Digby was taking a big risk offering an opinion, but he was at a loss as to what to say.

'Don't be an arse, Minister! Send it back and have some pimply school-leaver in a big white hat phlegm up on it out of spite?' Ingmar pushed his breakfast away and called a waitress. 'Bring me a large, single malt whisky, any bloody brand, and four soluble aspirin. Right then,' he continued after the girl had gone, 'what do you want?'

'I'm sorry?' Digby, somewhat taken aback by this abrupt enquiry.

'Come on, come on, come on Minister, I'm a busy man, what do you want?'

Of course Digby did not like being addressed in this fashion by a Civil Servant, but he was as likely to object as to slam his tackle in the waffle iron which had just been placed at his elbow. Ingmar Bresslaw's power was awesome and he wielded it with the scruples of a bed bug. He was the Prime Minister's hit-man, the toughest thug in Whitehall, and Ingmar's dark shadow in your door spelt terror to any member of the government. What's more, the higher you got, the more terrifying he became, because it was his job to make sure that no one ever got close enough to challenge his boss.

However, Digby could not help but feel rather put out and honour bound to stand up for himself.

'Uhm I'm awfully sorry Ingmar. I mean really, sorry, but it was you who summoned me surely?' he said meekly taking a piece of toast.

'Was it? Oh yes. Don't bother buttering that toast, I haven't much to say,' replied Ingmar.

Digby had just stuck his knife into a curl of butter. His arm was stretched across the table holding the knife. He did not know what to do for the best. Withdraw the knife, in which case the curl of butter might come away with it and Ingmar might imagine that he was being disobeyed, or else lay down the knife in the butter where it was, which would be sloven table manners and Ingmar might feel that insufficient respect was being shown. In the end, Digby remained frozen, conducting his short interview with Ingmar Bresslaw arm outstretched across the table with his knife into the butter. Bresslaw did not notice as he did not bother to look at Digby.

'Right Minister,' he growled, his great wet boozy eyes still staring glumly down at the bacon. 'Your speech to conference, all prepared?'

'Oh yes Ingmar, I'm very pleased with it,' replied Digby.

'I didn't ask how you felt about it, I asked if it was bloody well prepared,' snapped Ingmar Bresslaw. 'You haven't messed about with it? Changed anything since we wrote it for you?'

'Well . . . I did add a joke,' confessed Digby.

'Ye Gods, Saints preserve us, a joke! What bloody joke?'

'Well . . . it's about a donkey . . .' said Digby, his arm beginning to quiver with the strain.

'Well if it's the one I've heard about the donkey, your resignation will be requested mid-speech,' said Ingmar. 'Not that I care. The point is, just make sure you don't get carried away and add anything of substance that hasn't been agreed, all right? Above all, don't mention the road plans, they're political dynamite, all right? The BritTrak stuff is quite a hot enough potato for one conference. That damn anti-road rally yesterday shows people suspect a pretty radical plan, but, as you well know, they don't know the half of it. So it's damned important how we present ourselves on this one. A silly move now would kick up a stink we couldn't handle and ruin the most important bit of legislation since we sold the NHS to American Express.'

Despite the pain in his arm, Digby swelled with pride. He knew his road projects were big stuff but to have the mighty Ingmar Bresslaw speak so seriously about them was a high commendation indeed.

'So have you got that?' said Ingmar. 'Talk rail. Keep off your bloody roads. All right. Goodbye, Minister.'

'Goodbye, Ingmar,' said Digby, and he got up and left. To avoid further embarrassment he took the butter knife plus the bit of butter with him.

A WARNING IGNORED

Outside the hotel the rail lobby finally got their moment with Digby, they converged on him one step ahead of the press. They were pathetic, like beggars, they knew the Minister would give them nothing and they harried him in a defeated, dispirited fashion. Except Sandy, Sandy lobbied with cool, confident simplicity. Wearing a neat suit and dark glasses he pushed his way through the throng and confronted Digby head on.

'Minister,' he said firmly. 'I am going to say this only once so you had better listen. In your speech today, *don't* announce the formation of BritTrak.'

'Another bloody Scot,' thought Digby to himself, ignoring Sandy and getting into the limo. 'They're all train mad, it comes from living so bloody far from anywhere decent, that's what it is.'

CROSSED LINES

Despite the fact that he had been up late telling Deborah his story (and making rather a meal of it, it might be added), Geoffrey was up bright and early on Monday morning. And just as Digby was dealing with the train lobby in Brighton, Geoffrey was getting ready to phone the Office of Patents in order to get back the designs of his brilliant invention.

As has been said, the telephone was one of the great banes of Geoffrey's life. Communication is rendered infinitely more difficult when you cannot see the person to whom you are speaking and Geoffrey had to be on particularly good form to make himself understood. On this morning, what with the excitement, the loss of sleep and everything else, he wasn't.

'*Urgh, urgh,*' he said into the receiver on hearing that he was connected.

'Aaaargh! We've got a sicko!' screamed Dolores.

The Whitehall department Geoffrey was phoning, despite being the repository for the very latest inventions, was itself last fully refitted just after the war and it still boasted a nice old-fashioned exchange staffed by nice old-fashioned girls.

'I dunno,' she explained to her anxious colleagues' enquiries, 'he just sort of went *urgh, urgh*.'

'Dirty bastard,' chimed Maureen, 'probably gets his filthy kicks going urgh urgh. You shouldn't have screamed Dolores, that's what they like. It makes 'em all excited to hear a girl scream.'

'I couldn't help it,' claimed Dolores. 'He went urgh.'

'Yes, well, you have to be strong Dolores,' asserted Maureen. 'You owe it to other women.'

The phone rang again. Maureen answered it. 'Hello Whitehall Office of Patents.'

'*Urgh, urgh, urgh*.'

'Aaaargh!' screamed Maureen, slamming the phone down. 'It's that *urgh – er*.'

'I thought you said don't scream,' complained Dolores. 'That wasn't very strong. Coo, I'll bet he's excited now. I'll bet he's as excited as anything. I'll bet he's rolling round on the floor rubbing himself with a washing-up glove and going *urgh*. You've gratified him Maureen, that's what you've done, you've given him gratification.'

'Oh shut up, Dolores,' said Maureen.

Geoffrey summoned up all his concentration and dialled again. But this time the girls were ready for him. Maureen possessed a rape alarm and they had sworn that the very next time anyone went *urgh* at them, they would let him have it.

'*Urgh*,' said Geoffrey and an ear shattering shriek shot out of the phone, into his ear, through his brain, out of the other ear and ricocheted against a couple of walls before finally dying down in the goldfish bowl, giving Deborah's goldfish, Jaws, a nasty turn.

Geoffrey decided he would have to wake Deborah and ask for her help. Being a student, Deborah was able, to a certain extent, to make her own timetable. Her timetable this morning had been to try and get some extra sleep, since she had got so little in the night, what with visions of imaginary burping axe murderers, followed by Geoffrey's tale of the real thing.

Deborah snapped into a bleary consciousness.

'What! Where! Don't sit on the Kiwi fruit!' she said, with one of those curious lapses of logic that sleeping or half-awake people specialize in when attempting conversation. Her eyes focused on Geoffrey who had brought her a cuppa, and was endeavouring to keep it steady.

'Geoffrey! It ain't five minutes since I finally prised you off the end of my bed, now you're back. What is it, a charity thing? You get sponsored for how much you can annoy me?'

'Sorry,' he replied. 'I brought you a cup of tea.'

'What's going on? Are Murder Incorporated here? Is it curtains for us, Bugsy?'

Geoffrey explained that there was no immediate danger, and Deborah enquired, far from soothingly, why then, he had woken her up after only a couple of hours' sleep, further adding that perhaps Geoffrey would like to take a hike and not return unless either the assassins or Elvis turned up.

'You have to ring the Patents Office,' said Geoffrey proffering her the extension phone. 'I've tried but they think I'm a raving sex beast.'

'Hmm,' said Deborah, 'they may have a point. Get your eyes off my front, Meathead.'

OH WHAT A NIGHT

'Get your eyes off my front, Meathead' was, as might be imagined, the phrase which Deborah used when she caught Geoffrey ogling, which was often. Deborah was as pretty as a picture, and what's more, a picture of something very pretty, and Geoffrey was so hot for her you could have boiled an egg in his Y fronts. Of course Geoffrey was hot for a lot of girls and Deborah often had to admonish him on behalf of a stranger they happened to pass. 'It's all very well taking a discreet glance,' she would say, 'but allowing your eyes to extend three feet on little springs and steam to shoot out of your ear-holes was a bit obvious.' Thoughts of sex play an enormous part in the make up of any individual, and for young men it is close to an obsession. Geoffrey was a young man and, being, as he was, at a disadvantage when it came to asking out girls, his obsession was a nightmare. Geoffrey, quite simply spent his entire life absolutely gasping for a fuck.

Obviously having a disability, even a severe one, is in no way necessarily an obstacle to leading a fulfilling sex life, but Geoffrey had never been lucky that way. In fact he had only ever had-it-off once, and that had been the result of a triumph of organization and bucking the system. It was when he was seventeen and living for a while at a special needs boarding school. There had been seven boys living in Geoffrey's dorm, all in their teens, and, as might be expected, all hornier than the brass section of the London Philharmonic.

They did not have the outlets that other young lads had, something as simple as masturbation was difficult for most of them. This problem consumed Geoffrey. His soul burned with a righteous fury over the injustice of it all. For teenage boys to be denied the chance to have a quick one off-the-wrist seemed too cruel even for one who had faced many deprivations in his short life. Something would have to be done.

Geoffrey Spasmo conceived a wicked, wicked plan. Under his direction, the entire dorm scrimped and saved for months and months and one dark and naughty night Geoffrey dug out his prized possession, a tatty copy of Penthouse, and skipping all his usual favourite pages, Cheryl, Janine, Wanda, he chose a number from the classified ads at the back.

The whole thing was a triumph. A very nice young woman arrived in a taxi, which Geoffrey met at the end of the school drive. At first she was reluctant but it would have taken a harder heart than hers to deny the longing in Geoffrey's eyes. They sneaked up to the dorm, which was now so highly charged that if the window hadn't been open the entire room would have short circuited itself, and the girl, who according to the back of Penthouse was called Suki, got straight down to it. Providing six professional hand jobs in succession, the whole thing took about a minute and a quarter.

'I have to tell you boys,' whispered Suki, 'that this is very easy money for me. I mean I only have to touch them and they go off.'

Finally it was Geoffrey's turn, and Suki was in a magnanimous mood. These young clients were considerably less demanding than blokes in airport hotels who wanted to do it in the wardrobe, then talk about their wives.

'All right Geoffrey,' she said. 'How about unloading your cherry? Reckon you're up to it?'

Geoffrey wasn't sure but it would have taken a tactical nuclear strike to stop him trying. Fortunately for him, Suki was a natural born therapist.

A THEFT DISCOVERED

But that had been long ago, and there had been many years of frustration since then. Whilst at university he had thought about paying for it a second time, but it really wasn't what he wanted. That first time had been a personal triumph, a great adventure. As an adult it would just rub in his inability to take a woman to bed without paying her.

Which was why, even though he was being sought by an anonymous murderer, Geoffrey could not resist a glance at Deborah's bosom as she took the phone from him, and her nightie afforded him a tantalizing glimpse. However, having been suitably admonished, Geoffrey averted his gaze and gave Deborah the number.

'Why so urgent?' said Deborah wearily. 'I mean OK, so somebody's stolen your invention from the lab. But I mean, hey, come on, they're not exactly going to have got it out of the Patents Office are they?'

But Deborah and Geoffrey were in for a shock.

'I'm sorry, but I have no record of any patent submission from any Geoffrey Peason. In fact, I have no record of that name at all,' the voice said and the voice was not lying, for the cover-up had happened way above the voice's head.

On the Saturday morning, when Deirdre Whelk, the Civil Servant responsible, had discovered exactly which patent application had been stolen, she had stormed straight over to see the Minister in a fury. 'Doing a Deirdre' as her minions called it, and her minions knew to keep well out of the way. Something Digby Parkhurst was not in a position to do, since Deirdre was standing four square before his desk, fixing him with an eye that could have cut diamonds, and what's more, diamonds that were still buried half a mile deep in the granite of the Kimberley.

'Now look here, Minister,' she snapped. 'I understand that your transport people need to keep up with design developments, which is why I have been prepared in the past to allow you a look at certain items of interest which my department finds itself in possession of. But my God, they're for your eyes only!'

'Of course, Deirdre, of course they are, and only I ever see them,' Digby lied.

'Minister, the bloody thing has been stolen. Did you steal it?' Deirdre asked.

'Don't be absurd, Deirdre,' replied Digby, trying to sound statesmanlike, but actually sounding git-manlike. 'Her Majesty's Ministers do not indulge in felonies, we . . .'

'Oh no?' interrupted Deirdre. 'How would you describe handing on government secrets?'

'Deirdre, you're being pompous,' said Digby, being massively pompous. 'Government secrets? A paltry patent?'

'The Office of Patents is a branch of government,' snapped Deirdre. 'Its secrets are a branch of government. I have broken the law, you have broken the law and whatever sordid oil baron you snitched to has broken into my department! Now for my own sake, and for my own sake only, I am going to screw the lid down on this, Minister. But you,

Minister, are a very stupid man.'

Deirdre stormed out of Digby's office and got to work on a cover up. The result being that when Deborah put the phone down to face Geoffrey she had to inform him that his invention had completely disappeared.

Geoffrey was truly stunned. The disaster befalling him was huge. First they had tried to kill him, now they had stolen both copies of his life's work, and he did not know who they were, or why they were attacking him. Geoffrey sat on Deborah's bed, trying to think what he should do.

'OK, Geoffrey, so give me the juice. What is this crazy invention?' asked Deborah, hauling herself up into a sitting position by means of the bar that was suspended above her head. 'You've always made a secret out of it like it was the recipe for coke. What could be so special? Have you discovered the secret of alchemy?'

'I did it for you Deborah,' said Geoffrey. 'It's an engine, and I designed it for you.'

'An engine?' enquired Deborah. 'That's nice, thanks. You mean like in a car?'

'Yes, exactly like in a car, except it doesn't use petrol. It's powered by hydrogen,' said Geoffrey and adding rather unnecessarily, 'it's a hydrogen engine.'

'Don't be stupid Geoffrey,' said Deborah. 'You can't run an engine on hydrogen.'

'You can run an engine on anything that is a

source of power, Deborah,' snapped Geoffrey. He did not normally snap at Deborah, in fact, even if he had wanted to he probably would not have had the guts, but he was in something of a turmoil. 'Anything at all, oil, electricity, coal, legs . . .'

'Some legs,' said Deborah. 'Mine couldn't power an electric toothbrush.' It had been almost three years since the arsehole in the Global Moritz had tried to rush the pelican crossing on yellow, but understandably she was still a little bitter.

'Yes, some legs,' admitted Geoffrey. 'But you can run an engine on any source of power. The only question is, how efficient is it? I wanted to make a clean engine, a light engine, an engine that could make you truly mobile Deborah. One where the fuel weighed very little but delivered an immense amount of power. When I first met you, I wanted to make an engine that would turn your wheelchair into a Thunderbird. I wanted to make you able to dance and fly. You were the inspiration Deborah, you concentrated my mind. You made me want to build an engine!'

'I have that effect on all the guys,' said Deborah.

Chapter Ten

BOY MEETS GIRL. BOY ANNOYS GIRL. BOY STANDS NOT A HOPE IN HELL WITH GIRL.

DECLARATION OF INDEPENDENCE

Since Deborah's friendship with Geoffrey was shortly to lead her into the most mortal danger it is worth taking a moment to discover how it was that they came to meet at all. It had happened some three years previously on the London Underground. Well not actually on the underground, but at the wall of ticket barriers that the authorities began to erect shortly after the King's Cross Fire, in the apparent hope that next time nobody at all would get out.

Early in the time of Deborah's burden, before she became cripwise to the system of apartheid under which she would be spending the rest of her life, she had attempted to take a tube. Later of course Deborah was to realize that she was as disbarred from such simple public activities as were black South Africans from municipal swimming pools in South Africa. Later of course, Deborah would come to realize that the only thing missing from doorways, steps, lifts, escalators, curbs etc., in London, were neat signs saying **ACHTUNG! No Disabled People Allowed**. However, this was in the springtime of her trouble. The Global Moritz was still a recent memory and Deborah was determined to stay in Britain, continue her education and square up to the slings and arrows of outrageous bastards.

Of course her parents had begged her to return to New York.

'What, you hate your Momma so much you won't let her look after you?'

'Momma,' Deborah had said, 'if I come to you now I'll never get out again. You'll glue yourself to my wheelchair and force soup down my throat for forty-five years till you die, and then I'll starve. Now is the time I have to learn to live my own life.'

'You don't *like* my soup?' said Momma.

FIRE HAZARD

And so Deborah had stayed in London and, on that fateful day when she met Geoffrey, found herself stuck at the ticket barrier at South Kensington station with a weary looking London Underground person approaching her. Deborah was very quickly realizing how naïve she had been in assuming that, with enough determination, she could roll where she wanted to roll. An enormous revelation was about to be demonstrated to her. A life-time sized truth was looming up at her wearing the uniform of London Regional Transport. Deborah, who before her encounter with the Global Moritz had been a young woman, was now a fire hazard. She had passed through a physical transformation. A transformation even more dramatic than that undergone by female stars in the US who, on reaching the age of forty-five, disappear for a month and re-emerge aged thirty, talking about feminism and being careful not to sneeze too hard in case they implode. Deborah's transformation had been greater even than this. For Deborah, once a warm and vibrant human being, exuding personality and soul, had become, a fire hazard. Fire hazard, and specifically fire hazard. Not obstruction, embarrassment or damn nuisance, but fire hazard.

The reason Deborah was so specifically a fire hazard was that in those two little words, the able-bodied community let itself off the hook. It would of course be churlish to deny someone access to a theatre or pub because their chair would be difficult to get up a flight of steps, or because they occupy more space than walking customers and are hence less profitable. On the other hand, to deny someone access because they are a fire hazard – well, there is a sensible and public spirited action. There is a fast route to the moral high-ground if ever there was one.

'Nobody likes it, love, but there you go.'

Should Deborah, or anyone similarly afflicted be

so selfish as to complain about their effective ostracism from social and cultural life, what would she be doing but wishing pain and death upon the able-bodied community. And let us face it, it is not their fault that she is in a wheelchair.

'It's the possibility of a panic that worries us,' people would patiently explain to Deborah. 'You have to ask yourself what your situation would be in the case of a rush and a stampede.'

Very occasionally Deborah attempted to argue her corner, pointless though she knew it to be.

'Listen, bud,' she had said, as politely as she could manage, to the slightly punky young man who was refusing to sell her a ticket to a play to be performed in the upstairs room of a pub . . . 'It is Saturday afternoon OK? and I have just negotiated the entire length of Oxford Street. I have dealt with it all; the tone deaf dickwit playing two of the three chords of "Blowin' in the wind", who kindly had his guitar case full of five pence bits spread across half the pavement . . .'

'Yeah, all right but . . .' interjected the young man, slightly offended. He did a bit of busking himself and often did a Dylan number or two, after all you had to cover the classics didn't you? However, Deborah was in no mood to be interrupted by a hippy, especially one who thought that having short, spiked hair meant he wasn't a hippy.

'I have got round ten broken paving stones that the council kindly put there to trip up blind people

and snag wheelchairs. I have avoided the one-and-
a-half million tourists standing in groups wondering
how they just managed to pay five pounds for a can
of coke.'

The punky hippy tried to interject, but failed.

'I have circumnavigated the thousands of thugs
from the city in pretend Armani suits who can't see
you because they're talking into their portable
phones. So they bash you in the knees with their
stupid brief-cases, with the reinforced steel corners,
that are absolutely essential to protect the bag of
crisps and a copy of Penthouse, which is all they
have inside the case.'

The punky hippy was amazed, this woman did
not seem to require oxygen.

'I have detoured round the gangs of bored youths
who hang around waiting for their balls to drop,
outside each and every one of the identical fast food
outlets offering identical crap in a bap and Tennessee
Fried Dog; the crocodile of French schoolgirls with
their beautiful Benetton jumpers tied round their
waists, just at a nice level to get caught in my face;
the endless men who stop dead directly in front of
me to turn round and look at the French schoolgirl's
asses; the road works; the bollards; the steaming
piles of plastic bin liners; the taxis taking a little-
known short cut along the pavement; the bloke who
stands around with a sandwich-board saying eat
less meat and protein; and the strange bearded
tramp waving his arms around and screaming fuck

off at everybody. All these things I have dealt with today, in a frigging wheelchair, bud. I think I could just about handle twenty-five assorted teachers and social workers making for the door of an upstairs room in a pub!'

'Hey,' said the punky hippy. 'Don't you ever have to breathe?'

'It's called circular breathing,' replied Deborah. 'The Australian Aboriginals developed it to play their didgeridoos, it means that they can keep blowing for ever. All New York Jewish girls are taught it, that's how we get to marry such rich men.'

The punky hippy was embarrassed. People in wheelchairs weren't supposed to crack dirty jokes. The idea of Deborah making gags about blow jobs embarrassed him . . . after all, he thought, could she? Would she still want to? People in wheelchairs are de-sexed by society, which is why they all have to use the same toilet.

BARRIER

So there she was, at the ticket barrier at South Kensington tube station, asking if she could be allowed through the gate reserved for those with luggage as her chair would not fit through the automatic barrier.

'I can let you through here love,' the man had said, 'of course I can.'

'Good,' answered Deborah.

'But what about the steps, eh? The steps down onto the platform, eh? Sorry love, but what about the steps?'

South Kensington is partly a ground-level station and the platform for the District and Circle lines are reached by a flight of steps. Deborah enquired whether there was a lift and was informed that not only was there not one, but this was exactly the sort of thing that she should have found out before setting out on her journey. London Regional Transport could not be expected to deal with this sort of problem at the drop of a hat. It seemed like a fairish point, but not when you consider the number of people in wheelchairs in London. The reason why requests like Deborah's were so rare is that most wheelchair users know the score and don't even bother to ask. In fact, if Deborah had phoned in advance she would merely have saved herself the trouble of going to the station at all, because there was no lift and no staff available to carry the chair anyway. And where was she going? Piccadilly? Well she might as well try to get to the Moon. There were the escalators at this end, the escalators at that end, the corridors, the steps, the crowds. It turned out, that in order for a person in a wheelchair to travel by tube they must arrange in advance to be met and helped by London Transport staff at both ends, and only travel at certain times, and only to and from stations where facilities are available.

Deborah realized that she was not going to be

allowed through, and resolved to turn away, vowing then, as she was to vow a thousand times a week for the rest of her life, not to consume her precious energy on anger and frustration. She could not allow herself the luxury that most people indulge in, of letting off steam by having a raving good whinge.

Who can honestly say that they have never been consumed by that intense annoyance, never felt that burning but wrenching tension and anger at life's petty frustrations. A barman repeatedly ignoring you; a screw head that has for some reason been made out of soft putty instead of steel; a traffic light which has a thing about the colour red – such tiny irritations make one ready to kill. What, then, would be the inner fury felt by a person who has lost the use of certain limbs? How terrible would be the endless turmoil to the stomach that simple inanimate objects and petty bureaucracy will engender? If that fury were given expression, the person in question would die of exhaustion within a week. Deborah was no mystic, but, since her encounter with the car, she had learnt to keep control of her Karma.

CREATING A SCENE

So, with a weary sigh, Deborah nailed a lid down on the fury bubbling up in her guts, and with a left-hand shove started the skilful process of extricating herself. Unfortunately, she now discovered that during her brief negotiations with officialdom, she had become the cork in a crowded bottleneck of people with suitcases and their own problems.

Deborah wanted the floor to open up and swallow her, and not just because this would have been a convenient way of getting down to the tube trains. She had never been fond of scenes and had already discovered that her new circumstances made her a natural centre of attention. In fact she sometimes felt that she was condemned to be either totally ignored or the object of all eyes and asked to choose between the lesser of these evils. Like most people, she would certainly have chosen the former. Since her encounter with the Moritz she had constantly been attracting people's notice; holding them up when trying to get through doors or into lifts; getting in their way when they wanted to carry drinks across the pub floor; being stared at by hundreds of people as she and her chair were manhandled into a concert. She hated every one of these little starring roles of life, just as she hated the one in which she was caught up at the tube station.

Deborah's reactions to all of this were no different to anyone else's. Who wants to be an inconvenience? Who wants to be in the way? Everybody knows the feeling of social villainy one experiences on getting out a cheque-book at a supermarket cash till and holding people up while you write it out. We have all felt the howling wind of that great communal sigh which emanates from the queue behind you.

You can almost hear them all thinking, 'He could at least have filled the name of the shop out while she was weighing his carrots.'

Well that was how Deborah was feeling now, except ten times more. She knew what they were all thinking behind her, it did not take much imagination. 'I wish this bitch would get the fuck out of the way.'

It was at this point that Geoffrey Spasmo made his appearance. Pushing through the small crowd, he lurched up to the London Underground person, and, concentrating hard so as to make himself clear, said in a loud voice:

'This is body fascism! You as a black man should understand what it feels like to be discriminated against.'

The London Underground man was indeed black and he did understand what it felt like to be discriminated against. Unfortunately, he didn't understand Geoffrey, the subtler aspects of Geoffrey's argument were rather lost in his guttural delivery. You had to listen carefully to understand Geoffrey, especially when he was shouting and excited. The only word that the London Underground man made out was 'black' and taking into account the confrontational attitude that Geoffrey was adopting, he not unnaturally presumed that race was central to Geoffrey's point. Which in a way it was but not in the way the London Underground man, whose name was Terry, presumed.

'Listen, mate, all right?' said Terry, pretty angrily. 'Don't come it with me, all right? If you come it with me, you're not going to be in a position to come it with no one else for a long time, right? You know what I mean mate, or what?' Terry did not give Geoffrey time to reply to this last enquiry, for he immediately expanded on this theme, producing, by a remarkable coincidence, an identical argument to the one which Geoffrey had been trying to put across himself.

'I mean you're a spastic, right? What are you doing with that racist shit? Don't you get your own discrimination, or what, I mean, *or what?*'

'That's what I'm saying!' said Geoffrey speaking slowly, and this time Terry understood. 'You should let this lady go on the tube.'

'I can't, can I, fuckwit?' replied the aggrieved Terry. 'What am I? Captain Kirk? Do you think I've got a transporter, or what?'

'In that case,' said Geoffrey, 'I think you should join me in some form of protest. In fact, I think everybody in the queue should. I think we should all sit down so that we can stand up for universal public access.'

Deborah could see that the only crowd cooperation likely to take place in the next few minutes would be Geoffrey's lynching.

'Forget it, pal,' she said. 'You can't get people to stand up for themselves, let alone anyone else. As far as they're concerned we're just a couple of crips holding up their day.'

'But that's the exact attitude we have to fight,' stuttered Geoffrey.

Deborah was beginning to warm to this insanely deluded young man. For one thing, she was grateful that she was no longer the only inconvenient, disabled person irritating a crowd of people. On the other hand, she, unlike her champion it seemed, still lived on the planet Earth.

'*You* fight it,' replied Deborah. 'I have enough problems fighting this chair.' At which point she reversed hard into a big suitcase directly behind her which had been slowly pushing her towards the barrier.

'Well excuse *me*!' said someone who wanted to get to Heathrow.

'Sit on it!' said Deborah, offering a vertical forefinger. She was angry, and tired, and completely stuck.

'You won't get anywhere feeling sorry for yourself,' said the Heathrow traveller, and all the other pushers and shovers turned away. They personally would be too embarrassed to *talk* to a cripple, let alone argue with one.

With a huge effort, Deborah managed to extricate herself from the mêlée and effect a partial escape.

'You mustn't fight the chair,' shouted Geoffrey, leaving Terry to get on with his day and scuttling after Deborah, 'it's part of you.'

Some explanation is required here.

Did Geoffrey leap to the defence of every person with disabilities whom he encountered? Did he run after everyone in a wheelchair trying to engender in them a positive attitude to their condition? No, had he done so there would have been no time for him to gain his Ph.D. in physics. The fact was, that from the first moment he saw her, Geoffrey was smitten by Deborah. This, obviously, was not because Deborah, like Geoffrey, suffered from a disability. A person's sexuality is not governed by their own physical condition but by that which they find attractive in others. When we see pictures in the colour supps of some half-dead, prunelike Hollywood mogul escorting a twenty-year-old blonde bombshell about the place, we do not say, 'Oh I thought he would have gone for somebody more half-dead and prunelike.'

Geoffrey fancied Deborah for the obvious reason that she was very beautiful. Lots of men fancied her and she had had a number of boyfriends. Of course, occasionally, her disability did confuse things, she had to watch out for the weirdos. Deborah soon recognized that there were some guys who got all mushy and romantic over what they saw as her helpless condition.

'You want to protect something? Get a job with Securicor,' Deborah had said to one misty-eyed suitor who had informed her that he wanted to build a nest for her to snuggle up in. There had also been one man who Deborah strongly suspected was actually turned on specifically by her immobility.

'I ain't being no new experience for some jerk who's into bondage,' she had told him. 'Go stick it in a slot machine,' and he had burst into tears.

Like most people her age, Deborah struck up relationships for the fun of it and had no interest in a long-term thing. Geoffrey, who would gladly have married her, had never got so much as a snog. This did not greatly surprise Geoffrey, as he was realistic and did not consider himself the world's most romantic catch.

A SERIOUS SITUATION

This first, tube-side, encounter had taken place three years previously. Little had changed since then: Geoffrey still loved Deborah and wanted her sauce, Deborah had come to love Geoffrey but definitely did not want his. One thing had changed of course, and changed very suddenly. They were now both in deep trouble.

Geoffrey was very silent after the phone call to the Office of Patents and it was not his Cerebral Palsy that was making him shake.

'Geoffrey, tell me what's going on?' asked Deborah.

His thoughts were far away. 'I was so concerned with building it for you, I never really considered how important it could be to everyone else. I was a bit of a dickhead I'm afraid Deborah, after all, it's obvious, it will change everything.'

'What are you gurgling about?' asked Deborah testily.

'Everything Deborah. The entire economy of the Earth, the political map, the military map. Everything.'

'Crap,' said Deborah, expressing her scepticism.

'Deborah, I've invented an engine that runs on hydrogen,' insisted Geoffrey. 'An engine which runs on hydrogen is an engine that *does not run on oil*. It could change the world!'

'So how come nobody invented it before?' said Deborah. 'Hydrogen isn't new.'

'People have been inventing hydrogen engines for years,' said Geoffrey, 'and biomass engines, and electric engines. The problem has always been that all of these methods carry much less energy density than petrol, hence less power. People *like* power. Most cars crawl along at fifteen miles an hour, but the drivers want the *potential* to be able to do a hundred. That's why engines using cleaner fuels have never been adopted.'

'And you've made your hydrogen dense have you?' enquired Deborah.

'Well, not dense, just more efficient, Deborah. I have invented a colossal thing. It costs nothing to run . . . it's environmentally harmless.'

'And then it turns into a pizza and you can eat it,' said Deborah. 'Come on Geoffrey, I know you've got a brain that gets stuck in doorways but . . .'

'I tell you it costs nothing to run, and it's environmentally harmless,' said Geoffrey, firmly. 'That's why they've stolen it; that's why they tried to kill me – it's too bloody good. The hydrogen is produced by the electrolysis of water . . .'

This sounded vaguely convincing to Deborah, she could dimly remember something from school about anodes and cathodes.

'And the beauty of it,' continued Geoffrey, 'is that it burns cleanly. All it produces is water. Not tetraethyl lead; not carbon monoxide; not nitrogen oxides – just water. It's a potential revolution as big as steam or oil itself!'

'But they've got it, whoever *they* are,' Deborah reminded him.

'Yes, they've got it,' Geoffrey conceded, 'and they're trying to kill me. God knows why. Why not offer to buy it off me, that's the way things are normally done isn't it?'

'I guess they must be nuts. But the point is, what are we going to do?' said Deborah.

'Well I think I'm safe here,' said Geoffrey, reasoning that it would be unlikely that his hunters would connect him to Deborah. No one at work knew anything about his private life. His colleagues had long ago given up even the pretence of making any effort to understand him. They were perfectly pleasant and friendly but they had their own lives to lead.

'Listen, they want you dead because you are a living copy of your invention,' said Deborah. 'Having robbed your work place, and your home, they presume that they hold all the hard copies, so all they have to do is kill you and it's theirs. But they blew it didn't they? So it's simple. Just write out some more copies of the secret and hand them round, give one to the police, put one in the bank, take out an ad in the paper. Once they realize what you've done, they'll also realize that there isn't any point in killing you any more because the secret is beyond their control anyway. They've shot their bolt Geoffrey; they've let you get away. Even if they find you again it will be too late.'

'Not if they find me within the next three months Deborah,' said Geoffrey morosely. 'Because that's my estimate of the minimum amount of time it would take to recreate the plans in any comprehensible manner, and that's if I can get hold of a computer.'

'Three months!' exclaimed Deborah.

For a moment, the seriousness of the engine situation was overshadowed by the seriousness of the having-somebody-crashed-on-your-sofa-for-three-months situation.

'Here's a pencil,' she said, 'I want you out in two and a half.'

Chapter Eleven

DÉBÂCLE

YOUNG DIGBY

Digby strode towards the podium, calm and confident, he was feeling good. The shock of the previous night was like a dream now, he was back in his element, wrapped in the warm cocoon of his party, and, as long as he avoided offending any major industrialists, he could remain there forever. They had given him a great slot for his speech, just after lunch. Everybody would be mellow and he had plenty of time to get it all on camera before the dreadful '*Play School* turn off' when the television stations ended their live coverage in order to do the kids' programmes.

'The Minister is no stranger to the platform,' said the BBC's political correspondent lovingly into his microphone . . . 'Old conference hands will perhaps recall his first appearance at the famous Blue Podium, when, as a plucky fifteen-year-old, he won many a heart on the floor with a little youthful commonsense. If memory serves, young Master Parkhurst even made one or two of the party grandees sit up and listen.'

The correspondent was referring to a particularly revolting occasion which had happened some twenty or so years previously, when, for a brief moment, Digby had found himself enveloped in the warm glow of uncritical press attention. It was one of those nauseating incidents which crop up periodically, when a youngster is deemed to have spoken with a simple clarity and insight that grown-ups, living in the complex world, had lost sight of.

'I just think,' young Digby Parkhurst (aka Shitsby Zitburst) had said, to a smiling and indulgent conference, 'that it's about time the unions pulled themselves together (warm applause). After all, we're all British aren't we, and I don't think that the men who fell in two World Wars would think very much of these strikes. My father works very hard and has never been on strike. It took him six years to pay for our car, and I'm extremely proud of that.'

Young Digby had been president of his school debating society. He had written an essay entitled 'England or Anarchy?' which had been published in a local newspaper, and, as a result, he had been invited to conference as a 'youth delegate'. The reason that this invitation had been made was that, at the time, the concern in Digby's party was that they had become out of date and were considered unfashionable amongst the young. Searching about for a solution to this problem the party grandees had decided that the appearance of fifteen-year-old Shitsby, school blazer tightly buttoned, hair parted and flattened, a soup stain growing slowly on his upper lip, would make them hip. This was a miscalculation, but conference loved it.

'When I'm set an essay at school *thnn thnn*,' young Master Parkhurst had said, 'I certainly do not go on strike! I jolly well write that essay, for I know that is the only way that the job will get done!' Loud cheers.

THNN THNN THNN

And again Digby was at the podium facing an expectant conference crowd. Rumour had got about that there was to be an actual policy announcement during the Transport speech, and actual policy was always a treat at conference.

'The Minister is playing to a packed house,' said the BBC correspondent. 'We are all certainly expecting something pretty significant. The rumour is *rail*. It is very unlikely to be roads with the depth of popular feeling on the subject at the moment. We shall simply have to wait and see, but it is certainly going to be a highly significant speech.'

Actually the correspondent knew exactly what was in the speech because Ingmar Bresslaw had given him a full text earlier so that he could write his copy in advance and meet his afternoon dead-lines.

'Yes,' he gushed, 'I feel confident that the Minister has some fairly spectacular policy changes to set before us.'

He knew it, the hall knew it, and Digby knew it, but Digby wasn't going to rush things. He was going to luxuriate in every moment of the build up, the audience would have to wait three-quarters of an hour for the big BritTrak moment. In the meantime, Digby regaled them with his uninspiring succession of humourless platitudes to which the hall responded with their uninspired repertoire of Pavlovian responses. They clapped joyfully, they nodded thoughtfully, they mumbled 'hear hear' sagely and scratched their bums and thought about the bar. Digby loved every minute of it. He positively glowed; the immaculate Brylcreamed hair, the shiny cheeks, the fat wet lips. He almost seemed to be glowing from within. It was as if he'd sat down hard on a thousand watt light bulb.

The Donkey gag went down a storm.

'A donkey and trap!' they repeated to each other. 'So that was what those Luddite environmentalists proposed! Ha!' They sniggered and grinned and clapped and leant over to inform each other that Digby was on terrific form. Oh yes, they all agreed, he might even, one day, be in line for the top job if he managed to avoid screwing his secretary and didn't get caught drunk driving or making multiple share applications.

Oh, how Digby was loving himself. The weight of all those years of toadying and being a despised little farty was lifting from his shoulders. If, as Kissinger claimed, power is an aphrodisiac then at that moment Digby could have coaxed an orgasm out of a concrete elephant.

'I hardly think,' he said again. 'I hardly think,' was Digby's absolute favourite phrase and probably the most accurate thing he would say in his entire political life. Digby *did* hardly think, but that wasn't how he meant it. To Digby, the phrase was a three word sneer, always delivered with a tiny laugh.

'*Thnn thnn* (tiny laugh), I hardly think . . .'

Whenever an audience heard that scintillating rhetorical combination they hugged themselves, for they knew that they were in line for a searing bit of ministerial wit. They knew that Digby was ready to sock it to 'em. And he was. He squared up and shot his big gag straight through the transparent autocue.

'*Thnn thnn* (tiny laugh), I hardly think that even the *looniest* environmentalist could be so *green* . . .'

Digby paused, it was his fantastic green/naïve pun. His people assured him it would be a major woof and they had coached him meticulously to pause at this point so as not to spoil it. But there was no laugh. Digby was in that terrible place which comedians fear most of all – the gag swamp.

He hit it again.

'*Ahem, thnn thnn* (larger laugh) could be so *very green.*'

Still nothing, the murky waters were closing over him.

'*Ahhhhhm, thnn thnn thnn thnn* (huge laugh, drum roll, drop trousers and sing *Mammie*) could be so green. By which I, of course, mean *naïve.*'

That was it, he'd got 'em. Digby was enveloped in that comforting cloud of boozy, cigary, lunch-laden whiff that indicates that a thousand conference delegates have got the joke.

'. . . So green and naïve, as to question the inalienable right of every man and woman to own a motor car, if they so wish.'

SOME MOTORISTS ARE MORE EQUAL THAN OTHERS

There are at present about five hundred million trucks and cars in the world and the Earth is literally staggering under the strain of them. Yet, in fact, only a small part of the world has yet been car colonized. Almost all of the five hundred million cars and trucks are located in the Westernized, developed world, eighty one per cent in fact.

It was lucky for Digby that the three or four billion inhabitants of China, the Soviet Union, India and South America did not turn up that afternoon at the conference and, having had their food bowls thoroughly searched, come into the hall to claim their inalienable rights. Should those populations ever achieve the levels of car ownership prevalent in the West it would undoubtedly and, as a matter of simple fact, destroy the planet. Hence, what Digby really meant was the inalienable right of every man and woman in Europe, North America and Japan to own a car if they so wish.

Fortunately for Digby his audience did not question this point. They were still explaining the green pun to each other.

Having established so eloquently the inalienable right of a person to own a car, Digby went on to argue his rights as a free born Briton to use it with the minimum of restriction.

'What is the point of a chap having the inalienable right to own a car,' he said, 'if he is not entitled to drive it where he pleases.'

This is a very worrying thought because the fastest growing area of the motor industry is that of four-wheel drive. With massively improved engineering, millions of cars now have an off-road capability. Are they to be allowed to use it? After all, the confines of a narrow road restrict a person's freedom. If a fellow is capable of nipping across a field surely it is his inalienable right to do so? If not, why build in the capability in the first place? Such an idea would not be inconsistent with present thinking. A transport policy which is prepared to happily allow a million cars into a city that physically only has room for half that number, despite the general suffering of all concerned, will eventually get round to allowing the owners of fun-top jeeps to chuck wheelies in Kew Gardens.

TROUBLE IN THE PIPELINE

'The private motor car is a cornerstone of our very civilization,' Digby opined. 'It is, I think, our greatest triumph.'

Triumphs of civilization cut both ways of course. Perhaps the greatest triumph of Roman civilization was the plumbing. The élite of Rome gloried in it and quickly came to ask themselves how they could ever have lived without it. The water pipes satisfied their thirst and washed away their whiffies. Unfortunately for the élite of Rome, these pipes were all made of lead and it is a fair historical supposition to make that within a few short generations the once all-conquering élite of Rome were dafter than a pair of one-legged trousers. This is why they started acting so strangely and became such easy prey for savage marauders. These savage marauders had no plumbing and hence, although extremely smelly, were not dribbling, fiddling and making horses into senators when it came to a world historical shift in the balance of power.

In fairness to the élite of Ancient Rome, they were unaware of the nastier properties of lead and when Caligula started chewing his toga and claiming to be a teapot they of course didn't think to blame the plumbing. We, on the other hand, suffer no delusions as to the catastrophic consequences of failing to address the crisis of the car. The car population is expanding faster than the human one. By the year 2030 there will be a billion of them. This is unlikely to result in the appearance of smelly marauders but the social and environmental consequences will make smelly marauders seem like welcome house guests. On the other hand, as Digby often pointed out, people need their cars, so what could he do?

A VERY PUBLIC SOLUTION

The solution of course is fantastically simple. There is a solution that would put a stop to the jams, clean up the air, massively reduce the human carnage, *and probably without even having to restrict anyone's car ownership*. The solution is public transport. But it would have to be public transport so good that most people would not dream of going to the expense of using their cars for mundane things like going to work. There would have to be tubes every minute and buses everywhere. Clean transport, safe transport with nice conductors and no chewing gum on the seats. It would have to be free if necessary, and the money saved by unchaining the cities would pay for it in time.

That is the solution; not toll roads, not private clamping firms, but public transport. Unfortunately

Digby's public transport policy was rather different, as he was about to show as he finally arrived at the crux of his speech, it concerned the railways.

' . . . And now, I come, if I may, to the subject of, *thnn thnn thnn*, Rail Transport.'

The audience shifted expectantly in their seats. This was it, the moment of excitement was approaching, they flexed their fingers and cleared their throats, ready to clap and cheer.

'Rail Transport,' Digby repeated, and he almost seemed to spit the words out. He could feel the hall go tense, it was as if the demon king had leapt up beside Digby on the platform. The faceless ones knew the villain had been introduced and they wanted to hiss and boo.

With the exception of a few sad, tired old boys at the back of the hall, the audience hated trains. Not because they were sometimes late, nor because they are often a bit dirty and the buffet runs out of everything except KitKats five minutes after leaving the first station. No, these apostles of a new morality hated trains because you can't *own* them and if you can't *own* something then how can it be worth having? That is the problem with public transport. The individual cannot own a train or a bus, they can only borrow it for the journey they want to make and at the end of it they have to give it back, and, horror of horrors, let somebody else use it. People have to share trains and also they have to pay for them, even when they are not using them themselves. The people that Digby was addressing did not want to share anything. They did not want to share health care, they did not want to share leisure amenities and they did not want to share transport.

'Trains!' shouted Digby, 'are an anachronism,' which, to give him his due was an extremely brave word to attempt in front of a thousand people and four channels of television.

'Contrast them if you will with the private motor car which is a gazelle. What do these great hulking dinosaurs have to offer us? Freedom of movement? no. Personal security and privacy? luxury, comfort and a status symbol of which the whole family can be proud? no. They offer us a form of transport where people are packed in like sardines, which is confined to narrow lines and is in danger of grinding to a halt at any moment at the behest of some horny-handed trade unionist. Let me tell you what this government intends to do with trains!' Digby thundered.

'Let me explain how we shall serve this cumbersome out-moded institution.' The audience strained forward, Digby was coming to that rare thing at a political conference, the announcement of a policy. They all knew what it was, and they could not wait. The Minister, *their* Minister was going to announce the destruction of the railways and they would give him a monumental ovation.

'What, you ask me, will the government do with

the railways?' shouted Digby, eyes wild now. Yes, yes, yes, they did ask him that, that was what they wanted to know.

'What this government intends to do with the railways . . .' said Digby, rising to a frothing, spitting, fist-thumbing crescendo, 'is . . .!!!!'

Digby froze. For a long moment the audience believed it was a dramatic pause. Then, by the look on his face, they thought he had got so excited about dismantling one of the country's greatest assets that he had had a heart attack. 'Good way to go' some of them thought.

Then they realized that he had gone mad, because Digby's next word was . . .

'Nothing.'

A CHANGE OF PLAN

Sandy sat down again. People had been concentrating so much on the Minister's speech that they had hardly noticed the young man in the middle of the fourth row getting quietly to his feet to hold up a handbag. Out of the bag he took a red wig and a tape recorder. He held them for a moment, and then sat down.

Digby had got the message. He remembered the confessions of the previous night, and he remembered the young man who had confronted him outside his hotel. Above all, he knew that he could not announce the setting up of BritTrak. So there he stood, facing one thousand completely mystified and increasingly resentful delegates.

Where was the promised crescendo they asked themselves? Where was the rousing bit of policy that would bring them to their feet? This was what they attended conference for, or at least why they bothered to turn up for the speeches. They had done their bit by laughing at his jokes, where was the crescendo?

Digby was thinking desperately. He knew what they expected of him, but he did not know how to deliver. The whole of the rest of his speech concerned BritTrak and on that he knew he must be silent. He could see the young Scot sitting quietly in the fourth row, gently stroking a handbag. How alone Digby felt up there, how terribly exposed. He *had* to say something.

As the seconds ticked by he wracked his brains desperately. He was Minister for Transport, there must be something he could rouse them with . . . Bollards would not excite them, he doubted if zebra crossings would get them going . . . A thousand pairs of eyes were on him. The cameras of the nation turned. Digby could almost hear the commentators licking their lips.

It was an appalling moment. Complete public humiliation in front of the entire nation is a prospect likely to make a man reckless, desperate even. So it was with Digby. Into his mind drifted a vision; a vision of great beauty; one that would excite and enthrall as no dull railway policy ever could – it was the vision of a man stroking the model of a motorway flyover. And, suddenly, with the eyes of the world upon him, Digby threw caution to the winds and madness overtook him.

'What are we going to do?' he cried, breaking a silence that had lasted an eternity. 'I shall tell you what we are going to do. We are going to build roads! We are going to build roads, roads and then more roads! We are going to build roads to tunnel under roads, roads to fly over roads, roads to fly over roads flying over roads. Roads, roads, roads, roads, roads!!'

Digby could get no further. The conference was cheering and shouting, some even took up the chant, 'roads, roads, roads, roads . . .' In the television and press galleries the scribblers and wafflers went wild. This was news. This was controversial. This would split the country, it might even split the party. On the platform it was quite easy to see that there would be a split in the party, but only a small one, with Digby on one side and everybody else on the other. But that was something which Digby would face later. For the moment he was fired with evangelical fervour.

'I have plans,' he shouted. 'I have plans to make every city in Britain ten times more accessible to traffic, twenty times. Where will we put the cars you ask?' They weren't asking, they were too excited, but Digby was going to tell them anyway. 'In the parks, that's where. They're called parks aren't they? Let them live up to their name.' This also received a huge cheer, although one or two milder souls did begin to wonder. Certainly Ingmar Bresslaw wondered, as did the Prime Minister. They could see their carefully calculated plans disappearing in a wave of public protest. Digby, on the other hand, was completely intoxicated with the response he was receiving.

'Once the Channel Tunnel is fully working, people in the City, north of the Thames, are going to need ready access to that tunnel and the European Currency Units beyond. But they won't get it will they? And why not? Because South London's in the way that's why! Well not for long! I'm going to pave Brixton! I'm going to tarmac Wandsworth! I'm going to concrete Clapham! Every city centre in Britain is paralysed because you can't get your car into the shops, so what am I going to do? Shall I tell you what I am going to do? I shall knock down the shops that's what. Then I shall build huge multi-storey car-parks and put the shops on top of them.'

COMEUPPANCE

Digby received a wonderful ovation, and, feeling rather naughty but fully justified by the response he had received, he returned to his seat on the platform. Except he didn't because there was no seat to return to – it was gone. The place was still there, between the Ministers for Housing and Health, but the chair had been removed.

'I say, have you seen my chair?' said Digby to the Minister for Housing.

Perhaps it was the noise of Digby's ovation, but the Minister for Housing did not seem to hear . . . 'My chair, have you seen it at all?' Digby shouted at the Minister for Health, but again he received no reply. Neither of his colleagues even looked at him, it was as if he was not even there.

Digby had no other choice but to leave the platform, he could not very well hang about like the last turkey in the shop. He gathered up his papers and walked with brisk dignity towards the steps that led down from the platform. He attempted in his manner to appear that he had other more urgent business to attend to and could not afford to sit about all day. Whatever impression Digby was trying to give, the one he actually gave was one of a bumbling loser . . .

He did not notice how he came to trip up, it might have been a ruck in the carpet, it might possibly have been an outstretched foot, but there he was, face planted in one of the tasteful potted plants that had been placed about the stage as the central initiative of the party's green policy.

Digby's ovation was over and the Chairperson was moving onto other business as Digby struggled to his feet grinning weakly. He reached for his briefcase. Digby distinctly remembered shutting the clips, but they were open now, and, as he picked up the case, his papers, along with a Mars bar, a little pack of tissues and a biography of Joan Crawford, flew about the platform. The Chairperson ignored the kefuffle Digby was making as he scrabbled about on the floor in front of a thousand delegates. Indeed, everybody on the platform ignored him, for Digby was now a non-person. The party's revenge for boat-rocking is swift and terrible. Without a word being said, all of Digby's colleagues knew that the oily little shit, Parkhurst, was no longer 'a member of the club.' He had opted for the wilderness and he was to be treated as a pariah.

As Digby struggled to retrieve his Mars bar, he felt a painful kick in the behind. Nobody saw it happen, the Minister for Health who delivered the blow had, like the rest of the cabinet, been to a good school and was hence highly skilled in the secret art of kicking an oik without authority being aware of it.

Digby got to his feet, his half closed briefcase under his arm, and managed to leave the platform without further incident. At the bottom of the steps Ingmar Bresslaw was waiting in terrifying silence. Ingmar's large, boozy face was red with rage. He nodded towards a small interview room just off the main hall. As Digby scuttled towards it, he began to consider for the first time just how serious his situation might be. In the heat of the moment, with a thousand delegates, first staring at him in disbelief, and then cheering him to the rafters, the size of his crime had genuinely eluded Digby. One look at Bresslaw's twitching, whiskyfied face had put him right.

'You stupid little shit,' said the Prime Minister's top henchman as he closed the door on Digby's condemned cell. 'Do you really think you can steamroller us?'

'No really, Ingmar, it's not like that,' pleaded Digby. You see, I uhm . . . I lost my notes about BritTrak so I . . . I just filled in with a bit of harmless waffle about roads . . . Went rather well I thought.'

'Harmless waffle! You ruddy fool.' Ingmar's big bushy eyebrows quivered with indignation like two chilly black mice. Digby thought he could actually see blood vessels bursting on the man's nose as he spoke. 'That roads policy is absolute political dynamite. Half of our own party are going to be bloody uneasy about it.'

'But they . . .' Digby tried to protest.

'Cheered?' barked Ingmar Bresslaw. 'Is that what you were going to say? Cheered? Of course they cheered! This is a party conference you ruddy arse! They're supposed to bloody cheer. But wait till they start seeing lorries tearing past their garden gates. They won't all be cheering then.' Ingmar suddenly threw out two great hairy hands and grabbed Digby's lapels. Digby was almost too astonished to be scared.

'This was a back-door initiative, Parkhurst; a

Civil Service operation! The politics of confusion and deceit, a nod here, a wink there. Now you've told the entire bloody world and we will have every shitty little protest group in the country on to us. Even our own wets will summon up the courage to table a question or two. There will be protests, commissions of enquiry, the whole thing will take decades, if it ever happens at all.'

'I . . . I just thought . . . a few hints, for the faithful,' muttered Digby.

'Shut up, Parkhurst,' snarled Ingmar, his big frame tensing up so that Digby thought he might be about to be punched. 'I've heard enough of your bloody girl's voice to last me a lifetime. I never want to hear it again, do you hear? For God's sake man, what came over you? Acting independently of the party line? Who do you think you are? Winston Churchill? You got the job because the Prime Minister needed a faceless bloody nobody to front up a very delicate, and secret operation, but you got delusions didn't you? You . . . you utter . . .' he struggled for a fitting expletive . . . 'turd.'

Ingmar was truly offended by Digby's stupidity. After all, if you couldn't trust a talentless, feature-less, arse-kissing git with a government ministry, who could you trust? Ingmar hauled Digby almost up onto his toes and delivered the final chop.

'You've let us down, Parkhurst, and you're finished. The Prime Minister wants your resignation by midnight, all right? Now crawl away and die.'

The big man released Digby's lapels, turned on his heels and went off in search of whisky, leaving Digby stunned.

It was so brutal, so sudden. Surely he had not given away all that much of the road plans, he had only been playing to the gallery, pleasing the troops so to speak. But a couple of hours later in his hotel room, he knew, he saw the extent of his madness. His speech was the number one story of the day, it was described as 'extraordinary' and 'maverick'.

There he stood again upon the platform, 'destroy, knock down, demolish . . . Pave, concrete, tarmac,' he shouted out of the television screen, fist thumping the air. Sitting watching it Digby was forced to confess that it did sound rather radical. Worse was to come. The Prime Minister appeared extremely cross, denying everything and deliberately getting the interviewer's name wrong. For the Prime Minister to be personally involved in the Damage Control operation showed just how seriously Digby had screwed up.

The story the party were offering was that Digby was a brilliant but erratic personality. His deep sense of public duty and extraordinary political flair, had, perhaps, combined to create a slight imbalance in his political outlook. The Opposition of course were not buying it. They claimed, as did all the environmental groups that there was no smoke without fire and that the government should come clean about its plans. This time it was Ingmar

Bresslaw who appeared, admitting that of course there were road building plans, but nothing on the scale . . .

Digby would have liked to have wept for the fate of his beautiful models but he had no tears to spare, he was weeping for himself.

Chapter Twelve

THE ROAD TO RUIN

PART OF THE FURNITURE

Back in London, Deborah's TV was tuned to the same news broadcast that Digby was weeping over. Deborah wasn't really watching it though, she was more concerned with why Geoffrey had lain down on the carpet and was tinkering with her chair.

'What are you doing Geoffrey?' enquired Deborah. 'In fact, don't tell me what you're doing, just get the hell away from my chair all right?'

Deborah was rather sensitive about people touching and fiddling with her wheelchair as if it was an ordinary piece of furniture. She had noticed in pubs and crowds that friends sometimes used it as a coat-hanger. She knew that they meant well, they wanted to show that the chair was not an issue to them and that it did not make them feel uncomfortable, but they were also glad of somewhere to put their coats while they went off to dance. Deborah hated the way she always became the receptacle and guardian of everybody's property at a disco and she knew it was the solid fact of her chair that created this position. Another thing she had noticed was that at pub gigs, whilst watching a band or perhaps a comic, if it was a crowded, standing gig, little knots of people formed behind her, the chair (and Deborah in it) providing breathing space in an otherwise crushed room. All this was OK within reason, but Deborah's chair was not a part of the furniture, it was a part of Deborah and she didn't like it being fiddled with.

'I'm measuring it, Deborah,' stammered Geoffrey, his eyes a little hurt behind his thick glasses. 'I have to, I'm going to arm it.'

'Geoffrey,' said Deborah. 'It's a wheelchair, I don't want it to have arms, they'll get stuck in doorways.'

'I don't mean arms as in "arms",' Geoffrey replied firmly, although Deborah did not really register this firmness because Geoffrey's chin was bashing against his collar-bone and she was having enough trouble following what he was saying without trying to work out the subtlety of his intonations.

'I mean arms as in arms dealer, arms race, arms treaty,' said Geoffrey.

'You mean guns?' said Deborah horrified.

'Well, guns might be difficult, but weapons certainly,' Geoffrey stuttered. 'Listen Deborah, I mean really, listen. I'm putting you in a lot of danger here, those men really did try to kill me.

Satan is dealing from a rigged deck and some sucker's going to draw the dead man's hand. I have to make sure that the sucker isn't you.'

'If you're going to keep saying "sucker" Geoffrey, go get a saucer. You can't say it without dribbling,' Deborah replied. 'Personally I think you're being melodramatic.'

'Well, maybe about Satan and the dead man's hand,' conceded Geoffrey, 'but not about the danger. It's real Deborah and it's coming for us . . .' He snapped shut his tape-measure and, using his good hand, wrote down figures in a school exercise book which he had wedged under a wheel of Deborah's chair. Of course, on reflection, Deborah didn't really think it was that melodramatic either. After all, they did both seem to have been thrust into a web of murder and deception. She supposed it was not an entirely unreasonable thing to consider protecting one's self.

'OK James Bond, so what are you going to give me, I'm all out of machine guns,' said Deborah.

'Oh there's lots of stuff around the house that I can improvise with.'

'Great,' said Deborah. 'What do I get? A mounted ballistic food processor, maybe I can blend them to death. Perhaps you could tune up the Hoover, I could suck the guns out of their hands. Listen Geoffrey, if things really are this dangerous, I think we need to make some plans here. For instance, once you've designed the engine, what then?'

'I'm going to sneak out at dead of night, maybe in a raincoat and a Homburg hat, and take it to Greenpeace or Friends of the Earth.'

'Why?' said Deborah.

'Well I just think that sneaking secret inventions around is very Dick Tracy and it's important to make the effort.'

'Not the hat and coat, why the green thing? What's it got to do with a bunch of lentil munchers?' Deborah said.

'Well, it's a pretty clear bet,' said Geoffrey conspiratorally, 'that someday soon my stolen invention is going to be introduced to the world by a part of the car industry. When that happens it's going to revolutionize private motoring. It will be worth millions to whoever claims to have thought of it.'

Deborah still couldn't quite follow the green angle.

'So what you have to do,' she insisted, 'is to reinvent it double quick and sell it to the motor industry yourself, you could do with a few million. Believe me bud, the rent on this place gets higher every minute.'

'If you do a deal with the devil,' said Geoffrey piously, 'you had better be ready to end up being impaled on fiery stakes and having your sweaty bits nibbled by his tiny crawling demons.'

'What?' enquired Deborah, not unreasonably.

'If I sold my engine to Dagenham or Detroit they

would use it on private cars and nothing but private cars and, if it's as good as I think it is, which is bloody brilliant, twenty years from now we'd just have a world clogged up with hydrogen cars instead of petrol cars.'

'So bully for the world, Geoffrey,' insisted Deborah. 'You said yourself that these engines burn cleaner. Call me an earth mother and stick my face in a vegetarian casserole if you like, but that sounds like good news to me.'

'Oh yes, and where would that leave us?' asked Geoffrey.

'Rich.' Deborah was a practical girl.

'But you'd still be a prisoner in your own city,' Geoffrey said. 'People like you and me are the best example of how too many cars isolate people. You can't use a bus, it's tough to get on a train, a lot of taxis can't take chairs, and that's because all anybody cares about is cars, cars, bloody cars.'

'Yes but I'm disabled Geoffrey, remember? Not everyone is like me.'

'Everybody is disabled by cars!' insisted Geoffrey.

'Geoffrey excuse me, but did you leave a door open in your brain here? Cars carry people around you know? They don't disable people, they *enable* them to get around – especially people like me. What's more, if you were rich you could buy me a great big car, a limmo with a chair lift and a chauffeur and a bar and a swimming pool. So just cut the philosophy OK? and hurry up and reinvent your stupid engine because the sooner I'm outta my converted Ford and into a stretch Mercedes the better.'

And with that, Deborah wheeled herself into the kitchen and filled the kettle from the hose attached to her tap. Her kettle could not move because it was attached to a clever little tilting platform that made pouring easier. Geoffrey followed Deborah into the kitchen.

'Do cars *enable* the woman with a ton of shopping waiting at the bus stop for the bus that never comes?' he shouted.

'So now he's onto Communism already,' said an exasperated Deborah, struggling with the lid of a new coffee jar that would have given Mr Universe a limp wrist. 'They tried Communism in Russia, Geoffrey, their buses were worse than ours and everybody had to eat cabbage for the rest of their lives.'

Geoffrey would not be side-tracked by red, red herrings.

'Do cars *enable* the people who live on main routes and have to listen to traffic all night? Do they enable old people who can't cross roads, or have to walk miles extra to find a crossing? Do they *enable* the five thousand people killed each year in Britain, or the forty thousand in the US? Above all Deborah, do they *enable* the hundreds of thousands of people stuck in jams every day? I mean do they really? or do people just think they do?'

Having finally got the lid off the coffee, Deborah was attempting very gently to penetrate the foil vacuum seal with her thumb. After she had done that she had to brush away all the coffee that had exploded into her lap . . . 'I think they spring-load these mothers!' she moaned before returning to the topic of the day. 'Listen Geoffrey, get real OK? People love cars, I love cars and if you manage to stop your engine being used, I'm here to tell ya, they'll just carry on making dirty old petrol ones.'

'Deborah, look at yourself,' said Geoffrey. 'You can't walk, and the reason you can't walk is because of a car that caught you at a pedestrian crossing. They called it a pedestrian crossing, but it wasn't built for people. It was built for cars, just like everything else. Whoever I sell my engine to . . .'

'Presuming you can reinvent it before these murderers get you, which isn't going to happen while you're delivering the sermon on the mount,' said Deborah. She was struggling with a milk carton and it was only after she'd had to resort to trying to chew it open that she realized that she'd been attacking the bit that says 'open other side'.

'Yes, always presuming that,' conceded Geoffrey. 'Whoever I sell it to is going to have to sign a contract saying that it will only be used to make buses . . .'

'What!' Deborah could not help but laugh.

'Or . . . or, I don't know . . . for every ten cars they make they've got to make a train coach, or at least that only one can be sold to each household,

185

or that it can't be used in heavy freight lorries, I don't know, something. Don't you see Deborah, it's a question of beginning to change people's attitudes.'

'Look, Geoffrey,' said Deborah, deciding to have a can of Diet Coke instead. 'You can't force people to build buses. This is the free world, they can build what they like.'

'Not with my bloody engine they can't,' announced Geoffrey. 'Have you ever heard of Gridlock, Deborah?'

'Geoffrey, I come from New York, of course I've heard of Gridlock,' she snapped. Gridlocks had indeed originally been a US phenomenon. They emerged for the first time in Los Angeles in the late seventies and occur when the grids of roads (or spaghetti of roads as they are in towns like London) become jammed at a series of junctions, meaning that cars cannot escape. The jam then feeds back, blocking more junctions and hence causing further jams. The size of the Gridlock is dependent only on the number of cars feeding into the jam and how quickly the police can close the roads leading into it.

'London is heading for a super-jam,' said Geoffrey, 'so is every car city in the world. It would only take a couple of accidents to happen at the same time in peak traffic; a jack-knife on the Cromwell Road, a couple of smashes on the bridges, a pile up at the mouth of the M1 or Shepherds Bush maybe

– virtually anywhere actually. It would only take a coincidence and the whole city would be massively disabled. Just like us eh?'

'Very funny,' said Deborah.

At that point the front door slammed and a footfall was heard in the hall. 'It's only Toss, Geoffrey,' said Deborah. 'Come out from behind the sofa.'

HIGHWAY MAN

The door opened and in walked Toss in his traffic warden uniform. 'I have to tell you guy, that I was wicked today.' He threw his traffic warden cap onto a hook and put on a baseball cap – actually he missed the hook and the cap hit the ground.

'Toss,' said Deborah, 'pick the damn hat up.'

'OK guy, it's happening, y'nah what I mean?' replied an aggrieved Toss. 'But like you know, it's only my warden lid, its not a bomb or nuffink, right Spas?'

'Right Toss,' replied Geoffrey emerging from behind the sofa. 'Personally I'm into spatial anarchy. Mess is God's way of telling us we have too much stuff.'

'Totally good point, Spas,' said Toss, getting a litre of juice from the fridge. 'You're a philosopher you know that? You should have your own show on Channel Four.'

'What am I talking to, the three wise monkeys

here? Listen Toss,' said Deborah with quiet menace, 'I have told you till my tonsils have worn out that the reason I don't want your stupid stuff on the floor is because it snags my stupid wheelchair. If you left a hat and a coat on the floor in every room of this stupid flat I would not be able to fuck'n' well move!' Deborah's voice was rising to a crescendo. 'I don't *enjoy* having to talk like I'm your fuck'n' mother, Toss! I'm only twenty-one-years-old! Twenty-one-year-olds should not have to spend their time worrying about whether little scheisters like you pick their hats up or not, but I do have to worry about it because otherwise I shall become trapped for ever in a cave made entirely of your socks and stinking underwear! So *pick things up*! Or I swear I shall personally get two shoe boxes full of wet cement and stick them on your feet when you're asleep. See how you like being anchored to the carpet!'

Toss picked up his hat, 'Nice speech Debbo, happening. I appreciate the point, although, right, it's not necessary to chuck a total mental.'

Toss was Deborah's lodger, he had been home to his mother's for the weekend, which was why he had not been there the previous night.

Deborah had taken a lodger the moment she found her place. She knew that her compensation would take years, and money was tight. Money is incredibly important to people with disabilities. You will never ever hear a person with disabilities say 'money doesn't mean much to me'. Money means mobility, money means independence and personal dignity. Yet, for a person with disabilities, money is much more difficult to come by. Toss had been a lucky find. A year younger than Deborah, he was kind and easy going.

His job had surprised Deborah at first.

'What do you do?' she had asked.

'I hang out, girl. I chill,' replied Toss.

'No, I mean for a living,' said Deborah, wondering about somebody who hung out and chilled's ability to pay the rent.

'Oh that, right? I'm a traffic warden, and I am *wicked with a ticket*, girl, all right? Just the best. Don't mess with Toss when he's got his cap on because I take no prisoners!' said Toss proudly.

'A traffic warden?' This had not been what Deborah had expected at all.

'You have a problem, girl? Are you some kind of libertarian geezer who reckons it is her democratic right to park on top of babies' heads? Is that it? Because then I am your enemy, girl, and you'd better hide right now, because the ticket of Toss has your number on it,' said Toss.

Actually, being a person who could not walk and who lived in one of the busiest cities in the world, Deborah had good reason to support those who enforced the parking laws, particularly those laws concerning disabled parking places which people often pinch. It is, however, important to remember that they do not do this out of any desire to nab a convenient space. Of course not, no, they do it out of a morally courageous desire to pay back the charlatans, scroungers and malingerers who they personally *know* to be in possession of ninety per cent of all disabled car stickers.

Of course they accept that there are *genuinely disabled* people and they would not *dream* of depriving them of a place, but really, sometimes, you *do wonder*. After all, are these people *really* so disabled? Lots of people get aches and pains, they don't all go putting stickers on their cars.

It was because of this type of thinking that Deborah had no objection to traffic wardens, she was merely surprised to discover that Toss was one.

'I just thought that a cool, black guy like you, would be a DJ or something,' she added.

Toss looked at Deborah slightly pityingly, as a fond uncle might look at an idiot child, or an MP might look at a constituent.

'Listen, girl, you're not thinking straight right? You have not thought this one through at all. Let me ask you this. If all the cool geezers was.doing the Scratchin' and the Mixin' and the 'ooh get down-in' right? Then who would there be to get down? Who would there be to strut? No one, that's who. Check out the theory, girl, it's watertight.'

'So why a traffic warden?' asked Deborah, who could not fault Toss's disco theory.

'Because, girl, I like the streets. I like to cruise around and hang and chill and check things out.

This way I get to do it all day, *and* I get a wicked uniform, know what I mean,' and Toss laughed, 'aha ha ha.'

'Is your name really Toss?' asked Deborah who wanted to get everything sorted out at once.

'Nah, it's Tosh, Harold Wilson Tosh. But all the kids at school, right? they called me Toss. Which is understandable, y'nah what I mean? Because like Tosh to Toss is only one letter change to turn it into a wicked joke you see, girl? So I said to them, I said OK guys, you can call me Toss right, because right, and get this, because right, *I don't give a* . . . Wicked riposte, right? Aha ha ha.' Toss had clearly told this one before, and it had not improved with age.

'Quite wicked,' said Deborah rather doubtfully, and she let Toss have her spare room. That had been three years ago and Toss had not changed.

'Toss,' said Deborah, 'Geoffrey's going to have to stay here for a while. There are some people trying to kill him,' Deborah added.

'Don't worry about it, Geoffrey,' said Toss. 'You'll get used to it. I'm a traffic warden, I have people trying to kill me every day.'

'No, Toss,' said Geoffrey. 'Really trying to kill me.'

'Exactly, guy, that's what I'm saying,' replied Toss. 'I need a gun, I need armour and a gun. A traffic warden is at the *sharp end* of the twentieth century guy. When the dust settles, we *are* the enforcers, the last line of law. After us man, it's anarchy. We are *that* close to the edge,' and Toss proferred his thumb and forefinger to emphasize his point. 'They should do a film you know? it would be wicked! Clint Eastwood as a traffic warden, right? He gives this car a ticket OK? thus keeping open the city's life-lines, and letting the ambulance with the little girl in a coma get to hospital, right? Then the geezer who owns the car comes up with his portable phone and his cheese and ham croissant, and his Psion organizer . . .'

'Yeah, Toss . . .' Geoffrey attempted to interject, but Toss was on a roll.

'And the guy starts crying right? He says "Oh go on mate, let me off, I've only been gone three and a half days, I'll move it now. Go on mate, be a mate". And Clint says, "Sorry Guvnor, but it's the law. I'm really sorry, but I have to do it." And the guy says, "Well you little fucking shit, give 'em a uniform they think they're fucking Hitler. I hope you die of cancer, Cunt!" And then Clint gets out his Magnum and says, "I keep the city alive arsehole, and you're dead." Then he shoots the geezer and has his VW Golf crushed up into a tiny cube. It'd be a brilliant film, wouldn't it?'

Toss spent his entire day being either pleaded with or vilified, and, like many people in high-stress jobs, he tended to take his work home with him.

'It is mayhem out there! The minute word goes round that anything above fifteen inches of London kerbstone has become vacant it is a battle zone, guy! They're all screaming "mine, mine" and spitting and snarling and throwing boiled sweets and road atlases at each other. People will *kill* to park! They will kill *themselves* to park. There are geezers out there will eat their own *testicles* to get just one wheel within a yard of the pavement, you hear what I'm saying? We are talking Conan the Barbarian in a Vauxhall Astra! He is growing horns and a forked tail here! He is a *Panzer Commander*! Left hand down, right hand down, left hand down, right hand down, left hand down, right hand . . .'

'Toss!!' said Deborah.

'Both hands down at the same time.'

'The point is, Toss,' said Geoffrey 'there's just too many private cars.'

'You telling me!' said Toss. 'It's like trying to get fifteen heads into the same hat, it *cannot be done*!!'

'Well exactly,' said Geoffrey, 'and what we as a society have to do . . .'

Deborah could stand it no longer and decided to go out for a drive.

CAREER STALLED

Having turned off the news Digby sat alone in his hotel room for hours, until eventually steeling himself to the awful task of writing a letter of resignation – a letter that would end his meteoric political career. Wearily he crossed to the writing desk. The chocolate wafer which the maid had left beside the kettle, and was going to be his treat, seemed hollow now (it was), the neat little soaps occasioned him no glee, his life was over.

'My Dear Prime Minister,' he began, pausing to consider the correct wording for such a momentous letter. 'Deeply though I regret that our long association . . .' There was a rustle of paper. Somebody had pushed a note under his door. Digby picked it up and read it, there was not much to read.

'From the Office of the Prime Minister. Please be informed that your resignation as Minister for Transport has been accepted.'

It was the cruellest blow of all. Not even an 'I shall always appreciate your friendship'. Drink/Drive resignations were treated more kindly than this. Tears welled up in Digby's eyes and as they dropped onto the Prime Minister's note, or rather the note from the Prime Minister's office for it was not even signed, Digby had but one thought in his head – to get Sam Turk, the man he wrongly believed had destroyed him.

Why had Turk done it? Hadn't Digby apologized enough? Why destroy him? and in such a cruel cynical manner too. Such a wicked, vicious blow to deliver; to destroy him over railways! What vindictive irony, to force Digby to sacrifice his entire career in transport over a railways announcement!

Digby could not even take any satisfaction from the thought that Turk would be as irritated, by the spoke that Digby's improvised speech had put in the road wheel, as Ingmar Bresslaw had been. All he knew was that Turk's punishment of Digby for ticking him off over the Patents Office break-in had been terrible indeed. A huge, cruel, unjustified punishment far in excess of Digby's crime. Digby swore he would remember Sam Turk for what, Digby supposed, Turk had done. And Digby did.

CRISES IN THE BUNKER

Way way above Digby's head, in every sense of the word, at the top of the hotel, in the Prime Minister's penthouse bunker, a crisis meeting was in progress. The Prime Minister and the Home Secretary were listening to Simon Rodney Butterface in gloomy silence. Ingmar Bresslaw was also in attendance, plus one or two other Ministers – empty suits so lacking in distinction that at times it was possible to forget that they were in the room at all.

Simon Rodney Butterface was the Chairman of the Party. He was considered an intellectual, which, by the sad standards of the cabinet of the time, meant that he knew who Shakespeare was. It was Simon Rodney Butterface's job to ensure that the party would be re-elected at the next election. A job which, up until now, had merely involved delivering the official pompous sneer at anything that the Leader of the Opposition said and sending his long, damp tongue slithering along the corridors of certain 'proudly independent' British newspapers until it located an editor's anus in which to gently insert itself. Not arduous tasks by any means, and Simon Rodney Butterface had, up until the evening in question, had plenty of time to work on a slim volume of verse he was compiling entitled *The Glory that is England*. However, tonight was different. The party was in crisis and Simon Rodney Butterface's plump face sweated under his Brylcreemed hair.

'Parkhurst's speech was a disaster, Prime Minister,' he was saying. 'As I know you are aware, we were absolutely counting on the secret Road Building Agenda to provide a short term financial stimulus in the run-up to the next election. The sort of plans we were preparing to sneak through would have provided up to half a million extra jobs. If we cancel our plans, the result will be that we will fight the next General Election with the true state of the economy obvious to the electorate, in which case of course we will lose.'

The Prime Minister visibly blanched at this gruesome reminder of political mortality.

'Oh I'm quite sure we could never lose with you at the helm Prime Minister,' slobbered one of the faceless, empty-suited Ministers on the fringe of the meeting.

'Who the hell are you?' enquired the Prime Minister, noticing the speaker for the first time.

'That is your Minister for Agriculture, Prime Minister,' murmured Ingmar Bresslaw.

'Don't shout, Ingmar,' said the Prime Minister, a murmur from Ingmar Bresslaw being something akin to a town-crier who has been given a packet of throat pastilles and a megaphone for his birthday.

The Home Secretary spoke up.

'We have to cancel the plans. They were dependent on the legislation we've been pushing through Committee on reducing the influence of the public on public enquiries. Thanks to Parkhurst everyone will be able to see that for what it is now, a transparent ploy to pave the way for unrestricted road building. Even if we force it past our lot by getting the Whips to chew a few backbench bollocks, the rural lords will junk it, they don't want motorways through their game parks . . .'

'But Prime Minister,' pleaded Simon Rodney Butterface, 'we have to press on and damn the reaction. Quite apart from the fact that if we don't there will be nothing to cover up the recession, there is the road lobby to consider. Road lobby contributions to party funds are some of the most generous we receive. I can assure you we shall lose those contributions if we renege on our sworn promise to deliver road contracts.'

'Prime Minister we have no choice!' insisted the Home Secretary. 'The public will never accept such radical plans.'

'Then the public must be forced to accept them,' said the stern voice of Ingmar Bresslaw.

'Ingmar,' replied the Home Secretary testily, 'I

bow to none in my appreciation of your power and influence, but I fear that even the mightiest mandarin in the Civil Service cannot force the British public to accept the wholesale concreting of their country.'

'I can make them plead for it, Home Secretary. And I am going to.'

'And how, may I ask, do you propose to do that?' enquired the Home Secretary.

'People have got it too damn easy at the moment,' replied Ingmar. 'What we require is a transport crisis. A transport crisis of such proportions that the apathetic public will scream for action, drowning out the shrill voices of the environmentalists.'

'So what do you propose to do?' asked the Home Secretary. 'Sit around and wait for a gridlock, hoping it falls before the next General Election?'

'Oh I think we can be more specific than that,' replied Ingmar.

Chapter Thirteen

SERIAL KILLER

THE PINTO PROBLEM

Whilst Geoffrey Spasmo camped out at Deborah's place, working on the transport of the future, Sam Turk, the man who had forced him into hiding, was considering the problems of the transport of today. He was in his hotel conducting a cost evaluation exercise with his lawyers. Inwardly, of course, he knew that once he set in motion the grand plan, of which Geoffrey's engine was the centre, problems such as the one he was presently dealing with would be small fry indeed.

However, he was still head of Global Motors UK and there were appearances to be kept up.

The debate surrounded the Mark II Crappee which was to be released four years hence. Anti-lock, non-skid braking really should be included, but it would be expensive. What Sam wanted to know was, would Global Motors be in any way liable for the higher levels of death and injury which would inevitably follow from not fitting the brakes? and if yes, would the damages that ensued be greater or less than the enormous cost of retooling?

This simple debate Sam, who knew his motoring folklore, called the Pinto problem. The Pinto problem was first pointed out by a man named Ralph Nader who noticed that the Ford Pinto had a fuel tank located under the sill of the boot, which would turn the car into a fireball when hit by even quite gentle shunts. Ralph reasoned that, since Ford must know that they had a problem, they must be debating whether it was cheaper to change the car or let people die and fight the damages in the court.

That was the Pinto problem, and Sam was facing it again, just as he faced it with every new car launch, because, in fact, the anti-lock braking under discussion had been around for forty years. The question had always been whether it was worth putting it in. So far the answer had been 'no'. It was 'no' with the Crappee and it had been 'no' with its predecessor, the Moritz, which was why Deborah faced a lifetime without the use of her legs.

RECYCLING

Yes, the Global Crappee had killed before and would kill again. It had been killing for years. It had not been caught and brought to book because it had committed its earlier crimes under a different name. Then it had been known as the Global Moritz.

But surely not? After all, as anyone remotely interested in cars knew, the Moritz was a classic of the old school and the Crappee a modern upstart? How could anyone possibly equate the two cars in any way, let alone suggest that they are to all intents and purposes the same car?

The Mark I Moritz had been introduced in 1965 and it was considered by those who love it to be the greatest flower in the Global garden.

The Mark II, which followed in 1971, is also held in deep affection. In some inner cities it is known as the Blackman's Rolls Royce because it is favoured by slick and cool young Blacks. The Mark III, although much more recent and hence less imbued with irrational nostalgia also has its *aficionados*. Basically, the Moritz, originally conceived as an unglamorous family car, had, with the passage of time and the adoption of second and third hand models by groovy youths, become very cool. It is certain that none of those who love and cherish the Moritz, who polish it, tune it and hang fluffy dice from the mirror of it, would be seen dead in one of these crappy new Crappees.

'Not as throaty,' they would say, 'not as gutsy,' they would add, 'no bollocks to speak of whatsoever.' Which shows just how stupid people blinded by style can be, because the Moritz and the Crappee are definitely the same car.

This fact came about as a solution to the principal problem that all mass car manufacturers encounter, which is the colossal cost of retooling their empires to produce something actually new. Consider the dilemma faced at Global Motors UK in 1971, some six years after the Moritz had crashed onto the market and established itself as the top selling family four-door in Britain, and some eighteen months since a disturbing fall in sales had first been noted. A drop of sales which strenuous market research revealed having been caused by a growing perception that the Moritz was rather old hat and very much a sixties car. The young seventies family man listening to Bowie's 'A Space Oddity' on his eight-track cartridge player was loathe to purchase the same car that his fifty-five-year-old father might own.

The solution was simple, of course: produce a new family saloon. Six years had, after all, seen definite innovations in performance and safety. Unfortunately this solution was entirely out of the question. Global Motors UK had hundreds of millions tied up in equipment and facilities that could only produce the Moritz. To start all over again with an entirely new car would mean re-equipping all their factories, and re-designing all the machinery. Faced with this horrendous prospect the Global executives decided to forget about the idea of a new car and just carry on making the old one.

And so, in 1971, came the Mark II Moritz. It looked like a new car, it was advertised as a new car, but it was in fact the same car with much more curve over the wheel arches and different shaped brake lights.

In 1977 came the Mark III, exactly the same car again, except this time, rather squarer and carrying major glove compartment innovations. This sold well until 1984 when with great fanfare Global Motors again introduced to the world exactly the same car but with radically improved rear wind-screen shape and on the Ghia model, a challenging third ashtray.

Certainly there had been improvements, of course the technology surrounding cars had changed, but basically, it was the same car.

And so, after four versions of the Moritz, Global Motors UK arrived at the nineties and the momen-tous decision to cancel the old faithful, to put an end finally, once and for all, to a much loved motoring legend. There were nostalgic articles in the papers, an unpleasantly trendy documentary 'appreciation' on the telly, where a lot of expensively hair-cutted journos, singers and comedians established their working class credentials by going on about how much they cherished the memory of their Mark I Moritz and what 'a bleeding serious motor' the Mark II had been. All in all, there was a deal of ballyhoo and the Moritz was regretfully laid to rest never to appear again. . . . Until the following month when the Moritz Mark V was introduced, except it was called the Crappee. And what Sam Turk had to decide was, when they brought the

Crappee out again in a couple of years' time, should they fit better brakes?

THE FRIDAY CAR

One Moritz is particularly relevant to this story. It was a blue Mark III, bought new in 1978 by a Mr and Mrs Sinclair who kept it till 1985. This particular Mark III was what they call a 'Friday afternoon car', i.e., a car that has endless niggling problems and is hence deemed to be a car made in a rush on Friday afternoon when everybody is really bored with the work and no longer gives a toss. Actually the car had been assembled on a Tuesday morning and had endless niggling problems because everybody was really bored with the work and no longer gave a toss. It was Henry Ford who invented the Friday afternoon car, and also the Tuesday morning car.

After Henry Ford, every car was built on a metaphorical Friday afternoon when everyone was really bored with the work and didn't give a toss. For it was old Hank Ford who, after deep thought and much experimentation, perfected a brilliant system whereby the life of a car worker could be rendered catastrophically boring. After years of painstaking research Henry invented a process so brilliant in reducing the quality of millions of people's working lives to crucifyingly turgid, tedious wage-slavery, that he was rewarded by becoming

one of the world's richest men. True, he paid well
and his assembly line methods made it possible to
produce cheaper cars, hence making them widely
available (a rather mixed blessing as things turned
out), but the human price was considerable. With
his revolutionary production line process Henry
reduced his workers to being merely the most
sophisticated machines on the factory floor.

Having introduced the production line, Henry,
like most other car makers was surprised by the level
of industrial militancy he encountered. Auto workers, over the years, have often gone on strike.
Almost exclusively, these strikes have been over
wage claims, causing many, not least the employers,
to complain that auto workers are concerned with
nothing more than money, caring not a jot for either
company or product. In this complaint the
employers are, of course, right. However, in expecting *esprit de corps* on the production line they are
pushing it somewhat. It is too much to ask of an
individual who has been deprived of every possible
emotional and intellectual connection with the job
he is doing that he should then take a pride in it.

S'GONNACOSTYAGUVNA

So the Sinclairs had their Tuesday morning/Friday
afternoon car for seven years, during which time it
led a pretty unremarkable existence. It went to
work, helped with the shopping, did Europe on four

occasions and spent an inordinate amount of time at various garages where men in blue overalls would stare at it sadly, suck in their breath through pursed lips and say, as if it broke their hearts, 'S'gonnacost-yaguvna'.

Mr Sinclair had heard the phrase 'S'gonnacost-yaguvna' so often he felt it should be his epitaph. He informed his wife that when he died he wished to be cremated, for fear that any preparation for burial might involve a pimply, eighteen-year-old undertaker poking around the corpse for a while before sadly informing Mrs Sinclair that the job would take a fortnight and that he couldn't guarantee a result seeing as how the corpse had clearly been carelessly handled in the past, and above all, it was definitely gonna cost her.

BACK SEAT WRITHING

The Sinclairs were careful drivers and during the seven years they owned the dodgy Moritz they bucked national trends by having no accidents in it at all. The car itself suffered one minor scratch at the hands of Sean, the Sinclairs' eighteen-year-old son. He was in the process of getting down to things with his girlfriend when their clumsy writhing about accidentally released the hand brake and the car rolled a few feet backwards into a tree.

This accident is important because it may serve partly to debunk one of the most enduring myths of motor transport. The myth that it is comparatively simple and also deeply desirable to have it off in the back seat. Anybody who has found themselves trying to do the business with one foot out of the window, the other one stuck in the glove compartment and the gear stick up the arse, will know that they have been conned.

In the USA where the legend began, back seat banging was once possible in comparative comfort. There was a time when Detroit turned out great football-pitch sized cars with enormous, bench-back seats and open tops to allow for the ecstatic extension of a leg. Way, way back, in the great American decade you really could do it in a Buick, get pawed in a Ford and have it away in a Chevrolet – certainly then, but not now. Sadly, you can do fuck all in a Vauxhall.

Yet the myth remains, the goal to which the whole of adolescent America seems to have aspired these four decades past, hasn't changed and, since what is teencool in the USA is by definition teencool everywhere else, the shagg'n' waggon lives. Cars are still sexy.

TURBO CHARGED TACKLE

The great racer Stirling Moss claimed that there are two things a man will never admit he does badly, drive and make love. Which is a strange irony, because most people are not particularly good at either. None the less Stirling was probably right, it is difficult to imagine a bloke in a pub saying, 'I nearly caused an accident last night then went home and couldn't get it up'.

It isn't just adolescent dreams that connect motoring and sex. It is a reality re-enhanced through every aspect of marketing from bikini clad girls at motor shows to husband/wife power games in Renault ads. The sales people would have us believe that the connection is that, like sex, motoring involves surging, powerful rhythmic motivation, ease, space and freedom of movement. This, of course, had nothing to do with most people's experiences of driving, or indeed sex. Perhaps a more realistic explanation of why driving is like sex is because it involves an awful lot of hanging around, followed by a bit of vague shunting, a great deal of frustration, and a brief, desperate surge before grinding to a dirty, sticky halt again.

It is said that the car is a phallic symbol. It is often claimed that the shape and aerodynamics of sports and racing cars are reminiscent of the penis. Well, whoever it was who first coined this extraordinary equation must have packed something very strange indeed in his pants, or else possessed a car that was slightly banana shaped. The E-type Jaguar is reckoned by car image makers to be the most phallic of all cars. Well all right, it's longer than it is wide, but really and truly it's about as phallic as a coffee-table. When people look at an E-type, they might marvel at its slick lines and wickedly smooth contours, but it is only conditioning that would make any bloke ever say 'that looks like my nob'. In fact there has only ever been one popular (as opposed to image-created) equation between the sexual organs and a motor car and that was in the 1950s, in the USA, when Ford produced the Edsel, the greatest single failure of any car ever. Years in preparation, meticulously conceived and designed: it none the less completely flopped. Market research produced the stunning revelation that the radiator grill reminded people of a vagina and that was why they weren't buying it. No doubt, if the E-type Jag had *really* reminded people of a todger they wouldn't have bought that either. The moral of the story is that people like their sexual organs in their underwear, not in their garage.

THE MORITZ FULFILS ITS DESTINY

Anyway, the Sinclairs had the dent, that Sean's ardour had caused, hammered out and it cost them. A year or two later, they decided to purchase the all new Mark IV Moritz, and sold their Mark III to Bob, a watch salesman. Bob already had a nice new company car. The Moritz was to be for fun, he was going to customize it, which he did, jacking up the rear end and installing a huge bendy aerial that stretched in a great loop from one end of the car to the other.

Bob was a great driver. He had had numerous prangs and near misses in his motoring life and *not one* of them had been his fault. It was an extraordinary thing but whenever he was forced to swerve, or the other bloke was forced to swerve, or brakes were jammed on, or horns were beeped, not once, ever, had it been Bob's fault.

'Did you see that stupid bastard?' Bob would say to his long suffering girlfriend, 'Chelle.

As Bob often said to his mates, he was content to drive at high speeds because he knew that he could handle a motor. What did worry him, however, was that some stupid bastard who should not be allowed on the road, might cause an accident in which Bob was involved. Bob's mates all agreed wholeheartedly with this fear, it haunted them too.

Another aspect of Bob's extraordinary powers behind the wheel was that drink did not affect them. Bob *strongly* disapproved of drinking and driving. He detested it, after all, a kiddie might be involved. Yes, he felt it was a disgusting practice, *for those who could not handle it*. If you couldn't handle your booze then you were a bloody idiot to drink and drive, that was not negotiable. Bob, however, could handle his booze, obviously not to ridiculous excess, although he would admit that he had driven completely legless on more than one occasion, but he conceded that that was naughty and he certainly did not do it any more. But two or three pints, maybe four, followed by just a half, 'because he's driving', did not affect Bob. No, if he, or his mates watched their drinking when they had the car it was simply to avoid being nicked. *No way* were they unfit to drive. In fact, Bob reckoned that he was a considerably better driver when pissed than most of the wankers on the road when sober.

Anyway Bob did the Mark III Moritz up a picture and slammed it straight into Deborah. The Sinclairs' dear old car, which had only had one scratch in twelve years, suddenly, out of the blue, crippled a young woman for life.

Of course, it wasn't Bob's fault, *no way* was it Bob's fault. This arsehole in front slammed on his anchors at a crossing, right? Even though it was green, Bob swerved to avoid him and hit this American bird who shouldn't even have been there!

In fact, what had happened was that Bob was approaching a pelican crossing which he guessed would be green by the time he arrived at it. There was a car in front stopped at the crossing, but Bob presumed that this car would be underway at any moment, thus relieving Bob of the necessity of actually stopping. Bob was hoping to do the whole thing without having to drop lower than third gear.

However, as he approached the lights, the car in front failed to move. Despite the fact that the orange signal was now flashing it remained stationary. Bob had not seen anybody step onto the crossing so why was the wanker not moving off? It was of course the old explanation, thought Bob, people were such terrible bloody drivers.

The reason Bob had seen no one start onto the crossing was that Deborah had actually begun to cross a few moments previously and she was struggling with eight new books which she had just bought. One of the great student thrills at the beginning of the first term is buying all the important looking books on the reading list. Most of the books remain unread forever of course. All ex-students have a few books on their shelves that are basically brand new, except the price on the back is 35p. None the less, it is a great buzz to buy them and feel like a real intellectual, just for a moment. Deborah having had great fun in the shop acting terribly earnest and brainy was trying to get her haul home when she dropped one of the books on the crossing and was forced to try and pick it up without upsetting all of her other purchases. This process, of course, took a few moments and by the time she had finished the little green walking man had changed to the little red standing man. However, of course, Deborah had no choice but to proceed.

Bob couldn't believe it as he neared the lights. The yellow had stopped flashing and the light was actually *green*, why did the stupid bastard not pull away? Well one thing was for certain, Bob was not going to stop just because some other wanker did not know how to drive. So he slammed the Moritz down into second, accelerated round the stationary car, just as Deborah emerged from in front of it, and broke Deborah's spine. Bob of course tried to brake but, perhaps due to the absence of an anti-lock system, only succeeded in skidding.

Deborah had only been in England for a fortnight.

Chapter Fourteen

THE MAN AND THE DOLL

MOTOR CITY

Sam Turk took Concorde to New York and then a private Lear Jet to Detroit.

'Welcome to Motor City' a sign said, and some wag had sprayed 'Greetings honourable colleague' over the word 'welcome' in a reference to the manner in which the once mighty US motor industry now found itself desperately aping the Japanese.

Industrial dominance was a hard thing to fathom, Sam thought to himself as he took the chopper to the Global building. Why, it wasn't thirty years since the USA was such an economic power it didn't seem as if it could ever end. How do these things happen? A hundred years before, the British had been the Japanese, so to speak. After them, in the middle of the century, the people of the United States were unquestionably the Japanese. These days, perhaps rather ironically, the Japanese themselves were the Japanese. Who would be the

Japanese next thought Sam? Probably the Germans, but you can never tell.

LIVING DOLL

From the Helipad, Sam went directly to the palatial office of his boss, Bruce Tungsten, 'Mr Automobile', the President of Global Motors.

Sam had not been expecting to be greeted with open arms and nor was he. 'Bruce, Bruce, Bruce,' he said affably, striding across the huge office to greet his long-time colleague and boss. 'Bruce, Bruce, Bruce,' he added as he continued to cross the huge office until finally, exhausted, he stood before the great oak desk that Doug Global himself had once used.

'Good to see ya, old pal,' Sam added and, leaning across the huge desk, offered his hand. Bruce did not accept it. He stared hard at Sam for a few moments through eyes that gave nothing away, and then said:

'I hear that you have allowed the first car out of Global UK since you took over to be called the Shitty.'

Sam was disappointed, he had not seen Bruce for many months and they were, after all, old friends.

'The Crappee, Bruce. If you put the emphasis on the last syllable it sounds kind of Italian.'

'Sam you couldn't make that name sound Italian if you stuck it in a gondola with a plate of spaghetti.'

Bruce was very tired. He had been boss of Global Motors for two years, having been appointed to head the dying giant by a board of receivers after old Doug Global's dissolute grandson, Karl, had brought the company to the edge of extinction. Karl's last act as President had been to insist that the wing mirrors on Global cars be fitted parallel to the road so that people could snort drugs off them.

Since that time, Bruce had been fighting to turn round the company, and indeed, since Global Motors was so big and so important, turn round the whole US motor industry. He had been banking on Sam to penetrate the European market, where import quotas still kept the Japanese vaguely at bay.

'Sam, for two years I've been working sixteen-hour days to make this company, which you and I love, a viable institution,' said Bruce wearily. 'Europe is fantastically important to us. It's a market we're already established in, with an independent British firm. We've finally sorted out our industrial trouble there and you bring me a car called Shitty.'

'Crappee, Bruce, Crappee,' Sam corrected rather defensively. 'We're hoping to get that fat opera singing guy to do the voice-overs,' and Sam attempted an exuberant Italian accent, 'You will be so ha-*pee* in a Cra-*pee*.'

Bruce Tungsten repeated the phrase, as if not quite able to believe what he was hearing. 'You will be so happy in a Crappy, Sam?'

'No Bruce,' asserted Sam. 'Ha-*pee* in a Cra-*pee*. The Global Motors Crap*pee*'.

'Global Motors,' said Bruce sadly, and clapped his hands. Instantly a little doll that he had on his desk burst into electronic laughter.

'Cute,' said Sam, 'maybe later we can have a game of Twister.'

'This isn't a toy, Sam,' said Bruce Tungsten. 'It's a challenge'.

'Yeah, I guess it must be,' Sam replied. 'Can you keep the little sucker on your desk a whole day without smashing it to pieces.'

'Did you ever hear about Henry V, Sam?' asked Bruce.

'One of the Ford boys was he?' enquired Sam. 'Let me see, there was Hank II, and Edsel, they named the car with the grid like a snatch after that loser . . .'

'Henry V of England, Sam,' corrected Bruce.

'Dagenham?'

'He didn't make cars, some people don't, you know. He was an English King, and his great rival was France, and, in order to taunt King Henry, the Dauphin of France sent him a bucket of tennis balls.'

'Nice taunt, that would have taunted the hell outa me,' said Sam.

'It was apt, because Henry was new to the crown but he was already talking big, talking about taking out France altogether, busting up the whole operation. The Dauphin was showing Henry that he was just a stupid kid who should still be playing games. Do you see Sam?' enquired Bruce.

'Sure, I know history stuff,' said Sam rather huffily, 'although I ain't too sure where the dolphin fits in.'

'Dauphin, Sam, it means crown prince in French. The prince sent Henry tennis balls because he was laughing at him Sam, you understand? He was laughing at him. Well the same thing has happened to me.'

Sam was astonished.

'A French Dolphin has sent you sports equipment because he finds you funny?'

Sam suddenly felt sorry for his old friend, he had clearly flipped under the pressure.

'Listen, Bruce, I ain't no analyst, I'm a car man, grease and steel. Maybe you should see a shrink or something.'

'Two years ago I received this, Sam,' and Bruce indicated the laughing doll. 'Take a good look at it old friend and try to think of it as my balls.'

Fortunately for Sam he was not expected to answer this one for Bruce ploughed straight on with his explanation.

'It is made by the Tintandu computer-game people, who as I am sure you are aware, are part of the Hirohato group – Japan's biggest car manufacturer.'

'Those fucks don't make cars, they make toys,' Sam sneered vehemently, happy to be back on a subject he understood. 'I'd like to see a guy fence a ranch and bring home a steer in the back of a "Hirohato".' Sam put huge and contemptuous inverted commas round the very name.

'People don't want to bring home steers, they want to bring home groceries Sam and Hirohato outsell us even here at home in the States by three to one.' Bruce was angry.

'When I took over at Global I announced to the world that one day I would humble the great Hirohato giant. I said that the United States still had a great industry and, like a phoenix, it would rise again.'

'The Phoenix was a General Motors machine wasn't it? Had three tail fins I recall.'

'The Phoenix I am referring to is an allegorical fucking myth Sam. It was a bird that got barbecued but walked away from the griddle, shook off the seasoning and flew ever higher. That Sam, is what I said I would do for Global, that I would make it rise again.'

'I remember Bruce, we were all damn proud. Some of the showroom girls cried so hard they nearly slid off the bonnets of the cars.'

'Well,' continued Bruce, 'after I said that, the next day, the Hirohato people sent me this,' Bruce indicated the little doll. 'They sent it with instructions for me to say "Global Motors" and to clap my hands.'

'Little slimes. We should have dropped more bombs,' said Sam sympathetically.

'Global Motors,' said Bruce, and clapped his hands. The doll began to laugh. 'Global Motors,' said Bruce clapping his hands again and the doll laughed louder, at a third clap it laughed louder still.

'And now!' said Bruce, rising to his feet, his voice quivering with emotion whilst the doll, still laughing, added a macabre weight to his words. 'And now! My top man in Europe, a guy who goes back with Global as far as I do, brings me a car called a Shitty!!!'

'I brought you something else Bruce,' said Sam with a big smile.

'Stop grinning like that,' snapped Bruce, 'you look like the damn Jap puppet.'

'You're going to be grinning too in just a minute here Bruce. I got something that is about to turn you and me into billionaires.'

And Sam Turk explained to Bruce that he had in his possession the plans for a hydrogen engine.

THE BIGGEST THING EVER

Bruce scarcely dared hope that what he was listening to was true. It was too extraordinary, too wonderful. It was, without doubt, the biggest thing he had ever heard. Could it be true? an engine that did not require petrol? He knew that Sam was extremely unlikely to joke about something as important as a motor engine, after all there were some things about which you just simply did not joke. None the less, there must be a catch, it was just too wonderful.

'It's true all right Bruce. I had it stolen from the British Office of Patents,' said Sam, proudly lighting a cigar.

'You stole it!' enquired Bruce. 'Was that strictly necessary?'

'Sure it was necessary. I hate to negotiate, it's demeaning.' Sam was enjoying the manner in which power had switched in the conversation.

'But what about the team who invented it?' asked Bruce. 'Have you started an industrial war here?'

'There's no team, Bruce, no industrial combines. This thing was invented by one mad professor guy, like Eddison,' said Sam. 'There ain't gonna be no war.'

'One guy! That is incredible: one guy changing the course of US industrial history. One guy.' Bruce, who was used to vast research teams, consuming even vaster budgets in order to come up with a new hub cap, could hardly believe it. 'One wonderful guy. I want to kiss him. I want to leave Maureen and marry him. Where is he?'

'He's dead, Bruce,' said Sam, 'but I'm sure he would have been touched by the offer.'

'Dead?'

'Dead or nearly dead, Bruce,' Sam assured him.

'European contractors ain't quite as efficient as the boys in Detroit, but if he's *only* nearly dead, he's *very* nearly dead.' Bruce's face was such a picture of shock and horror that Sam felt perhaps some further explanation was required. 'We stole his engine Bruce, no way was the guy going to take that lying down. What was I supposed to do?'

'Buy it off him for God's sake,' snapped Bruce. 'Couldn't you have just bought it off him like a human being? You say the guy may not have got it yet . . . ?' Bruce grabbed a phone and thrust it at Sam . . . 'Phone them, phone them now, call it off.'

'Bruce, this is the biggest thing ever, we do not need complications. Better to just take the guy's work and bump him off.'

Bruce was astounded at his old friend's coldness, but then he did not yet know the half of Sam's plan.

'Besides,' Sam continued, 'the guy would never have sold, Bruce. We checked him out, he's a public transport nut.'

Sam was trying to soothe Bruce and he had hit the right spot. Bruce was no more a lover of public transport than Sam.

'What, you mean a tram freak?' asked Bruce, relieved to hear that the condemned man was at least an evil person. 'One of those guys who wants half the damn freeway reserved for buses?'

'Exactly,' said Sam. 'Can you believe the sickoes God put on the Earth? When I get to heaven I'm

gonna ask him what the fuck he thought he was
doing.'

'Sam, can you imagine it?' said a very worried
Bruce. 'The kind of damage a man like that could
do, with all that evil engineering genius combined
with his perverted communistic politics?'

'That's why I had to kill him, Bruce,' said Sam
sanctimoniously. 'The guy didn't deserve to live.'

'A guy like that would have us all doing the same
thing; going to the same places; looking the same;
acting the same – like some kind of Chinese farm
collective.'

'Exactly, and I ain't wearing no boiler suit for
nobody,' replied Sam triumphantly.

Bruce was trying to convince himself that murder
was justified. He did not really manage it, but the
deed was done he told himself, or almost done.
Besides, there was the man's legacy, his engine: the
saviour of Global Motors. He would live on through
his work.

'All right,' he said, 'let's forget the egghead for the
moment, when can I see the engine?'

'We don't have an actual engine as such, just the
plans,' replied Sam, 'and I have to tell you, they are
kind of complex.'

'Then get them over here, to Detroit, right now,'
said an increasingly excited Bruce. 'The sooner we
get a secure lab working on producing a prototype
the better.'

'A prototype,' asked Sam, rather surprised.

'Sure a prototype,' replied Bruce. 'You don't think we can build an engine without a prototype do you? Everything needs a little test. Remember when we tried to rush the Cossack? Nobody noticed the design team had drawn the wheels oval shaped to make it look slicker.'

'I was just wondering why we need to build an engine at all,' said Sam.

'What you mean franchise it!' Bruce asked, astonished. 'Let some other company produce it! What are you turning into Sam, some kind of fruit? Am I going to have to buy you a handbag here? You gonna start wearing lipstick? Franchising is the first step to wanting to go to bed with guys, Sam. We make our own fucking cars. Global Motors build 'em and Global drivers fill 'em . . .'

Sam was staring hard at his boss. 'I don't think you've grasped the full potential of this thing Bruce,' he said quietly.

'Grasped it, Sam? I can taste it!' Bruce was nearly dancing with glee, all qualms about the inventor's well-being having disappeared. 'If this engine performs the way you promise, fifteen years from now it will be the *only* engine! It will take the Japs and the Krauts easily that long to catch up. Global and the US will be on top again, and we'll be environmental heroes too! Oh my God! I love you Sam, once we've got this engine on line I'll be able to take this doll to Hirohato and tell him to stick the head in a pencil sharpener then commit *hara-kiri* with the damn thing. Laugh at us will they? I'll make them laugh!! Global Motors, ha ha,' and he clapped his hands with glee. The doll began to laugh with him . . . Global Motors' Hydrogen Engine! Ha ha.' Bruce clapped his hands again and the doll laughed louder. 'The Global Motors Hydrogen Engine, which rubbed every Japanese, every German and French nose in the mud. Yes, and Ford, and GM. Sam! Sam this is the beginning of the second age of private transport, and we'll be it Sam, we'll be it!'

Sam sat down and tugged at his cigar. He looked his friend up and down for a moment while Bruce caught his breath. When Sam did speak, he spoke gently, almost with a hint of humour.

'There ain't gonna to be no Global Motors Hydrogen Engine Bruce,' he said. 'Fact is, there ain't gonna be any hydrogen engine at all.'

'What . . . ? What are you talking about? You said . . . ' 'I know what I said Bruce,' said Sam gently, 'and there ain't gonna be no hydrogen engine. So put your stupid doll back where it was.'

Bruce stared at Sam aghast for a moment. His fists clenched.

'What is this, a joke?' hissed Bruce, 'some kind of stupid trick? You going to go down the bar and tell all the guys you sold the boss on a story about an engine that didn't drink petrol? If you've been joking Sam, I swear, I'm going to kill you, then I'm going to sack you.'

Bruce strode around his desk, the veins on his

neck standing out. He was a trim, lean looking man, and he looked ready to bury a fist like a forty ton truck in Sam's not inconsiderable gut.

'I ain't been kidding you, Bruce, so just wash off your war paint, OK? The design exists, I just said the engine ain't going to get made.' Bruce was too stunned to speak. 'Listen old pal, what do you and I make if we bring a radical new machine into the corporation? Huh? One that turns round the fortunes of the whole company?'

'Well,' said Bruce thoughtfully. 'In theory, of course, nothing. After all, it's our job to bring new ideas into the company and I guess we're paid pretty well as it is. But if it's money you're worrying about, I'm sure I wouldn't be overstating things if I was to talk in terms of million dollar bonuses.'

'Million dollar?' enquired Sam.

'Yes, I should imagine it could run as high as that, possibly more,' Bruce assured him in his best President of the Company manner.

'Listen Bruce, we've known each other a long time, and I don't want to sound offensive but you're talking like a pathetic small-minded little fuckwit,' said Sam, not wanting to sound offensive but failing rather badly.

'Now listen here Turk . . .' said Bruce.

'This engine is worth billions,' said Sam, 'many, many billions. Do you hear that, Bruce, not one million but many *thousands* of millions. The two single largest industries in the world, motor and oil, could be utterly destroyed by it.'

'Oil, maybe,' cried Bruce, 'and good riddance to 'em. Fuck those fat Texans and those anti-American towel-heads in the Gulf. But the motor industry! It will be the phoenix I predicted, rising out of the flames of its dead self to an even greater strength.'

'Maybe,' said Sam, 'after a minimum fifteen years of retooling, re-educating, re-equipping, fifteen years of total and utter confusion, you and I will be dead before the damn thing starts to show a profit. Christ it took compact discs nearly ten years to make any real money. Switching from oil to hydrogen will be as big a revolution as cars were in the first place.'

'So what are you saying?' said Bruce, who was beginning to guess at what Sam was saying, and it made him gasp.

'You want to know where the *real* money is in this invention? The *now* money, not the next year money. You want to know where *our* money is? Not the shareholders' of Global Motors money, but *our* money? You want to know where that is?'

Bruce knew.

'The real money is in *not* producing the engine Bruce,' said Sam, a heavenly happiness bubbling beneath his outer calm. 'That's why I need you; I need a partner with contacts a lot better than mine; a guy who I can trust to make the best deal; to help play both ends off against the centre – to grab the sale of the century. People know I'm kind of rough and ready, I need someone smooth in there, that's you, Bruce, ol' pal. Otherwise, obviously, I would have rowed you out and gone it alone.'

'Thanks Sam, I appreciate your frankness,' said Bruce. 'What's your plan? Take it to the Japs and the Krauts, tell them we got an engine that'll blow them out of the water and ask them if they want to buy it?'

'Maybe, yeah, maybe we'll put 'em in the frame, just because we're going to be rich don't mean we shouldn't be picking up the peanuts.'

'Peanuts? They'll pay billions,' protested Bruce.

'Peanuts,' said Sam firmly. 'Think bigger Bruce. This engine would score bigger losers than Honda and BMW. After all, in the end they can retool, eventually they'll pinch the design, ignore the patent, they'd come back. They've done it before haven't they? the bastards. Bavarian Motor Works wasn't worth fuck in '45 was it? No Bruce, they're the peanuts. Who really stands to lose from the hydrogen engine, old pal? Who'll never come back?'

'My God, the oil companies,' gasped Bruce. 'BP, Shell, Texaco, Esso! They'd be nothing without the petrol engine, nothing.'

'Nothing, old pal,' reiterated Sam. 'Might be a few bucks left, making fire lighters and heating town halls. Imagine it, the mighty Shell standing on the street corner selling petroleum jelly to fruits.'

'It's an incredible concept. A trillion-dollar industry, and its shirt is open, there is a big target painted on its chest . . . We could kill it Sam . . . We organize a meeting, we make 'em pool their resources – we could take them for a billion each!'

'You're right, Bruce, and we will,' answered Sam. 'But it's still peanuts old pal, it still comes dry roasted in a jar.'

'Don't be absurd,' snapped Bruce. 'A billion is not peanuts in anybody's language.'

'Oh yeah,' asked Sam. 'How about Arabic?'

'Oh my God,' said Bruce sitting down. For the first time his big chair made him look small.

'How about Venezuelan? Russian? . . . How's about Texan, yew good ol' boy yew,' said Sam in an accent which he intended to have come from Dallas but, being no actor, it could have been Scottish. Returning to his real voice, Sam returned to his original point, 'But most of all, most most of all Bruce, how about Arabic?'

'You want to hold the Gulf states to ransom?' said Bruce, and it was almost as if the room got darker as he spoke.

'I do,' said Sam. 'That is exactly what I want to do. Texas has other assets besides oil, the Russians don't even know how to pump theirs properly, but what do the Arabs have? They ain't got nothing but oil . . . Think about it, Bruce. We, the controlling figures behind America's biggest car maker, possess a secret engine, an engine that will blow those Arab kingdoms and Muslim republics all the way back to the Dark Ages. In fifteen years, if we so choose, they could be selling perfume and spices again. We could destroy their entire world. I say we *have* to be looking at a minimum of ten *billion* a piece. I guess we could be the richest men on Earth.'

The room was swimming before Bruce's eyes, after all, he had not had quite so long to adjust to the idea as Sam had. Sam was continuing his thesis . . .

'That's the real reason why I have to kill the Einstein guy. If we're asking for that kind of money, we have to be able to guarantee that, when we hand it over, those Arabs are getting the only copy in existence.'

'Sam,' Bruce tried but failed to keep the fear from his voice, 'what do you think the President would do if somebody tried to blackmail him over the entire economy of the United States?'

'Well I guess he would probably have the CIA try and bump the blackmailer off,' replied Sam.

'Yes,' said Bruce, 'and I have a kind of suspicion that that is exactly how we can expect the Gulf states to react as well.'

'Hey, hey, hey, Bruce. Who said anything about blackmail? Did I mention blackmail? You mentioned blackmail, I didn't. All I am talking about here is a simple deal, that's all. We are simply offering certain oil producing parties the first refusal to buy out the rights of a certain engine type that is in our possession. It happens all the time.'

'Well, that's true I guess,' conceded Bruce. 'But I still think they'll try and kill us.'

'Which is why there needs to be two of us. Only one of us ever goes in, the other sits tight, lays low, maybe we even tell them there's more of us. But they won't get rough, I swear it, not with Bruce Tungsten pitching them. Sure they might try and bump me off as a punk on the make, but with Mr Automobile himself they'll know it's just business. A straight deal. We have an invention which they can purchase if they wish. Listen Bruce, until they have the world rights to that engine they have to play ball, and once we have the cash what are they going to do? Mug us? The money will be the bank's problem, there'd be no point in killing us. Besides, ten billion each buys a lot of protection.'

'These people know people who blow up airplanes Sam! They take hostages! You don't know what you're getting into here . . .'

'What I am getting into is asking a group of countries to give me twenty billion dollars, minimum, so as not to destroy them. I'll tell them to think of me as a country myself if it makes it easier for them. Come on Bruce, we're big boys, I guess those kind of stakes have to be worth a little risk.'

'And if I don't want any part of it?' asked Bruce.

'Then you will never see me again. At least, when you do, it will be on the front of Business Week,' Sam replied.

'OK, I'm in. When do I get to see the plans?'

'Oh, whenever we can arrange it, ol' pal,' said Sam. 'Global Motors,' he shouted and clapped his hands at the little doll.

Chapter Fifteen

HACKS AND HATCHETS

SUPPING WITH THE DEVIL

As a politician, Digby should have realized that he who sups with the devil should use a long spoon, but Digby was rather a silly politician and he burned with fury at what he mistakenly believed had been Sam Turk's part in his political undoing. Digby had therefore decided to get back at Turk by attempting to expose him in the press. He would inform the world that the President of Global Motors UK was in the habit of stealing patents.

Digby's original idea had been to deal with what is known as a 'quality' paper. He had written a rather pompous letter, on House of Commons note paper, to the editor of a rather pompous newspaper of the type that is too large to read successfully on the lavatory – unless of course you are an expert in origami. The letter purported to be a public-spirited tip-off from a concerned MP, regarding a clear case of corporate criminality. However, the editor was a professional, expert at reading between the lines, and in the case of Digby's letter there was an ulterior motive between every one of them.

'Absolutely transparent,' the editor had remarked, describing the letter at a dinner given by his publisher. 'The spiteful little so and so's trying to smear Turk, God knows why. Must be something that happened while he was Minister. Pathetic effort, the story's unusable, nothing more than an unsubstantiated libel. Global Motors would sue us into an overdraft.'

Also present at the dinner party was Christian Corbet, the editor of another newspaper, owned by the same publisher, the *Sunday Word*. A journal of a size convenient for taking to the lavatory but for which, once there, a far better use could be found than reading it. Corbet was a man for whom the only good thing about the word 'conscience' was the first syllable.

'Would you mind if I took a look at that letter?' enquired Corbet. 'We might be able to make something of it.'

And so it was that Digby found himself in communication with the *Sunday Word*. At first he was suspicious, understandably, but Corbet (the editor himself, a point which appealed to Digby's vanity) protested such good faith and genuine interest in the story that Digby was eventually wooed. Besides, as Corbet pointed out, Digby *had* written the letter, surely he was honour bound to discuss the accusations therein, and, if possible, substantiate them. Another option, Corbet darkly hinted, might be for his newspaper to discuss the matter with Turk. The editor was forced to point out to Digby that a top motor executive suing an ex-cabinet minister for libel, also made for good copy.

Digby went to discuss his story with Corbet at the offices of the *Sunday Word* – an act comparable to a frog hopping into a French restaurant and offering to do a deal.

'So you see, Christian,' Digby was saying, as the jaws closed over him. 'Obviously the Patents Office kept me informed of any interesting developments in the field of motor engineering, and, perhaps rather foolishly, I let slip something of what I knew to Samuel Turk, the Chief Executive at Global Motors UK. Very silly of me of course. After all, careless talk costs lives and all that, aha ha ha ha, *thnn thnn thnn.*'

Digby laughed because his last comment was intended as a light witticism. It wasn't of course, but even if it had been the funniest thing since Coke tried to change their recipe, Christian would not have laughed. Being a tabloid editor, he knew that the only form of humour in the English language worthy of recognition is the pun. 'We say "peas off" to French greengrocers' for instance or, 'Trudi's no good at sums but the fellahs can tell her she's got one figure absolutely right.' Years of the ruthless pursuit of the pun had rendered Christian completely oblivious to the possibility of any other form of humour.

'Anyway,' Digby continued, oblivious to the fact that he was staring down the throat of a man who picked the likes of Digby out of his teeth at the end of the day. 'Within a very short time, the documents to which I had foolishly alluded were stolen from Whitehall. I was absolutely certain that Mr Turk had been instrumental in the theft and I confronted him furiously at party conference. He denied it of course, as any common rogue would, but he later found ways to hit back at me, demonstrating, I feel, that my accusations had found their mark. I am convinced, Mr Corbet, that a major industrial company is in the habit of breaking into government offices and I feel that despite my own unfortunate, although entirely innocent, connection with the scandal, this is a matter of which the public should be made aware.'

'Of course, Mr Parkhurst, of course,' replied Christian, through a languid, half-closed mouth, which was the way he always communicated. Some thought it was to appear relaxed and urbane, actually it was to hide his fangs . . . 'And you feel that the proof of Mr Turk's guilt in this matter is that, after you had "confronted" him, Mr Turk conspired against you personally, causing you to be severely embarrassed at party conference?'

'Yes, that is the case,' said Digby, leaping and snapping at the bright, shiny hook which Christian

Corbet dangled before him.

'How did he manage that, Mr Parkhurst, I wonder?' Christian's lips scarcely seemed to move. 'What method did he use to conspire against you and hence cause you such distress?'

'Ah . . . ah . . . now you see, I thought you'd ask that Mr Corbet,' said Digby, trying to appear wise to any journalistic tricks, but actually looking like a man with a sign on his trousers saying 'here is my arse, please kick it' . . . 'Oh yes, I was very certain that you would ask that.'

'And I did ask, Mr Parkhurst,' replied Christian.

'And I uhm, I decided that it was not relevant to the scandal I am offering you and hence have decided to say no more about it,' said Digby in his firm voice – a voice so lacking in firmness you could have spread it straight from the fridge onto fresh crusty bread.

'Oh I think it is relevant, Mr Parkhurst. I think it is the very first thing that the public will wish to know,' Christian assured Digby.

'It's really a matter of very little interest or importance to anybody,' said Digby, in a voice which was now attempting to appear relaxed but which sounded about as relaxed as a paranoid neurotic who's just sat on a box of fireworks.

'So you don't want to talk about the fact that he was blackmailing you?' said Christian.

'Blackmail! Who said anything about blackmail? It's preposterous, I never mentioned blackmail,' Digby spluttered.

'Mr Parkhurst, a week ago you were a senior minister; now, as a result of a conference débâcle, you are sat on the back benches with nobody wanting to sit next to you. He must have had something pretty juicy on you I'd have thought.'

'I can assure you that you are wrong, Mr Corbet,' said Digby. 'Now you have your story and I consider it a damn good one. So if you will excuse me, I am a very busy man.'

Digby rose to go and Christian Corbet allowed him to leave without further questioning.

'Well, well, well. Sometimes God smiles even upon us lowly hacks,' said Christian Corbet to himself, as he watched Digby's figure retreat across the mighty news floor of a great and historic British newspaper; past the top investigative teams, hard at work trying to find connections between prominent homosexuals and Aids sufferers; past the picture desks, where highly skilled graphic artists were diligently touching up the gussets on the latest pics of some minor royal with the wind up her dress; past the little corner where George Wood, 'The voice of sanity', sat twitching in his strait-jacket, waiting to be unleashed to tear off another completely barking article about lesbians being paid for by Labour councils; past all the honourable scriveners of the fourth estate – and out of the vipers' nest.

'Galton,' said Christian to his news editor, who had silently attended the interview with Digby.

'What do you think it is that I wish to know?'

Digby had hardly noticed that Galton was in the room. He was a prim, fastidious, ferretlike man, who instinctively stood in shadows and corners avoiding the light.

'I would imagine, Chief,' Galton replied, consulting the notes he had taken in his neat, precious handwriting, 'that you would like to know what it was that happened to Parkhurst, after the reported ill feeling at the road lobby reception, that would make him so radically cock-up his speech.'

'That is correct, Galton,' said Christian, and you could not have squeezed a forged fiver between his clam-like lips. 'That is exactly what I wish to know. You may unleash the pack.'

ARMS BUILD UP

'A flame thrower! What is this, a war? Are we going to Iwo Jima? My Momma did not raise her girl to be a soldier.'

Deborah was protesting at having a canister of gas hung beneath the seat of her wheelchair.

'Listen girl,' said Toss, who was helping Geoffrey with the heavier work, 'I always reckoned the best, right, instruction in the world was one word, right? "Run", that is the world's best fight instructions, and let me tell you, if these heavy geezers ask me where Geoffrey is I'm going to say "He's over there guy, the little bloke who can't keep his head still," and then I'm going to run. But you can't run Debbo, and so if they cut up nasty, girl, you will have no alternative but to fight, and, like, I don't want to cast aspersions, but a chick in a wheelchair ain't the most scarifying sight for a ten ton thug with a meat axe and garrotting wire and an insane, maniacal grin, who enjoys inflicting pain on the helpless – know what I mean?'

'You're a very eloquent man, Toss,' replied Deborah. 'You must remind me to call you next time I need help filling out my nightmares.'

'OK, Deborah.' Geoffrey emerged from under the back of the chair like a mechanic at Brands Hatch. 'I reckon you'll be able to throw a sheet of flame about eight to ten feet from between your legs.'

'Now that is a neat trick,' said Deborah, 'and one every girl should be taught by her mom.'

'But whatever you do, make sure you spread your knees apart, otherwise, four hundred cubic centi-meters of burning gas could disappear up your backside. Now Toss, help me depress the flat-iron.'

The flat-iron was exactly that, a small, old-fashioned solid flat iron welded to the jointed arm of an anglepoise lamp. Deborah, like many people, loved buying crap at markets; old fizzy pop bottles, odd cups and saucers and, in this case, a flat-iron. Toss had a great deal of trouble depressing the arm down into its niche on the inside side of the arm of Deborah's chair, because Geoffrey had replaced the springs that had been on the lamp arm with some from a Bullworker, which Toss had bought in one of those hopelessly optimistic exercise fits which occasionally consume normally rational people.

THE BENDS

'I am going to seriously tone up my body, guy,' he had promised himself. 'I'm going to pack so much power, when I ripple a muscle, the *building* is going to shake. It is going to show up on the *Richter* scale!'

Toss was convinced, as millions had been before him, that if he bought an exercise machine, he would definitely use it, and what's more, use it every morning. He had of course used it once, and then rather unimpressively. 'Ten minutes a day' the booklet had said and Toss had grabbed up the machine with joyful enthusiasm.

After what Toss was convinced must be well over ten minutes, he glanced at the clock. To his astonishment less than two minutes had passed. 'No pain no gain, guy,' he murmured philosophically, and continued his workout. The next time he allowed himself a glance at the clock, after what seemed an eternity of pushing and pulling, scarcely another minute had passed! Toss was amazed, time seemed to be virtually standing still. He stared at the second hand on the clock, willing it on, but the more he tried, the more it appeared to be actually slowing down until eventually coming to a virtual standstill.

From Newton to Einstein there has been much fascinating discussion on the various factors that affect time. These include speed, mass, weight, distance and strange phrases like 'quantum mechanics' which scientists make up in order to sound important and convince the rest of us that we are thick. However, for some inexplicable reason, despite all this racking of the brain, no serious research has been done into the commonest and most radical 'time bender' of them all, which is, of course, exercise.

It seems that Einstein claimed that time travels more slowly at the speed of light, or he claimed something like that anyway. He made it rather difficult to be absolutely sure what he claimed, by deliberately and maliciously employing equations that nobody understood in order to put people off the scent and stop them contradicting him. Anyway, if he did claim that time travels more slowly at the speed of light, and let us presume for the purpose of argument that he did, it is difficult to see why anybody ever thought it such an earth shattering observation, because the deceleration involved pales into insignificance when compared to the rate at which time passes at the speed of an exercise bike or a gentle jog. Twenty minutes on an exercise bike can take anything up to a year of ordinary time. The seconds crawl past as if they were anchored to the clock face. A fellow might set off for a 'quick half hour run' and return to find his children grown

old and his house replaced by an amusement
arcade. Even then, he'll only have done twenty-six
minutes and will have to fill out the remaining time
with a few desultory push-ups.

The fact that exercise makes you live longer is
not, as many believe, a biological circumstance, but
a law of physics.

BACK TO THE ARMS RACE

Anyway, Toss gave up exercising within three Earth
minutes of beginning it. Then, a considerably older
and wiser man, he hurled the machine he had
bought into a corner and there it had languished
ever since, staring at Toss contemptuously and
whispering, 'Nice body tone, Pigeon Chest. I can't
exactly feel the buildings shake'.

Finally, to Toss's delight, the Bullworker had
found a purpose. He dismantled it with sadistic
pleasure and gave the springs to Geoffrey, thus,
providing Geoffrey with the means to propel the flat-
iron through a right hook of considerable pressure.

Eventually, Toss got the arm folded down beside
Deborah and the little catch Geoffrey had designed
clipped over it. Geoffrey explained that, were
Deborah ever to release that catch, she was to be
extremely sure that there was somebody standing
over her to absorb the blow. For were the iron to
merely swing wildly and unchecked to the full
stretch of the arm, it was most likely that the force

would topple Deborah's chair.

'Great,' said Deborah, 'so this one's for putting me out of action is it? I tell the murderers not to worry, that I'll just fling myself on the ground to make their job a little easier.'

'It's for close quarters fighting, Deborah,' said Geoffrey.

'Yeah,' added Toss excitedly, 'you have to imagine that the geezer is standing over you, right. He's come across the room, right, saying, . . . "I'll waste the bitch, I'll cream her sweet arse. She is history. She is dead meat. She is . . ."'

'Yeah, OK, Toss, I'll imagine my own death if that's all right by you.'

'Just trying to get you used to heavy geezers, Debbo. Know what I mean?'

'Toss, till I was eighteen I lived in New York City. In New York if you don't get threatened occasionally you go see a therapist and ask him why you have no charisma. Where I used to live you asked someone "how was their day", they'd say it was fine, nobody shot at them. People in New York go to Beirut for a break.'

Deborah was aware that New York was not actually quite the war zone she described, but she rather enjoyed massaging the paranoid prejudices of foreigners.

'All right,' said Toss, 'we'll forget the character stuff and get to the point, right. He is standing over you with a blunt machete, saying that he's going to fillet you, dice you up and leave you marinating in a puddle of gore, unless you hand over the plans. What do you do?'

'I hand over the plans.'

'Well, yeah, that's right, but if you don't have the plans or an unexpected fit of bravery comes over you, that's when you flick the switch – but don't do it now, all right, because it packs a wicked hook.'

Geoffrey went on to explain that once the punch had been delivered, if time allowed, Deborah should put the arm across her and attach the iron end to the opposite arm of the chair so that the elbow of the jointed anglepoise arm pointed out in front of her like the prow of a ship. Having done this, there was a small wire coiled up in the end of one of the chair arms, Deborah should stretch this across and hook it onto the other arm, thus forming a draw-string to the anglepoise bow. Geoffrey had concealed two nasty looking bolt-like arrows in the uprights of Deborah's seat back.

'Stick an apple on your head, Toss,' said Deborah, 'I feel like some target practice.'

'Later,' said Geoffrey, who was behind Deborah fitting something into the back of the chair. It was a battery which Toss had pinched for him from a temporary traffic-light. Geoffrey wired this up to the handles of the chair, adding a small charge-convertor which made it possible for Deborah to deliver all the electricity in the battery in one hit, if she so desired. Geoffrey reckoned that there would be enough power to seriously scare any enemy who grabbed the handles of Deborah's chair.

'Especially if you can manoeuvre him to stand in a puddle,' Geoffrey added.

'Well, I'll sure try and remember that,' replied Deborah.

'And finally there is this,' and in danger of cutting himself and Deborah, Geoffrey put a nasty, vicious looking hatchet into a niche down by Deborah's leg.

'Oh yeah, and how does that work?' asked Deborah.

'Uhm, well, you have to grab it and chop the bloke with it,' admitted Geoffrey rather shame-facedly.

'That's OK, Geoffrey,' said Deborah. 'It can't all be Star Wars. I'm kinda pleased you left a human element in there. When I kill, I like to feel the guy die. So what about you Geoffrey? What weapons of death have you equipped yourself with?'

'Oh I'll be all right. I have to get on with the engine,' said Geoffrey. 'I wanted to see you all right first, after all I can run, sort of.'

Deborah hoped that Geoffrey was right.

SAM'S NET CLOSES

The murderers that Sam had commissioned to find and kill Geoffrey had found a willing source of information in Denise, the woman at Geoffrey's place of work with the 'You don't have to be mad etc.' sticker on her desk. She did not know much, but what she did she was happy to divulge.

'Well, he keeps himself to himself really,' she wittered, meaning that he was generally ignored. 'A very quiet man, terribly brave. I mean if I looked like him I'm not sure I'd want to go on really, would you? being a burden and all. Anyway, we haven't seen him for a week or so, he rang in sick. Probably still hung over from Suzi's leaving do. That was the last time I saw him. He had a *lovely* time, you could tell by the way he twitched. Everyone just treated him as one of the gang. They're a wonderful lot that work here you know. Mad of course, oh yes, we're all completely potty, but wonderful. Friends? Well not really that I noticed, I think they like to be more with their own kind really, don't you? Less embarrassing for them. I did see a lady in a wheelchair come and pick him up once or twice in her car. Lovely isn't it that they can help each other like that?'

RATTLING THE SKELETONS IN DIGBY'S CLOSET

Sam Turk's hired thugs were not the only people involved in investigations. The hack pack from the *Sunday Word* had descended on the Royal Princess Hotel, Brighton, where the upper echelons of Digby's party had stayed during conference week. Not the upper upper echelons, but Digby level echelons.

On arrival, the dedicated journos had proceeded to interview everyone, buying drinks and slipping tenners about pretty liberally.

Of course the *Word*, like all the scandal sheets, had its regular spies, whom it kept on retainers, at any venue where the famous might be found. Every hospital has its porter alert for the arrival of an overdosed sporting personality or a newsreader with a Coke bottle stuck in some important little place. All the top drinkeries have a waiter on the look out for any celebrities who seem to have a weak bladder and who always return from the toilet rather cheerful and with a small white moustache. However, regarding Digby, the regular spies at the Princess Royal knew nothing, and so the search was spread further.

'That ex-minister, Digby Parkhurst,' the hacks would ask, 'the one who resigned in disgrace. Remember anything about him the night before his speech? Anything that might have upset him?'

The hacks heard of the dressing down Digby had received over breakfast from Ingmar Bresslaw. They heard how the previous evening Digby had arrived late for the launch of the Global Crappee and how he had seemed very angry with Sam Turk. Eventually the hacks got lucky. From a receptionist, they heard that a barman knew about a maid who had a funny story about a bloke wandering the corridors of the hotel, late at night, in drag.

'I couldn't believe it, well you wouldn't, would

you?' the maid said, accepting a gin and tonic. 'I mean it was obviously a man, it's all this European influence I reckon, all the blokes are turning into poofs.'

The maid explained that the fellow had been in full drag and drunk as a lord. She had met him as she came out of the lift, it had been on the top floor where the suites are. The hacks knew already that this was the floor on which Digby had stayed. Sensing a scoop they asked the girl to describe the man in drag.

'Well, I must say, he made quite a presentable woman,' she recalled. 'Slim he was, good looking I expect, under the make-up. I remember thinking it was a shame he was a poof. I can tell you there weren't many good looking men staying in this hotel during conference. Lot of fat bastards and no mistake.'

'Anything else about the bloke?' the anxious reporters asked, 'anything to distinguish him?'

'Not really, no. Except, of course, that he was definitely Scottish.'

'Scottish,' the hacks confirmed.

'Oh definitely, he called me a wee lassie.'

Chapter Sixteen

OIL, ROADS AND ENGINES

OLD FRIENDS

The elegant Dutchman was almost white with shock. Not many things in this wicked man's life had shocked him. Things that would cause a normal person to have to sit down for a minute and have a cup of tea, left Cornelius Brandt completely cold. He headed an enormous oil-based multi-national that had, for a century, abused human rights and fundamental employment practices worldwide – but Cornelius was unmoved by this. His company, Imperial Oil, had tenaciously hung on in South Africa through the worst excesses of apartheid. This, Cornelius thought merely good business. He had personally and happily dealt with Pinochet's brutal regime in Chile; he had fuelled the aircraft that had got Samosa out of Nicaragua, and never had Cornelius Brandt turned a hair, let alone been shocked. You could have crept up behind him and burst balloons in his earhole from now until the end of time and he would not have twitched – but now, Cornelius Brandt was shocked.

He gripped the arms of his chair with pale, transluscent knuckles, the bones, seemingly, trying to burst from his grasping, clawlike fingers. 'We have known each other many years, yes?' he said, in that peculiar sing-song accent with which the Dutch speak English. An accent which is normally kind and pleasant, but coming from Cornelius, it sounded like the authentic voice of a henchman of the devil.

'Sure, we go back, Cornelius,' answered Sam Turk with his usual easy charm. Sam was a bluff, straightforward Yankee who could say 'You're fired, your desk has been cleared' in such a manner that people often did not realize what had happened until they had left his office. It was this easy tone that had been in Sam's voice when he had informed Brandt that Global Motors would, without question, destroy him and Imperial Oil within an absolute maximum of fifteen years.

'We can run cars on hydrogen, Cornelius,' good ol' Sam had drawled. 'It's happened. The alternative is here, oil is history.'

'Oil is history . . .!' Tell Cornelius Brandt any three words but those! Say to him 'your wife's dead', that would be fine. 'Is it in?' Cornelius could handle at a pinch, but never 'oil is history'.

'Samuel, you and I, we have fought many good battles together, we are old and good boys, you and

I!' Cornelius was trying to sound as relaxed as Sam but the piece of concrete in his larynx was making it difficult. 'Is it thirty years since you and I lobbied congress, side by side, over the super highways?'

'Thirty-five Cornelius.'

'Don't let us be fighters to each other Sam. It would be sad, no?'

'Ain't gonna be no fight Cornelius, not unless you call putting an old hound to sleep a fight. You're the past, my old friend, you ain't got nothing to fight with.'

Cornelius dropped the Mr Nice Guy act.

'Listen, Turk, you may think you've grabbed my curly short ones, but I've got a tiger in my pants and it's going to bite you, old pal! We'll lobby to licence fee this engine out of existence. We'll push for twenty years of safety tests. We'll blow up your fuck factories . . .'

'Cornelius, once Mr and Mrs USA realize that they can drive to Alabama without paying a penny in fuel . . . Once the President realizes he ain't never going to have to kiss ass to any Arab ever again . . . Once the EEC sees the possibility of complete self-sufficiency . . . You know better than anyone how unstable the oil supply is. Every damn week there's somebody about to start a war in the Middle East. The day after we demonstrate this engine to the world, you get your death sentence, pal, and you just sit around waiting to die.'

Cornelius said nothing. Very slowly he swallowed

an aspirin, sipping from a lead crystal goblet inscribed 'stay on side, we need you,' and signed Richard Nixon.

'Of course, it doesn't have to be that way,' said Sam.

NEW BROOM

Druscilla 'Corker' McCorkadale entered the Ministry for Transport with a firm, purposeful tread. Everything about her suggested that she had lots to do and no time to waste. This was actually an illusion because Corker had just had her car driven around for fifteen minutes until the photographers arrived. Corker had specifically asked the press office to invite some cameras, in order that her first bustling day as Minister for Transport might be duly recorded.

'Tell them it will be a super photo,' Corker had said.

'Will you be making any kind of statement, Minister?' the press officer had enquired.

'Don't be silly,' said Corker. 'What on Earth would I want to do that for?' The Prime Minister had chosen Digby's replacement well.

Just around the corner from the Ministry, Corker had her driver stop the car and remove from the boot a collapsible bicycle.

'Have you got the yellow reflector sash?' Corker whispered.

'Yes, Madam, here you are.' The driver handed it over and Corker pushed off. 'Ching ching,' went her bell. 'Shifto you chaps, I've a department to run,' she shouted cheerily, wobbling towards the hack pack on her unaccustomed steed.

'This way, Minister! Look this way please,' they shouted as the motor drives sprang into action. Corker reluctantly allowed herself to be stopped by the cameras. Ever the professional, she could not prevent a modest portion of still-shapely thigh peeping out from beneath her rising hem line, as an elegantly shod foot perched on the pedal.

Druscilla had been known as 'Corker' since the first day she entered government, when the *Sunday Word* had headlined a four-year-old photo of her in a bikini with the phrase 'Coo what a Corker!' She made a great fuss of demanding to know the source of the photograph, but colleagues suspected that she had sent it herself. Until her promotion to transport, Corker had been a junior minister at the Department for Health and, despite her relatively lowly antecedents, she was already extremely well known to the public. The reason being that she was a voracious publicity vulture. Corker had once fainted in Dixons, having hyperventilated at the sight of so many cameras.

FISH BURGERS

It had been Corker's brilliant media intervention

254

that had saved the government over the great fishy beef scandal.

The feeding of fishmeal to British livestock appeared to be causing cows to go a bit scaly and spend an unhealthy amount of time sitting in puddles. This has led some scientists to propose the possibility that, since the average British teenager eats his or her weight in hamburgers every six hours, pretty soon now we might expect a few of them to start going 'glop, glop, glop', breathing through their armpits and spawning half a million eggs. Once this possibility hit the news stands ('OH COD! BEEF HAS HAD ITS CHIPS!'), there was, understandably, a degree of panic, and, for just a moment, it actually looked like the farmers might have to sell their Rolls Royces. However, at the last minute, Corker, the Junior Minister for Health, had saved the day. Not by introducing any new guidelines regarding the rearing of cattle, but by taking a posse of photographers to the Tower of London where she allowed herself to be photographed standing between two Beefeaters, eating a hamburger.

It was this genius for damage control that had led the Prime Minister to promote Corker to a senior ministerial post, in the hope that she would smile winningly whilst the Civil Service sorted out the Digby mess.

THE ROAD TO NOWHERE

'We've got a complete environmental panic brewing, Mrs McCorkadale,' Ingmar Bresslaw had said to her during her breakfast briefing the previous week. 'Would you call that sausage cooked? I wouldn't call it cooked. What is wrong with this sodding country? Even the bloody dagoes can cook.' Ingmar took a pull at a hip flask, whilst Corker sympathized diplomatically. She knew not to get on the wrong side of Ingmar Bresslaw.

'An environmental panic, you say, Ingmar? It's not the bloody greenhouse effect again is it? I just don't understand that one. For centuries all the British have done is moan about the lousy weather, and when we *do* get the chance of a bit of sunshine everyone starts bellyaching that Southend will soon be under water. Honestly, who *cares* whether Southend is under water or not. Nobody I know lives there. Do you know anybody who lives at Southend, Ingmar?'

Ingmar admitted that he did not. Corker was very much his kind of minister; obscenely ambitious but without any particular political principles to justify that ambition. Corker simply loved being famous and she would do *anything* to get in the papers. This was a minister who would climb Churchill's statue and sit on his face for six column inches.

'No, it's not the greenhouse effect, Mrs McCorkadale,' answered Ingmar, giving his sausage the sort of bristling, eyebrowish look that made the bowels of young back-benchers dissolve and put them in severe danger of losing their deposits. 'It's roads.'

'Oh yes,' said Corker. 'That's *fascinating*,' she added, wondering how her lip gloss was holding up. There was an awful lot of it on the rim of her coffee cup, so there couldn't be much left on her.

'This government has a massive road building plan,' Ingmar was saying. 'Truly colossal. A plan that, if fully implemented, will create traffic jams well into the next century.'

'Sorry Ingmar, small point,' said Corker, grabbing a chance to show that she was listening and on the ball . . . 'You mean rid us of jams.'

'No, Minister, I mean *create* jams,' said Ingmar, lowering his voice to slightly less than its usual boom. 'The purpose of building roads is to stimulate the economy. If we were ever to arrive at a system of roads which was jam free there would be no excuse to build any more, which is the language of recession and I hope you have no wish to hear that kind of language in your ministry, Minister. Traffic jams are a necessary factor in continued economic growth.'

'You're kidding me,' said Corker.

'I am not kidding you, Minister. Why do you think motorways are constantly covered in bollards and contra-flows, restricting traffic to snail-like single lanes?' enquired Ingmar.

'Uhm . . . road-works?' Corker answered, weakly.

'When did you ever see any actual road-works being carried out behind those walls of bollards, Minister? Perhaps once a year. Is it not more common to see mile upon mile of pristine tarmac bollarded off for no apparent reason at all? The reason for that, Minister, is to create jams, jams that will persuade the public to accept further road building.'

'Coo,' said Corker, absolutely astonished. She had, of course, noticed that there has never been a major road built, ever, that did not end up constantly jammed, but she had never realized what a good thing it was . . . 'I suppose all this is a bit of a secret though, is it?' she added, trying to look professional.

'Yes, it is a secret,' said Ingmar, 'as, indeed, is our whole road strategy. There was considerable public disquiet anyway, but now that bugger Parkhurst has panicked the entire country, we are going to have to lie very low.'

'Yes, it's all off, isn't it? I heard the Prime Minister denying everything at conference. Did you have a good conference, Ingmar? I had a marvellous conference. Perhaps you saw that photo of me on a donkey? It was gruesome, I hated it,' said Corker, who had had it framed.

'Yes,' said Ingmar, pursuing his point with a weary sigh, 'As far as the public are concerned it is all off. It is your job, Mrs McCorkadale, to continue to reassure the public that we never even entertained the sort of road plans that the imbecile Parkhurst revealed at conference.'

'Right ho,' said Corker putting on her serious face. 'All off . . . never even on. Got it.'

'Until such times as you are told otherwise, the Prime Minister wishes you to present the friendly, socially aware face of our transport policy to the general public.'

'You've got the right girl, Ingmar.' Corker couldn't believe her luck, she was in the fast lane and it was easy street. Ahead of her lay years of photo calls, years of adoring profiles in the women's mags about keeping her make-up straight through a workaholic sixteen-hour day. By the time she'd finished, if she wasn't Prime Minister, she would certainly be able to get her own chat show, and that would be even better.

'In the meantime,' said Ingmar, fixing his fiery, bloodshot eyes on Corker's, in order to intimidate her with the awesome seriousness of the situation.

'The old bugger fancies me,' thought Corker, giving him a wry, flirty little smile, all subtle innuendo, with a hint of white teeth.

'In the meantime,' repeated Ingmar, 'and kindly stop grinning at me like a simpleton, Mrs McCorkadale.' Corker laughed as if to show that she knew Ingmar was only joking . . . 'In the meantime,' Ingmar continued, 'the Prime Minister wishes you to allow for the massive road building preparations to continue.'

'Uhm, which road building preparations would these be, Ingmar?' enquired Corker.

'The ones which do not exist, Minister.'

'I see.'

'The ones which have never existed and which you must deny at all times.'

'Right ho.'

'The ones which your senior Civil Servants are working on as we speak, looking to the day when the public will be persuaded to accept the necessity of thousands of new roads.'

'And how are they to be persuaded of that, Ingmar?' enquired Corker.

'Never you mind about that,' declared Ingmar. 'I shall attend to the manipulation of public opinion. I have methods.'

And by the scarily sinister way that he said it, it seemed to Corker that Ingmar was probably intending to individually torture each and every British subject until they called for the paving of the Home Counties.

'Well, that all seems pretty straightforward,' said Corker.

And thus it was that Corker McCorkadale came to be demonstrating the environmental face of government transport policy by cycling the last hundred yards to work and flashing her legs for the cameras. Whilst behind the walls of Whitehall,

Digby's precious models continued to spread across tables, over filing cabinets and out into corridors.

MOTOR-VATION

It was hot and sweaty in Detroit that night. Bruce Tungsten was sitting up late, alone in his vast office. All the lights were out, but Bruce was occasionally illuminated by a burning flash or a shower of sparks at his window. Bruce's office overlooked the vast Global Motors works and even though everybody bought Japanese these days, the long, hot night rang to the sounds of American industry. Global Motors, an enormous corporation, dedicated to the art of making losses with out of date machinery and out of date cars. Out of date? Of course they were out of date, the Japanese innovated every five minutes, damn it.

'Global Motors,' Bruce said, and clapped his hands. The little doll that Hirohato had sent him laughed in the darkness of the night. It laughed at him, it laughed at the company he'd been with since he got out of the army, and it laughed at the United States of America.

Bruce clapped again, 'Global Motors.' He could not hear it enough even though it burnt into his soul. Again and again he clapped and the doll kept laughing. Bruce got up and strode about the office. Each time the laughter died he tormented himself anew, shouting the name of his company into the silence and clapping his hands till they were sore.

Bruce snatched up the doll.

'One day Hirohato,' he spat. 'One day soon, now, I'm going to take this little doll and stick it so far up your butt you'll need a stethoscope to hear it laugh.'

The phone rang, as Sam had said it would. Bruce picked it up and the voice on the other end spoke immediately.

'Is it true, this nightmare? Is it real? Does it exist, this damnable engine?' the voice asked, and Bruce recognized it as Cornelius Brandt's.

'Yes, it's true,' Bruce replied.

'I did not really doubt it,' said a weary Cornelius, his voice dry and choked. 'But Turk is such a gangster, I needed to hear it from you.'

'Well, you've heard it,' said Bruce, 'and now you're going to do exactly what Sam and me tell you.'

Chapter Seventeen

DIGBY RUMBLED

Christian Corbet and his creature, Galton, sat in Christian's office at the *Sunday Word* staring at the big television screen.

'That's it,' said Christian, freezing the video, 'best shot we're going to get. You're sure the BBC won't give us any of their tapes?'

'After what George said about them in last week's *Voice of Sanity*?' Galton shook his head. 'Of course he was right, they are nothing but raving communistic, lesbian-loving Stalinists. One day Sir, one day we shall settle scores with our television "colleagues". We shall show them that the true meaning of the word "balance" is that the scales will always tip to favour the strong and ruthless.'

'Yes, all right, Galton,' said Christian, who knew that once Galton got going it was sometimes difficult to stop him. 'Anyway, it's of no importance, this picture tells me the story plain as day.'

The image on the screen was of the moment at the party conference when Digby had stalled mid-speech. The point at which he had promised to announce government rail policy. The point just prior to his ditching his speech and ending his career with a disastrous improvisation about roads.

Galton had reported to Christian the results of the Royal Princess Hotel investigation. It seemed extremely likely that the Scottish transvestite who had been spotted near Digby's room, late on the night before the speech, was the means by which Digby believed Sam Turk had intimidated him. However, if this was the case, why was it, Christian asked himself, that Digby had appeared perfectly composed throughout the following morning, and had, indeed, delivered the first half of his speech with what was, for the average cabinet minister, considerable aplomb – meaning that he actually faced in the right direction and got the words in the right order?

'It's as if something hit him half way through his speech,' Christian had mused. 'Well, the party tittle-tattle is that it was a naked power bid, Sir,' said Galton. 'It is their belief that he felt, by exposing secret policy and gaining for it popular support, he could push the policy and himself to the forefront of the government, possibly even presenting himself as a potential leadership contender.'

'That's what they say, is it, Galton?' enquired Christian, his mouth now actually shut.

'Yes, it is presumed, Sir, that he was seething.'

'Seething?'

'Seething at the fact that Department of Transport policy had to be conducted in such an underhand manner; secret contracts; constant lobbying; the real power lying with the Civil Service. As an ambitious minister, he is deemed to have seethed, Sir, and yearned for popular approbation.'

'Galton, even Digby Parkhurst must have known that announcing plans to relocate St Paul's Cathedral behind a DIY centre in Essex would not bring him popular approbation.'

'They also think he must have been on the piss, Sir.'

But Christian knew better, he knew that something must have happened to make a dull, featureless minister screw up his career and party policy so spectacularly. This was why he had called for the video tapes of the day's events. He had watched Digby leave his hotel to be confronted by the members of the rail lobby, he had watched Digby arrive at the conference hall and he had watched Digby's speech, particularly the point of confusion. Christian had watched Digby shout, 'What this government intends to do with the railways is . . .' and he had touched the freeze-frame button. Then, taking a ruler to the screen, he attempted to follow Digby's eye line to find out what the minister had seen at that precise moment.

It was blurred, and almost off the corner of the

screen, but it was unmistakably there; a young man, standing up in the fourth row holding up a handbag.

'That's our transvestite,' said Christian. 'Bloody cheeky, eh? Fingering Parkhurst mid-speech.'

'Rather strange behaviour on Turk's part too, I feel, Sir,' added Galton. 'After all, it was the precise timing of the hit which led to Parkhurst's road speech, and the subsequent débâcle over secret government policy. Sam Turk, as a prominent road lobbyist, must be kicking himself that in bringing down Parkhurst he inadvertently brought down the biggest road building plans in British history.'

'Sam Turk had nothing whatsoever to do with the incident,' said Christian, decisively, and he called for a second television and video recorder. The equipment having arrived, he inserted into the second machine the news tape of Digby's departure from his hotel and his encounter with the rail lobby. He froze the tape at the point at which the forceful young man pushed his way through the crowd . . . Through the general babble he could be heard warning the minister not to announce the formation of BritTrak, what's more, he had a Scottish accent. Christian looked at the frozen image of the man outside the hotel. He turned to the image of the man in the fourth row, one business suit is much the same as the other, but none the less, it was clear that the two men were the same person. 'Well, well, well,' murmured Christian through a mouth that was positively imploding. 'So Digby Parkhurst got stitched by a queer train nut.'

Chapter Eighteen

THE ENGINE SLIPS FURTHER OUT OF REACH

ASSEMBLING THE LAB

Toss was out traffic wardening, Deborah was at college sitting an exam and Geoffrey had the flat to himself. He was hard at work in the little work area that Toss had helped him to set up in Deborah's laundry-room. This was a partitioned area at the back of the kitchen which housed the washing machine, tumble drier and ironing stuff.

Most of what Geoffrey required to re-design his engine, was in his head. The only tool which he really needed was his home computer, a machine specially adapted to Geoffrey's needs. This, Toss retrieved from Geoffrey's flat at his first opportunity, which was the Tuesday evening after work. This meant that two days had already passed since Geoffrey had discovered that his invention had been hijacked. Toss also grabbed books, notes and whatever other stuff he was able to lay his hands on amongst the mess. This was not very much, because

Toss was forced to operate without putting on any lights. The reason for this was because it was clear to Toss, having strolled past the place a couple of times during his lunch-hour, that Geoffrey's flat was being watched.

Toss knew this, because, in the course of his years tramping about with his traffic warden cap on, he had come to know every type of loafer, trader, ne'er do well, and poser that hung out on the streets of London.

'I'm cool, guy, you understand. My eye is like an eagle and I am totally happening,' Toss had pointed out when asked by Deborah how he could be sure that the two men he had reported had actually been watching the house.

'It is my personal style to be hip to whatever is going down, yah nah what I mean?' he added. 'I know when a guy is just chillin't out right? Just catching rays, watching the fine ladies and hangin' OK? I know if he is a thief, right, a beggar, a pimp, a copper's nark. I have to tell you that I am so wicked to the street life of this city that I can tell you what people had for breakfast, yah nah what I mean! And the geezers outside of Geoffrey's flat was watching it, girl. They weren't selling chestnuts and they weren't delivering nuffink, they was watching.'

'All right already, so your cockney intuition assures us that they were watching,' said Deborah. 'I had no idea you were such a Dickensian character Toss. Anyway, the question is, what are we going to do about it? Geoffrey can't exactly reshape the world with a ball point pen and pad.'

Geoffrey sat twitching on the sofa, wondering whether he should point out that greater men than he had done just that, but he couldn't be bothered to formulate the sentence.

The upshot of the conversation was that Toss had returned to the flat as dusk fell, pushing a pram. Geoffrey lived on the ground floor of a large old Victorian house, the sort where the old family living-room had been divided into six 'desirable maisonettes' and the understairs cupboard had been converted into 'a totally separate and enclosed living area suitable for a young couple'. Geoffrey was fortunate that, being a moderately well paid professional person, he was able to afford a whole floor, but the great mass of bell buttons on the front door indicated that above him dwelled many souls.

'Listen, Fleur!' Toss shouted into the intercom, having pretended to push a button . . . 'It's me, doll, and I'm back for good all right. Livingstone needs his mum . . . Now don't give me that, doll, yah nah what I mean?' continued Toss, enjoying his performance. 'Just open the door and get me dinner on all right? And then you'll have to wash me shirt cos Livingstone's just pissed on it and that shirt is wicked threads, girl . . . What's that, doll?' Toss leant in, pretending to listen to the intercom . . . 'Loves yah? Course I loves yah, I fucks yah, don't I?' This triumphant bit of characterization completed, Toss leant in, to disguise his movements, and deftly unlocked the door with the key that Geoffrey had given him . . . 'Thanks doll,' Toss shouted into the uncomprehending Tannoy as he pushed the pram into the gloom of the hallway.

Having closed the door he let himself into Geoffrey's flat. He shuddered slightly to see that the white outline that the police had drawn round the body of one of the men who had been unwise enough to take on Geoffrey Spasmo, was still visible on the floor in front of the sideboard.

'That Geoffrey is a wicked geezer,' Toss said to himself, as he began to load the pram with Geoffrey's computing equipment. Toss had decided to stay the night at Geoffrey's place because he considered that the watchers might smell a rat if he emerged with his pram only half an hour after entering. A character such as the one Toss had created, would certainly stay for supper and a shag at least. It wasn't so bad. As Geoffrey had promised, there was plenty of booze in the place, so Toss got his chicken and chips out from under the pram, plus his cork-screw . . . He didn't fancy using Geoffrey's, in fact, he shuddered at the very sight of the evil spike which he knew to have inflated the bottom of the man around whose body the police had drawn their sombre line.

'Wine, food, vibes,' mused Toss, putting on his ear-phones and settling down in the darkness. 'It is time to forget the dead, and chill out.'

REVISION CRISIS

Toss did his job of collection well and the little laboratory which Geoffrey created was sufficient to his needs, and, for a week, the little community at Deborah's place settled into a routine. Geoffrey slept on the sofa and never went out, spending almost every waking moment in his little lab, redoing his sums on top of the washing machine, earnestly working out weight-to-power ratios in equations so long that they stretched the length of an entire ironing board and constructing anew his specifications for light-weight alloys and revolutionary lubricants. The theory was all still in Geoffrey's head, but the retrieving of it was complex and time consuming, and, of course, there was the washing to do.

'We need to wash our stuff, Geoffrey,' Deborah protested. 'The world may be on the verge of a transport revolution, but we still need to have clean underwear.' So Geoffrey reluctantly moved all his papers and Deborah loaded the machine, swearing, yet again, that next time she really would clean out the fluff filter.

Unfortunately, Deborah's constant presence in the flat proved rather a distraction to Geoffrey's work. Despite being in danger for his life and working against the clock, he still could not help his mind wandering to the girl who was, after all, the inspiration that had got him into the whole mess in the first place.

It was doubly distracting for Geoffrey because Deborah was at home much more than usual. It was the period of her final examinations, and hence her presence was not required at college. She was constantly in and out of the kitchen and whenever he heard her, Geoffrey's heart ached. Each day she thought of new things to wash, or iron. It was not that Deborah wished to distract Geoffrey, but it was the last week before her history of costume exam and Deborah was in a revision crisis.

Revising for exams is always hell. The mind wanders, panic wells up, lethargy sets in, the TV beckons. Deborah tried to concentrate, each day she tried, and yet, constantly she caught herself coming to with a start having been reading a book for five minutes and yet not having taken in a single word. Throughout the week, Deborah, who was normally so positive and so lively, mooched and slouched about the flat, made coffee, offered to make Geoffrey coffee and watched the mid-day news. She rang friends on the same course to assure them that she was not getting any work done. They rang her to assure her that they were also not getting any work done. All over the country demoralized young people were ringing each other up to assure their friends that they had managed to do no work at all, while secretly suspecting that their friends must have done loads, and loads, and loads of work.

On the third day of her torment Deborah realized, with only four days to go until the dreaded paper, that she must really pull herself together, therefore she did what all the other tormented revisers around the country did, she made a timetable. She made a detailed timetable of how best she would organize her revision time in her last four days. She drew neat squares indicating the remaining mornings, afternoons and evenings, and in these squares she neatly wrote things like 'eighteenth century French court dress' or 'work clothes as fashion', thus indicating at which time she would be revising what subject. This completed, Deborah wearily returned to the article she had been reading in *Woman's Own* about which member of the royal family had lost the most weight. Each morning Deborah read the paper from cover to cover, arguing to herself that this was a serious and legitimate use of her time. Secretly, of course, she knew that this was simply another anti-revision prevarication. Under normal circumstances, she often skimmed the paper, occasionally not even opening it at all. On revision mornings, however, she even read the situations vacant pages. Deborah was always interested in employment opportunities.

Ever since the Global Moritz had paralysed her from the waist down, she had been aware that forging a fulfilling career was going to be just that little bit harder for her than for most. Because of this, despite being currently a full time student, curiosity often led her to check out the job market. Finding out which employers claimed to be equal opportunities employers – not that that meant much because, of course, it only meant equal opportunities for human beings, not fire hazards.

'Look at this, Geoffrey,' said Deborah, breaking into the middle of some mile long equation forming in Geoffrey's mind and causing all the numbers to fly out of his ears.

'Global Motors UK are looking for graphics people in their design deparment. Maybe I should apply, do you think they'd give me special consideration seeing as it was one of their cars that put me in this chair?'

'Deborah, please,' said Geoffrey, 'I'm trying to concentrate.'

'All right already, for God's sake, one little word. I'm sorry,' Deborah snapped back. 'I have work to do too you know,' and she wheeled herself back into the sitting-room, past her lecture notes and started to watch a programme for the under-fives which asked Deborah whether she'd like to pretend to be a puppy dog along with Trudy and Sean.

THE BELL TOLLS

Finally, the morning of Deborah's exam had dawned and she had gone off, in a rare old state, at about eleven. Toss had been gone for ages as he was on the early morning shift that week so Geoffrey briefly had the place to himself. He went through into his little workroom and prepared to concentrate his massive mind. Unfortunately for Geoffrey, he was not the only one who had been waiting for him to be alone in the house.

Blissfully unaware that terrible danger was stalking him, Geoffrey became immediately and happily engrossed in his work, so much so, that he almost did not hear when the tiny glass bell tinkled at his ear informing him that somebody was messing about at the back windows. Deborah, living as she did, on the ground floor, and being even more vulnerable than most, had done her best to make her flat secure. Toss was not always around, and, as he himself pointed out, he 'wasn't no Mohammed Ali, girl'. Hence, Deborah had had bars fitted to the rear of the flat and an alarm system installed. Geoffrey reckoned this offered him a fair degree of protection, but, as an added precaution, he had fitted an extra electronic element to the alarm, whereby, if the alarm circuit was overruled or the bell silenced by some skilled hand, the tiny little crystal bell would ring, thus informing Geoffrey that intruders were about without letting them know that their presence had been announced.

Deborah was glad that the bell had found a function, it had been one of the numerous gifts she had received whilst in hospital from relatives she scarcely knew she had. The only thing to commend the bell, in Deborah's opinion, was that it was small, unlike the six-foot teddy bear that a cousin who worked at Bloomingdales had sent. When you're in hospital for eight months people have time to send things by sea, and Deborah's relations had made good use of this service.

'Do you want to know what's embarrassing? I'll tell you what's embarrassing,' Deborah had moaned from her sick bed, in a letter to a friend. 'Being a girl from an extended Jewish family, seriously ill in hospital. I can no longer look the nurses in the eye. It ain't the treatment, having my orifices stared at in disappointment by students I can handle, peeing through a tube I'll live with, but being the cause of the postman getting a hernia, this I cannot take. The man has grown old bringing me my daily sack of presents. First he stooped a little, then he went grey and had a hernia, finally the poor guy ends up in hospital himself. They buried him last Tuesday, killed by the American shopper.'

The endless gifts had made Deborah terribly uncomfortable, not least because there are so many lonely people in hospitals, people who have no visitors and get no presents because they are old and their lives have died around them. Eventually, fortunately for Deborah, the daughter of a family of Soho/Italian restaurateurs appeared two beds up and even Deborah's family's efforts paled into insignificance – but not before she had received the bell from an aunt in the Bronx. 'Anytime, anywhere, beautiful girl,' the note had said, 'you ring

277

that bell and God will listen. You ring it, you say, let's talk, and you talk. Believe me, beautiful baby, he will be listening.'

Deborah had been rather surprised that God had so little on his hands, but she did not make this point to the kind aunt in her thank you note.

Geoffrey knew the story of the bell, and very much hoped that God was paying attention now. He knew that the intruders were attacking the back of the house, for the signal he had rigged up to the front of the house was the tiny beeping of an electric watch. Somebody, in the privacy of the back garden, was working away at Deborah's bars, and they were very good at their job, because Geoffrey could not hear a thing.

However, he trusted his warning system and so decided to institute the hiding plan.

THE HIDING PLAN

Geoffrey, on considering what it was he should do if ever the hidden hand that pursued him were to arrive at his door, had decided that it would be unwise to try and fight. He was realistic enough to realize that on the previous occasion he had been monumentally lucky, and, it would be foolish indeed for him to go about under the impression that he was in a position to get the better of enormous, heavily armed thugs whenever he so chose. Therefore, he had prepared a hiding place behind the ironing board.

Deborah's laundry was, of course, equipped for a person who did things sitting down, a conventional ironing board was far too high for her, besides which she would have found it extremely difficult to set one up. She would, of course, not have been alone in this. Everybody finds ironing boards extremely difficult to set up. The reason for this is that they were designed by a mad octopus, the same mad octopus who designed deck chairs.

Anyway, Deborah's ironing board was set into the wall, and hinged at the bottom, so that, when it was required, it could be simply pulled down. The wall it was set into was the partition wall between the laundry and the kitchen, which had originally been a single width of reinforced hardboard. However, on Geoffrey's instructions, Toss had spent the previous Sunday morning adding a second hardboard face to the kitchen side of the wall, thus creating an eight-inch wide cavity, access to which could be gained by lowering the ironing board and climbing through the ironing-board-shaped hole.

This Geoffrey did, and not a moment too soon, for the intruders had now dealt with the bars and also the glass at the rear of the house. As Geoffrey pulled up the board behind him, he could distinctly hear somebody climbing into the back bedroom, which belonged to Toss.

It was a brilliant hiding place, the two intruders missed it completely and were very soon satisfied that the flat was empty.

'So,' said Jurgen, a German employee of Euro Despatch. 'It is a pity, yes? No sign of our quarry.'

'I don't think he's home, Fritz,' replied Noddy, who wore a bobble hat and was from Wolverhampton. Noddy had named himself after the lead singer of Slade, Wolverhampton's contribution to the rock and roll hall of fame . . . 'What we going to do? Wait?' he enquired, leaning against the clothes drier in the laundry-room.

'I think not,' said Fritz, who wore a black polo neck and wished he had a duelling scar. 'Possibly one of the other two might return first. Let me remind you that the spastic fellow is our only target. Our employers do not wish to attract any more interest than is necessary.'

'Well, let's piss off up the pub then,' said Noddy, shrugging his shoulders.

Geoffrey, in his hiding place, was of course delighted with the turn events were taking, although he knew that he would now have to find a new safe house, which would deprive him of the society of the girl he loved. Still, it might make him concentrate.

TRAITOROUS BODY WORK

Unfortunately, Geoffrey was rejoicing too soon, for his cerebral palsy, which had saved his life on a previous encounter with the forces of evil, now let him down terribly. His head jerked and banged against the cavity wall, then it did it again and after that, a third time. Probably this rhythm solo would have gone on for some time, but at that point, Jurgen pulled down the ironing board to reveal Geoffrey twitching behind it.

'So what have we here?' said Jurgen, all icy and cool.

'I think it's the spastic bloke we're s'posed t'kill,' replied Noddy, not realizing that Jurgen had asked a rhetorical question.

Geoffrey climbed out immediately, without being told to, he knew that his chances of survival were small whatever he did, but trapped inside a wall cavity they were zero. His body was uncooperative enough without further restricting it.

The laundry was necessarily a cramped space and Noddy was leant against the drier, whilst Jurgen was in front of the washing machine. Between them and Geoffrey was the little stool Geoffrey had been sitting on while his computer sat on top of an upturned laundry basket.

Jurgen was a professional killer, and the first maxim of professional killing is, not to talk about it, but to get it over with immediately. He knew the story of how this strange little twisted fellow had already got the better of his two colleagues. Looking at Geoffrey, he found the story difficult to believe, but he was taking no chances and intended to get his job over with at once. However, pose was also important to Jurgen. He reached inside his jacket for the silenced pistol with a languid hand, the other dangling casually down beside him, limply hanging inside the open lid of the top-loading clothes washer.

TOUGHER THAN THE REST

Geoffrey was one of the coolest people in London, he was brave as a lion, smarter than a rat and in his whole life he had never allowed himself to be beaten. If you're spastic you simply can't, because if you did you would be beaten the minute you tried to get out of bed in the morning.

Of course, nobody ever really understood just how cool Geoffrey was. Even Deborah and Toss, who knew him well and also something of his deeds, could never fully comprehend just what an extraordinary individual he was, because the social conditioning is simply too strong. No matter what Geoffrey achieved it would always be a spastic achieving it and his future potential would always be doubted because it was the future potential of a spastic. Spastics just don't look like they're up to much and when, as so often they do, they prove that they are, other people are still secretly suspicious.

Geoffrey had a matter of a second in which to act. The controls of Deborah's machinery were wall-mounted, it was Geoffrey himself who had designed this. It saved Deborah having to try to reach out of her chair and lean across the top of the machinery. Many people in wheelchairs employ concertinaed, extendable arms with grips on the end, but Deborah did not need too, she was fortunate enough to have an electronics wizard for an admirer.

Geoffrey dropped his hand down and turned on the tumble drier, it jerked and rumbled behind Noddy. For a split second both Noddy and Jurgen were distracted, it was the old 'look over there' routine, but done much more effectively with a remote-controlled clothes drier.

There was a cup of washing powder on a shelf attached to the wall in which Geoffrey had just been hiding and, in the split second he had earned himself, Geoffrey brought his good hand up to grab it. As his hand came up it flipped the washing machine onto heavy stain wash. Deborah's water heater was one of those over-enthusiastic ones that heat the water so effectively that you could virtually make tea from the hot tap. A jet of scalding water spurted over Jurgen's hand, he shouted in pain, Noddy turned to him, eyes wide with surprise, and Geoffrey flung the powder in Noddy's face.

That was it, Geoffrey had exhausted his armoury and in the momentary confusion that he had created, all he could do was run like hell, or as much like hell as his unruly body would allow him.

By the time Geoffrey was through the living-room and into the hall, Noddy had recovered, and, despite streaming eyes, had drawn his gun and was in pursuit. Geoffrey wrenched open the front door, which set off the front alarm. The clanging made

Noddy pause for a moment which allowed Geoffrey to get out into the front path. The cool air of freedom hit him, he was going to make it, the crowded street was only a few feet away. Toss was just turning in through the gate.

'Wicked, Spas, what's happening?' he enquired of the figure jerking towards him, with its head bobbing against its shoulder and one arm performing a strange modern ballet all of its own.

But then there was no head, and no arm. Both simply disappeared mid-jerk, each absorbing the terrible impact of a barrel of Noddy's double-barrelled sawn-off shotgun, which Noddy fired the moment he had reached the doorway. For a moment Geoffrey's poor twisted, now virtually headless, body remained standing. Then it collapsed.

Noddy was gone, Jurgen too, they were out of the back before Toss could even understand what had happened. He just stood there staring at the corpse of his ruined friend.

Geoffrey Spasmo was dead, and the secret of his great invention had died with him.

Now Sam Turk really did hold the only ace.

Chapter Nineteen

THE CASUALTIES MOUNT

THE JOLLY GRIDDLE

Springer had been desperate for a chance to talk to Sam ever since Sam had got back from Detroit, but he had had to wait almost a week because it had been agreed that any discussion of their secret project should take place very discreetly. There should be no chance of anyone following them or overhearing or even knowing that the meeting had taken place.

To this end, Sam had arranged that they should meet at the Jolly Griddle Family Restaurant on the A40 just south of Oxford. He judged this a sufficiently anonymous venue. Travelling salesmen stopped there all the time, two men deep in discussion would certainly not be noticed. Everyone was always too busy discussing how awful the food was.

Only in Britain could the Jolly Griddle chain not only survive but prosper. Only we could eat the stuff they dish up. On the road into hell there is a Jolly

Griddle Family Restaurant, and even there, where the fires of Hades burn with a fearsome heat, the fish is still frozen in the middle when it arrives at your table.

They just can't cook *anything* at these places and one is forced to wonder whether they do it deliberately. Surely it must be as easy to microwave a portion of baked beans right, as it is to microwave it wrong, so why do the beans always arrive congealed and with a skin on them? One would have thought it would be as easy to put the bit of lemon on top of the fish *after* heating as it is to do it before, so why does the bit of lemon always arrive dried up and microwaved to death? It is *almost* as easy to shake the water out of a portion of peas before dumping them on a plate as it is not to bother, so why does one's food have to arrive floating in an eighth of an inch of water?

Is it a conspiracy? Is it a joke? Is Mr Jolly Griddle screaming with laughter in his mansion? saying to his wife, 'I don't believe it, these people will eat *anything*!! What shall I try next? I know, ring the local shoe factory and ask them for a million individual lasagnes.'

COLD INSIDE

'I don't believe this, the fish is still cold inside,' said Sam. 'Hey kid, come here,' he motioned to a bored dispirited adolescent. 'Kid, the fish is frozen on the inside, it is hot on the outside, but frozen on the inside. Half done is not done at all. You want me to eat the breadcrumbs, is that it?'

It was absolutely clear from the lad's expression that he did not give a tiny toss what Sam did with his meal. At the end of the week he would take home less than sixty five quid, if he hadn't still been living at his mum's he would have starved.

'I'll take it back then, shall I?' he said.

'It has already been back, kid, you took it back once, but it is still cold, how can that be? Did you forget what the problem was on the way or something? It is still cold.'

'Is it?' said the waiter, 'I'll take it back then, shall I?'

'Hey Sam, why don't you just eat your French fries,' said Springer, who had been under the impression that the whole point was that they were not supposed to draw attention to themselves.

'French fries? These are not French fries, Springer, these are *English* fries, which is why they are white, bendy and soaking up water from the peas. OK kid, forget it, life's too short,' Sam motioned the waiter away.

'Sam you told me this was all hush hush,' said Springer slightly reprovingly as the waiter retreated. 'Why did we drive fifty miles to eat garbage if we are putting up a sign saying we are here?'

'Springer,' said Sam, 'look at this stuff. That kid must get asked to take back every second piece of fish he serves. If I *hadn't* have complained, now that would have drawn attention.'

This of course showed how, despite his year in the country, Sam still knew very little about the British, because the British would rather die than cause a scene. Very little food was ever sent back at Jolly Griddles. Thousands of mums and dads sit in these family restaurants, seething with anger, swearing they will say something, but, unless the fish actually bites the children, they rarely do.

Sam and Springer's conversation turned to Sam's visit to Detroit.

'So you saw Tungsten? Gosh I'll bet he freaked, I'll bet he did a back flip,' said Springer.

'Yeah, he was pretty excited,' conceded Sam.

'Excited, I'll bet he was excited. He is going to be the most important car maker since Henry Ford. The three of us are going to be American heroes! I guess even if they learnt we had to bump off the little professor they'd forgive us.'

Sam looked at Springer with the same quizzical look he had used on the beach in Brighton.

'Not that anyone's ever going to find out of course,' Springer quickly corrected himself.

'Bruce's reaction was kind of strange, Springer,' said Sam. 'He had a kind of different plan to ours. I don't know, it took me back a little I confess, but it sort of has its points.'

'What plan could there be other than to make the engine?' asked Springer, mystified.

'Well, to not make the engine of course. Bruce wants to suppress the whole thing and sell the designs to the oil people, to the Arabs. Get paid off in billions and pretend there never was a hydrogen engine.' Sam was watching Springer carefully. It took Springer a moment to reply, he was too surprised to speak.

'Why the dirty, rotten little bastard,' he said eventually. 'I can't believe this! Bruce Tungsten? Mr Automobile? I thought the guy was a car man! I thought the guy was an American! Jesus Christ, Sam, what is he? some kind of drug addict? This engine means Global is back! It means the USA is back! Big beautiful babes rolling out of Detroit and across the world. It will be like the Japs never happened! . . . I don't believe this! Jesus . . .' Springer was lost for words.

'It would mean an unimaginable amount of money,' murmured Sam.

'We make our dough from making engines, besides you couldn't spend that much. Sam, you got to talk to him.'

'Yeah, I know,' conceded Sam. 'I just felt honour bound to give you his plan, and you're sure you're not interested?'

'Hey, what do you think? Get outta here! We've made cars together for twenty years. I'm a car man.'

'Good. OK,' said Sam. 'I'll talk to Bruce, I guess he'll come round.'

They paid the bill and walked out into the car-park together.

'Nine, two, four,' said Springer, following a custom that they had observed for all their years as a team. It meant that, not including their own, there were nine cars parked, of which two were Globals and four were Japanese. Given something to stand on, Springer could do the trick almost instantly with up to a hundred cars.

'A few years from now, nine, nine, zero, huh?' said Springer, getting into his new Crappee.

'Sure thing, old pal,' said Sam. 'You got a pen?'

Springer wound down his window, Sam leant in and shot him dead.

Springer's car had been parked in the corner of the car-park, it was four whole days before anyone even noticed something was wrong. No one remembered a thing. Sam, who of course had arranged a watertight alibi, was not even questioned. What possible motive could he have for killing his old pal and trusted employee?

Sam had never meant this to happen. He cursed himself for having been so foolish as to let Springer in on the secret at all. Bruce he needed, Springer he did not. Of course, at the point he had taken Springer into his confidence, Sam had not yet fully worked out the enormity of his plan, it had just been instinct, he and Springer worked together on everything.

Sam's ruthlessness surprised even himself.

'Dough is strange stuff,' he mused to himself as he drove back to London.

LEARNING THE HARD WAY

Digby sat down in the driving seat of his beautiful Panther Chief Executive (Kevin Class). It was the last night he would have the car, back-bench MPs are not provided with ministerial limousines and Digby had received a curt note to return his to the Westminster car pool forthwith. The chauffeur had already gone. As he turned the key in the ignition he reflected on how quickly fate can lay a person low. Only a fortnight before he had been driven down to Brighton in this very car, rehearsing a speech which he hoped might lay the foundations of a leadership bid. Now he was a disgraced back-bencher, his career in ruins. That, however, as Digby well knew was not the half of it. His current situation would appear quite idyllic once the news-papers hit the doorsteps in the morning. What's more, Digby knew that he had only himself to blame. It wasn't just his appalling naïvety in going to the press, for which he was chastising himself, it was the craven and cowardly attitude he had adopted to his whole bloody life. There was, he knew, no question that his imminent exposure in the *Sunday Word* as a homosexual (what's more a homosexual with rather camp theatrical tastes), would be rendered infinitely more cruel by the lifetime of denial which had gone before. It was not just that he had always portrayed himself as a jovially sexist rogue either, far worse was his utter failure to attempt in any way to change the prejudices of society, prejudices to which he was about to fall victim. He had not only denied the fact of his own body, he had actually conspired against it. Digby's party, despite harbouring many a closet gay, was rabidly homophobic and Digby had gone along with all the slurs and prejudices. He had snorted with laughter at the queer jokes that regularly delighted the members' bar and eagerly joined in campaigns of slander against local councils who sought more tolerant attitudes towards sexual minorities. All this was going to make Digby look pretty pathetic in the morning when four million newspapers appeared with the headline 'DIRTY DIGBY IS A RAVING WHOOPSIE'. You just don't mess with the press, that had always been the dictum. How could Digby have forgotten it?

He had learnt of the terrible consequences of his pact with the devil only that morning. Astonishingly, he had actually woken up feeling perkier than at any time since he had received the Prime Minister's acceptance of a resignation he had not then even proffered. The sun was shining, the toast was hot and as he indulged in the tiny sensual pleasure of pushing down the plunger in the coffee maker, Ingmar Bresslaw's terrible anger was beginning to fade from Digby's mind.

Contemplating life as a back-bencher again, Digby could see its good side. It wasn't a bad old life, if you had a decent sized majority and your constituency party still supported you, which Digby's did, (after all, they reasoned, better to have an ex-minister for your MP, than one who had never held real power at all). Digby sipped his coffee, and mused, almost eagerly, on the jolly, irresponsible lot of the back-bencher. He would be able to whoop and holler and shout 'shame' and flick ink pellets at the opposition and cheek the new oiks, just as he had done before high office had dampened his high spirits. He would be able to get as drunk as he liked before debates without being in any danger of having to make a contribution, the only constraint imposed on a back-bencher's drinking being that he remains sufficiently sober to go through the right lobby at division. Yes, Digby could indulge in all the Boys' Own fun of the back of the House without that irritating anonymity which is the lot of most of the six hundred. He was an ex-minister, he would be able to strut and boast about the place posing as a rebel ('I play a lone hand, and I'm nobody's lap dog'). Having rubbed shoulders with power he would always be in demand as an after dinner speaker, people like hearing about power ('I recall once saying firmly to the Prime Minister, whilst I knew the Foreign Secretary to be listening . . .'). He was still young, he could become a socialite, dining out with celebrities, telling them what the Queen was really like ('two words: gracious lady').

Besides all this, he would be well off for the first time in his life. As an ex-minister there was no doubt he would be able to pick up numerous lucrative directorships. Already his name had been linked in the papers with Cornelius Brandt, and people were talking about him as a possible titular head of the British Division of Imperial Oil. It is a curious thing, but when ministers resign there is much press speculation about what they will do for a job. This speculation continues until, after much horse trading, they emerge as a director of British Telecom or something similar. The fact that the ex-minister in question is still an MP and, hence, already has a job, representing the tens of thousands of people in his constituency, passes without comment. This was the case with Digby. Renowned git though he was, to those in the know, he was still considered to be eminently employable. As far as the party was concerned he had resigned in disgrace, but to the public at large he was the outspoken champion of the road who had been forced out of office. There would, no doubt, be numerous petrol pumpers, car manufacturers and motoring organizations eager to improve their profiles by giving the fiery and quixotic ex-Transport Minister a position on the board.

Then the doorbell rang, shattering Digby's happy reverie forever.

Digby answered the door himself, his treasure

who 'did' for him had not yet arrived ('she is *marvellous*, I would have been *submerged* long ago without her. Can't speak a word of English, of course').

'Mr Parkhurst,' said Galton, and despite the fact that the sun was shining strongly, he did not disintegrate into a pile of dust as blood sucking vampires are supposed to do.

'Yes, Digby Parkhurst, can I help you?' replied Digby, rather stiffly.

'I see you don't remember me, Sir, that's all right, I'm used to that, Sir. We were introduced. Galton, of the *Sunday Word*, I attended the interview which you gave for Mr Christian Corbet, my editor.'

Thinking about it, Digby did recall a shadowy figure lurking in the shadows.

'Hmm, yes, well have you prepared your story?' Digby asked. 'I shall not hesitate to offer it to a rival publication.'

'Oh we've prepared it all right, Sir. Out tomorrow in fact. I wonder if I might have a few words, Mr Parkhurst. Just to clear up one or two details?'

'I really cannot see why that should be necessary,' replied Digby. 'Now if you'll excuse me, I am an extremely busy man.'

'All right Digby, boy, I'll cut the crap, shall I? We know you take it up the arse and we know that on the night before your speech one of your bum boy pals visited you in your hotel room wearing a dress and false eyelashes. We also know that the following day he blackmailed you into cocking up your career. Here's his picture. He's Scottish.'

It was moments like this that made Galton's day. Digby went from white to green. He actually gagged and croaked as his stomach turned over with fear and loathing.

'May I come in now?' enquired Galton.

'What for?' asked Digby, in a ghastly whisper.

'Well, it might be possible for us to add a slightly more favourable slant to what is, after all, a pretty seedy story, if you were able to see yourself clear to confessing everything exclusively to the *Sunday Word* and giving us the background of your queer ways, you know. Did some wicked old bugger have you when you were a kid and set you on the path to frightfulness? Very mitigating that, Digby, very mitigating.'

For a moment Digby even considered it, making up some awful fiction about being forced to be gay at school, pleading with Galton to go easy. But then a spark of sanity, perhaps even honour, bubbled its way to the surface and Digby realized that there was not a chance in hell of Galton going easy, and anyway, he had been lying for too long.

'I have nothing further to say,' replied Digby.

'We shall have to go with the story as it stands, Digby,' said Galton.

'Go to the devil,' said Digby, slamming the door, but Galton had sold his soul that way a long time before.

CARBON MONOXIDE

The beautiful Panther Chief Executive had been
running quite a while now, but Digby wasn't going
anywhere. He just sat there, with the car in neutral
and a hose-pipe running from the exhaust pipe in
through the top of the slightly open passenger
window. Digby's eyes were closed. The internal
combustion engine had claimed another victim.

Chapter Twenty

DOWN BUT NOT OUT

Deborah and Toss had not spoken much in the week since Geoffrey had been murdered. Neither of them could think of anything to say, the shock was too great. Toss, who had actually seen him die, could not expunge the vision of Geoffrey's last seconds from his mind. Deborah, who had loved Geoffrey, and felt as one with him in the colossal battles of his life, was quite simply bowed down with grief.

Whilst there was still the police to deal with, they had both held up quite strongly. Deborah had tried desperately to interest the police in the disappearance of Geoffrey's invention, but since the Office of Patents vigorously asserted that they knew nothing of any invention and Deborah could not produce anything to substantiate her claims that an invention had ever even existed, the police were inclined to believe that Geoffrey lived in a world of fantasy and delusion, probably chemically induced.

'Drugs Sir, gotta be,' DC Collingwood opined to the Superintendent as they left. 'These Spasos, well, they got nothing to live for have they? Not surprising a few of them turn to the honeyed oblivion of drug induced ecstacy. The bloke couldn't pay for his trips and hits and pops, Sir, so he got done, simple as that, I reckon.'

COMFORT IN THE LORD

Deborah had hoped that Geoffrey's funeral might provide a catalyst whereby she might come to terms a little with the dreadful mourning which haunted her, but it didn't.

'After a lifetime of struggle and torment,' the vicar had said, trying to be nice, 'our brother Geoffrey is happy in God.'

Deborah squirmed, even in death, Geoffrey was being defined by his disability. The vicar, nice bloke though he was, was offering comfort in the idea that, in a sort of way, death was a release for Geoffrey. Without saying it, he was suggesting that it must be so bloody awful being a spastic that, in a way, even having your head blown away with a sawn-off shotgun was sort of preferable. Deborah knew Geoffrey was not happy in God, he had never wanted to die. He hadn't wanted to be a spastic either, but that was beside the point. He had definitely never wanted to die. He wanted to work, write, drink, enjoy his friends and, if possible, have it off occasionally. None of which, Deborah imagined, you could do with God. It just wouldn't be right.

'As we all know,' continued the vicar, 'Geoffrey rose magnificently above the burdens that God chose to place upon his shoulders. The Lord moves in mysterious ways and we can never know what purpose he had in so afflicting Geoffrey. Perhaps he understood Geoffrey's strength, and wished to use him as an example to others who were not so strong.'

'That makes sense,' thought Deborah. As tears streamed down her cheeks, her thoughts flooded with the occasions when Geoffrey's indomitable spirit and wit had proved to her how strong she could be herself, even from her chair.

'Whatever purpose God saw for Geoffrey upon Earth, it is done now,' the vicar concluded. 'For Geoffrey's struggles are over, and he is at peace.'

But Deborah knew that he wasn't. She wanted to shout. She wanted to scream to them all that Geoffrey's immortal soul was about as peaceful as Beirut. She gripped Toss's hand as anguish flooded through her. Geoffrey's work, his engine, the one he had designed for her, was gone. Gone forever. How could he ever be at peace? Everything he had dreamt of had been stolen and he wasn't there to put it right.

At the graveside they watched Geoffrey's small coffin being lowered into the grave.

'Leave plenty of room, guy,' murmured Toss

under his breath, 'because the geezer is going to be doing a lot of turning in the grave. He is going to spin.' Toss's thoughts were along similar lines to Deborah's. He knew that Geoffrey had failed, they had all failed.

READ ALL ABOUT IT

In the days after the funeral the torment had increased. Deborah could find nothing to do with herself, nothing to occupy her mind. It was the weekend and she had decided that she would seek grief counselling on the Monday, the victims support group had been in touch and she had got the number of an analyst from a friend.

'I know it seems kinda New York to be going to an analyst,' Deborah had said to Toss, her eyes red with a week of crying. 'But I can't go on like this. It's worse than when I was crippled. He came to us for help. Now he's dead and his engine's gone and we don't know who did all this to him, Toss. We've no one to fight, no one to blame. It's the impotence that's killing me inside. If we had just one clue, Toss, just something to think about, something to do, I think I would be all right, but we don't. We've got nothing, and we never will, we're tiny people and we've been stepped on.'

That had been Saturday night, the Saturday that Digby turned the key of his ex-ministerial limmo. As Digby breathed himself to death, Deborah cried herself to sleep.

By Sunday morning Digby's suffering was long over, but for Deborah there was no relief. Often, at times of great unhappiness, a person will wake up and check themselves, wondering for a brief second, ecstatic with potential, whether the load has been lifted, only to realize a moment later, as the liquid lead runs into the stomach, that nothing has changed.

Deborah hauled herself out of bed and went through into the kitchen to make coffee, imagining, as she did every time she entered her kitchen-cum-laundry area, Geoffrey's last terrible dash for freedom.

Some people had recoiled at Deborah wanting to continue to live in a flat, in the garden of which a close friend had had his head blown off only a week before. These people had no idea what it is like to be a paraplegic. Deborah could not simply move in somewhere else. Her home was her haven. There, everything was designed as much as possible to work for her, as opposed to the exact opposite, which is how everything is designed in the outside world. Deborah needed that home, and anyway, it was hers. She would not leave it just because some evil low-life had invaded it. Toss, on the other hand, would have liked to move, but he stayed for Deborah's sake. He didn't like it, he wanted desperately to get away from the gloomy presence of tragedy and the constant reminder of the appalling moment in the garden. But he had to stay.

Toss was still asleep as Deborah made the coffee, but his paper had been delivered. He favoured the *Sunday Word*. 'Just for a laugh, know what I mean. See who's screwing who.'

Deborah always claimed to be stunned that Toss would pay good money for such drivel. However, like everybody else, she would flick through a copy herself when she got the chance.

And there it was. The clue she had been wishing for. Deborah did not realize it at first, she was merely reading with interest the surprising secret life of an ex-cabinet minister. Halfway through the article, however, she came to the meat of the matter. A sideline issue to most readers, nothing like as interesting as the stockings and suspenders, but it was life and death to Deborah.

Having got through its story that Parkhurst was being blackmailed by a Scottish transvestite railway nut, bent on hijacking the government's BritTrak scheme (probably the most accurate front page the *Sunday Word* had ever printed), the newspaper went on to explain . . .

During the *Sunday Word*'s painstaking investigations, the minister made a cowardly and dishonourable attempt to throw us off the scent. Explaining his conference cock-up by claiming that Samuel Turk, the Chief Executive of Global Motors, had been blackmailing him. The reason for this, nervous Parkhurst claimed, was that Turk had stolen plans for a 'miracle motor' from the Office of Patents, and that Parkhurst had been on to him.

The *Sunday Word* approached Mr Turk, who strenuously denied the accusation. We also contacted Deirdre Whelk, the senior Civil Servant at the Office of Patents, who denied any knowledge of a miracle motor. There had been a break-in, she admitted, but nothing had been stolen.

An hour later, when Toss wandered in wiping the sleep from his eyes Deborah had already decided what she had to do.

'Toss, the time has come to fight back,' she said, in a firm, decisive voice. He looked at her in surprise. It seemed to Toss that Deborah had been speaking in a sombre weepy monotone for so long that he had forgotten what her usual voice sounded like.

'Yo, girl,' he replied, 'what is happening with this new-found decisiveness? Has an alien with a positive attitude taken over your body?'

'Toss, I know who has Geoffrey's engine designs . . . it's all here in the paper. It's a guy called Sam Turk, an American I am shamed to say.'

'Well, they can't all be like you and the Statue of Liberty,' said Toss, kindly.

'Thanks, I hope I look as good as she does when I'm a hundred years old. Listen, this guy is the head of Global Motors, and I am going in there, and I am going to get Geoffrey's engine back.'

Chapter Twenty-One

BIG DEAL

Later that same Sunday, the unwitting target of Deborah's increasing wrath was in Geneva facing the representatives of the world's oil producers. They were a powerful crowd but Sam Turk eyeballed them without a flicker of nerves. Turk had been Global Motors' principal union-breaker back in the fifties. During those heady days, he had thought nothing of having decent men beaten and the frighteners put on their families. He had been one hundred per cent in bed with the mob, kept a baseball bat on his desk and stood as God-parent to the children of made men. Sam prided himself that it took quite something to scare him. He didn't know it, but as he sat staring down at the oil men, that something was sitting in a wheelchair in London staring at his face in a newspaper.

THE UNION

The Union of Oil is the loose cartel by which many of those states which produce petroleum products organize their affairs and attempt, when they're not at war with one another, to prevent damaging competition.

Never had a U of O delegation been organized so quickly as the one which Bruce Tungsten and Cornelius Brandt had brought about. Even when they were fighting, Union of Oil diplomacy happened at a fairly leisurely pace. Decades of sucking out of the ground a liquid for which the whole world thirsted had led to a lack of urgency, perhaps even complacency, in its dealings. Another block to the Union operating in a time-effective manner was the disparate nature of its membership. It was made up of a mixture of feudal monarchs, military dictators and elected prime ministers. In fact, such were the differences of principle and method within the group, that everybody knew that anything the U of O decided, might, at any time, be completely ignored by one or other of the countries involved.

Not only was it extraordinary that the U of O had assembled so quickly, but it was extraordinary that it had assembled at all, because at the time of their meeting with Sam, the Union of Oil was supposed to be hopelessly divided. The conventional wisdom amongst diplomatic circles was that it would be months, perhaps years, before they could be persuaded to even talk to each other. The problem being that one of their number had invaded a neighbour, the aggressor claiming that the neighbour had been stealing its oil by means of long bendy pipes that tunnelled deep and looped under the border.

None the less, all the member states sanctioned this meeting, including the two belligerents whose soldiers were at that moment locked in mortal conflict. The reason being that when figures as senior to Western oil interests as Bruce Tungsten, America's Mr Automobile, and Cornelius Brandt, the boss of Imperial Oil, shuttle red-eyed from country to country announcing that oil will be economically dead inside two decades unless immediate action is taken, even the slothful U of O gets its arse into gear.

The meeting was, of course, conducted in the deepest secrecy. The current war had caused both the United States and the European Community endless diplomatic and military inconvenience. The leaders of those powers would clearly have been none too pleased to learn that after months of refusing to meet, representatives of the two belligerents were now having tea together. Of course the other, even more important, reason for secrecy was that the meeting involved the suppression of an invention which could bring great benefits to humankind. The last thing anybody needed was moral dilemmas to muddy the deal.

A LESSON IN DIPLOMACY

Cornelius Brandt had been surprised when it was Sam Turk, not Bruce Tungsten, that he met at Geneva airport. Cornelius was extremely tense, it is never any fun having to tell the people upon whom you rely for your livelihood that they are about to get stung for a gigantic amount of cash. Of course it was not Brandt's fault, but none the less he could not help feeling that the affair, once concluded, was likely to sour his business relationships for some time to come. Perhaps it was the tension that made him so brusque.

'What are you doing here, Turk? Yes?' he snapped. 'They are expecting Tungsten, they want the master not his dog.'

If Sam was stung by this rather rude remark he did not show it.

'Well, ol' pal,' he grinned, 'I decided I needed the trip.'

In fact Bruce had also been extremely surprised when Sam had announced that he would convey a sample of Geoffrey's design to the Geneva meeting, and strike the deal himself. Bruce had argued forcefully that, since he had set up the meeting, it should be he that chaired it.

'I don't see that, Bruce,' Sam had said affably. 'Setting up the meeting was where the influence and credibility were required, but now you've done that, why it doesn't matter a damn who actually shows them the engine. Ronald McDonald could do it and the results would be the same. The engine does the talking, ol' pal.'

This had prompted Bruce to, again, make the point that he himself, as co-conspirator, had yet to set eyes on these magical designs. Sam protested that he wasn't exactly going to fax them to the States, but assured Bruce that his curiosity would be satisfied the moment he got to London. However, by the time Bruce did arrive in London, Sam had already arrived in Geneva, where he and Cornelius Brandt were getting into a limousine.

'Take us up around the lake a little,' Sam said to the driver, explaining to Brandt that he required privacy in order to offer Brandt further information. Brandt said nothing and sulked.

Soon they were amongst the countryside and Sam got out of the car.

'You go hiking if you want,' said Brandt, staying put, 'I hate trees.'

Sam walked round to the driver and gave him five thousand American dollars.

'That's to have your panel beaten out and fix your paintwork, son,' he said, before walking round to Brandt's side of the car. Brandt's look of surprise soon turned to fear as Sam dragged him out of the car by the collar, threw him face down over the bonnet of the big Mercedes and bashed his head a couple of times against the beautiful, smooth metal.

'You got yourself a bargain, kid,' said Sam to the astonished driver while still holding Brandt face down on the bonnet, 'they build these Mercs like fucking panzers. Why I don't think I've scratched it. If this had been a British car his head would be buried in the road.'

Sam pulled Cornelius Brandt round to face him, there was a huge nasty bruise on his forehead and his nose was bleeding.

'OK, listen up, little Dutchman!' said Sam, still with the same big smile and easy manner. 'Don't call me a dog, OK? Don't put me down and be mean, you understand, I hate it.'

Sam pushed Cornelius Brandt back into the car and ordered the driver to head for the private villa where the momentous deal was to be discussed.

TEA PARTY

On arrival at the villa, Sam and Cornelius had been met by the chief technical officer of the Union of Oil. Sam presented him with a copy of Geoffrey's plans and he took them away for study by a team of top engine brains and fuel heads. After that, Sam and Cornelius waited. They knew that they would not be received by the Union representatives themselves until after the engine's credentials had been established.

The hours passed, lunch was served, and then tea. Not a word passed between Sam and Cornelius.

Conversation is always a bit stilted between two people, when one of them has recently beaten the other up. But Sam was a naturally gregarious soul and the silence really got on his nerves. As the long hours ticked away, he began to wish that he had not dealt so roughly with Brandt. Eventually he could bear it no longer.

'Hell, if I'd a'known we were gonna be sat staring at each other all day, I never would have buried your ugly mug in that car hood,' he said by way of conciliation.

Cornelius said nothing, refusing even to look Sam in the face.

'What, are you going to sulk all day?' said Sam. 'OK, so I bruised your head. Here, look, does this make you feel any better?' and with that Sam leant his big body forward and head butted the table, making all the tea things rattle. 'How was that?' he enquired, a nasty bump already rising on his forehead. Still he was received in stony silence . . . 'Oh, yeah, I forgot,' Sam continued, 'I slammed you two times didn't I?' and again Sam whacked his head down on the table, this time making the top jump off the sugar bowl.

'Mr Turk,' the Dutchman said, as if speaking to the opposite wall, 'your football yob behaviour, which is like a thug or something, yes? is not edifying, it is not smart. You disgrace yourself, yes?'

'Aw diddums,' said Sam not very cleverly. And silence returned.

Another fifteen minutes passed, it seemed like fifteen years. Sam sighed, paced about the room, sat down, drummed his fingers, sighed, got up again, whistled a couple of bars of 'Forty Second Street', accompanying it with a little shuffle, sat down again, picked up his teaspoon, sighed, then started tapping his teaspoon against his cup. Now it was Brandt's turn to be consumed with irritation.

'Don't tap please, yes?' he said through gritted teeth.

Sam stopped tapping. Then after about a minute he started again. 'Ching, ching, ching,' went the teacup. Cornelius Brandt's face grew tense, but he said nothing.

Sam kept on tapping. He tapped and tapped and tapped. Having tapped out the 'William Tell Overture' on his cup about fifty times, Sam decided he could do better than that. He stopped tapping and rolled up a little pellet of bread, which he flicked at Cornelius, making a noise like a cannon. More pellets followed.

'Enemy sighted, Sir,' said Sam, playing at being a military commander. 'Little Dutch faggot, range eight feet. OK, let's hit 'em with a thermo-nuclear, inter-continental ballistic bread pellet from Uncle Sam. Ready, aim, fire.' The pellet hit Brandt on the nose.

Sam upgraded his technology. He employed a knife to improve the force and accuracy of his projectiles. He used up all the bread on his own plate in some twenty or thirty pellets. 'Peow,' he said, followed by the sound of an explosion whenever he managed to hit Brandt's head.

'Excuse me,' Sam said, leaning across, 'could I have your bread if you're not using it? Mine is all through.'

Cornelius cracked, he snatched up his teacup, which happened to be half full of cold tea, and hurled the liquid into Sam's face. Sam then emptied the contents of the pot over Cornelius, a teabag ending up perched on top of his head.

Silence fell again and not another word was said between the two men until an emissary arrived to inform them that the Union of Oil was ready to talk.

THE DEAL

The gathering was not as large as Sam had expected. Not every country involved was individually represented and only the four largest oil companies had sent delegates. However, those in attendance had authority to speak for all, so the atmosphere was heavy with money and power.

'My science officer informs me that Mr Tungsten did not exaggerate, and nor did you Mr Brandt.'

The bearded and berobed prince was attempting to play it very calm and regal and was not doing a bad job of it. However, Sam, who had seen a hundred men bluffing in his time, could see that the oil potentate was badly shaken.

'You undoubtedly have in your possession a technological breakthrough which could, we agree, one day produce a viable alternative to the petrol engine.'

'Oh, is that so?' said Sam.

'Yes, it is, and we congratulate you,' answered the Prince.

'Well that's nice, your Highness, but congratulations, even from a big cheese like yourself, trade pretty light against the US dollar.' Sam was standing four square, a big bruise on his forehead and tea stains on his collar.

'Yes, we have no doubt that if you continue along the lines that your research has taken you so far, one day, in as little as perhaps ten years you may produce a viable prototype. A prototype which would undoubtedly put in question the long-term future of the petro dollar. We thank you most sincerely for bringing the matter to our attention.'

'Well, thank *you*, your Highness,' said Sam rather nastily.

'You were right to think that we would be interested in aquiring the world rights to the research you have conducted so far. We concur that it is essential to the Union of Oil's long-term interests that we maintain control over such developments . . .'

'Excuse me, your Highness,' Sam interrupted the Prince. The Prince was extremely surprised, having never been interrupted before. In fact, the Prince was on the verge of ordering ten lashes for impudence, but he was reluctantly forced to recognize that he did not have the authority at the present time. The Prince's surprise and irritation was to turn to anger, moments later, as Sam's tone became clear.

'I wonder if I might just dig out my big shovel here, Prince, and start to shift a little bit of this bullshit,' said Sam. Cornelius Brandt instinctively stepped away from him, half expecting a bolt of lightning to put an end to Sam's impudence. The Prince raised an elegant eyebrow.

'Explain yourself, Mr Turk. If possible without recourse to the language of the gutter,' he said.

'Oh, I'm sorry, Prince. I didn't realize a guy who would cut off a thief's hands for stealing a goat would be quite so sensitive.'

'Kindly keep your tired and unimaginative prejudices to yourself, Mr Turk, and stick to the point. What have I said that you consider to be so foolish?'

'Oh, it's just something in phrases like "one day", "in ten years", "prototype", those kind of words, Prince. Words that sort of give the impression that you're trying to bull me about how much you reckon what I got is worth.'

'On the contrary, we accept absolutely that you are in possession of a major breakthrough. We wish to acquire the rights and we are prepared to offer yourself and Mr Bruce Tungsten eight million

United States dollars each, for the world patent.'

'So long, guys,' said Sam, heading for the door.
'Get yourselves a copy of the next issue of *Scientific American*, the death warrant of your industry is going
to be on the cover. You can keep those designs if you
like. We're registered in the US and Bruce Tungsten
will have the damn things rolling out of Detroit
before you know it.'

'Mr Turk,' spluttered Brandt.

The Prince nodded a tiny nod and Sam's way was
blocked by two gentlemen in suits who had been
standing by the door.

'Listen, towel-head,' said Sam, spinning round.
'You know that if I don't report back to Tungsten
tonight, or one of my secret partners, we go ahead
with the engine.'

'Do not judge everyone by your own loathsome
standards, Mr Turk. You are not in any danger,'
said the Prince, and he probably meant it, although
a glance round the room would quickly have
informed Sam that certain other Union members
might not be so considerate.

'So how come you're blocking my path?' asked
Sam.

'Because I have come a long way to conduct these
negotiations and I must insist that you have the
courtesy to complete them,' answered the Prince.

'In which case have the courtesy not to crap me,
OK? You know damn well that my engine is at
production level. There ain't gonna be any more

research or development. We are ready to roll, and if we do you had better buy yourself a herd of goats, because we are sure as hell gonna derail your private gravy train, Prince.'

The Prince looked about at his colleagues, all of whom were empowered to negotiate on behalf of their states. Their faces were resigned. None of them had expected the bluff to work, and it hadn't. They would have to pay.

'Twenty billion dollars you say?' enquired the Prince.

'Oh hot, damn!' said Sam. 'You see I've been working in London, England, this last year or so. I think in *pounds* these days. Have to ya see, so as I can compute how many Ecus to charge for my product!'

Cornelius Brandt shook with anger. 'You're mad, Turk. Don't ask it,' he stammered.

The Prince remained outwardly calm, but he too was shaken, everyone was. Sam had even surprised himself, he had not been planning to nearly double his demand.

'Am I to understand that your price is twenty billion *pounds*?'

Sam was a gambling man, he read the faces of the people in the game and he decided to chance raising the stakes. 'The price for the world rights in perpetuity to the Global Motors hydrogen engine is now fifty billion United States dollars. Payable in gold, securities or cash. What's more, it goes up five

billion every two and a half minutes from now on,'
Sam looked pointedly at his watch.

'Mr Turk,' even the ultra cool Prince was now
showing his emotions. 'This is no way for civilized
people to conduct negotiations.'

'I ain't civilized, your Highness,' said Sam,
thumbs in waistband. 'I'm an American car man
and proud of it. I wasn't born, I was beaten out of
a quarter-inch steel panel in Detroit. We never set
much store by being civilized down on the auto line.'

'Oh *please*,' said Cornelius Brandt.

'Now listen up, all of you, OK?' Sam barked.
'We all know that you have no choice whatsoever.
Your people have checked out the plans and you
know how extraordinary they are. Can't think why
nobody figured out the secret before. Lucky for you
they didn't, or you'd never have got as fat as you
did.' This was rather rich coming from a man who
himself sported a belly you could have plumped up
and got cosy on. 'Maybe they did figure it out,
maybe I ain't the first guy you've had to buy off.
Whatever, if the engine goes into production you
know that you're all peasants again. Personally, I
reckon you're getting a bargain here at fifty billion.
Mind you, gentlemen, I feel obliged to inform you
that in about a minute the price will be fifty-five
billion.'

'Mr Turk,' said the Prince, in a lifeless voice. 'The
member states of the Union of Oil, in conjunction
with the major petroleum refining and distribution

companies' (at that Cornelius Brandt gulped) 'hereby undertake to purchase from you, Samuel Turk, managing director of Global Motors UK, the exclusive world rights, in perpetuity, to the hydrogen engine developed by the Global Motor Company. The Global Motor Company will, in their turn, undertake never to build a single unit of the said engine, or divulge the secret of the engine to any third party. The price agreed is fifty billion United States dollars.'

'Sorry,' said Sam checking his watch, 'twenty seconds too late, it's fifty-five billion.'

'What!' the Prince, so icy a moment before, positively spluttered.

'Too much pompous bullshit, Prince. All you needed to say was "deal" but you had to dress it up like some kind of fucking international treaty. Well, I warned you.'

The whole room erupted in furious protest.

'Mr Turk!' Cornelius Brandt shouted, 'this is absurd! Unjust! You cannot possibly . . .'

'I can do just what I damn well like,' barked Sam. 'Because I've got you guys over a barrel with your balls in a clamp, so don't tell me nothing, OK? Now I like you guys, and so I'm going to do you a big favour, by reminding you that in less than a minute the price goes up from fifty-five to sixty billion.'

'Deal,' said the Prince.

NEAR TO DEATH

After Sam had gone, the Union of Oil and the big petrol pumpers had a conference. At first everyone shouted at once and the result was a confused babble. However, one thing was clear as crystal, if Sam had entertained any hopes of receiving a birthday card from the assembled group, he was going to be disappointed.

Soon it became clear that there was a distinct group who favoured direct action. The loudest voiced in this group was a tough looking man in military fatigues.

'This man cheats and insults us. He is a bully, a braggart, I am confident that General Ali will want him dead.'

General Ali was the military dictator who had invaded his neighbour, and no slouch at the bullying and braggarting game himself. A very different type of leader indeed to the people that the Prince represented, he thought nothing of using military force and terrorism to achieve his ends. All in all he was a very scary man. It was well known, about the Gulf, that you did not mess lightly with General Ali.

'Killing Turk would be pointless,' snapped the Prince.

'Oh yes?' enquired the man in fatigues. 'Then perhaps you would like to be the person who informs the General that we have just negotiated a fifty-five billion dollar pay-off and that he is expected to contribute.'

'Gladly. I will phone him now,' the Prince boldly replied.

'Why the hell not kill the man?' the hawks in the group pressed. And the doves explained that it would do no good, for some other conspirator, Tungsten for instance, would take over control of the engine.

'Well, we'll kill him as well,' announced the man in fatigues.

'We have no idea who is a party to this invention,' snapped the Prince. 'It is absurd to suppose that we would be able, with absolute certainty, to suppress it by force. The only way that we can be one hundred per cent certain that this engine will never be produced, is to own it ourselves, and the only way to do that is to purchase it legally. If we start to chase it you may rest assured that very quickly it will emerge somewhere, and then it would be unstoppable.'

There was no doubting the logic of this and the hawks sulkily agreed that the legal way was the only sure way.

'But we could kill the swine anyway,' said the General's man, hopefully, 'and deal with Tungsten.'

Fortunately for Sam, he was outvoted. Unfortunately for Sam, General Ali had never had a great respect for democracy.

Chapter Twenty-Two

MR AUTOMOBILE, SUPERWOMAN AND THE GENERAL

WAITING ON THE WORD

Bruce Tungsten had been jittery ever since he got back from his mysterious trip to the Gulf, everyone had noticed. The company was in the midst of a massive catalogue update, bringing a series of new models and improved classics onto the market. By rights, Bruce Tungsten should have been at his sharpest and most involved. He wasn't though, he was preoccupied, his mind was clearly elsewhere. In vain, the top design team tried to get final approval on the results of years of labour. Particularly urgent was the new four-wheel drive, off-road Rancheroo Prairie Cruiser, it was all ready to roll off the line. The media blitz was poised and the ads had been made. The car was to be targeted at young, urbane executives and city bankers, so the advert featured a rugged cowboy gone hunting in Wyoming: lean and silent; alone by an open fire with his dog.

'Will ya just look at the final cuts boss,' they

pleaded. 'Ranger and Toytana are both snapping at our heels here. We believe Toytana are offering a four-by-four that can cross rivers up to four feet deep and Ranger have a winching line that could drag a bus out of a swamp.

'Well, those should be useful features for picking up the groceries at the Seven Eleven,' murmured Bruce, fingering the strange little doll that always stood on his desk. His staff were most surprised at this. Mr Automobile had never been cynical about a car before.

They clamoured at him to make the decisions they required, but Bruce was evasive. He was waiting for the phone to ring. Eventually it did, the secure line, Bruce knew that it was Sam Turk.

'Meeting's over, boys,' he said to his astonished employees. A collective 'but boss' was on the tip of their combined tongues, but you didn't 'but boss' Bruce Tungsten. They dutifully trooped out and Bruce spoke to Sam.

'What's the story, Sam? I had Cornelius Brandt on line an hour ago saying you were an animal, but he wouldn't tell me anything else.'

'Oh he's just a little touchy because I put a teabag on his head,' replied Sam. 'Bruce, ol' pal, we have pulled off a deal so big and so mean you could put a saddle on it and ride it in a rodeo. They had no choice pal, no choice. Guess what I stung them for, go on, guess . . . guess, you have to guess, go on, guess.'

'Sam, I have no idea,' replied Bruce. 'I haven't even seen . . .'

'Forty billion dollars.'

The phone almost fell from Bruce's hand.

'You have to be joking, Sam,' he replied, white-faced.

'Ye-e-e-e-s, I am!!!' screamed Sam Turk. 'Fifty-five billion Bruce, twenty-seven and a half each. What are you going to do huh? I think I'll just buy myself a little country in Central America and set myself up as a dictator, that way I get my own army and also I can give the President a hard time whenever the Democrats are in.'

'Sam, I've never even seen this damn engine,' said Bruce.

'No, that's right, you haven't at that,' said Sam, cheerfully, 'but you don't have to see it partner, they've seen it, and they want to buy it.'

'I want to see it, Sam,' said Bruce.

'Now listen here, Bruce. The deals have been done and you're damn lucky I'm not the kind to cheat on an old pal. It would be very easy for me to have just conveniently forgotten about any partners I might have had . . .'

'I know that, Sam,' said Bruce apologetically.

'Now, I don't know if you're having any crazy thoughts about this engine.'

'Sam, I was just curious, that's all.' Bruce was now less apologetic. 'I'm a damned car maker, and an engineer, I want to know how it works.'

'And I'll tell you sometime Bruce, believe me I will,' placated Sam. 'We'll sit down in some good old bar and I'll map the whole thing out with a couple of boxes of matches. But right now it's money that matters Bruce. We have to be in a position to receive fifty-five billion, in gold, bonds, assets and cash. And what's more, we have to do it by next Tuesday, which is when I told them I wanted to exchange.'

'That's quite impossible, Sam. The logistics would never fall into place. You can't just deposit it at a bank, it's just too much money. We are talking about the sort of assets that could destabilize an entire economy.'

'I know,' and Bruce could actually hear Sam grinning, 'isn't it beautiful?'

'Sam please, think about it. Adequately preparing to place fifty-five billion dollars on the world money markets cannot be done by two individuals in four days.'

'It has to Bruce, ol' pal. The longer we leave them to sweat over this, the more likely they are to start sticking bombs through letter boxes.'

'Sam, it can't be done.'

'Oh yes it can, least ways it had better, and it's *one* individual by the way. This is your job Bruce. I don't have the influence, or the clout to pull it off. No bank would take my word on those kind of figures. No brokerage would listen to me. So let me tell you how it's going to be Bruce. There's fifty-five billion coming in. That's two lots of twenty-seven and a half. Except the Gulf states pay on Tuesday, and what they can't unload they take back with them. So my share, ol' pal, is the *first* twenty-seven and a half they can invest on your instructions, and yours is the second, anything you can't find a home for, you lose.'

'Sam, by Tuesday!' protested Bruce. But the line was dead.

Bruce touched the intercom button.

'Michelle,' he said, 'cancel everything for the next five days.'

'But Mr Tungsten,' came the astonished reply. 'You can't possibly . . . Sir, this is the most important . . . Why the whole new range . . .'

'Cancel everything, Michelle,' said Bruce. 'A few days from now it won't matter a damn.'

SUPERWOMAN

As Sam put the phone down on Bruce, something which he had never done before, in another part of the great Global UK building an employment officer was also putting down the phone having spoken to Deborah.

'Global Motors UK is an equal opportunities employer,' the paper had said, and as Deborah dialled the number, she wondered.

'They don't mind about murdering people with disabilities,' she said to herself, 'I'll bet they ain't so eager to give them a job.'

Paradoxically, Deborah's disability made it easier for her, on this occasion, to at least gain an interview. Global was a huge corporation, public relations were an obsession with them, the last thing they needed was some loud-mouth crip' kicking up a stink about discrimination. Always interview the cripples, that was the rule. Then, when you turn them down, you can say it's because they just aren't right for the job, nothing to do with the wheelchair.

So when Deborah rang the number, somewhat exaggerating her qualifications, and pointedly asked about disabled access, the employment officer at Global UK agreed to put her in with the first batch of interviewees to be seen the following Monday.

That evening she told Toss.

'You're mad, girl!' he exclaimed. 'Why don't you just bell the geezer and say you know all about the miracle engine and about him killing Spas and all that. He'll shit himself. I mean he'll have to see you because he doesn't know what you know, does he?'

'He doesn't care what I know either, Toss,' said Deborah. 'The guy has the designs right? What proof do we have that those designs were originally Geoffrey's? Turk can just claim he designed them himself.'

'Yeah, but I mean somebody must have known what Geoffrey was working on, and could back our story. Someone at his work, or whatever.'

'Nobody knew about Geoffrey's engine but Geoffrey. The guy was a spastic, Toss, people didn't talk to him. Besides, he kept it a secret, even from me, until it was stolen. The stupid jerk left no tracks at all. We've tried to get the police to believe the story, so did Geoffrey. Christ, Toss, it's been published in a newspaper! Nobody gives a damn and Turk knows it, he has nothing to fear. Which is why the only chance I have of getting those designs back is to tackle Turk unawares.'

'Well I have to say, girl,' said Toss, forlornly, 'at the risk of sounding negative, your chances are kind of tiny. "Infinitesimally small" are words that are not out of place here. The geezer will kill you.'

And yet again he tried to dissuade Deborah from her chosen course, as he had been doing almost continuously since the previous morning when she had read the *Sunday Word* article.

'Deborah, these people blew Geoffrey's head off! I mean they *blew it off*! It was like some sort of Robert De Niro thing, except they didn't use real ketchup, they used blood. They have no respect for the sanctity of human life. None.'

Toss was absolutely convinced, not unreasonably, that Deborah was going to get herself killed. So fearful was he, on her behalf, that he had even, with the greatest reluctance, volunteered to attempt the mission himself. He was honest enough with himself to concede that he was relieved when Deborah said that it wouldn't work.

'This is the one time when being in a stupid wheelchair gives me the edge. Somebody has to get into the Global building right? and once in, get around it. That person is me. People don't like to *talk* to people in wheelchairs, let alone kiss them off. They're embarrassed too, so they grin weakly and ignore us instead. I have to tell you, they do not have a similar problem with young black guys. It is conceivable that you might get the job interview, but if you start wandering round their building uninvited, you are going to have the FBI and the National Guard and the Ku Klux Klan on your back in two, maybe three, seconds maximum. They will slam you against the wall, spread your legs and say hurtful things like 'Freeze Nigger mother fucker' or, seeing as how we're in London, 'Orl roit Sambo wotcha want?'

Deborah, like many Americans was rather proud of her cockney accent, which was strange because she couldn't do it at all. The American cockney accent is taught via 1940s Sherlock Holmes B movies, where actors from the Bronx sit on top of hansom cabs saying 'Cor blimey, wot a toff! Arf a crahn to roid ya to tha trine styshon.' This accent reached its glorious zenith with Dick Van Dyke's extraordinary performance as the sweep in *Mary Poppins*.

Dialect aside, Deborah's point was a forceful one. She pressed it home.

'Now little old me, on the other hand, Toss.

Who's going to press me against a wall? A poor pathetic girl in a chair? What possible danger could I be? Crippled you see, good for *absolutely* nothing. Such a shame, so young and yet so *useless*, what harm could she do?'

Toss could see the logic in this argument. But only as far as it went.

'All right, Debbo, I am happening to your point that you have got slightly more chance than me. But considering, girl, right, that neither of us have any chance whatsoever, I mean, none, right? your advantage is kind of academic.'

'That's beside the point. I have to try.'

'Listen, you're not bleeding Davy Crockett, girl, you don't have to remember the Alamo. You are going to be wheeling yourself into the lair of a killer right. And for what? So you can ask him for your engine back. Do you know what he'll say, Deborah? He'll say "no", that's what.'

But there was no dissuading Deborah, her mind was made up. Geoffrey's mission had become her mission. After all, in a way, it was *her* engine that had been stolen, Geoffrey had designed it for her. He had wanted to make her fly, and now this Turk guy had stolen her wings and she intended to get them back. What's more, she was going to demonstrate to Sam Turk that you did not deposit the heads of her friends in her flowerbeds and expect to get away with it.

It wasn't entirely personal. Since his death,

Deborah had thought hard about Geoffrey's self-imposed mission. He had intended that his engine should be used for good, that through his work transport in the next century would be prevented from destroying the planet. Deborah's backbone was always a bit stiff on account of the fact that she spent her days sitting down. At the thought of Geoffrey's dreams, however, it stiffened further, stiffened with iron resolve.

'Toss,' said Deborah, 'I am on a mission to save the world.'

THE GENERAL

Sam was plotting with Bruce, Deborah was plotting with Toss, and the man in the battle fatigues was plotting with General Ali.

General Ali had a lot of problems. He was an army officer who had come to power via a military coup. His position had always been rather shaky. In fact, he had started up the recent war with his neighbour by way of rallying popular support. It is one of the great paradoxes of history that leaders who find themselves in difficulties at home, often start wars in order to make their people love them. Although, why anyone should feel deepening affection for someone who has exposed them to being bombed, gassed, shot at and invaded, has never been explained. However, be that as it may, the General remained in a fairly precarious position. He who rises by the coup is often condemned to fall by the coup and many terrible rumblings were to be heard in the country – although these may have had something to do with the fact that, due to war rationing, the bread was now fifty per cent sawdust.

The once beautiful city was devastated, the army was weary, its best men were gone, and the people were hungry. The last thing the General needed was to have to stump up the seven billion US dollars that the Union of Oil had designated as his country's contribution to Sam Turk's buy-off.

'We're busted, Colonel,' the General informed the man in military fatigues who had attended the Union of Oil meetings. 'Seven billion dollars? Where am I going to get it from, taxation? What is there to tax? People will say "OK General, take the rubble that used to be my house, take the food out of the empty larder." Listen, Colonel, you remember when we took power? You remember what I said?'

'You said that heads must roll because the state was bankrupt and could no longer afford to pay its soldiers or feed its babies,' the Colonel replied.

'Spot any irony?' enquired the General.

The Colonel remained silent on this one.

'You know what I think?' said the General. 'I think we can sort this out more cheaply.'

Chapter Twenty-Three

INGMAR'S EFFORTS

THE EIGHTH MAN

Whilst Deborah and General Ali plotted against Sam Turk, Ingmar Bresslaw plotted to fulfil the promise he had made to the Prime Minister that he would bring the road building plans back into public favour. He was absolutely determined that the public would be persuaded, by fair means or foul, that they wanted nothing less from their government than an epoch making era of public road building.

A plan had been forming in Ingmar's mind, almost since the very moment that Digby had disgraced himself. It was an outrageous and audacious plan, requiring meticulous detail in its planning and split-second timing in its execution. Ingmar had held long and deep discussions with engineers, town planners, publicists and lobbyists and was now ready to assemble the undercover team that would be required for the job. It was for this purpose that Ingmar had gone to visit Bill 'Bogus'

Bottomley, a senior operative at MI5.

'Look, I'd love to help, Ingmar, you know I would,' said Bogus, 'but we really do try and avoid the dodgy stuff these days. Can't risk it you see. Do something dodgy, next thing you know, there's a book out about it, have to be terribly careful. Actually, I've got a book planned myself for after I retire, all the blokes have, it's terribly competitive. In fact, I've been meaning to ask you a favour on that score. You see the truth of the matter is, my book's going to be rather dull I'm afraid, never even met a Russian, let alone engaged one in a deadly game of bluff and counter-bluff. Spent my whole life listening in on students doing their year pretending to be socialists, damn dull. What I need is an edge, something to drum up a bit of interest. So I was just wondering if you could put it about that the PM thinks I might be the eighth man.'

'The eighth man?' enquired Ingmar.

'You know,' said Bogus, 'in the Burgess/Maclean, their trade is the treachery business. Nothing substantial, just a rumour, wouldn't half bump up my measly book advance.'

'Bogus,' said Ingmar, 'I require the assistance of Her Majesty's Secret Service on a very sensitive issue of grave national importance. I do not wish to discuss publishing.'

'But the Secret Service *is* publishing these days, Ingmar,' insisted Bogus. 'Nobody does anything any more without thinking about how it's going to look in their book and to be quite frank, old boy, roads won't sell, Russians do. Listen, be a sport, I can't even get a Sunday serialization, and with the Soviets going and collapsing on us, like the bastards we always knew them to be, the Burgess business will probably finally die in a year or two. I really need to get my claim in now. The Chief's bagged pretending to be the sixth man, so that's out, he's bought a couple of homosexual screen prints and a little bust of Lenin to leave lying round his flat. Damn clever, wish I'd thought of it. Then there's a chap over at MI6 who's written a book called *The Seven Dwarfs*, claiming there were seven of them, I'm certain the bastard started with the title. Even says Moscow Control was known as Snow White, and of course Penguin love that. Anyway, he's backing the Chief's claim to be the sixth man, I'm convinced money changed hands there incidentally, and he's proposing that the Queen Mum was the seventh. Not bad that, she always was a bit of a fag hag, friend of Noel Coward's etc. Anyway, I'm going for the eighth, and a hint from the PM, or even the Foreign Office would be wonderful, could put twenty-five thou' on my advance. Go on Ingmar, you could swing it.'

Ingmar Bresslaw made his excuses and left. If he wanted dirty tricks performing he would have to go elsewhere . . .

ANGRY ALF

. . . Which was why he was to be found the next evening dining at the House of Lords with 'Angry' Alf Higgens, who had, some years before, become Lord Higgens of Hackney. Angry Alf was a trade union man born and bred, and, despite the fact that his politics had been drifting steadily rightwards all of his life, his worker credentials were something of which Alf was inordinately proud. He was the type of man who considers that the fact that his unfortunate mother was forced to bring up him and six siblings without the benefit of an indoor lavatory, imbued him in later life with an omniscient insight into the minds of working people.

'Don't tell me how to run a union,' he would instruct colleagues, 'I never had a pair of shoes until I was eight.'

Angry Alf's trade unionism was the politics of power and posture. Throughout his years of influence, he loudly boasted that his job was simply that of 'doing deals for his boys'. He gave short shrift to anyone who dared raise in his presence the broader principles of trade unionism.

'Don't give me any of that bollocks about solidarity,' he would brusquely instruct them, adding that, as a child, he had to rise at five o'clock in order to help out on a coal round before school. It was Angry Alf's narrow perspective and singleness of purpose that had made him, in his years of power, such a respected figure in the road lobby. Roads meant more work for Alf's workers and so roads had no greater champion.

Alf had long since retired, but he had kept up his connections with some senior road lobby figures and he still had influence within his old union. It was for this reason that Ingmar Bresslaw had sought him out. Ingmar's huge plan required skilful, well-motivated operatives. If MI5 could not supply them, perhaps Angry Alf could.

'The planning has already been done, your Lordship,' Ingmar assured Alf. 'All I require is the services of about twenty men. They must be of the best type of course. Utterly reliable, you understand, courageous and resourceful. Will you do it?'

Angry Alf was doubtful, life was very pleasant in the House of Lords. He had no great desire to immerse himself in Ingmar's schemes.

'I don't know, Bresslaw,' he mused. 'If we were rumbled I'd probably lose my ermine. This is social engineering you're talking about.'

'I am talking about bringing the public to their senses, Alf,' said Ingmar. 'Britain needs more roads, you know how important that is, but since Parkhurst's speech, the anti-road movement has held the moral high-ground. We have to do something now. If we're not damn careful, there won't be a square foot of tar laid in Britain for half a decade.'

Ingmar was talking a language Alf found difficult to resist.

'All right,' he said, 'I'll make a few calls, see how the land lies. But it's a dodgy game we're playing here. If we lose, or worse, get found out, they'll lynch us.'

Chapter Twenty-Four

MONDAY MORNING

A COP AT THE END OF HIS ROAD

It was Monday morning and Chief Superintendent Barry Ross was completing a letter to Corker McCorkadale, the Minister for Transport. It was a very sad letter, a letter from a proud and disillusioned man. Barry Ross had controlled London's traffic for fifteen years, but he had grown old and tired in the job. This was the day he was to take premature retirement and he felt the need to explain why.

Minister, (he wrote) I have to tell you that my reason for seeking early retirement is because I am absolutely convinced that it cannot now be many months before the job I have loved will become, quite literally, impossible to perform. I am a proud police officer and will not be the man who presides over the moment when London quite simply ceases to function. Please let me assure you that this is now an inevitability. The long-feared gridlock, which has been my constant nightmare, will become my successor's reality since I see absolutely no political will to face up to the cataclysmic scale of the problem.

The problem is, of course, pure and simple. It is the private car. I have devoted my life to the rights of the private motorist and still believe in them one hundred per cent. But such rights become rather theoretical, don't you think, when traffic moves at a snail's pace and it is impossible to park? Minister, in order to protect the private motorist of the future, action must be taken now. The pollution, the road carnage and the insane inefficiency have to be dealt with. There is one answer, Minister – the rigorous promotion of public transport. Nobody has to park a bus.

Barry would be sorely missed, he was the best traffic planner in the country and had just about kept London moving, against virtually impossible odds, for years. Now he had had enough. Despite being a Monday, this was to be his last day.

HEADING FOR TROUBLE

On that same Monday morning, Deborah and Toss left their home together and headed for the Swiss Cottage area of London, where the UK headquarters of Global Motors were located. Deborah was as sure as she could be that this was where Sam Turk was to be found. Discreet telephone enquiries during the previous week had shown Turk to be a diligent man who arrived at his office early and left late.

Deborah parked her converted car with its disabled sticker bang outside the mighty Global building. It was on a double yellow line with prominent signs about the place saying that parking was prohibited at all times. Deborah felt that she would be OK though, because riding with her was her own tame traffic warden. Toss was in uniform, and it was his job to wait by the car, ensuring it remained there, unclamped, for that ill-defined time when Deborah would be making a getaway.

'You might be hours,' complained Toss. 'I'm going to look a bit of a dickhead spending all day putting a ticket on a car, girl. I am a flash! I am lightning! Nobody books them like El Toss.'

'Listen Buster,' replied Deborah, 'you ain't the one walking into the lion's den. Just wait by the car because I got a feeling that if, and when, I get out of this place, I'm going to be in a hurry.'

And with that, Deborah wheeled herself up the ramp which Global Motors had thoughtfully provided outside their building. Unfortunately, at the top of the ramp were swing doors, and the conventional ones to either side were too stiff to open. They had dropped very slightly on their hinges and hence dragged on the metal bases as they swung. This, of course, meant that Deborah had to sit outside the building (it was now raining), trying to attract the attention of someone inside, whilst hoping someone might come along. Eventually someone did.

'I hope you ain't on the judging panel for this job,' Deborah said to the person. 'Because if you are, I just lost it.'

Once inside, Deborah found the Global building pretty well-equipped, and, having reported to reception, Deborah was escorted in a spacious lift to the appropriate floor.

'Jeez, eighth floor,' said Deborah, casually. 'I would have thought only the big boss guys got to ride this high.'

Her companion merely grinned, as if humouring an idiot. Deborah tried again. 'Maybe the great Sam Turk himself will get in. I could ask him for a job direct.'

'I don't think so,' said the girl with a patronizing smile. 'there's a private executive lift to the penthouse offices.'

Deborah had feared as much. Still, at least she knew where his office was, and hence where he was most likely to be. However, she could not strike out for it just yet. Deborah had decided that she would have to go through with the mock interview for fear that she would be missed and a sympathetic search party sent out for 'the poor stupid girl in the wheelchair.' Fortunately for Deborah, she was called first.

'Getting me out of the way early,' thought Deborah, cynically, as she was ushered solicitously into a room containing three earnest looking people, their faces a picture of heartfelt solidarity and support.

THE CHAIR GETS INTERVIEWED

'Hi, I'm Rod. Step right in and take a seat.'

Aaaahhh! Rod wanted the floor to open and swallow him. What was he saying? What was he doing to this poor girl? just rubbing in her terrible, horrible disability.

'Sorry, stupid thing to say.'

'Pardon?' said Deborah, positioning herself next to the empty chair that had been placed in the middle of the room to accommodate interviewees.

'Uhm . . . about stepping right in . . . Uhm, stupid, silly . . . Obviously I meant wheel right in . . .'

Rod looked around for a razorblade with which to slit his wrists.

'Wheel right in!' Rod was a soggy croûton in a *faux pas* soup, a croûton going under for the third time. He was a nice, caring man, a liberal. Whilst a student he had even been a Communist for a week and a half. He just wanted to show this poor pathetic girl that he was massively aware of her catastrophic inadequacies in the leg department but, within the bounds of practicality, he would not judge her too harshly on them.

'Look, what I'm trying to say is just forget about it, all right? God knows, we certainly have.'

'Forget about what?' asked Deborah.

'Your . . . your . . .' Rod could not bring himself to use the word wheelchair. It seemed so brutal, just drawing attention to the poor girl's appalling predicament. As if she didn't have enough to put up with without insensitive oafs like him idly dropping the word 'wheelchair' about willy nilly . . .

'Your non-walking status,' he said, in a flash of particularly uninspired inspiration.

'Oh,' said Deborah. 'OK, Rod, I'll forget about it,' said Deborah.

'Will you?' said Rod, his face a picture of concern and admiration. 'Will you really?'

'Sure,' said Deborah.

'That's *super*,' said Rod, delighted at having put her at her ease.

The interview began. Deborah explained that she had just taken her examinations in graphics and design and went on to expand on how she felt that this training would provide a good grounding for work in promotions.

But Deborah knew that, as she spoke, her chair was growing. Its arms were expanding upwards to envelop her, the wheels creeping outwards across the floor. She almost seemed to be shrinking into it as the handles behind her head touched the ceiling and the foot rests crept towards the panel, and began to push against the table, behind which her three interrogators sat.

Before long the chair was as big as the room, it

was forcing Rod and his two colleagues against the wall. Such was its size and dominance that it took a great deal of concentration for them to make out Deborah at all, perched far back, as she was, in the giant seat.

Every time the interviewers attempted to shrink the chair it got bigger, backing them further and further into the corner . . . As Deborah improvised a pretty good argument as to why she would make a good promotions woman, the panel's minds raced along the myriad of problems which they saw ahead, regarding the employment of that chair. Would it fit between the desks? How would it travel to showrooms and displays? Could it get in when it got there? How many demands would it make on other workers? How would a car buyer feel confronted by a piece of transport for the lame? Would it depress people?

The answers to all these questions were depressingly negative. How else could they be, considering that the chair now filled the entire room, the foot rests sticking out of the windows and the handles cracking the plaster on the ceiling. Eventually, after what seemed like a lifetime, an acceptable twenty-three of the allotted thirty minutes had passed and Rod drew the proceedings to a close.

'Thanks, Deborah,' he gushed. 'That was marvellous, really fantastic. I mean really fantastic,' and Rod meant it. He found the fact that Deborah could talk at all, most impressive, and also very brave. 'We still have quite a few people to see but really, I mean, *really*, you were terrific.'

Rod leapt up gallantly to open the door for Deborah, attempting to imply with his body language that holding the door open for a cripple was not something he expected any gratitude for, it was just something he was happy to do as one person to another, because obviously Deborah was a person.

After Deborah had gone, the three panel members, out of a mutual sense of guilt, went through the motions of discussing *her* rather than the chair. She was a charming and intelligent girl, they assured each other, each attempting to outdo the others in demonstrating how much they had attempted to look at Deborah's candidature in a positive light.

Having done this for a moment or two, with anguished reluctance, the panel moved onto the *practicalities* of employing Deborah, addressing themselves, as they felt they must do, to whether it was fair to the company, to other employees. Rod even wondered whether it would be fair to Deborah herself, but he was never called upon to expand further on this curious worry because the intelligent nods that he received belied any further explanation.

Finally, and with the utmost reluctance, it was agreed that there was no place for Deborah at Global Motors, if for no other reason than that she was a fire hazard.

Actually, Deborah's position at Global was about to rise with remarkable speed. Her interview having concluded early, Deborah emerged from under Rod's protective arm to discover that her minder had not yet returned to escort her out of the building.

'Could you tell the lady that I made my own way out,' she enquired of the two other candidates who were sitting waiting. They promised to do this through sympathetic smiles, which hid the fact that they were thinking 'Bet she gets it because she's disabled'.

UP IN THE WORLD

Once on the loose, Deborah set about finding the executive lift. She guessed that it would be somewhere in the same area of those lifts provided for the common herd. After all, it would be an exclusive lift indeed that had its own separate shaft. Sure enough, on returning to the lift area, Deborah spotted the discreet, unmarked sliding door beyond the stand-up ashtray and knew that there lay her only route to the penthouse offices. As Deborah had suspected, a key was required to summon the lift. Ostensibly, this was a security measure but, of course, the real reason was to avoid the pristine executive environment being polluted by the foul, rank and stinking air of non-executives.

This little example of corporate élitism is one of

the numerous ways by which the pecking orders and promotion structures are defined in commercial life. It is rather difficult to properly gauge rank and status when everyone wears much the same suit, so little signs and symbols have been devised. You can't tell a colleague how much you earn, but you can make a point of visiting the loo at the same time as he does, and then grandly disappearing into the senior management lav. This confirms your relative status. There are just as many drips on the floor of the executive bog as in the ordinary one, but the point is, they are *executive* drips.

The most meaningful badge of rank in any large company is, of course, what car they give you. The motor that you park in the company car-park tells everybody what you earn and who you can boss about. One day business people will probably dispense with confusing terms of rank such as 'under manager' and 'junior executive', and will simply define people's status by their cars.

'Well son, you'll start off as a Ford Escort, like every young lad, but if you work hard and keep your nose clean, who knows, in ten years you could be a Granada, perhaps one day even a Jaguar like me.'

This snobbery is, of course, wonderful news for the car makers who delight in endlessly producing minor variations of the same car so that the fleet managers of large companies can go mad trying to assess the career implications of awarding someone an electronic radio aerial or alloy wheels whilst his furious colleagues only get a lockable glove compartment. This method of promotion is also a good way of saving money, because it is possible to honour an employee much more cheaply than by giving him or her a pay rise. One can simply replace his Ford Sierra with a Ford Sierra TP (Toss Pot), thus allowing him to rush home shouting 'Darling they've given me the tinted sun-roof!', this small reward being much magnified by the fact that Roger and Bill's new cars do not even have electric windows.

BRIEF ENCOUNTER

Anyway, the immediate upshot of this corporate snobbery was that Deborah would require the assistance of an executive with a key to the lift in order to reach Sam Turk.

Deborah's first problem, of course, was to avoid running into her minder, who would no doubt shortly be coming to pick her up. To this end, Deborah summoned a non-executive lift in order to begin her mission on a different floor. The list on the wall went 'ping' to show that a lift was coming and Deborah prayed, as the doors opened, that the minder would not actually be in it. Her prayers were answered, and, struggling to conquer the fear rising in her stomach, Deborah disappeared upwards into the building. She decided to alight at the floor marked 'Accountancy and Contracts'. Deborah was seeking a floor teeming with executives anxious to use their executive lift and she felt that 'Accountancy and Contracts' sounded like the sort of activity where seniority might be required. Whilst in the lift, Deborah had donned the costume which she and Toss had prepared on the previous evening. It was hidden in the bag she kept hung behind, between the handles of her chair and consisted of a peaked cap marked 'Comet Telecommunications', a small tool bag and Deborah's laminated student union card which she clipped to her breast pocket. Close inspection of this card would, of course, beg the question of why a third year design student, who was entitled to access to all bars and leisure facilities, should necessarily be qualified to mend phones at Global Motors. However, as close inspection would require someone leaning over her and peering down her front, Deborah reckoned she would get away with it. Again Deborah was relying on her apparent helplessness to allay any suspicion. She only hoped that she would not be collared by some flustered employee saying, 'Just the person I need. Everytime I try to phone in for the cricket score I get a recorded tape about Mandy, who says she's a naughty girl and would I like to hear about her melons?'

And so Deborah sat by the lifts of the 'Accountancy and Contracts' floor of the Global Motors building and waited for an executive. Non-executives came, and non-executives went, until eventually her patience was rewarded.

'Say, listen, can you let me back in this thing?' she said as a purposeful man with a key approached the unmarked door. 'They have a fax up on the top tomatoes' floor which seems to be getting messages from Mars, and kinda enigmatic ones at that. They let me in at reception, but I goofed and got out here.'

They seemed to like their executives rude at Global. The man did not even answer Deborah, he simply nodded her into the lift and then followed her. He punched the top floor button for Deborah but himself alighted on the next floor up from accountancy and contracts. Deborah did not attempt to thank him, the man clearly was not in the mood for small talk.

ENGINEERING A CONFRONTATION

The executive floor was rather luxuriously carpeted. This was a bit of a blow for Deborah as carpets slow wheelchairs right down, also, unless the carpet is extremely securely fitted, it is very easy to drag the thing up into a ruck whilst turning. Still, there was nothing she could do about the interior design. Deborah had a job to do and the job was to unearth Sam Turk, confront him and wrest from him Geoffrey's design. A tall order indeed, but Deborah, who regularly had to do battle in the supermarkets of Swiss Cottage, knew a thing or two about tall orders.

'Excuse me, I have to check some phone wiring in the corridor outside Mr Turk's office,' Deborah said to a passing executive-level secretary . . . 'His automatic dial keeps ringing the Finchley Road Pizza Shed and they're threatening to sue.'

'Well I haven't heard of . . .' the secretary attempted to say, but Deborah interrupted her.

'It's just in the corridor, I have to run a volto-joule reverse-current meter over it,' she said, holding up a big cooking thermometer on a spike that she used once a year for roasting the Thanksgiving turkey. Deborah always celebrated Thanksgiving. She considered herself an American (US) first and a Jew a very very long way second. The thermometer, a highly credible piece of technology, was sufficient to convince the hesitant secretary and she pointed the way to Turk's office.

It was only now that the full terror of the situation began to weigh a little upon Deborah. Shortly she was going to have to act, only a wall separated her from her prey. She felt a little like a mouse stalking a lion and an almost overwhelming desire to make a bolt for it welled up inside her.

'Courage, Deborah,' she whispered to herself. 'Courage, you schmuck. If more people would'a had courage, Hitler would'a stayed a corporal.'

All her life Deborah had been taught that those who fail to stand up for what is right share the guilt for the wickedness of the world with those who actually champion evil.

'Easy to say, Poppa,' Deborah whispered to herself as she positioned her wheelchair by an electric wall socket. 'But these people blew my pal's head off with a sawn-off shotgun. You come stand up to 'em.'

The memory of Geoffrey's demise lent an equal measure of both courage and fear to Deborah's emotions, so all in all, the memory of Geoffrey's demise was not a lot of help.

Deborah could hear discussion going on inside Sam's office, so she knew that she would have to wait. Tackling one able-bodied murderer would be difficult enough, she did not want him surrounded by henchmen. Slowly but surely, the room began to empty as earnest looking executives emerged from Sam's office door. They passed Deborah, who was earnestly waving her turkey thermometer at an electric plug socket and scratching her head with a screwdriver. They all gave her a little smile, feeling rather proud that Global, unbeknownst to them, pursued such an equal opportunities policy. Deborah prayed that Sam himself would not emerge and depart for some fifteen-course executive lunch, leaving her with the necessity of pretending to be fixing a telephone line in an electric plug socket with something that belonged up a turkey, for hours on end.

Chapter Twenty-Five

THE BATTLE BEGINS

DO NOT DISTURB

Eventually, Sam's meeting seemed to be over. No one had emerged from the office for a full ten minutes and Deborah could hear no talking from within. With sinking heart she realized that Sam was alone, the time had come to do it.

'If I'm going to take this mother,' Deborah said to herself, attempting with little success to stiffen her resolve with tough talking, 'the time is now.'

She took from her bag a neat little sign that she had made. It said **'DO NOT DISTURB UNLESS YOU WANT YOUR BUTT KICKED CLEAN TO DETROIT'** and was signed, Turk. Deborah had done enough research to have a vague handle on Sam Turk's way of communicating. Very gently she hung her sign on the door handle, of course she was aware that this was not the usual method by which executives ensured that they were not disturbed. Under normal circumstances, when a top dog required absolute privacy, if for instance, they wanted to shag an employee or prise up a floorboard and count their ill-gotten tax concessions, they would bark curtly into an intercom and the door would instantly be guarded by a stern-faced private secretary with a severe bun and an armour-plated brassière. None the less, Deborah, whose whole strategy was based on bluff, thought that there was a fairly good chance that any minion, faced with her little sign, would think twice before disobeying it.

Deborah took a deep breath, reminded herself one more time that if the worst came to the worst she must remember to keep her legs apart, and opened the door.

Inside the room Sam Turk was sitting with his back to the door, and as it happened he was communicating curtly via an intercom with a stern-faced private secretary with a severe bun and an armour-plated brassière.

'If anyone from the Union of Oil turns up you send them straight through OK? No coffee, no how are yous, nothing, just send them through.'

The stern-faced private secretary in the outer office was rather surprised at this instruction. In the past she had noted that Sam was rather irritated by her stern manner. In Detroit Sam had been guarded by a blonde Californian called Farrah who gave off such a positive charge she could wipe the data off a floppy disc. Everything in Farrah's world oozed with sun-drenched enthusiasm, she could never have simply offered someone a coffee, rather she would announce that she had some *great* coffee . . .

'I also have great de-caf, plus I have sugar. I have half sweetener, or I have whole sweetener, and I promise no bitter after-taste, I use it myself. I have great cream which is in this cute jug here, but I also have great milk, skimmed, or full if you prefer. The pot's hot so just yell for more. Enjoy.'

By the time Farrah had finished offering you a cup of coffee you felt like you'd had a massage. It is a little known fact that the reason for the dramatic reversal in fortunes of the awesomely powerful US economy is that they simply let their language get out of hand. So much time is spent greeting each other, describing the coffee and sending out for 'those great chocolate-chip diet muffins they have at Bronski's', that there is no time left to keep up with the Japanese.

THE MOUSE AND THE LION

Sam heard the door and swung round.

'What the hell do you want? My phones are fine, get out,' he barked.

'I ain't no telephone engineer, Mr Turk,' said Deborah. 'My name is Mary Hannay. I'm with the FBI.'

'Sure you are, little girl, why and I bet you have a Superwoman costume on under that cute blouse,' answered Sam, and, having no time to deal with lunatics in wheelchairs pressed the button on his intercom. 'Miss Hodges could you please . . .'

'The Bureau is kinda interested in your hydrogen engine, Mr Turk,' snapped Deborah. Sam Turk looked at her thoughtfully.

'Forget it, Miss Hodges,' he said, taking his finger from the button. Sam looked at Deborah thoughtfully some more, he did not know what to make of her. She certainly did not look like a federal agent.

'So what is the FBI doing rolling around in wheelchairs dressed up as telephone engineers?' he asked, not unreasonably.

'We have no authority in this country,' said Deborah, desperately improvising. She knew this nonsense would not lead her far, but she needed to get a little closer to him.

'I guess that's so,' said Sam, walking round to the front of his desk. He did not know who this woman was, but there was one thing of which he was already certain: she was no FBI agent. If the FBI wanted to talk to him they would knock on the door and say 'Hi, it's the FBI' and they certainly would not send a smart arse chick who looked barely out of her teens. However, as she had mentioned the engine, Sam knew that he must tread a little carefully.

'Kind of an inconvenient cover, ain't it?' he enquired, leaning against his desk. 'A wheelchair.'

'The wheelchair isn't a cover Mr Turk, I'm paraplegic. The FBI is an equal opportunities employer,' answered Deborah.

Deborah always made a habit of confronting every assumption she came across regarding the incongruity of a paraplegic being somewhere or doing something. On this occasion it was unfortunate, because Sam remembered something. 'Paraplegic' is not a word one encounters all the time, but Sam had come across it only a few days before. It had cropped up in a conversation that he had conducted over a scrambled telephone with the head of Euro Despatch after the successful conclusion of Sam's commission regarding the despatch of a certain gerbil named Geoffrey Peason. Euro Despatch were an efficient firm and they offered a degree of background information on the jobs they carried out. Sam had learnt that the gerbil Peason had eventually been discovered at the home of a young female American paraplegic student and a young black traffic warden. He even remembered her name.

'What do you want, Deborah?' Sam asked, but Deborah was too astonished to answer.

'Sure I know who you are, kid,' Sam continued. 'You're the friend of a guy I may have had a little business with recently. But you have nothing on me and you know it, or you wouldn't be here, you'd be with the law. So what do you want?'

'Well I . . .?' for a moment Deborah experienced a sensation almost unique in her experience, that of not having anything to say.

'Go home, little lady. I'll get them to order you a cab.'

Sam was acting very casual and unconcerned but that was only because he did not wish to have to have Deborah killed in his office. That would be extremely inconvenient, especially on the day before his monumental deal when the situation was tense enough. However, underneath he was hugely put out. How on Earth had this girl worked out his connection with the engine? She must also know about his connection with the death of her friend. Given time to think, Sam would probably have remembered the article in the *Sunday Word* and figured things out from that, but, for the moment, the girl in the wheelchair seemed almost clairvoyant, and terrifyingly so. Of course Sam knew that she could prove nothing, not unless she had another copy of the engine plan. None the less, the whole situation was pretty disconcerting. Sam resolved to get her out of his office immediately and then to contact Euro Despatch to arrange her murder that very afternoon.

'Miss Hodges,' said Sam again, touching the intercom button.

'I have a plan of the engine!' blurted Deborah. 'He drew up another before you had him killed, and your thugs didn't find it!' Deborah's mind was racing, she was running out of ways to stall him, she just had to get him close enough, but how?

'Forget it, Miss Hodges,' said Sam again, taking his finger off the intercom button. 'You have another copy?' he asked very quietly, all his dreams of unimaginable wealth hanging on how he dealt with this girl.

'Yes, I have it right here in my blouse,' said Deborah.

Sam could scarcely contain himself, the relief was incredible. He leapt forward joyfully to tear the supposed plans from Deborah's clothing. Sam Turk never imagined that he could possibly be in any danger, but he was. He was the mouse and Deborah was the lion.

TRUSSED TURKEY

Crack! Geoffrey's dead fist in the shape of a small Victorian flat-iron leapt out of the arm of Deborah's chair and swung hugely and horribly into the side of Sam Turk's head, the spindly anglepoise arm delivering the sort of blow that no human arm could muster – no matter how many steroids were pumped into it. Sam Turk folded up like a deck chair, i.e., in a confused heap with everything bending the wrong way.

'Jeez, Geoffrey,' muttered Deborah, addressing her dead companion at arms, 'I hope this guy has a thick skull. He's no use to me dead.'

Sam was not dead, he lay at Deborah's feet, the side of his face a throbbing purple tribute to the awesome ballistic power contained within an anglepoise lamp arm, an old flat-iron and a couple of Bullworker springs. The weapon now lay collapsed and limp across Deborah's lap. She leaned forward painfully doubling herself up over it, and stretching down in front of herself with all her might. Clutching at the turn-ups of Turk's trousers she finally managed to get a hold of his feet and pulled them up onto her lap. Producing some of the telephone cable that had played a prop part in her brilliant portrayal of the telephone engineer (she accepted that the FBI agent had been rather two dimensional, but she was proud of the engineer), Deborah proceeded to tightly secure Sam's feet. This done, she felt a little safer.

'That's evened the score a tad, bud,' she muttered to herself, perhaps a little vindictively. 'Now neither of us can walk.'

Letting Sam's feet fall from her lap, Deborah manoeuvred her chair towards Sam's hands. Of course the carpet rucked itself up under the wheels of her chair and as she struggled to free them, Sam seemed to stir. With a huge effort Deborah got herself into a position whereby she could lean forward and reach Turk's hands. First though, since she wished to tie them behind his back, Deborah had to roll the big body onto its face.

'Why didn't that clutz Geoffrey think to fit a fork-lift onto this thing?' thought Deborah, as she leant over the side of her chair and attempted to heave the unconscious Turk over without toppling herself over, which would of course mean the end of everything.

'You never hear of Jane Fonda, you bastard?' Deborah enquired of the non-comprehending Turk . . . 'It wouldn't hurt to exercise a little, maybe cut down to fifty hamburgers a day.'

Eventually Deborah got the large car maker where she wanted him, with his hands and feet firmly tied, and, what is more, his tied hands tied to his tied feet. Deborah then got herself into position and threw a jug of water at his face.

INTERROGATION

When Sam Turk came round he could be forgiven for being a little surprised, he was in fact positively astonished. The very last thing he remembered was towering menacingly over a helpless girl in a wheelchair, and now, the very next thing, as far as he was concerned, was that he himself was being towered over. He was trussed up like the guest of honour at a sado-masochist ball, and his head appeared to have been used to stop a Network South-East train that was in danger of actually arriving on time.

More to the point, and point being the word, he was staring at the front end of the bolt on what appeared to be some kind of wheelchair-mounted crossbow. 'Don't move,' said Deborah, rather unnecessarily, considering the position that Sam Turk was in.

'Or say a word,' said Deborah, as Sam appeared

to be opening his mouth to speak. In fact he had been trying to breathe properly. In consequence of the years spent wheeling herself around, Deborah had very strong arms, and she had trussed Sam extremely tightly. His shoulders were being pulled back and down, putting a considerable strain on his chest.

Deborah stared at him across the raised arm of the anglepoise, which now served as the bow of the weapon which Geoffrey had so ingeniously designed. She had the wire, which was stretched between the arms of her chair, pulled back tightly against her chest, a short arrow, or bolt, lying gently across the bow, its point fashioned from the thin, shining spike of an electrical screwdriver, the blade of which Toss had filed down to a vicious chisel-like edge.

'Now listen to me, suckhole,' Deborah said very slowly. 'You killed my friend, OK? I know you did, so don't deny it. You killed my friend who, with one twitch of his spastic shoulder, was worth more than every beat your heart ever made. Nothing beat my friend, nothing! At least not till you, you evil little fuck! He overcame everything life ever put in his way, and that was plenty. But he couldn't overcome you, could he? and you know why? 'Cos you're too low, that's why. My friend never looked anywhere but up, and to see a slime like you, you got to look way down low. Now I'm only telling you all this so you need have no doubt that if you don't cooperate with me, I'll kill you without even thinking about it.

I mean it, I don't want anything more than to kill you and I could do it right now. Right now, do you hear! All I have to do is let go of this wire and you're dead! Nobody noticed me come in, nobody would notice me go. I'd be out of here. And I want to do it, Mr Turk, believe me, I really, desperately want to kill you. All I need is an excuse, and you can give me that any time you feel like it.'

'Why don't you then?' asked Sam, painfully.

'Shut the fuck up,' said Deborah, and Sam could see her thumb and forefinger quivering as she held back the bolt. He hoped she did not have sweaty hands. 'I told you not to say anything and I meant it. One more word, just one, unless I say so, and I'll kill you, you understand?'

Sam nodded as best he could from his difficult position.

'Now the reason I'm not killing you straight off is because I ain't a murderer, much as I'd like to be,' Deborah continued. 'Besides which, you have something that belongs to me, and I want it back. I want the designs of the hydrogen engine that Doctor Geoffrey Peason designed. He designed it for me! You understand! For me! I was his fucking inspiration! Have you ever inspired anyone Turk? Maybe to puke up, I guess, that's about the best effect you could hope to have on anyone, to make people sick. But I inspired an engine and I'm taking it back, because you are never going to use it just to put a billion more private cars on the road.'

Even in his prone state Sam felt a vague pleasure that at least there was something about him and his plans that this appalling girl did not know.

'Geoffrey wanted his engine to be part of a new way of doing things and that's exactly what it's going to be.'

Sam did not attempt to answer, he was happy to let Deborah keep talking. They would be discovered at some point and, seeing as how they were at the nerve centre of a huge industrial conglomorate in the middle of a working day, he reckoned it would happen sooner rather than later. Deborah knew this too and so she decided to get to the point.

'OK, this is what you have to do now. You have to give me your key to the executive lift and you have to tell me where the plans to my engine are. You can talk now, but only about the key and the engine.'

Sam Turk could scarcely resist a smile.

'Well, the key is right there on the desk,' he answered, indicating a key card which Deborah recognized as the same as the one which her rude companion in the lift had used . . . 'Use it, kid, get the hell out of here, by the time I get loose you'll be long gone. As to the engine, I'm afraid . . .'

'Let me save us a little time here, Turk, because we're both busy people right?' said Deborah. 'You're about to tell me that the plans ain't here, that they're somewhere else, which would be good news for you because poor old Miss Paraplegic ain't likely to get the rise on you a second time. Well, I have to tell you that I doubt that those plans are elsewhere, because I can't think of a more logical place for Sam Turk's magical new Global engine to be than in Sam Turk's office at the Global building.' Deborah was, of course, unaware that Sam did not see Geoffrey's plans as the new Global engine at all. 'Now you had better hope I'm right, Mr Turk, because either I get the plans in my hands in the next five minutes or I'm going to kill you.'

'Ah now, come on, kid . . .' Sam began to protest, but Deborah was not in a listening mood.

'I told you not to speak unless I said,' she hissed. 'One more word, just one, and the negotiations end with a bolt in your neck and I'm outta here. You ain't the only one with a stomach for murder, Turk. Now listen, this is my one chance, OK? My one chance to get back my property and to revenge my friend, right? Well believe me, if I can't do the first I will sure as hell do the second. So bite on this.'

Deborah accompanied this by leaning across her bow and, with the hand that was not holding back the bolt, flinging a scarf over Sam's head. 'Go on, I said bite on it, suck it into your puss and bite it!'

Sam had no choice but to work the scarf into his mouth as best he could without the use of his hands.

'Go on, all of it!' Deborah commanded. 'Get it in your mouth, the whole damn scarf. Do it, bastard.'

Sam sucked in the cloth until it filled his cheeks and he began to gag. He did not mind, he certainly was not going to be able to tell this stupid girl where the plans were with a scarf in his mouth.

'You biting it, Turk?' demanded Deborah. Sam nodded. 'Biting it hard?' again he nodded. 'Good,' she said and let go of the wire.

The bolt buried itself deep into the fleshy part of Sam's thigh, it was not a terribly serious wound but it was a painful and bloody one. Sam's head swam, he wanted to cry out with the shock and the pain. But of course he could not, now he understood why Deborah had made him stuff the scarf. Deborah drew the shaft of a second arrow back towards her chest.

'You want to know something, Turk?' she said, 'I wish I was in your position, I really do, because you may be hurting in your leg, but at least you can feel something. If that was me, I wouldn't feel a thing. Do you know why that is, you little scheister? You disgrace to the American flag! I'll tell you. My legs can't feel because the brakes on the Global Moritz were of the absolute minimal standard that you people could get away with at the time. Global could have fitted better brakes, but they didn't, and that's why I can't walk, and why I wouldn't feel no arrow in my leg. Now, I shot you, Turk, so that you know how serious I am. It was a hard lesson, but I guessed you have a pretty thick skin, also I am only giving you one warning so I wanted to make it good. The next arrow, you get in the face. OK, this is what happens now. I'm going to pull the cloth out of your mouth, and you ain't going to scream and you ain't going to shout. If you do, in that moment, you're dead, OK, just like my friend, you're dead, and I'm gone. The only sound you are going to make is to tell me where the plans are, and if you even hint that they ain't here, I'll kill you instantly. No further discussion, no negotiations of any kind, if they really ain't here then I lose, but you lose worse. OK, here goes.'

Keeping a firm grip on the shaft of her arrow, Deborah leant forward and, taking hold of a protruding corner of the cloth, gently pulled it out of Sam's mouth. Sam was a gambling man, but he was not foolish or impetuous. He weighed the odds of a situation carefully. In this circumstance he knew that there was a chance that if he called Deborah's bluff she would not kill him, but he could see from the bloody mess on his trousers that there was a real possibility that she would. There was also, of course, the possibility that if he gave in to her demands and gave her the plans, she would still kill him, but he didn't think so. Sam knew that his best bet was to gain more time. Deborah's position of power could not last forever, the odds would have to change soon, he had to humour her until then.

'In the safe,' he whispered. 'Seven-nine-two-zero-four – twice.'

Chapter Twenty-Six

THE SHIFTING BALANCE OF POWER

THE ODDS CHANGE

Very carefully, and keeping the bound Sam in her sights the whole time, Deborah slowly reversed her chair towards the wall with the safe in it. This was a complicated process, she only had one arm for motivation, she required the other to keep tight the bolt which she was training on Sam. This meant that, to avoid simply going around in circles, Deborah was forced to continuously change hands, performing tiny arcs and thus slowly backing away.

Eventually she arrived beneath the safe. Fortunately it was set low in the wall and, reaching up, Deborah was able to shift the dial, her eyes flicking upwards to the dial and back to the prostrate Sam between each number. Click, click, click, seven-nine-two-zero-four-seven-nine-two-zero . . .'

'I got one more number Turk, if the door of this safe don't swing open, I shoot you immediately,' said Deborah. Sam nodded to show that he understood.

'Four!' The door clicked open and swung forward upon its beautiful German-made hinges. Deborah almost dropped her arrow in relief. She couldn't think what she had been expecting, some sort of booby trap perhaps, but Global Motors was a respectable business, they did not have exploding safes.

Without taking her eyes off Sam, Deborah's hand groped upwards and backwards into the safe. She could feel a sheaf of papers tied up with string. Taking a firm grip on them she dragged them out over her head and down into her lap. Reaching backwards again she discovered a couple of larger rolled up sheets, these too she awkwardly dragged out. One glance at the top page of the sheet was enough to convince her that she had struck gold, *'Notes on the Principles of Hydrogen-Powered Internal Combustion* by . . .' and the name was crudely Tippexed out. 'Not even his name remains huh?' said Deborah wheeling back towards Turk. Sam tensed, why the hell had nobody disturbed them yet? What did he pay these people for? Actually, it was not so strange, it had in fact been less than fifteen minutes since Deborah had first appeared and a combination of Sam's enigmatically forestalled intercom messages to Miss Hodges, plus the sign that Deborah had put on the door had so far dissuaded everybody from risking Sam's famous wrath by disturbing him. Sam wondered what his chances would be if, bound as he was, he attempted to roll towards Deborah's chair and topple her. Deborah read the fear on his face.

'Don't worry, I ain't going to kill you, less you make me,' she assured him. 'Just you nuzzle down to the piece of cloth on the floor there and suck it back into your mouth, OK?'

Sam did as he was instructed as Deborah tortuously rolled her way back towards him, employing the same alternative thrust method that she had used to get to the safe. When her chair again stood in front of Sam, who now cut a pretty pathetic figure, bleeding and sweating and with his cheeks stuffed with cloth, Deborah produced some heavy-duty insulation tape from her prop tool-bag. Fumbling it open with one hand and her teeth, a rather difficult thing to do, she leant forward to Sam for the final time and firmly taped up his mouth.

Finally she relaxed her hold on the arrow.

'I'm going now, Mr Turk,' she said, taking up his lift key from the desk, 'and let me tell you that by tomorrow there will be a copy of my engine in the post to every environmental group in the country. Whoever makes this engine is going to consider the Earth first and profit second. I've won, you murdering schmuck.'

But Sam could not hear her, the birds were singing too loudly in his aching brain for Deborah's voice to penetrate, for behind Deborah the door had quietly opened and through it had come the one man who could ignore Sam's 'do not disturb' signs without risking the sack, Deborah's recent lift companion, Bruce Tungsten.

CONFLICTING PLANS

Bruce strode quickly up behind Deborah and grabbed at the anglepoise arm, wrenching one end out of its clip on the arm of Deborah's chair and bending it right back, breaking the hinge on the other arm from which had been launched the first blow against Turk.

'OK, little lady,' said Bruce, grabbing Geoffrey's plans from her lap. 'Keep your hands on the arms of your chair where I can see them, don't you move them now. By the look of things around here you're a mite too resourceful for my liking.' Bruce had a pistol. Even in his state of blissful relief at being rescued in the nick of time by his co-conspirator, Sam Turk could not help wondering why Bruce had brought along a pistol.

'Well, well, well, Sam,' said Bruce, jovially, whilst none too gently pulling the tape from his mouth and allowing Sam to spit out the cloth. 'This one's going to be a barrel of laughs to tell the boys down in the locker-room. The day ol' Sam Turk got trussed up and seriously wounded by a young girl in a wheelchair.' The girl under question moved her hands slightly, she wanted to spread her knees apart and the only way she could do this was to haul them apart with her hands.

'I said keep your hands exactly still, Miss,' said Bruce waving his gun at her. 'My old pal Sam here is a very tough guy indeed, in fact he's one of the meanest men I know, and yet you got the better of him. That makes you a very formidable woman as far as I'm concerned, so just keep yourself real still OK? Or I shall be forced to tie you up like you did to Sam here.'

'Speaking of which,' grunted Sam, who it must be remembered was still lying bleeding on the floor with his arms and legs pulled backwards and bound behind him. 'For God's sake get me out of this before I bleed to death.'

Bruce ignored Sam's plea, instead he placed a little doll on top of Sam's desk.

'I have to thank you, Miss, whoever you are,' he said. 'Personally I was scared to confront old Sam here myself, I was fearful he'd get the better of me. That's why I've spent two and a half hours going to every top man in this building enquiring, hoping that one of them might have a clue as to the whereabouts of our new miracle engine. Of course it wasn't any use, none of our senior management were aware that we even had a new miracle engine. Kind of selfish of you to keep it to yourself Sam, considering it represents the entire future of our industry.'

'You can't double-cross me you bastard,' said Sam. But, of course, seeing as how he was saying it whilst trussed up and stuck to the floor with his own blood, it was palpably obvious that Bruce could do just about what he wanted. Sam changed his tack.

'Fifty-five billion bucks, Bruce,' he pleaded. 'You are holding fifty-five billion bucks in your hand, that's what the oil people will pay! You can't throw that kind of bread away just to make cars!'

Deborah could not believe her ears, the duplicity of it astonished her.

'You mean you weren't even going to make it!' she gasped. 'You were going to sell my engine to the oil people so they could put it in the trash!'

'He was, I wasn't, and keep your hands where they are!' said Bruce, noticing that yet again Deborah's hands were straying towards her knees. 'You damned idiot, Sam, did you really think I was going to let the greatest engineering breakthrough in a century just disappear? I'm a car man for God's sake, I make cars. These plans go back with me to the USA, tonight. Lord almighty man, do you have no vision at all? No soul? I'd rather be a multi-millionaire national hero than a multi-billionaire nobody, schmuck. I'm disappointed in you Sam. You need something to help you get motivated. Keep my doll, it was good for me . . . Sam Turk,' he said loudly and clapped his hands. The Doll began to laugh. It was still laughing when the windows crashed open and three masked figures in combat fatigues, balaclava helmets and carrying machine guns sailed in as if from nowhere. One knocked the pistol from Bruce's grasp, another threw him to the floor, while the third covered the room. Deborah they ignored, and she used the opportunity to haul apart her knees to the sides of her chair.

MULTI NATIONAL ETIQUETTE

Along the corridor, in Miss Hodges' office, some of the younger girls wondered whether they should go and investigate what the noise was.

'Absolutely not,' replied Miss Hodges. She had only a few minutes before been instructed specifically by Bruce Tungsten himself, the President of the entire international group, to leave him and Turk absolutely alone.

'Gentlemen from the American mid-west often conduct business by smashing things,' she assured the nervous girls. 'I believe it's hormonal, like stags rutting and parallel walking. They must be left to get on with it or else they might take it out on their wives when they get home.'

FOUR PARTY DISCUSSION GROUP

Inside Sam's office the balance of power had changed radically again. The chief terrorist was speaking.

'So it looks like you done half our job for us,' he said, nodding towards the prostrate Sam. 'The general wants you alive, which is bad news for you my friend, let me tell you. I don't know what you done to make him mad, but he's sure mad. You are luckier,' he said, turning to Bruce. 'You we will kill now, and the secretary.' For the first time he acknowledged Deborah. 'It is very convenient of you to be here Mr Tungsten, we did not expect to see you here at all. We thought we'd have to go to Detroit to kill you. OK, give me the plans and we'll make it quick huh?'

Bruce's mind was racing, but unfortunately he could not think of anything clever. 'Come on, come on,' said the terrorist. 'I can shoot you then take them if I like, but I don't want to get them all bloody.'

Still Bruce hesitated, his burning passion to get the better of Hirohato urging him to do anything to save those plans, throw them out of the window, try to swallow them, anything. His own life meant nothing, but he had to save the engine and pay Hirohato back for that doll. Then Deborah spoke.

'Just toss the plans over to me, pal,' she said. 'I'm a fellow American, you can trust me.'

'Shut up!' snapped the terrorist. Then, turning back to Bruce, he said, 'Give me the plans.'

'C'mon bud, you've got nothing to lose,' said Deborah quietly. 'I can get them out, somehow the thing'll get made. Trust me, I got special skills, I can do it, better I have them than him. C'mon.'

Not really knowing why, Bruce turned and tossed

the plans to Deborah. She caught them and the terrorist shot Bruce, although fortunately, because the terrorist was also turning to look at Deborah, Bruce was only winged. The other two terrorists were already moving towards Deborah to retrieve the plans. It was then that the whole room received an enormous shock, for a sheet of flame suddenly burst forth from between Deborah's legs engulfing both men in a inferno, just below the knees. Instantly their trousers were alight and both fell to the floor beating at their burning legs. Deborah revolved her chair. Suddenly she was facing an astonished and terrified terrorist chief. Again fire bounded forth from under her. Now there were three men writhing around beating their legs and searching for a vase of flowers.

'So long,' said Deborah, and wheeling her chair round, she smashed through the door.

DECISION TO DISTURB

Down the corridor Miss Hodges was on the horns of a dilemma.

'It sounds like they're shooting at each other now,' one of the girls had said.

'Must be having an awful row,' another added.

Miss Hodges was inwardly furious, she had never warmed to Sam Turk's manners since the day he had first arrived at Swiss Cottage promising people, for some reason known only to himself, that he intended to kick their bottoms. Fortunately, in Miss Hodges' case, at least he had never carried out this threat but breaking windows and conducting shoot-outs during office hours was nearly as bad. It was such a terribly poor example to the younger girls.

She pressed the intercom connecting her to Sam's office, but there was no reply. 'Wait here,' she instructed the wide-eyed under secretaries. 'I shall enquire if they require coffee.'

Deborah was waiting by the executive lift when Miss Hodges rushed past her and into Sam's office. There she discovered a scene straight out of Dante's *Inferno*. Both the President of the company and the Chief Executive of the UK division lay wounded on the floor, one bound, and three militaristic, Middle Eastern looking gentlemen were writhing about the place desperately trying to put their trousers out.

'Mr Turk!' said Miss Hodges. 'Installing a bas-ketball net and a golf putter in your office is one thing, but sado-masochistic orgies is quite another. I resign.'

'The girl! The girl in the wheelchair,' shouted Turk. 'For Christsake stop her!' Miss Hodges was a highly professional woman and knew full well that Sam was entitled to a month's notice of her departure. She remained therefore his senior perso-nal assistant. Turning on her heels she rushed back into the corridor. The girl in the chair was still there, but she would not be for long. Ping! The executive lift arrived. The girl slipped a key card into the slot and the doors opened, but not before Miss Hodges had bounded down the corridor and grabbed the handles of Deborah's chair to prevent her rolling into the lift.

It was then that Miss Hodges received the shock of her life, quite literally, for Geoffrey's ghostly hand was still hovering over the woman he loved, and if there is a heaven, still loved. Deborah's hand dropped to a little switch that Geoffrey had installed, and sent the entire contents of the traffic-light battery shooting up poor Miss Hodges' arms. She wasn't standing in a puddle and it wouldn't have been a strong enough charge to do her any harm even if she had. However, it was enough to make her leap backwards in fear and surprise, and at that time Deborah disappeared into the lift and pressed ground floor.

Chapter Twenty-Seven

GETAWAY

A GENUINE HAZARD

Toss was extremely glad to see Deborah emerge from the Global building (again she had had to enlist help to cope with the sticky door). Toss liked to think that he was only pleased because Deborah was still alive, but he could not deny that he was almost equally relieved that his period of guarding the car was over too. Three hours trying to look like you're booking the same car would have tested the histrionic powers of Sir Henry Irving.

None the less, it had been worth it. The getaway car was still in place and Deborah and Toss's departure was unobstructed. If Deborah had emerged a few minutes before it would have been a disaster. Toss had left his post for a moment in order to stroll up the ramp to the door of the Global building to see if he could sort of will Deborah along by meeting her half-way. When he returned, after what he considered to be a matter of seconds, busy shoppers had parked their cars to either side of Deborah's and a third had actually boxed it in. The reason that the three drivers had felt justified in this outrageous bit of attrition parking was that they had all *put their hazard lights on*.

The invention of the hazard light is one of the few genuine changes which have been introduced to cars since Benz and Daimler first realized that the explosion of volatile liquid vapours inside a piston cylinder attached to a gear system and a drive shaft, would be a wonderful way of sitting in a traffic jam. Hazard lights are, as the name suggests, a hazard. They provide certain drivers with such a combined sense of inner peace and moral justification for their actions that a casual observer might presume Jesus Christ was at the wheel.

Some people think that hazard lights excuse *anything*. If you want to stop in the middle of an urban clearway to pick up six kids and an antique kitchen dresser, no problem, bung on your hazards, that will make it all OK. Contemplating a U turn across a dual carriageway, but worried it might be a little dangerous? Not if you have four orange lights blinking simultaneously at the corners of your car, that will provide you and other road users with all the security and protection required.

There are some drivers who genuinely believe that there is no manoeuvre, no matter how dangerous, that having both indicators on at the same time will not justify. Parking on top of a bus queue, driving into the reading room of a public library, the day is surely coming when bank robbers will plead in mitigation that the getaway car had its hazards on.

Toss had given all three offending cars tickets, an action which genuinely outraged the drivers when they returned, it simply was not fair to give them tickets, they had not been gone long, besides which *they had had their hazards on*.

Anyway, by the time Deborah emerged from the Global building, the way was once again clear.

'Yo, girl, what's happening?' enquired Toss as Deborah rolled down the ramp towards him. 'So you managed to persuade him not to blow your head off then?'

'I've got it,' screamed Deborah, 'I've got it! I've got it!' She shouted, waving the plans around.

'Wicked,' said Toss, opening the driver's door for her. 'But Debbo, please try to be cool, I have a reputation in this town. Hysterical women screaming that they have "got it" at me could be misconstrued.'

'I can't believe it,' bubbled Deborah hurrying to shift herself from the chair to the driving seat. 'I went in there and I knocked Sam Turk to the ground, tied him up and tortured him until he told me where Geoffrey's plans were.'

'Cor,' said Toss, momentarily so impressed that he forgot to say anything cool. 'That's right, and I took out three guys with my flame-thrower,' Deborah continued as she leant sideways out of the car, folded up her chair and tucked it in behind her.

'Totally happening, girl,' said Toss. 'SAS-ville,' he added. Toss had regained his composure because he no longer believed a word Deborah was saying.

'Get in the car, Toss. We are on a mission to unchain the highways and byways of the world.'

As Toss got into the passenger seat a car drew up behind them. It was a big, left-hand drive, American Global, a Supreme Class Over-Cruiser.

'Here, do you think I've got time to book that flash bastard?' enquired Toss.

'I don't think so,' said Deborah, her expression suddenly changing from exuberance to fear. 'We have to move.'

Sam Turk, limping hugely, but very much on his feet, had just barged through the swing-doors, he was carrying Bruce's pistol. Sam had cut an alarming figure rushing through the building, having been untied by a deeply disturbed Miss Hodges. There was a huge blood stain on his trousers and the side of his head was swollen up like a rugby ball, the shape of the flat-iron being still clearly visible. However, when one is watching fifty-five billion dollars disappear over the horizon, it is a finicky man indeed who gives much thought to sartorial matters. Sam didn't, and his appearance would have shocked a Vietnam Vet. It certainly scared Toss.

'Girl, I dunno what you done to that geezer, but he looks well agitated. Let's scarper right now, 'cos

I don't want to meet him, girl, no way.'

'Me neither, Toss. We'd better hope his driver doesn't know London,' replied Deborah, and with that she twisted the hand accelerator and beeping wildly barged into the traffic. Looking over his shoulder Toss could see Turk running as fast as his wounded leg would allow him towards his limmo.

MOVIE CHASE

Our entire lives are dominated by fantasy, every time we turn on the TV a deceit of one sort or another is perpetrated upon us. Mostly we recognize them as deceits and they do no real harm. We understand for instance that the 'serving suggestion' on the front of a box containing frozen food is a sort of culinary version of the picture of Dorian Gray in reverse. The more aged, putrid and dissolute the food inside is, the brighter, shinier and more delicious the picture on the box will appear. Interestingly, the 'serving suggestion' deceit was originally devised by the press office of the Kremlin prior to Gorbachev's presidency. The more utterly dead the leader became and the more his face seemed to resemble a de-frosted lasagne, the brighter and more luminous became his official portrait.

The serving suggestion trick is a fair, innocent deceit. If popping a sprig of parsley behind Brezhnev's ear made him look slightly more alive on the podium in Red Square, at least it gave the KGB something to laugh at. However, some media deceits are more dangerous, and the mournful mortality rate amongst teenage joy-riders suggests that the movie car chase is one of them.

The movie car chase is second only to back-seat shagging as the greatest car myth of all. Car chases in movies are like sex in movies, they seem to go on for ever, continually jump cutting from one completely impossible position to another and apparently involving no personal risk whatsoever.

All week people sit in traffic jams. Sometimes, on a Friday night, they go to the movies, on the way they sit in more traffic jams, they miss the first part of the movie because they can't find a parking place. Then they sit in a dark cinema and watch a man drive a car through rush-hour traffic, clear across a city at eighty miles an hour. If the man had turned into a six-foot banana we would say it was a stupid movie, but a man driving a car through a crowded city at eighty miles an hour we not only accept but remark to each other how brilliantly done the car chases were.

Nothing can stop the hero in his car. If he meets another car, he drives round it, or maybe over it, or just possibly through it. He goes on the pavement, he crosses into opposing traffic lanes, he hurtles down empty alleyways. His car can jump, his car can roll over, it is more like a performing dog than a ton and a half of lifeless metal. If you offered it a biscuit it would probably sit up and beg.

The fact that this display bears as much resemblance to driving as the lasagne of Dorian Gray does to food, is irrelevant. The fact that it was shot at 5.30 a.m. on four successive Sunday mornings, means nothing. The fact that if you actually tried any of that stuff for real you would not get twenty yards before ploughing into a bus queue and killing thirty innocent pedestrians, is not a part of the equation. The fact that Moses may have been able to part the Red Sea but he could not do more than ten miles an hour in London, doesn't matter. Movie car chases remind us of how much we love cars.

When the movie is over, everybody goes and sits in a jam again.

REAL CHASE

Deborah and Toss were stuck in traffic on the Finchley Road; about thirty cars behind, Sam and his driver were also stuck.

'He had a gun,' said Toss nervously.

'I should have killed him when I had the chance,' said Deborah, causing Toss to look at his friend in a new light. A nervous silence descended. Finally Toss said 'I can't believe this traffic.'

It is a strange thing that, despite the fact that the traffic jam has become an absolute fact of modern existence, people still say 'I can't believe this traffic' whenever they find themselves in one, which is all the time. The reason for this is probably because, every now and then, very occasionally, one has a decent journey and actually gets lucky with the traffic. These journeys then exist in our memories like childhood summers in which the sun always seems to be shining. The fact that it pissed down almost continuously for most people's childhoods is irrelevant, there were wonderful summer days which stand out in our memory for their glorious uniqueness, until eventually they are all that can be recalled, it's the same with jam-free journeys.

'Can't we go any faster?' said Toss.

'Sure, Toss, sure,' snapped Deborah. 'I'll just drive right under this truck in front of us shall I?' Of course, if they had been in a movie she could have done, or perhaps instead, she would have driven through a fruit market, scattering fruit everywhere but curiously injuring no one. Or she could have simply screeched across into the other lane and woven her way forward through the bumper-to-bumper opposing traffic, causing police motor-cyclists to fall off in dramatic slides, then get up and scratch their heads.

Deborah, of course, could do none of those things, she could just sit and edge her way forward like everyone else. Back up the line, Sam Turk was in the same position, and was suffering a terrible car dilemma. Should he jump out and run up the queue on foot, and, if so, would the traffic instantly leap forward at speed, thus allowing Deborah to disappear into the distance? This dilemma is similar to another classic taxi dilemma, that which consumes every taxi passenger at the point at which they enter the last traffic jam of their journey, perhaps only two hundred yards from their destination. The gruesome question is, will the wait be a short one, or a long one? Would it be quicker to sit it out or pay the cabbie off and leg it? Sadly, it has been decreed that the traffic will only leap forward if the passenger leaves the cab. If he stays put, the last hundred and fifty yards will take twenty-five minutes.

'I can't believe this traffic,' said Sam.

Chapter Twenty-Eight

NIGHTMARE

Actually, the traffic was heavy even by London standards, and Toss and Sam were not the only people who could not believe it.

Chief Superintendent Barry Ross was staring at his great big flashing map, the source of so many of his grey hairs, and wondering why God hated him the way he clearly did.

Just two hours before, Ross had been a reasonably contented, if rather sad, policeman. The morning traffic had just about made it in and found somewhere to park, there had been the usual ulcer-growing half hour between eight and eight-thirty when it really did seem to Ross as if it simply would not be possible to squeeze any more cars into London – he felt that way every morning, and somehow the miracle was always achieved.

'They get there in the end, Janine,' he would say wearily to the policewoman who brought him his morning tea. 'Late, furious, double-parked and worrying about their paintwork, but they get there.'

'Yes, Sir,' said Janine.

'Apart from the casualties,' Ross continued, 'they won't get there, no I'm afraid not, they won't get there at all. Not with their mangled limbs and suchlike, and their massive internal bleeding and their being just plain, old-fashioned dead. They won't get to work at all will they? And it's my poor lads as has to scrape them off the bonnets and get their heads out of the steering wheels, what's more.'

'Yes, Sir,' said Janine, feeling a bit sick. She liked Ross, but hated it when he got morbid, which he often did, because years of being the grand orchestrator of London's single most effective killing machine had sucked the happiness out of Ross. He had become grimly familiar with death, he had forgotten the social reserve which most of us apply to the subject. Ross and his wife were seldom invited out to dinner any more because of Ross's unfortunate habit of remarking that the meat course reminded him of something his boys had hosed off the Old Kent Road that morning.

'Natural wastage, Janine, my dear, natural wastage,' Ross mused. 'The toll may be terrible, but it has been decreed acceptable by those who know about these things. We may thank our stars, Janine, that it is not you or I who are called upon to quantify an acceptable death toll. Ours not to reason why, ours but to cut them out of the bodywork.' Ross took a thoughtful cup of tea.

'Do you know that the United States of America loses nearly as many citizens each year on the roads as it lost in the entire Vietnam war?'

Janine did know, because Chief Superintendent Ross often told her this type of fact. She knew the accident frequency on almost every junction in the city, which was why she found it hard to sleep at night. Janine's mother wished that Janine would go and work in a nice flower shop or something.

'Funny that, isn't it?' continued Ross, reflecting on his Vietnam statistic. 'You'd have thought there'd be more fuss.'

'I suppose people don't fuss, Sir, because they think it's worth it,' replied Janine. 'They prefer driving their cars to fighting the Vietnam war.'

'Don't let this job make you hard, Janine,' said Ross, reprovingly. 'Don't let it sap your humanity.'

About nine-thirty Chief Superintendent Ross pulled himself out of his reverie and went for a final ride in the chopper, surveying for the last time the vast mess over which he had presided.

'Quart in a pint bottle,' he murmured to himself, as he often did when contemplating the M4 as it poured cars endlessly into West London.

'Quart in a pint bottle.'

The helicopter flew along the still chock-a-block motorway, with its queues still reaching back towards Heathrow. They followed the near-stationary line of traffic through Hammersmith and

South Kensington and up to Hyde Park Corner, and that was when they saw it. Ross's nightmare, the heart of the gridlock.

'God help us,' whispered Ross.

'You must be joking,' God whispered back.

An articulated lorry containing drums of corrosive liquid had jack-knifed whilst trying to turn into Constitution Hill, somehow it had lost part of its load. A couple of cars had been damaged by falling drums and there was a serious spill steaming and bubbling on the tarmac. The incident was perhaps forty-five seconds old, the driver of the lorry had not even got out of his cab yet, but already cars were backing up.

'Oh please, not today, please,' murmured Ross, but as God had just pointed out, it was too late for prayers. Before his very eyes, Ross could see the traffic pouring into the jam. He watched as the lines feeding back along Park Lane, Knightsbridge and Piccadilly began to freeze. Ross could actually see the movement draining out of the roads beneath.

Ross did not yet know that he had just watched the birth of a gridlock, but he knew that the situation was serious. He grabbed the radio.

'Hyde Park Corner is out, repeat out, minimum four hours. Stranded artic', looks like corrosives.'

Ross needed to give no more instructions, his team had rehearsed their techniques and plans so many times. They had a damage control exercise worked out for every possible crash in London. Ross knew that seconds after he had informed the centre, patrol cars would begin to attempt to divert traffic away from the stricken area, the BBC and commercial stations would be informed and the fire and ambulance services would attempt to pick their way up to the scene of the crash. Ross knew that all these things would be happening, he also knew that it was like putting a sticking plaster on a shotgun wound. This one stupid accident would screw up traffic in London all day, there would be long delays and huge inconvenience, it simply could not be avoided.

'Let's go home and get a cup of tea,' said Ross wearily.

'Nice retirement pressy, eh, Chief?' said the pilot. 'Block on the corner couldn't really be worse could it?' But of course it could, as they would soon find out.

THE HORNS OF A DILEMMA

Down on the ground, in the frozen tentacles of the stricken intersection, countless human dramas were unfurling. Every car contained its degree of frustration, but some burned more agonizingly than others. The bride in the hired Daimler was assured by her father that it would be all right. He was wrong, it wouldn't be, and the embittered groom would later get drunk and, in a foolish attempt to hang his silk wedding boxer shorts on top of the church steeple, would fall and break his neck. Behind the Daimler was a fellow in a BMW who was rushing to meet a very important foreign client at Heathrow. His failure to do so put a black mark on his career ('You should have set off earlier.') which led him three years later to drive that same BMW off Beachy Head. Nearby across the countless smaller problems was a Mini in which was contained a beating heart, a beating heart that a small child lay waiting for in Great Ormond Street Hospital. That heart was destined to beat its last right there at the throbbing epicentre of the gridlock. Beeping its horn at the Mini with the heart, was an Escort van containing a plumber on his way to deal with a burst that would now sadly destroy the entire lifetime's possessions of an elderly widow. Behind the Escort, also beeping its horn, was a Mercedes containing three robbers who had just done a jewellery store near Harrods.

People's jobs, people's health, people's love affairs, people's futures were frozen in the traffic, and a great lament rose above the smoke and the growling engines, wailing in sorrow for the losses of the day. It was the hooters' chorus. In the British driving test one is informed quite clearly what the car hooter is there for, it is there to inform other road users of your presence. Well if that was what people were using their horn for around Hyde Park corner on the day of the gridlock, then they were wasting their time, everybody already knew everybody else was there, that was why no one could get anywhere. The truth is, of course, that, in the drama of the moment, people were forgetting the Highway Code and were not using their horns to say 'I am here' but were using them to say '*Why* am I here?'

Horns serve no practical purpose: they are there to alleviate personal frustration and to insult and annoy other road users. Their only real use, the one defined in the driving test as 'announcing your presence', is rendered completely useless by the fact that they are used so often to say 'fuck off' that that is the only message which other people hear. Horns are like alarm bells: one hears so many of them that it never crosses anyone's mind to take any notice of them.

DREADFUL COINCIDENCE

When Chief Superintendent Ross arrived back at his command centre, Janine had a cup of tea ready for him.

'This is an unexpected treat, Janine,' said Ross. 'You don't normally bring me a second cup until elevenses. Is this a retirement present?'

'Oh no, Sir, that's later, we've had a whip-round . . .' Janine stopped short, Gloria was glaring at her. Gloria was the girl in traffic control with the 'You don't have to be mad to work here but it helps' sticker on her computer. She had organized a presentation for later and was anxious that Janine should not give it away.

'No, sir,' continued Janine, 'I just thought you might need a pick-me-up. There's a huge bomb scare at Holborn Circus, Sir.'

'Oh dear,' said Ross, trying to disguise how deeply shaken he was. This was another classic accident scenario location, a major junction right in the financial district. 'I suppose traffic's backing up over the river?'

'It's got as far south as Lambeth, Sir, and it's spreading back west, down the river to Waterloo.'

Ross sipped his tea.

'Have you sugared this, Janine?' he enquired.

'Oh yes, Sir, three as usual,' she replied.

'Funny,' said Ross, 'it tastes bitter.' And well it might, for Ross knew that with the Corner and Holborn Circus blocked out, there would be paralysis through the West End to the City. What a way to leave. 'You heard about old Barry,' they would say in years to come. 'London's top traffic man couldn't even get home on his last day.' Ross gripped his mug tightly, deliberately allowing it to burn his hand a little so that his whirling senses might have something to fix upon. Janine was still standing before him. He looked at her enquiringly.

'Is there something else, Janine?' he enquired.

'Yes,' she said, in a nervous squeak. 'A load of ball-bearings has come off a French lorry at the top of the Marylebone Road underpass, and a tall coach has got itself wedged at Blackwall, and . . .'

Ross raised his hand to silence Janine. He gently put down his teacup and went over to the big flashing board, the board which had been his ball and chain for so many years, and was now his executioner. The big board was flashing away like a panic full of perverts.

'Well?' he asked.

'We're trying to contain it, Sir,' said a sergeant. 'It's just there's so much traffic feeding in we can't cut it all off and so the crisis area keeps expanding.' Ross could actually watch the jam grow as new light trails snaked across the map. 'Our cars are getting blocked in as we try to turn traffic away,' the sergeant continued. 'I'm afraid this one's really come to life, Sir.'

'Four crucially positioned accidents inside an hour,' said Ross. 'There is no God.'

And God replied, 'Not in peak traffic there ain't, mate.'

THE SHIVERING SNAKE

It was exactly an hour later that Deborah and Toss began their getaway. Central London was completely paralysed. Every escape route ended in a jam and hence became a jam itself. From the moment Ross understood the extent of his ill fortune in being presented with four crucials in one morning, he could have taken a pencil and a London streetfinder and charted the inevitable growth of the super-jam across the entire length and breadth of London. In fact, this is exactly what he did. It was a pointless exercise of course, rather like the captured Christians of Ancient Rome drawing up a detailed rota as to the order in which they would be fed to the lions, but there was little else for Ross to do. The puny defence and control initiatives which he had planned for circumstances such as these, were all in place, his officers stood bravely on the expanding edges of the grid vainly attempting to staunch the never ending feast of cars that flowed in to feed the monster's insatiable appetite, and there was nothing Ross himself could do. All morning he sat at his desk fiddling with his coloured pencils, mapping out the growth of his nightmare, struggling feebly to keep his predictions ahead of the terrible reality outside.

'Dean Street and Old Compton should be solid within the next five minutes,' he would shout to people who already knew. 'That means Soho is completely locked now.'

Then Ross would relapse into silence for a while, before shouting, 'I imagine Baker Street will be stationary by now, that means that Hyde Park and the Marylebone Road jams have officially linked.'

Perhaps the process of charting the uncontrollable gave Ross the vaguest feeling of having some control over it. If it did he was kidding himself, traffic flow has a life of its own. Occasionally Ross would attempt a positive suggestion of some sort, just for the sake of form.

'The Regent's Park ring road will be solid by now. Eventually people will take to the grass, phone the park authority to tell them to put guards on the flower-beds and warn the Zoo, maybe they could put cotton wool in the animals' ears or something.'

Ross was right, out on the streets (and on the grass) the rules were getting stretched. It takes quite a lot of provocation for most people to start breaking laws, but some cars had already been stuck for nearly two hours, and that is quite a lot of provocation.

It starts with a collectively shared paranoia that one is in the wrong lane, that the outside lane, or the inside lane, is moving whilst one's own lane is not. So, out goes an arm and a car attempts to switch lanes. Instantly the paranoias of a hundred other motorists are confirmed. 'So the other lane *is* moving faster,' and a hundred arms go out and the traffic, which is scarcely moving forward at all, attempts to make up for this by executing a pointless series of edging, bobs, slides and weaves, virtually on the spot. The effect, from the police helicopters above the turmoil, is that of a long, still, snake, shivering in its sleep.

TO BE YOUNG AND FREE

The fruitlessness of the lane shiver, combined with the gut-wrenching tension of trying to physically drive through a taxi without scratching your paintwork, leads some of the more impetuous souls to delude themselves that the problem can be solved by more direct action.

These poor dupes, suckled on a diet of motoring images of freedom and individual triumph, convinced by generations of car makers, oil men and politicians that the car is the ultimate symbol of individual liberty and self-expression, simply cannot believe that the car is also a terrible trap. A trap which, far from confirming the individual's splendid isolation and independence, condemns the individual to a dronelike conformity of movement, or, as is increasingly the case, paralysis. Far from celebrating the freedom of the individual, more and more the private car is becoming the ultimate leveller, reducing us all to a dull conformity – identically frustrated, identically furious, identically stuck.

This hard truth is of course too much to bear for all the young Steve McQueens fuming in the jam. In their anger they decide to fight back. Surely that is what being a free individual is all about? Struggling for one's rights against impossible odds. Suddenly and completely irrationally they say, 'OK, fuck this, I'm getting out,' and with a satisfying roaring of gears drive straight up a cul-de-sac, or else, perceiving a modicum of movement in the oncoming traffic, start trying to force their way into it by attempting to execute an impossible three-point turn, thus bringing the opposite lane to a standstill as well.

KNOCK-ON EFFECTS

Back at the control centre, Ross was fielding endless furious calls from the emergency services, who were, of course, completely unable to service emergencies. Fires were left burning out of control, the ill and injured were left to die, there was even the beginnings of some looting as enterprising souls realized that the police were having to respond to calls on foot, and anyway they were completely tied up dealing with half a million purple-faced motorists. There were calls from big businesses and financial institutions, desperately enquiring when the paralysis would lift as commerce was impossible under these conditions. Eventually there came a call from the Prime Minister's Office.

'What the hell is going on, Ross?' shouted Ingmar Bresslaw. 'The damned city's ground to a halt. The Prime Minister's trying to conduct Question Time and only six government MPs have managed to get to work! The only way we got the PM in was by police helicopter . . .'

'Yes, Mr Bresslaw . . .' attempted Ross.

'The other lot have got a hundred of their people in because half of them came by tube. The smug bastards are having a lovely time,' exclaimed a furious Bresslaw. 'Do you realize that the Prime Minister is outnumbered by a hundred to seven because of you. The opposition are desperately trying to introduce crapulent Private Member's Bills while they've got a majority. Fortunately, the Speaker's stuck on Waterloo Bridge.'

'Because of me, Mr Bresslaw?' protested Ross, who had spent years issuing fruitless warnings concerning exactly what had come to pass.

'Yes you, you clueless, clod-hopping PC Plod, damn you!' Ingmar seemed incandescent with rage. 'You're the top traffic cop. God knows what the Frogs and the Krauts will make of our efforts to be capital of Europe now. I just hope you have no aspirations to an honour Ross, because let me tell you, after this you're going to be lucky to keep your pension.'

Ingmar slammed down the phone. His voice had been filled with fury and frustration. Strangely though, as he sipped his whisky Ingmar's bloodshot old eyes were smiling.

Ross also put down the phone and looked again at his big map, the lights of which were now creeping up around Swiss Cottage and West Hampstead.

Chapter Twenty-Nine

IN A VERY SERIOUS JAM

For the previous five minutes or so, Deborah's little car had at least been vaguely edging forward. Toss knew this because the empty litter-bin completely surrounded by hamburger wrappers, kindly offered to the people of the Finchley Road by McDonald's, had moved from the front of the car to the back. Now, however, they had stopped completely. Both were painfully aware of the enormous danger behind them. Theirs was one of the more horrendous human dramas being played out in the gridlock that day.

'Try up towards Hampstead,' suggested Toss.

They were positioned opposite an open-right turn which the courteous driver in the other lane had left clear. The turn headed up Frognal a long, steep, quiet residential hill that pushed up from the Finchley Road to Fitzjohn's Avenue. 'It will take that Turk bloke ages to get up to the turn, girl. We'll

404

be outa here,' he added, warming to his subject. 'We'll be dust, we'll be a memory, history baby. Don't look for us, girl, because we'll be long gone.'

'Don't call me baby, Toss,' said Deborah, 'not now, not ever.'

'It was a general expression, girl,' answered Toss.

'Oh yeah, well, I only see me and you in the car, Toss, and I ain't nobody's baby.'

Deborah was still feeling rather gung-ho after her extraordinary triumphs in Sam's office. This, combined with being completely terrified and stuck in a traffic jam, was making her rather prickly.

'Hang the left, girl,' admonished Toss. 'We have one chance, let's take it.'

But sadly there are no chances in a gridlock, no opportunities for individual initiative, no way to get lucky and beat the system. Deborah and Toss soon found that they were not alone. The first thing people do when faced with a block in the main arteries is to branch out into the rat-runs, the quiet residential streets, thus clogging up local traffic too. Within moments the road into which they had turned was hopelessly clogged, cars following Deborah in, cars appearing in front from other side streets.

'Oh for God's sake!' screamed Deborah, hammering her horn. 'We have to get away!'

She beeped, the people in front beeped, the people behind beeped, but not an inch did any of them move.

'Debbo,' said Toss, 'I think we have to do a runner.'

Deborah and Toss were about to do something that would be almost unique in that whole long desperate day. They were going to abandon their car. This is something that people find extremely difficult to do, understandably. Cars are very expensive items and most of them are only a quarter paid for. You can't just leave your most precious bit of property hanging about in the middle of the street. You have to stay with it, protect it through its time of trial. During a traffic jam the car owner is completely disabled, he cannot walk, he is incapable of movement. As the incidence of jams grows around the developed world, more and more people are choosing to voluntarily disable themselves for many hours each week, preferring to sacrifice the use of the very legs God gave them in exchange for the illusion of carefree mobility.

MEAN WHEELS

Deborah's wheels were some of the few still rolling in London by lunch-time that day. With a considerable wrench, for as has been said, one does not abandon a car lightly, Deborah agreed with Toss that they should try to get up the hill towards Hampstead tube station.

'That geezer was real angry, right?' said Toss. 'It ain't going to take him forever to realize that he can leave his driver guy, right? Stroll up the jam, stick his gun through our window and do us in without anyone being any the wiser, right? He could do that, and I reckon he will.'

It was a persuasive argument.

'Also, I reckon if we go now, we might lose him before he gets parallel with the turn.'

They were fortunate, Deborah wrestled her wheelchair out from its position in the car while Toss stood around authoritatively, his uniform lending their actions legitimacy.

'Just popping to the lav, guys,' he shouted as people began to realize that a driverless car was about to be left in their path. Deborah got into her chair and they were off.

'Yeeha! Hi Ho Silver, away!' shouted Toss as he began pushing Deborah up the hill. They must have travelled a good hundred yards and Toss was beginning to puff when Deborah shouted for him to stop.

'We've forgotten Geoffrey's fucking plans!!' she screamed.

'Wicked girl, that's the kind of choice detail that makes the story worth telling in years to come,' observed Toss. 'Bung your brake on.'

Toss left Deborah where she was and tore back down the hill towards her abandoned car. Reaching in, he grabbed up the bundle of plans and was about to rush off again when a large fellow got out of the van that was positioned behind Deborah's car.

'Oi,' he shouted threateningly, grabbing Toss's arm, the frustration of his wrecked day fuelling his anger. 'What's the game leaving this motor then? When the traffic moves I'm sodding stuck ain't I?' Of course, the man was stuck anyway because he was in the middle of the biggest jam in history, but he wasn't to know that.

'So what's going on then, eh?' he enquired menacingly.

One or two other drivers wanted to know the same thing, and, leaving their cars, they surrounded Toss.

'I got no chance of picking up a fare with this bird's motor in my way, have I?' enquired an irate cabby, rhetorically.

'She really can't just leave her car there, and I don't care if she is disabled, I take medication myself,' said a plummy-voiced Hampstead woman, getting out of her convertible gold Mercedes. 'My husband is a Justice of the Peace,' she added.

'What is the game?' said the original van driver, fingering a nasty looking spanner.

Toss was hemmed in by aggression. He reacted magnificently, hitting back with all the authority his little peaked cap imbued him with.

'Bald tyre, guy, that is what the game is, bald tyre,' said Toss. 'Makes me weep, I mean, just totally weep. You're lucky, guy, cos I'm gonna book you and that way maybe you'll learn your lesson before you kill a little innocent child.'

'Now you listen to me, mate,' shouted the driver, veins bulging on his huge neck.

'No!' Toss shouted into his face, something which required him having to stand on tiptoes. 'You listen to me! All of you. Here on the streets I am the law! You understand? I carry a badge!'

'Yeah, a traffic warden's badge,' the taxi driver pointed out.

'Traffic warden "K" class,' shouted Toss, indicating the registration number on his shoulder which happened to end in a K. 'Do you have any idea what that means guy! It means killer traffic warden, kommando traffic warden, kung fu traffic warden! Bad driving is a disease. Meet the cure.' Toss spread his legs and stuck out his chest. 'You! Bald tyre,' Toss shouted at the van driver 'You! Cracked off-side mirror reducing visibility,' he shouted at the taxi driver. 'You! Seriously tasteless colour, reducing everybody else's visibility,' he shouted at the lady with the golden Mercedes. 'And all of you illegally jay-walking on Her Majesty's highway. Now get back to your cars or I call a chopper!' Toss took a bar of Cadbury's Dairy Milk chocolate from his pocket and held it to his ear. 'Yo! this is the Cobra, request special weapons group.'

Faced with a lunatic, Toss's inquisitors were unsure how to act next. Toss knew exactly what to do. Taking advantage of their confusion, he suddenly pushed past the big van driver and charged back up the hill towards Deborah. Sadly, by this time the advantage had been lost. Sam Turk had, as Toss predicted, decided to abandon his limmo and continue on foot. As Toss turned away from the angry motorists he saw Sam appearing at the bottom of the hill, the gun flashing in his hand.

Toss rejoined Deborah.

'Maybe we should face him out, Debbo,' he said. 'There's loads of witnesses and everything, what could he do?'

'Toss,' replied Deborah, 'he'll shoot us both and nobody will even get out of their cars. Let's go.'

The race between good and evil was fairly evenly matched. Toss was pushing a loaded wheelchair, Sam had a bloody wound in his thigh. But both teams, despite their disabilities, were making considerably better progress than any of the cars on the road, or indeed anywhere else in town. Abilities and disabilities are relative quantities.

OBSTACLE COURSE

Hampstead is one of the highest parts of London and the approaches to it are steep. Toss's heart was pounding as he laboured to push Deborah's chair up the higher reaches of Frognal towards the village. The endless exhaust fumes from the great chain of stranded cars they were passing made him sweat and choke. Every broken paving stone, every curb was a drain on his strength. None the less, Sam too was labouring, he had been smashed in the face with an antique flat-iron and received a nasty flesh wound in the leg, he was fat, in late middle-age and now he was trying to run up a steep hill. Slowly but surely, Toss, whose muscles were toned by countless weekend raves of shaking his bottie down to the ground (and then a bit untoned again by lying around half-stoned drinking Red Stripe Crucial Brew), was increasing the distance between him and Sam.

Then human nature intervened and dealt the front runners a terrible blow. They were running up Frognal which leads to Church Row, which leads to Hampstead Village, where a tube train, or a policeman or some form of assistance, would be available. However, in order get to Church Row you have to dog leg across Frognal Road, which was of course blocked. The cars had not moved on this road for about twenty-five minutes. Actually, that is not strictly true, the cars had been moving, they just had not been getting anywhere, it was the old shivering snake again. All the drivers, for want of anything better to do, had been kidding themselves that they were making progress by shuffling their cars together, closing the gap between bumper and bumper. This always happens in queues of traffic and never a thought is given to the needs of pedestrians, let alone wheelchair users.

'Shsffllit,' said Toss. This was intended to be 'shit' but he was too knackered to speak properly.

'Don't you bastards *ever* think of people like me!!'

Deborah shouted at the drivers of the cars, for once not minding about making a scene. The drivers turned away, looked at the ceiling, stared into the distance, and did all the other things that intensely embarrassed people in cars do. They all looked as if they'd just got caught in the middle of a junction when the lights changed.

'You've gotta leave, Toss. We can't just go sideways, it's just more streets full of houses, he'll catch us in the end,' said Deborah.

'Nowahgg,' gasped Toss, which Deborah understood to mean 'no way girl'. 'He'll kill you,' Toss continued, becoming a little clearer.

'He won't, not if I don't have the plans. Why should he? Now get going!' shouted Deborah.

'I'm not leaving you!' shouted Toss.

Deborah put her brakes on. 'Get going, you fool! It's the engine that matters,' shouted Deborah, thrusting the plans at him.

'I've told you, no way, he's already killed Geoffrey,' said Toss, releasing the brakes again and beginning to push Deborah along the traffic, looking for a gap that was not there.

Sam Turk was close now, Deborah was desperate. Suddenly she remembered the vicious hatchet that Geoffrey had placed down by her leg as a low-tech part of his defence plan. She drew it, and twisting back, waved it within an inch of Toss's astonished face.

'Toss! Take the plans and *fuck off*!!' she shouted.

Toss stopped pushing. 'OK, girl, OK, there is no need to get so radical,' said Toss. He took the plans from Deborah, then spun round and fell against the bonnet of a white Mini Metro.

'Get it together, Toss, *please*,' implored Deborah.

'Hey!' shouted the irate driver of the Metro. 'That black bastard's bleeding on my bonnet! What is it? Is he having a haemorrhage? That's drugs done that to him, that is, bleeding drugs. Dirty bastard!'

Toss rolled round to look at Deborah, and a red streak appeared on the white paint work beneath his shoulder.

'Fucking hell,' said Toss, in a stunned sort of way. 'He shot me.'

THE PLANS CHANGE HANDS

Sam had not wanted to risk gun play, but he had no choice. He was very tired anyway, and when he perceived that the young, able-bodied fellow in the uniform had grabbed the plans and hence was obviously about to ditch the wheelchair, Sam knew that he would have to act.

He knelt down on the pavement, steadied the pistol against the forearm of his non-trigger hand, and fired. It was a good shot, he did not wish to kill the lad, but he wanted to stop him. Toss took the bullet in the shoulder and was lying on the bonnet of the Metro in agony.

'Can't somebody help him?' shouted the Metro

owner. 'At least get him off my bonnet.'

Of course any movie could show us what Toss should have done. Being merely wounded in the shoulder, he should have gathered up the plans in his good arm and rushed off like an Olympic runner. Movie wounds are much like movie car chases, they are completely harmless. Real ones, however, are different, they traumatize and disable. It would be a few minutes before Toss was sufficiently collected to make any kind of move, and that was too long.

Sam staggered up, puffing, panting, bleeding and bruised, but carrying a gun. The irate owner of the Metro attempted to hide in his glove compartment. Sam leant down and snatched at the papers from the ground where Toss had dropped them, having been shot. Deborah lunged forward with her little axe, but Sam was wary of her this time. He jumped out of the way of the swinging hatchet, and, grabbing the side of Deborah's wheelchair, toppled her over onto the ground. Deborah tumbled out helplessly onto the pavement, missing the traditional English dog turd by an inch. This was, in fact, extraordinarily lucky, the chances of tipping a person out of a wheelchair on to a London pavement and not hitting a dog turd are small indeed.

Sam looked down at Deborah's immobilized form.

'What, you mean you can't fly?' Sam panted. He was feeling good, he had the plans, and he was pretty certain that anyone who realized a shot had been fired would prefer not to get involved. He was home free.

'You done good, kid,' gasped Sam. 'Makes me proud to be an American.'

'You make me sick, asshole,' replied Deborah, helpless on the ground.

Sam turned on his heel and began a leisurely jog down the hill.

THE WHEELS OF VENGEANCE

For a moment, Toss and Deborah were alone. She on the pavement, he on the bonnet. Then one or two people from nearby cars who understood that something had happened, nervously wandered up.

'That guy!' shouted Deborah, 'that guy down the hill, he has stolen my stuff. It's very important! You have to stop him.'

It was a futile request, people were fairly happy to assist the wounded but there was no way they were going chasing gunmen to retrieve somebody's purse. Besides, how could they leave their cars?

'Can I give you a lift somewhere?' enquired one woman sympathetically, forgetting for a moment that she had now been stationary for forty-five minutes.

'I've called the police, and an ambulance on my carphone,' said a man who was clearly extremely pleased with himself for having done this.

'Get me up,' said Deborah, calmly, 'please get me

415

up and into my chair.'

'Well . . . uhm . . . how . . . ?' they all dithered, not really knowing how to manhandle a paraplegic.

'Just stand up the chair,' instructed Deborah firmly, 'Grab me by the shoulders, and haul me into it, OK?'

'OK,' they said. There was a pause.

'NOW, PLEASE!' shouted Deborah. It is difficult to be intimidating and authoritative whilst lying helpless on a pavement with a dog turd only inches from your head, but Deborah managed it. The onlookers had her back in her chair in an instant.

'Thank you,' said Deborah. 'So long, Toss,' and she pushed herself off down the hill.

'Deborah,' shouted Toss who was just coming round, but she was gone. The last chase was on.

Chapter Thirty

HELL ON WHEELS

Deborah's hands burned as she attempted to restrain the chair for the first part of the chase; she had a corner to turn to get back onto the main hill and she could not afford to topple over in the process. By putting her brakes on and off she traversed the thirty or so yards back to the junction with Church Row without mishap and, pushing her left hand down, as she swung round into the hill she could see the figure of Sam Turk jogging away a hundred yards or so below her. He was already halfway back down Finchley Road. Once he was down, she would have lost him for she had no speed on the flat.

It takes a pretty large measure of courage to launch yourself down a hill in a wheelchair, particularly when you will be rolling over treacherous, broken paving stones and having to negotiate terrifying kerbs, more so, even, when your final objective is a deliberate crash with an armed murderer. But Deborah was not short of courage, so she hit the wheel arches on her machine and prepared to burn rubber.

'Well Geoffrey, you wanted your engine to make me fly,' she muttered. 'Here goes.'

She gathered speed quickly, and was forced to hang heavy on the anchors as she sped past, bumping over and occasionally even managing to avoid, the great wedges of broken pavement that hurtled towards her, every one a potential gravestone with her name on it. Sometimes a jet of water would shoot up as Deborah rolled over one of the pivoted pavements which had puddles hidden underneath. People watched amazed as Deborah sped past their windows with a grim look on her face, smoke rising from where she gripped the wheel rims. Deborah had gathered up the ends of the sleeves of her jumper in her hands in an effort to protect them, but these were quickly burning away.

There were two side streets that joined the hill down which Deborah was hurtling. The first kerb she had to negotiate was passable, the council having kindly provided a sloped stone on both sides of the road. Unfortunately, there was a car in the way. It had not been there on the way up with Toss, both the side streets had been pretty loosely packed, and it had been fairly simple to find a way between the cars. Even as Deborah started her down-hill dash to catch Turk she had seen a gap still available, but at that point frustration got the better of some pratt in a Mazda. The sleeping snake shivered, and even as Deborah headed for the precious gap, Mr Brand New Mazda rolled forward pointlessly to fill it. Deborah was by now doing about ten miles an hour, the car was only yards away, there was no way she could stop if she wanted to stay upright. It was teeth-gritting time. She shot down the kerb and slammed smash into the side of the car. With great good fortune her foot rests were high enough not to go under the Mazda, they hit it just beneath the door, thus protecting her knees. The chair tipped forward and the arm rests bashed into the car just at the level of the door handle, followed by Deborah who took the impact of the passenger window on her chest. Fortunately, the foot rests and the arm rests had taken up most of the force and, although very winded, Deborah was unhurt. She saw immediately that the Mazda had only edged forward to the stop line, there was just room in front of the car to get round between it and the stationary traffic pointing up the hill.

With a huge effort Deborah pushed herself away from the side of the Mazda, wheeled her right hand down and turned sharp left to get round the front of the car squeezing between it and the side of a Cortina, trying, by sheer lung power, to suck in the sides of her chair. As she was doing this a furious Mazda driver was jumping out of the other side.

'Now look Miss, what's the game?' he said trying to be calm. 'I hope you're insured because that was quite a thud and I'm afraid . . .'

The driver was walking around the other side of the car to meet Deborah, he intended to block her way and get the details of her vehicle. The man was in for a shock.

'Aaaaaarrrrghhh!' screamed Deborah, holding up the hatchet in classic psycho-killer pose. 'Aaaaarggghh!!'

Her hair was wild, her eyes were wild, everything about her was wild, the backs of her knees were probably wild. Understandably, the Mazda driver leapt out of the way and Deborah, slamming her arms into first gear, pushed off again, curving round the front of the Mazda, remounting the pavement on the sloped stone and powering on down.

She was closer to Turk now. Unaware that he was being followed he had slowed to an exhausted walk. Bumping and jumping, concentrating desperately, Deborah slid down the hill. She veered along hedges as a way of slowing down, throwing her torso this way and that to guide the accelerating chair past the hazards. So concentrated was she on the ground immediately in front of her, that it was nearly all over shortly after she left the Mazda. Fortunately, Deborah suddenly remembered from her trip up the hill with Toss that there had been a British Telecom obstruction on the pavement, Toss had had to squeeze her past on the road. Looking up, Deborah realized that it was almost upon her, the pavement was blocked, the kerb at that point was a good nine inches high. She was hurtling along, there was absolutely no way she could get down onto the road without a crash, Deborah had seconds to make a decision . . .

People who saw what Deborah did cheered and beeped their horns and, for once, the beeps were meant kindly: it was a magnificent manoeuvre. There was a lamp post on the pavement right by the little Telecom tent, between the lamp post and the nine-inch precipice was a further foot or so of pavement. As Deborah plunged towards the Telecom tent, she hit hard down on her right hand wheel, incinerating the last of her jumper sleeve and most of the skin on her right hand. The chair spun left and headed straight out off the kerb and into the road, but just as it appeared that Deborah and her chair would fly head first into the nearest bonnet, Deborah flung out her right arm and hooked it around the lamp post, nearly dislocating her shoulder in the process. The left wheel and most of the chair sailed out over the cliff edge, the chrome flashing in the watery sunlight, but the right wheel remained on the kerb and Deborah managed to haul the chair round with scarcely a drop in speed.

Looking down the hill, it seemed to Deborah that Sam was nearly on the Finchley Road and that all her efforts would end fruitlessly in her shooting out at the bottom and decapitating herself under a stationary articulated lorry that spanned the junction. However, Deborah could not have stopped herself at this point if she'd wanted to, so instead she spurred her chair on, removing any remaining skin on her hands in the process. The second of the two side roads loomed up before her. The gap was still there, just. With careful aiming, she could get between the cars. Unfortunately the gap was not adjacent to the ramp, if she wanted to get between the cars she would have to go off the kerb at a high point and, what is more, mount the other side at a high point too.

Deborah was now rocketing along, there was no way that she could risk a repeat of the Mazda performance. At the speed she was now doing, slamming into the side of a car could well kill her.

Deborah wiggled her body, touched the wheels and headed for the gap. As she left the kerb, flying into thin air, she leant back in order to avoid landing on her face. Even as she did this she was planning her assault on the opposite kerb, always presuming her aim was true, and she landed between the cars and managed to roll between them.

The aim was good, and it certainly was a shock to the lady in the Range Rover when a girl in a wheelchair crashed down in front of her. Deborah and the chair bounced forward under the momentum and again Deborah threw herself backwards. It was a tricky equation, she had to get her front wheels up high enough so that she would hit the far kerb with her large rear wheels and, hopefully, roll onto it, but not so far that she would topple over backwards. The kerb was not high and Deborah was on the final sprint, she had Turk in her sights and to her delight and astonishment he seemed to have stopped.

AT BAY

By a small irony Sam had actually stopped at the point where Deborah and Toss had been forced to abandon the car. The reason for this was that even the pavement was blocked. It was blocked by the van owned by the man with the bald tyres. The frustration of the gridlock had got to the point where uptightness had completely conquered sanity and it was pavement mounting time. In the centre, where the gridlock was two or three hours older, they had already started to try and drive through shops.

The man in the van, faced with Deborah's empty car in front of him, became more and more agitated about the fact that when the jam finally cleared in his lane, if the opposing lane remained jammed, he would still be unable to move. This had weighed ever more heavily on him until it had become an obsession.

Eventually, in the jammed driver's mad desire to take some action, any action, he mounted the kerb. There was never any way he was going to get round, but at least he was doing something. Of course, the space the van vacated was instantly filled from behind, creating an endless, rippling knock-on effect as car after car shuffled forward to fill the couple of feet of tarmac that the van's partial occupation of the pavement had provided. Hours and hours later, miles away on the other side of the river, cars which had been stationary all day would suddenly find themselves with an extra few inches to travel because of that van.

However, the immediate result was that, when Sam Turk huffed and puffed his way up to it, the pavement was blocked, as was the road. The cars had shuffled so close together in the excitement caused by the huge leap forward of the van that at this point of Frognal, there was no longer even room to walk between the cars.

Sam shrugged and put his foot on the bonnet of a golden Mercedes, preparing to climb over it.

'How dare you, you filthy tramp,' screamed the posh Hampstead lady. And it has to be said that by this time Sam did look pretty much like a filthy tramp, and what's more a filthy tramp who had been in a punch-up . . . 'Get your filthy feet off my bonnet, my husband is a Justice of the Peace,' the woman continued.

The van driver, delighted for a little diversion, leant out of his cab.

'Oi, shit face! You'd better leave that lady's car alone or I'll have you.'

Sam did not want trouble, he considered waving his gun around, but he knew that waving guns around can lead to big trouble. He was now very near the main road, movement was extremely restricted and there were bound to be police around, better to keep the peace, thought Sam, and look for another way round.

'Sorry,' he said, but no one was listening any more, they were all staring over Sam's shoulder, back up the hill, mouths opened, transfixed.

From behind him Sam suddenly heard the long drawn out cry. 'Baaasssttarrrd,' and he turned around to find out who it was who had so accurately summed him up.

EQUALIZING

Sam never stood a chance. He managed to raise his gun and even got off a couple of shots, but Deborah was too close. The shots went hopelessly wide and the gun flew out of Sam's hands as he took the full force of a wheelchair containing an axe-swinging woman, hurtling downhill at over twenty miles an hour. The footrests cut his shins away from under him and a split second later he received Deborah plus her chair in the guts. Over the bonnet of the Mercedes they went, with Sam on the bottom.

All three of them, the wheelchair, Deborah and Sam landed in different places. The chair went through the windscreen of a Datsun, Deborah landed on the boot of the Mercedes and Sam on the roof of an old VW next to the Merc, pointing down hill.

As she cannoned into Sam's chest, Deborah, resourceful even in this supremely testing moment, had grabbed the plans which he had been clutching to him.

THE PLANS CHANGE HANDS AGAIN

There was a stunned silence, the shot and the action had shut up even the posh Hampstead woman, for the moment. Deborah spoke.

'I got it, Turk! I got it! I got my engine back,' one of her arms was broken, she shoved the plans under it, with her other arm she held up the hatchet which she had managed to hang on to.

'I'm keeping them, Turk,' she shouted through the shocked silence. 'You ain't got no gun now and you come near me and I'll stick this in you! I will, I'll stick it in you.'

There was a general gasp from the observers who were, understandably, finding this dramatic stuff.

'So you could fly after all, kid,' said Sam through clenched teeth. He tried to move, but only gasped in pain, his legs would not function. Deborah's foot rests had done their work and both Sam's legs were busted. Once she understood the situation, Deborah could not resist a cry of triumph.

'My God, you're crippled! You can't walk! Is that a beautiful irony or what! Wait till I get to a phone to tell Momma I believe in God again. We're equal now Turk, and I've got the plans!'

THE PLANS CHANGE HANDS AGAIN

The captive audience was riveted, this really was top notch Hollywood stuff. So absorbed were they, that they even forgot their fear, in fact many of them had begun to believe that the whole thing wasn't real at all, but some piece of elaborate street theatre laid on by trendy Camden Council to stop rioting during the traffic jam.

'Kid,' whispered Sam. 'In my time I've fought unions, Mafia and the United States Senate to name but a few, and you are without doubt the toughest, meanest daughter of a bitch I have ever had the misfortune to tussle with. I don't reckon there's been above fifteen minutes in this whole day when you ain't had the rise on me.'

There was even some small applause at this splendid speech.

'Fuck off, creep,' replied Deborah. And the 'tut tuts' were audible towards Deborah, whom most people now considered an ungracious victor.

In fact, Sam did admire Deborah in a way, but that was not why he was treating her to such honeyed words. The reason for this was that he was desirous of keeping her attention, having noticed Bruce Tungsten squeezing round the van behind her.

After Sam had left his office it had been a few minutes before Bruce had noticed that he had gone.

427

Bruce had seen Miss Hodges untie him, whilst Bruce himself tried to douse the three burning hostages and then staunch his own bullet wound, but it was not until after the security guards had arrived that he had realized Sam had gone. Bruce, at heart, was not a bad man and, faced with an office full of human torches and electrocuted secretaries, he tended to deal with the situation at hand. Sam, of course, had kept his mind on the broader issues and gone chasing the plans.

However, once relieved of his responsibilities by two old blokes in peaked caps, Bruce quickly tracked Sam down, learning over the car phone from Sam's chauffeur that the car was stuck in traffic but that Sam had disappeared on foot up Frognal. Bruce had given chase.

And there he was, unnoticed by all but Sam, standing behind Deborah. Sam was attempting to keep Deborah's attention because he far preferred Bruce to have the engine than her. If Bruce had it then Sam might yet, at least be part of things.

'I'll take these then,' said Bruce, gently leaning in and plucking the plans from under Deborah's broken arm.

'Watch out for the axe!!' cried Sam, as a shocked Deborah squirmed round on the bonnet and lashed behind her with the hatchet. This time, however, her extraordinary combative powers deserted her, and she missed.

'Oooh,' gasped the crowd.

'If you ever manage to get out of this fix, Sam,' said Bruce, 'write and tell me how you managed it, I'll be interested. You'll find me in Detroit making engines.'

'Bruce,' pleaded Sam, 'get me a lawyer, a doctor, a drink! For God's sake, you can't leave me!'

But Bruce could and he did. Without another word he turned on his heel. Although, actually, he did not get very far. Not even one step in fact, because he got smacked in the face by one of the little flashing lanterns surrounding the British Telecom tent which Deborah had avoided earlier.

'Oooh,' gasped the crowd again.

THE PLANS CHANGE HANDS AGAIN

Toss leant down and grabbed at the plans.

'I got 'em, Debbo,' he shouted. The crowd was too riveted even to gasp. Once Toss had recovered from the shock of being shot in the shoulder, he had naturally set off after his friend. As he ran down the hill he saw the crash, and he saw a man creeping up behind the prostrate Deborah, which was why he had picked up the lantern, the only weapon that was available. It had been a good idea.

'Run, Toss, run,' shouted Deborah. 'Put them in a bank, the post office, Xerox them, stitch them to your body, but run.'

'What about you?' Toss shouted.

'Please Toss, not again, just *save Geoffrey's*

engine.' The appeal in Deborah's voice was sufficiently poignant to spur Toss to action. He turned around and legged it.

WIND POWER

Suddenly a huge beating noise filled the air, there were shouts and a rush of wind. Up from the Finchley Road came uniformed police. The man with the car phone at the top of the hill had done his job. He had reported gunfire on Church Row and *that* the police took seriously.

Beat bobbies had run along from Swiss Cottage Station and a helicopter of the Tactical Arms Group had been scrambled.

Since Toss was running up the hill he did not see the coppers behind him, and he had no time to stare at helicopters.

What the coppers saw, of course, was a bleeding man running away from what appeared to be a slaughter, carrying a parcel. Clearly he was worth having a chat with.

Toss was brought down with a neat rugby tackle and the engine plans leapt from his hand, bursting open on the pavement. The helicopter descended to hover only feet above Toss and the copper.

'No!' shouted Toss.

'No!' agreed Sam, Bruce and Deborah.

But it was no use, the winds from the blades scattered the precious plans for Geoffrey Spasmo's hydrogen engine up and away over the vast traffic jam that used to be London. Up over the rooftops, fluttering hither and thither across the paralysed city, landing in puddles, blown into drifts of sodden leaves, stuck to the windscreens of helpless, stranded cars, until very soon there was not a word nor a single figure of Geoffrey's designs left anywhere.

Chapter Thirty-One

THE QUEEN'S DILEMMA

It was the day of the State Opening of Parliament, with all its inane pomp and ludicrous majesty. The strange man in the black tights had bashed on the door. The procession of the bewigged living dead (also in tights) had passed without incontinence or cardiac arrest from the Lords to the Commons – or perhaps it is the other way round. The Prime Minister and the Leader of the Opposition had walked up the aisle together conducting their one private conversation per year.

'Go fuck yourself.'

'No, *you* go fuck yourself.'

'No, *you* go fuck yourself.'

All was ready for the Queen's speech. Except her that is, the Queen was far from ready. There were no circumstances under which she would be ready, because this speech was, without doubt, the foulest and most horrible that she had ever been required by duty to utter. Prince Philip, loyal and supportive as always, reminded her that she felt this way every year. Each time she was called upon to announce some vicious, petty cut in benefits and welfare, or some further dismantling of the resources of the state, she swore that she could not do it. Each year, as the Prince reminded her, the Queen wondered if it was worth provoking a constitutional crisis by simply refusing to recite the nauseating drivel, but the Queen knew she couldn't, *noblesse oblige* and all that. The State Opening of Parliament is the time when a constitutional Monarch gets real.

'This year it's different, Philip,' she whispered backstage as they inserted the huge metal support spike in the back of her dress to hold up the great big stupid looking crown. 'I really cannot say it.'

But she knew she would, she would have to. The public outcry after the great gridlock had been horrendous. Hundreds of thousands of Londoners had been left stranded in their cars for up to three days while the jam was cleared from the outside in. The knock-on effect had shot up the motorways and down to the Channel Tunnel, causing more horrendous delays. The complete shut-down of the capital for over half a week had affected business and commerce all over the country and into Europe. Countless deals had been lost, food had rotted, looting had occurred. The whole country had been absolutely astonished to discover what Chief Superintendent Ross had known for years, which was:

that we are completely and utterly helpless in the face of motor cars, they can cripple us, any day, any time. They are a monster that we have created, we worship them, sacrifice the riches of the Earth to them and we will die for them, the moment it is demanded of us.

'Something must be done,' the people cried. 'We need more roads,' many added. It was this charged atmosphere of national disaster that had forced the Prime Minister to request Mrs McCorkadale, the Minister for Transport, to produce a radical, new, emergency road plan for Britain. By an extraordinary coincidence, the Ministry for Transport had one all ready. Digby's models were dusted off and presented to the nation. In the near hysteria that followed the gridlock, environmental objections were set aside, the country wanted roads and the government was ready to rise to the challenge.

'My government,' the Queen said, a lump rising in her throat as big as her hat, 'will begin the total rebuilding of all our major cities so that they may better accommodate the needs of the private motorist . . . This will involve the widening of all motorways . . . All B roads to become A roads . . .'

The list went on and on, and it broke the Queen's heart to read it.

Afterwards, in the Cabinet Room at 10 Downing Street, the Prime Minister spoke to Ingmar Bresslaw.

'Terrible thing that Gridlock, wasn't it, Ingmar?'

'Terrible, Prime Minister.'

'Bit of luck for us, in a way, though, wasn't it?'

'Not really, Prime Minister, statistically it was bound to happen in the end. Ross had been warning us for years.'

'Yes,' agreed the PM, 'but it was a bit of luck, it happening right now, just when we needed to regain the transport initiative.'

'Yes, Prime Minister,' Ingmar conceded. 'That was a bit of luck. It couldn't have happened at a better time really. Almost as if it was planned.'

'How absurd,' said the Prime Minister.

'Yes,' Ingmar agreed, 'how absurd.'

'Thank you, Ingmar,' said the Prime Minister. 'Thank you very much.'

THE END

STARK

Ben Elton

Stark has more money than God and the social conscience of a dog on a croquet lawn. What's more, they know the Earth is dying.

Deep in Western Australia where the Aboriginals used to milk the trees, a planet-sized plot takes shape. Some green freaks pick up the scent. A Pommie poseur, a brain-fried Vietnam Vet, Aboriginals who lost their land . . . not much against a conspiracy that controls society. But EcoAction isn't in society; it just lives in the same place, along with the cockroaches.

If you're facing the richest and most disgusting conspiracy in history, you have to do more than stick up two fingers and say 'peace'.

0 7474 0390 2
GENERAL FICTION

GASPING

Ben Elton

Lockheart industries are making *senior* money. If *God* wanted to buy into their stock he'd have to think twice and talk to his people. They have a profit curve wound so far round the room it looks like a *Blue Peter* Christmas appeal.

But they're bored, they want more. New ideas, new products. That's when someone discovers *Suck and Blow* . . .

The marketing phenomenon of the decade has arrived! Designer air! *Perrier* for the nostrils!

But when the world starts gasping, only the biggest suckers survive . . .

0 7474 0889 0
NON-FICTION

BACHELOR BOYS:
The Young Ones Book

Ben Elton, Rik Mayall, Lise Mayer

Call it bad karma or anarchy in the UK, there's never
been anything quite like the cult-hit TV series *The Young
Ones* – totally bizarre, totally original, totally aggressive
and . . . totally TOTAL. So, here are The Young Ones in
their own write: Rick the Radical Poet, Vyvyan the
Psychopathic Punk, Neil the Suicidal Hippy, and Mike,
the Would-Be Spiv. The Young Ones offer a lifeguide for
survival in today's Thatcherite Britain, including
Vyvyan's useless tips for smashing up TV sets, the Joys of
Solitary Sex and the Diarrhoea of a Madman . . .

0 7474 5765 7
NON-FICTION/HUMOUR

Sphere now offers an exciting range of quality titles by both established and new authors. All of the books in this series are available from:

Sphere Books,
Cash Sales Department,
P.O. Box 11,
Falmouth,
Cornwall TR10 9EN.

Alternatively you may fax your order to the above address. Fax No. 0326 376423.

Payments can be made as follows: Cheque, postal order (payable to Macdonald & Co (Publishers) Ltd) or by credit cards, Visa/Access. Do not send cash or currency. UK customers and B.F.P.O.: please send a cheque or postal order (no currency) and allow £1.00 for postage and packing for the first book, plus 50p for the second book, plus 30p for each additional book up to a maximum charge of £3.00 (7 books plus).

Overseas customers including Ireland, please allow £2.00 for postage and packing for the first book, plus £1.00 for the second book, plus 50p for each additional book.

NAME (Block Letters) ....

ADDRESS ....

....

☐ I enclose my remittance for _____

☐ I wish to pay by Access/Visa Card

Number ⬚⬚⬚⬚⬚⬚⬚⬚⬚⬚⬚⬚⬚⬚⬚⬚

Card Expiry Date ⬚⬚⬚⬚